ALSO BY ELISABETH HYDE

The Abortionist's Daughter

Crazy as Chocolate

Monoosook Valley

Her Native Colors

In the Heart of the Canyon

In the Heart of the Canyon

Elisabeth Hyde

Alfred A. Knopf
New York
2009

THIS IS A BORZOI BOOK PUBLISHED BY ALFRED A. KNOPF

Copyright © 2009 by Elisabeth Hyde

All rights reserved. Published in the United States by Alfred A. Knopf,
a division of Random House, Inc., New York, and in Canada by Random House of
Canada Limited, Toronto.
www.aaknopf.com
Knopf, Borzoi Books, and the colophon are registered trademarks of
Random House, Inc.

Library of Congress Cataloging-in-Publication Data
Hyde, Elisabeth.
In the heart of the canyon / Elisabeth Hyde.—1st ed.
p.   cm.
ISBN 978-0-307-26366-7
1. Rafting (Sports)—Colorado River (Colo.–Mexico)—Fiction.   I. Title.
PS3558.Y38I5 2009
813'.54—dc22   2009013867

Manufactured in the United States of America

FIRST EDITION

FOR PIERRE

*For what you want, above all things, on a raft, is for everybody
to be satisfied, and feel right and kind towards the others.*

MARK TWAIN

All the greatest adventures begin with a mistake.

ANONYMOUS

THE CHARACTERS

THE GUESTS

Peter Kramer, age twenty-seven, a cartographer from Cincinnati

Evelyn Burns, age fifty, a biology professor at Harvard University

The Frankels, from Evanston, Illinois
    Ruth, age seventy-three, a painter
    Lloyd, age seventy-six, a physician

The Van Dorens, from Mequon, Wisconsin
    Susan, age forty-three, a guidance counselor
    Amy, age seventeen

The Boyer-Brandts, from Green River, Wyoming
    Mitchell, age fifty-nine, a devoted historian
    Lena, age sixty, a kindergarten teacher

The Compsons, from Salt Lake City
    Jill, age thirty-eight, a stay-at-home mom
    Mark, age forty, a businessman
    Matthew, age thirteen
    Sam, age twelve

THE GUIDES

JT Maroney, Trip Leader, age fifty-two

Abo, the paddle captain, age thirty-five

Dixie Ann Gillis, age twenty-seven

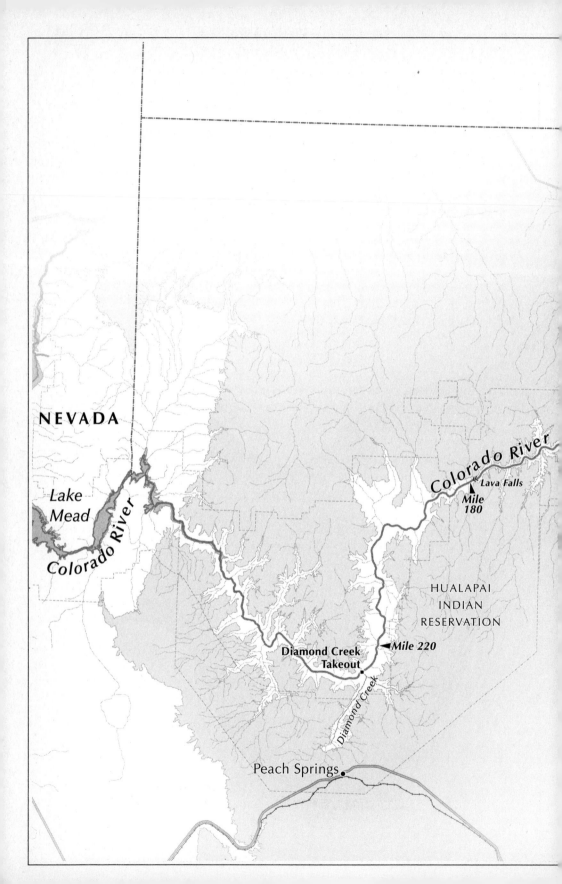

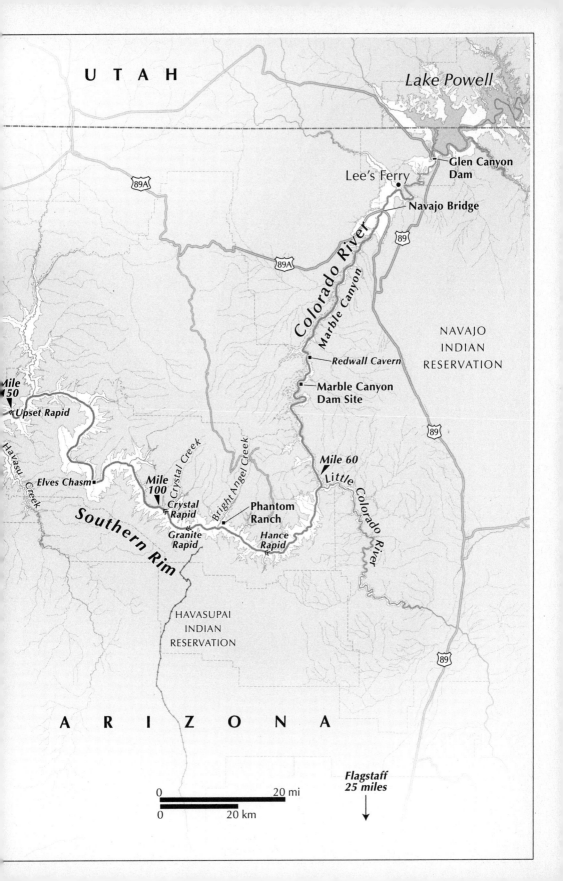

U T A H

Lake Powell

Glen Canyon Dam

Lee's Ferry

89A

Navajo Bridge

89

89A

Colorado River

Marble Canyon

NAVAJO
INDIAN
RESERVATION

Redwall Cavern

**Marble Canyon
Dam Site**

89

*Mile
50*

Upset Rapid

Havasu Creek

Elves Chasm

Crystal Creek

*Mile
100*

*Crystal
Rapid*

Bright Angel Creek

**Phantom
Ranch**

*Granite
Rapid*

*Hance
Rapid*

Mile 60

*Little
Colorado River*

Southern Rim

HAVASUPAI
INDIAN
RESERVATION

89

A R I Z O N A

0   20 mi

0   20 km

*Flagstaff
25 miles*

PROLOGUE

Down in the heart of the canyon, in the bone-baking heat, they put their lives on hold.

Most of the travelers had never experienced anything quite like it. Peter Kramer, whose year mapping the jungles of Central America included a monthlong stay in an unair-conditioned hospital with a fever of 104, found it impossible to suck down more than short little gasps of hot air. Evelyn Burns, professor of biology at Harvard University, spent the first day lecturing everyone about the tolerability of dry heat (105 in Arizona being nothing compared to 90 in Boston), then vomited five minutes into the first windstorm. Dr. and Mrs. Lloyd Frankel, river veterans, lay on their sleeping mats in stunned oblivion to the velvety orange wasps that scurried in blind circles on the hot sand between them. And Amy Van Doren, who unbeknownst to her mother had weighed in at 237 pounds on the hotel spa scale the night before the trip, rigorously shook the bottle of hot sauce over everything on her plate, for she knew that chile peppers made you sweat, which in turn would not only cool her off but enable her to lose a few pounds.

JT, the head guide, had seen it all before. This being his 125th trip down the Colorado River, he'd witnessed time and again the universal zombielike walk of his guests at the end of the day when they staggered up the beach in search of a campsite. He called it the Death Walk and always reminded his fellow guides not to expect much volunteer help in the first few days of any July trip, as guests acclimated to the suffocating conditions of the Grand Canyon. It was simply a matter of physiology: the human body wasn't designed to go from a comfortable air-conditioned existence to the prehistoric inferno of canyon life in a day. When his heat-stomped campers marveled at his energy, *he kept at what he was doing and raised an eyebrow and said, "You'll adjust."*

JT was a man of few words.

At night it was so hot you slept without a blanket, or even a sheet, for well past midnight the winds continued to fan the heat off the sun-baked canyon walls. In early morning, as people shook out their clothes for scorpions, the air could feel temperate, and they might be fine in just a bathing suit; but as soon as the sun's rays came barreling over the canyon walls, out came the long-sleeved cotton shirts, which got repeatedly dunked in the river, wrung out, and worn, soaked to chill, until sundown.

During the midday furnace, when even the guides crawled into whatever shade they could find and collectively dreamt of that first brisk morning in October when you could see your breath, JT himself would confront the heat head-on. Alone in his raft, he would kneel against the side tubes with his arms draped over the edge, staring in a kind of rapt hypnosis at the sheer walls across the river. Something in the flat midday light, he'd found, caused them to eventually start float- ing upstream, a mirage of the mind until he blinked, and then they would snap back into place until the next daze sent them floating upstream again. It was a game he played, a game he'd never reveal to anyone lest they think him soft, or spiritual, or just plain wacky.

But in fact he was all three. JT Maroney's heart was in those walls, and had been since his first trip thirty-five years ago when someone handed him a life jacket and a paddle and said, "Are you coming or not?" It was in the polished maroon cliffs of Marble Canyon, the dusty tan layers of Coconino sandstone; it was embedded forever in the shimmering black walls of the Inner Gorge, Land of the Giants. It was in the scorpions and the velvet wasps and the stinging red ants that sent you running for a vial of ammonia; it was in the feathery tamarisk trees and the canyon wrens' falling notes and the grumpy black- winged California condor he spotted without fail as they passed under Navajo Bridge the first day of every trip. It was in the tug of water around his ankle as he splashed about, rigging his boat; it was in the sunlit droplets that danced above the roar of big water.

Each trip changed him a little. This trip would change him a lot. It would change everyone, in ways no one could have anticipated.

But on the Fourth of July, at the beginning of JT's 125th trip, it wasn't about change. It was about drinking beer and eating pie and dreaming up new ways to fly the Stars and Stripes over the grandest river in the West.

In the Heart of the Canyon

1

Lee's Ferry

Mile 0

Up at Lee's Ferry, the night before the trip, JT sat on the side tube of his eighteen-foot neoprene raft, popped open a beer, and tried to remember exactly how many times he'd flipped his raft in Hermit.

Deep in the Inner Gorge, ninety-five miles downstream, the runoff boulders from Hermit Creek collided with the Colorado River to create one of the longest hydraulic roller coasters in the canyon, wave after wave of foaming madness that could buckle a raft in seconds. The fifth wave, in particular, had a tendency to curl back upon itself, something that could easily flip a boat. JT's goal was always to punch straight on through, aiming for just enough of a wild ride to give his passengers a thrill without actually flipping. Trouble was, sometimes the ride got ahead of itself, and JT hit that fifth wave with maybe too much weight in the back, and suddenly there they were, rising up, hovering in midair with water roaring all around and JT heaving his weight into the oars even as he felt them go back and over: down into the churning froth, getting maytagged and then popping up into the light, always disoriented until he spotted the white underside of his raft, which was usually right there beside him. And so it was, more than just a few times in his life as a guide, and although there were always a few who subsequently wanted *off, now,* what made it all worthwhile was seeing the expressions on the others' faces as he hauled them up onto the upturned belly of his raft—expressions of shock, adrenaline, joy, fear, joy, excitement, and did he mention joy? Because that's what it was, usually: the sheer exultation of surviving a swim in one of the most powerful rivers on earth.

JT tallied up the times he'd flipped. Five in all, if his memory served him well.

Draining his beer, he tossed the empty can onto a tarp on the beach and reached into the mesh drag bag for another. The sun was still high in the sky, the water a deep turtle green, achy cold if you left your foot in for more than a few seconds. Across the river, tan hills sloped up from the water's edge, speckled with piñon and sage and juniper; downstream, salmon pink cliffs marked the beginning of Marble Canyon.

JT was the lead boatman for this trip, the official Trip Leader, and as such he was the one who made all the important day-to-day decisions: where to stop for lunch, which hikes to take, whether they'd schedule a layover day. If there was a problem passenger, JT was responsible for reigning him in; if someone got hurt, JT decided whether to evacuate. JT figured he was good for two trips per season as lead boatman; you got paid a little more, but you never really slept.

Up on the beach, Dixie and Abo, his fellow guides, worked together stuffing tents one by one into a large rubberized bag. JT was tired and hungry and wished briefly that they were cooking him a good dinner instead. After a long morning spent loading up the truck back at the warehouse in Flagstaff, they'd driven the three hours to Lee's Ferry, where they worked the entire afternoon rigging their boats in the hot desert sun. The beach at Lee's Ferry was the only put-in point on the river, so it was crowded with people and boats: two fat motorized rafts, a dozen or so durable eighteen-footers, and a flotilla of colorful kayaks. The beach was littered with so much gear—dinged-up ammunition boxes, waterproof bags, paddles, oars, life jackets, water jugs—that it resembled a paddlers' flea market. Yet despite the mayhem, everybody seemed to know what was what and whose was whose, and JT knew that by ten o' clock tomorrow, all this gear would be stowed in its rightful place on the boats.

High in the sky, a turkey vulture slowly circled, its white-tipped wings spread wide. The people on the motor rig had set up lawn chairs and opened umbrellas for shade, but nobody was sitting down; there was too much work to be done, although they did it with a beer in hand. Up on the beach, Abo, his paddle captain, was now mending a book with duct tape, while Dixie, who would be rowing their third boat, was starting to assemble their picnic dinner. She wore a yellow bathing suit top and a blue sarong knotted low on her hips; wet braids curled at her shoulders.

"How come there are only five sandwiches?" she asked.

"Four for me, one for you and JT to split," said Abo.

"Well, someone's going hungry," said Dixie, "and it isn't going to be me."

JT smiled to himself. He was glad to have these two for his crew. Abo, who could always be counted on to loosen up a group, was thirty-five, tall and bony-legged, with bleachy-tipped brown hair and clear blue eyes. Nobody knew his real name. He was a farm boy from the Midwest who'd come out to study geology at the University of Arizona, then took a river trip and never went back to school. During the winter, he built houses and scavenged work up at the ski area. Reputedly, he had a son by a woman in California, a movie producer whom Abo had met on an earlier trip. He was a good guide, in JT's view; not only did he make people laugh, but as an amateur geologist he knew the pastry layers of the canyon better than anyone.

Dixie, whose real name was just that, Dixie Ann Gillis, was twenty-seven. She was relatively new with the company, and he'd only done one other trip with her, but he'd been impressed when he watched her rescue a private boater from the Rock Garden below Crystal Rapid. She had strong opinions about a lot of things, and JT liked that about her. If you caught him with his guard down, JT might admit that he was half in love with Dixie, but she had a boyfriend down in Tucson whose picture she kept taped to the inside of her personal ammo box, and JT wasn't one to mess with somebody else's good thing. Besides, after 124 trips, JT knew how things worked in the canyon, knew you could fall in love at the drop of a hat, literally, before you even got through Marble Canyon. It was a guide's life to fall in love, he knew; he'd done his share, but if there was one thing he understood these days, it was to stand back and not get caught up in things, trip after trip after trip.

JT unlatched the ammo box by his feet and took out the passenger list and scanned the names and notes. They were supposed to have fourteen passengers on the trip, but at the last minute one couple had canceled, which meant he was going to have to juggle the seating arrangements to balance out the boats. There were two vegetarians, three "no dairy," one "high craving for red meat." Most had no rafting experience, which didn't surprise him; but one couldn't swim, which did. There were two kids, which pleased him; kids usually brought a goofy spirit absent in adults, who too easily fell victim to excessive reverence for natural wonders. He made a mental note to assign the boys a job—can-smasher, maybe—so they could feel useful and independent from their parents.

He continued scanning. There was a couple from Wyoming, named Mitchell and Lena; Lena, he noted, was allergic to peanuts, furry animals, grasses, and pollen. Well, hopefully she was bringing along a box of Benadryl and an EpiPen or two. There was a mother and daughter, Susan and Amy. The one who couldn't swim was a young man from Ohio named Peter, age twenty-seven, traveling solo.

Noting Peter's age, JT glanced up at Dixie, who was reknotting her sarong. *Don't even think of it,* he heard himself telling Peter. *Don't even try.*

That evening, as the sky grew dark, boaters from all the groups gathered together and passed around a bottle of whiskey, sharing old stories, inventing new ones. Around nine thirty, JT, who'd passed on the second round, returned to his raft. He brushed his teeth, then unrolled his sleeping bag across the long, flat meat cooler that spanned the center of his boat. Even though it was dark, the day's heat continued to radiate off the canyon walls. JT strapped on his headlamp and sat down and carefully and methodically dried off his feet. He rubbed them well with bee balm, then pulled on a pair of clean socks to keep his skin from cracking. Finally he stretched out on top of his sleeping bag. He settled back and locked his hands behind his head and gazed up at the spattered current of stars above. A warm breeze fanned his skin, and he picked out constellations: the Big Dipper, Cassiopeia, the busy little Pleiades.

Up on the beach, a burst of laughter erupted from the revelers, but by now his eyes had begun to twitch and blur. He fought to keep them open, to watch just a little bit more of the star show, but within minutes he was fast asleep.

July 3

I'm writing in the bathroom of our hotel room because Mom is out there with everything laid out on the two double beds, FREAKING OUT that she might forget something. Tonight we had our orientation meeting. Mom and I were late and we walked into the room and everybody stared at me. Must have been my FAT CLUB T-shirt. Please please please don't make me go on this trip. There is nobody my age and all I'll do is eat. And it's going to be hotter than shit and I'll probably sink the boats.

Maybe if I throw myself out the window, she won't make me go.

We're supposed to get up at 5:30 tomorrow morning and the bus leaves at 6:30. I do not know what I am going to do with my mother hanging over my shoulder for two weeks. Why did she have to bring me along? I could have stayed home alone. Oh no Amy, I want some time with you, you're going off to college in another year. Oh no Amy, I wouldn't feel right. Oh no Amy, a serial killer might be able to figure out the twenty-two locks on our front door.

I think I've got food poisoning.

DAY ONE

River Miles 0–16

Lee's Ferry to House Rock

2

Day One

Lee's Ferry

Mile 0

The next morning JT woke up floating, as he did on every river trip. Fourth of July. Launch day. The air was temperate, the sky a dark peacock blue. JT estimated it was about five o'clock. At some point during the night, he'd drawn up his sheet. Quietly now, he sat up and pulled on a T-shirt, climbed over his gear, and hopped out onto the beach. He lit the stove and started a pot of water boiling, and when it was ready he dumped a baggie of ground coffee directly into the water and gave it a stir. How good it smelled, this bare-bones coffee in the canyon!

By now Abo and Dixie were sitting up, yawning, fumbling for clothes. When the grounds had settled, JT filled three plastic mugs and brought them down to the water's edge.

"Happy Fourth," he murmured.

Abo took his cup without a word and closed his eyes and blew on it.

"Thank you thank you *thank* you," said Dixie as he handed it to her. Her voice was soft, full of a sweetness and uncharacteristic fragility he tried to disdain but couldn't. "How'd you sleep, JT?"

"Slept great."

They sat very still and very quietly, taking in the shadowy blue-gray water, the silhouetted walls. A canyon wren called its plaintive cry, a long series of descending notes. A slight breeze lifted the hairs on his arms.

"I am so so glad," Abo finally said, his voice deep and gravelly with sleep, "that I do not have to be nice to anyone right away."

"How much of that whiskey did you have last night?" JT asked.

"What whiskey?"

JT left them and went to chat with the kayakers, who were straggling up the beach from their small camp just downstream. They were all related, it seemed: tall lanky brothers, along with their spouses and several children. JT asked them where they planned on camping that night; the key during these crowded summer months was for the different parties to stagger themselves that first night, so they wouldn't be on top of one another the whole trip.

"Haven't thought that far ahead," said one of the brothers. Though he couldn't have been more than forty, he had a full white beard. His name was Bud, and JT learned that they were all from Vancouver, where the temperature rarely rose above eighty degrees. Here, it was already close to a hundred. They were to be forgiven, he told himself, for not being the most organized group.

"Holler on the river if you need anything," JT told them.

By seven o'clock, the sun was already up over the low hills to the east, and the motor people were scampering about on the fat tubes of their rig, tightening their gear, and some of the day fishermen had arrived and were messing with their tackle by the side of the river. By eight o'clock, JT and Abo and Dixie had finished breakfast, and for the next several hours, they tightened straps and crammed hatches and rearranged gear so that all boats would be more or less equally loaded. They clipped bail buckets into their boats. The sun grew hot, and their shoulders burned, so they covered up with long-sleeved shirts. They guzzled water from old orange juice jugs.

At ten thirty, JT was lashing an American flag to his rowing seat—it was, after all, the Fourth of July—when he looked up to see an old gray bus rocking its way down the hillside. A cloud of dust roiled up from behind. Dixie squinted.

"Time to rock and roll," she said. "How're you coming, Abo?"

Abo, whose sleeping pad held a chaotic jumble of clothing, books, giant squirt guns, and camera equipment, stood in the well of his boat, brushing his teeth in the hot sun. He spat into the water. "I'm almost ready," he said. "Hey, can either of you fit some of this stuff in your boat?"

"Hell no, babe," Dixie replied. "You ready, JT?"

JT stood high on his boat and pissed a sparkling arc out into the river and wiggled himself back into his shorts.

"I'm ready," he said, hopping off the boat onto the sand. "Let's run this river."

3

Day One

Lee's Ferry

One by one, the guests staggered off the bus into the hot morning sun. Their clothes were clean, their hats straight, their skin pale and freshly shaved and smelling of sunscreen. Eager not only to be of use but also to make a good first impression on the guides, they swarmed the rear door of the bus, jostling to unload more than their fair share of gear. As best he could, JT matched people with the names on his list: Ruth and Lloyd Frankel, the old couple who'd been down the river more times than he could count; Peter Kramer from Cincinnati, who was doing much of the heavy lifting; the Compson parents, calling their two sons back from the river to help with the bags. The tall man with the flappy nomad hat must be the retiree from Wyoming, which would make the tiny woman with an identical hat his wife. There was the teenage girl, Amy—whoa, she was big—and the trim blond woman talking to her must be her mother.

There would be time for introductions later.

When the bus was empty and all the bags lay strewn about the beach, JT directed them to a heap of orange life jackets, and the three guides went around and checked their fittings, tugging on straps and yanking up shoulders to ensure things were sufficiently tight.

"I can't breathe," said the tiny woman.

"Good," said JT with a chuckle.

Then he called everybody over into the shade of some tamarisk trees for his orientation talk. He introduced himself with the fact that this was his 125th trip down the river. "Kind of a milestone, I guess you'd say," he said, glancing at the different faces. "But I'm as psyched now as I was on the first trip. I don't think it's possible for me to ever get tired of this place."

14

As he spoke, a fat yellow bumblebee lazily buzzed its way into the circle, then hovered in front of JT's face. JT grinned at the bee, and it scooted off.

"And it's way more than running the rapids," he said. "It's about hiking up into side canyons; it's about condors and mile-high cliffs and wild watercress and—well, you'll see what I mean."

He went on to remind them that over the next two weeks, they'd be getting to know each other pretty well. "I like to think of it this way," he said, hoping to instill good feelings at the outset. "There's no such thing as a stranger, just people we haven't met."

At this, the Compson mother nudged the two boys, who scowled and edged away. JT suspected he might have just reiterated some earlier parental lecture about being open-minded and making new friends; probably the boys had taken one look at all the adults and assumed they were in for two weeks of heavy scolding.

Well. Wait until those boys saw how adults could behave, two days into a river trip.

He squatted down and unfolded a well-worn topographical map on the sand. The group moved in closer. Using a stick, JT pointed to the upper-right-hand corner of the map.

"So: We're here at Lee's Ferry," he told them, "and we've got two hundred and twenty-five miles between here and the takeout at Diamond Creek. Some days we'll go ten miles, some days thirty; it'll all depend on the day. The only thing I ask is that you be flexible. Plans change, depending on a lot of things."

"I hope we're going to stop at Havasu," said the man from Wyoming. "Mitchell Boyer-Brandt," he added, extending his hand.

"Is Havasu the place with the turquoise water?" the mother asked.

"And vines and ferns and waterfalls," Mitchell said. "I've been waiting to go there since I was ten years old."

JT did not want to get sidetracked. "Havasu's beautiful," he agreed, "although with fifty people on the trail, it can lose a bit of its charm. But I'll do my best to stop there." Carefully he folded up the map. "Now: I see you all have a life jacket. Number one safety rule is you have to wear it *all the time* when you're on the river. No exceptions. When you get off the boat, clip it to something on the boat or a bush, whatever, so it doesn't blow away. Know what we call a passenger without a life jacket?"

There were nervous chuckles all around.

"A hiker," JT said with another grin. "Rule number two: Know where we keep the first aid box and take care of any nicks and scrapes. Wash them well. Put on some ointment. Use a Band-Aid. One little cut can quickly get infected, which definitely can ruin a trip."

"Are there rapids today?" one of the boys asked.

JT looked at the boy, who was squinting up at him. Then he looked at the boy's brother. Both light-haired, freshly buzzed. JT wondered if he would be able to tell them apart.

"What's your name?"

"Sam!"

"Put it here, Sam," said JT, and they slapped palms. "There are most definitely rapids today, and I want to give a little demonstration so everyone knows what to do in case you end up in the water."

"I sure hope *that* doesn't happen!" exclaimed the young man from Cincinnati. "Seeing as I can't swim."

"Well, it probably won't," said JT. "But in case it does, here's the routine. You might find yourself underwater for a few seconds, but I *guarantee* your life jacket will bring you back up. Once you're up, look around. Chances are you'll find yourself right beside the boat because the water's taking you down at the same speed. So grab on. Pull yourself up."

"What if you don't come up?" asked Sam.

"You'll come up," JT assured him.

"But what if you get sucked into a whirlpool?"

"I'll come get you myself, kiddo," he said. "Now, if for some reason you're *not* right beside the boat, you may have to swim on through the rest of the rapid. And then what you do is, it's very simple, see, you put your feet out in front," and he elevated one foot out in front of him and hopped a little for balance, "and kind of sit back, like this," and he leaned back from the hips with his arms out to the sides, "and just float on through the rest of the rapid, and we'll pick you up down below. Very simple. Pay attention. If somebody's waving at you to swim to the left, swim to the left."

"What if you're in a coma, though?" asked Sam.

"Oh, Sam," his mother sighed.

"But if you're in a coma, you can't do very much."

"Don't be a dickhead," said his brother.

"If you're in a coma, I'll take good care of you," JT assured Sam. "All of us guides, we're very good at taking care of people who are really hurt. But that's not going to happen. If you fall out of the boat, you're going to be just fine."

"But this raises the question," said Mitchell. "What happens if someone does get hurt?"

"We've got a satellite phone," said JT. "Usually they can get us a helicopter within an hour."

"And where's the nearest emergency room?" the mother asked.

"Flagstaff."

"Are there rattlesnakes down here?" asked Matthew, the brother.

"Yup. Don't bother them and they won't bother you."

"Scorpions?"

"Yup. Shake your clothes out in the morning."

"How about West Nile?" asked the boys' father.

"Nope."

"Lyme disease?"

"Nope."

"Hantavirus?"

JT held up his hands. "Whoa. Let's be positive, folks. You're probably more likely to get in a car accident on the way to the grocery store than get bitten by a snake."

"How hot does it get down here?" This came from a woman who looked to be in her early fifties, with a bowl-shaped haircut and no neck to speak of, what with her shirt buttoned up to her chin.

"And you are?"

"Evelyn."

"Ain't gonna lie, Evelyn. It gets pretty darn hot. And this trip'll be no exception. One fourteen at Phantom yesterday, I heard. But there's always the river for cooling off. Know what I say about the heat?"

The group waited.

JT raised an eyebrow. "If you're hot, you're stupid."

"What are the water levels running at, if I may ask?" said Mitchell.

"Lows are twelve, thirteen," said JT. "And for those of you unfamiliar with Bureau of Reclamation measurements, that means twelve thousand cubic feet of water are running past you every second. Highs are eighteen to twenty."

"Why the variance?" Mark asked, and JT explained that the operators of the Glen Canyon Dam released more water at certain times to satisfy the power demands of Phoenix.

"Kind of like tides," he said. "Not a big deal."

"How's the food?" Peter asked.

"Let me put it this way," JT said. "This isn't a weight-loss trip. We'll feed you well. Speaking of which, I want to get in a few miles before lunch, so let's get moving."

He tucked the map into its waterproof sleeve and told the group to make sure their water bottles were full, their hats secured. In response to his directions, the group filed out of the shade into the hot, bright desert sun. Last in the group was the teenage girl. She'd been standing in the back, and he got another look at her and realized she wasn't just big; she was huge. She was wearing an oversized green T-shirt from Jamba Juice, with gray athletic shorts that hung to the top of vast, dimpled knees. Her dark hair was parted in the middle and pulled back in a low, unflattering ponytail.

She hesitated, and JT noticed that her life jacket didn't buckle at the bottom.

"Let me adjust that for you," he said cheerfully.

Shyly she held her arms out and glanced to the side as JT tugged at the straps to free up a few more inches. Still the bottom buckle wouldn't clip. He checked to make sure the jacket was a size large. It was. He worked at the straps some more, and by squeezing tightly, he finally managed to clip the buckle shut. The girl winced.

"Too tight?" he asked, glancing up.

She wrinkled her nose.

JT frowned. "Well, you really need to have it buckled," he said. "Park regs. Put your arms down and let's see."

She lowered her arms. As soon as she inhaled, the buckle popped open. Instantly tears filled her eyes.

JT scratched the back of his neck. Regulations were regulations. If anything happened to her, it would be his fault. "What's your name?"

"Amy."

"Hey, Amy. Some of these life jackets have a little more give to them. We'll find you another one." He led her back to the pile, and they picked through the life jackets until they found one that buckled. Her arms stuck out cartoonishly, like penguin wings.

"I think a lot of it's just water weight," she offered. "My mother says it's from the altitude. My ankles are swollen too."

JT nodded, though he doubted her diagnosis. "Let's find you a good spot on one of the boats. Want to ride with me?"

"Okay," she said timidly.

"Come on, then," said JT, heading toward the boats. "You like the front or the back?"

"What's the difference?"

"Well, in the front, you might get splashed a little more."

Amy smiled. "Front, then."

He immediately realized that with her weight, the front of the boat was just where she *shouldn't* be. But he wasn't about to spoil the mood right now.

"Front it is," he said. "Come on. Mine's the boat with the flag. Where are you from, Amy? Wisconsin, isn't it? My gramma grew up in Wisconsin. You want some gum?"

"Thanks," said Amy.

"Welcome to the ditch," said JT.

4

Day One

Lee's Ferry

As the bus rocked its way down the gravel road to Lee's Ferry, Peter Kramer finished off the last of the watermelon he'd swiped from the breakfast buffet that morning. Peter had read in his sister's *Cosmo* that watermelon made your sperm taste better. He didn't know if he was going to get any blow jobs on this trip, but figured a quick adjustment to his own personal sugar levels wouldn't hurt.

Not that he had many hopes, after meeting his fellow passengers at the orientation session last night. There was a nuclear family with a clean-cut dad and weary-looking mom and two squabbling boys. A boxy, middle-aged woman, obsessing over whether she should bring her rain pants. A geriatric couple glued at the hip. A blowhard cowboy and his midget wife, both carrying large iced-coffee drinks. Last to arrive was a trim, stylish woman whose blunt-cut blond hair and wispy bangs gave her an ethereal Scandinavian look—but she came with her daughter, who was quite possibly the most obese girl Peter had ever seen.

Which had worried him: didn't they have weight limits, for safety reasons? What kind of an organization was this?

The trip had not been Peter's idea. Back in Cincinnati, he'd been moping for weeks, complaining to his sister that their mother was going to spend another entire SUMMER asking him to come over and water her PEONIES every other night and he needed a fucking BREAK from that woman. Just because he was out of work and just because Miss Ohio dumped him a year ago didn't mean he was available to step in as his mother's gardener.

Finally his sister got sick of listening to him complain, and she booked a last-minute spot with Coconino Explorations. She'd gone on a river trip with them the year before and loved it, and now wanted the whole world to go. Peter reminded her that he couldn't swim, that he didn't trust sunscreen, and that he was allergic to organized trips where you had to hold hands every time you crossed the street. Plus, canyons made him claustrophobic. Plus, he was trying to quit smoking.

"Peter. Stop. It's paid for," said his sister. "And it's really, really beautiful, and you'll come back a changed person, and some big map company will offer you a cushy job."

And so Peter got on that plane to Phoenix, if only to escape his mother for two weeks. He trusted his sister when she told him that the guides made everyone wear a life jacket, that his chances of falling into the water were slim. He told himself that Miss Ohio would hear about this and realize how adventurous he was and regret her decision to marry someone else. He was even all set to allow that perhaps he'd meet someone hot on the trip—until he walked into the orientation meeting and realized he'd committed himself to two weeks of forced group therapy.

Now Peter stepped off the bus into hundred-degree heat. It didn't seem very canyonlike. The beach was junky and crowded and noisy. They got a pep talk; he made it through Life Jackets and Gear Loading and River Safety and wondered if the bus driver would take him back to Flagstaff.

But then the Trip Leader introduced the other two guides, and everything changed.

She was wearing a beat-up straw hat and faded red shorts and a tattered pink shirt knotted at the waist that revealed her belly button. She had two braids that brushed against her shoulders and wore a silver charm on a leather band around her neck. She barely stopped to wave hello, though Peter couldn't take his eyes off her as she worked on her boat, lugging boxes and crates and yanking straps and coiling ropes; and when she dunked a bandanna in the water and tied it around her neck, he had to blink, to make sure it was real.

Was there any question, any question at all, which boat he was going to choose?

21

As soon as JT dismissed them, Peter casually wandered down to the shoreline and stood by her boat.

"Need some help?" he finally asked.

"Nope," she said, flashing a smile, and then she pirouetted from one boat to the other, bending and coiling and knotting and hoisting; what she was doing, Peter couldn't tell, but it seemed to require a good deal of expertise, and she finally pranced back to her own boat. Peter hadn't moved.

"Here," and she tossed him a snarl of rope, "untangle that, if you wouldn't mind. Hey Abo! Is this your bag? Don't make me haul your shit!" and Peter, whose mother had time and again asked him to untangle a skein of yarn only to have him scoff at the idea (for he had hoops to sink and weights to lift and a V-8 engine that needed revving), now found himself lovingly coaxing apart the strands of a white nylon rope that, for all the times it had touched Dixie's hands, had instantly taken on the intimacy of the entire contents of her top bureau drawer.

So that when the blowhard cowboy from Wyoming rounded everyone up for a group photo, he found himself smiling self-consciously, knowing she might be watching.

Day One

Miles 0–4

After JT's lecture, Evelyn Burns, PhD, found herself clambering on all fours across the rubbery tubes of Dixie's raft, trying not to slip as she made her way to the back. She would have preferred to ride in JT's boat, but the fat girl had just taken the front seat, and JT signaled Evelyn to find another boat. She reminded herself that a woman could row as well as a man and scolded herself for presuming otherwise.

But here they were, finally starting their journey! Evelyn had signed up for this trip as a gift to herself for her fiftieth birthday, and she'd been planning it for well over a year, reading guidebooks and history books and all the personal narratives she could find. A professor of biology at Harvard, she applied her vast research skills to scouting out the best equipment on the Internet—sunblock shirts and insulated water bladders and quick-drying pants that unzipped to become a pair of shorts.

Evelyn hated being unprepared.

Now, with an awkward lurch over a mound of gear, Evelyn found herself in the back well of the boat. The young man from Cincinnati was already sitting on one of the side tubes. Evelyn steadied herself and set her day bag down and wiped her brow.

"It's a bitch, isn't it, just getting in and out," he said.

Evelyn didn't want to think that she was in the same category as this young man, who had informed them all last night that he didn't know how to swim. Evelyn knew how to swim. She knew how to canoe and sail and kayak too. She just didn't have a lot of experience climbing in and out of big rubber rafts.

"So I forget—is this your first trip down the Colorado River?" Peter asked.

Actually, it was the first time she'd even seen the Colorado. She'd gotten her first glimpse earlier that morning, when the transport bus stopped at Navajo Bridge, which spanned the river just before the turnoff to Lee's Ferry. Lots of people liked to walk across the bridge, the bus driver told them. Evelyn got off the bus and joined the others, but midway she stopped and peered over the iron railing. There it was, five hundred feet below, a glassy blue ribbon flanked by green bushes and pink cliffs. Where were the rapids? Where was the roar of white water? All she could hear was the drone of cars crossing the bridge.

In fact, if she closed her eyes, she could have even been back in Boston. She thought of the man who'd left her six months ago with the briefest of letters, whose golden heart she still wore around her neck. She reached up and fingered the heart. It was smooth and warm, as familiar as a tooth. She recalled its red velvet box, the white satin inside. She remembered the touch of his bearded chin against her chest, how he bumbled with his glasses before they made love.

Suddenly, on a whim, Evelyn reached up and unfastened the chain. Dangling it over the railing, she pictured his face once more, then let go. Golden threads in midair, the heavier heart glinting below— Julian's gift evaporated in the hot desert air. And with it, she hoped, any gloom that was trying to seep in and ruin her trip.

"Yes, it's my first trip," Evelyn replied now.

"Mine too," said Peter. "I've never even been in a rowboat. Want some help?"

She was trying to clip her day bag to the web of straps that crisscrossed the pile of gear. She shook her head, but the straps were too tight, and she had to wait while he wedged his hand beneath to lever some space so she could slip her carabiner through.

"Tight little buggers, aren't they?" he said cheerfully.

No doubt wanting to imply that he had more experience than she! Down in the bilge, a puddle of cold water collected at her feet, and she wished she'd thought to get out her neoprene socks. But she wasn't going to go through the rigmarole of unclasping the carabiner and opening up her bag again.

So much work, just getting settled in a boat! How she hated being a novice!

Up front, the old couple had settled themselves efficiently, as though they'd done this a thousand times before. Meanwhile, Dixie waded knee-deep into the icy water and began coiling up the thick nylon bow line, which she then jammed into its own loop, giving it a fierce tug.

"All set?" she asked, and after getting nods all around, she gave the boat a push and hopped up and nimbly pranced across the piles of lashed-down gear to finally land with a little smack on her seat, where she wiggled herself into a good position and grabbed the oars and pivoted them out into the water. Deftly she gave two strong heaves with her right arm; the boat swung around, and to Evelyn's surprise, what she thought was the back quickly became the front as they caught the current and headed downstream.

"Good-bye, civilization!" Dixie exclaimed.

Evelyn gripped the straps. The sun bore down; the water lapped gently at the side of the boat. The river was a rich emerald green here, not blue as it had looked from the bridge, and it sparkled sharply in the sun, glinting where the current moved swiftly. Here and there, the water melted up into round blotches that simmered on the surface. Evelyn glanced back toward Lee's Ferry, where the motor rigs were still on the beach, and she thanked her lucky stars she wasn't on a motorized trip, for it seemed a clumsy and thoroughly illegitimate way to experience the river. Upstream, fishermen waded toward Wyoming, casting their lines.

With each stroke, the oarlocks creaked. Dixie sat facing forward and pushed on the oars, rocking at the hip. Choppy little waves splashed against the side of the boat as they headed into rougher water.

"Is this a rapid?" Peter asked as they jostled along.

Dixie leaned into the left oar to keep the boat straight. "Just a riffle. Why? You worried?"

"Of course I'm worried," said Peter. "I can't swim. Just how cold is this water, anyway?"

"Forty-six degrees," Dixie said. "Straight from the bottom of Lake Powell, courtesy of the Glen Canyon Dam."

"You really can't swim?" Evelyn inquired.

"Sink like a rock," Peter declared.

"Didn't you take swimming lessons as a boy?"

"I flunked."

Evelyn couldn't believe they let people come on this trip if they couldn't swim. And why was he here if he had such dread of the water?

"Trout!" hollered Lloyd from the back.

Evelyn searched the green water but saw no fish.

Dixie asked where everyone was from.

"Cincinnati," said Peter.

"What do you do in Cincinnati?"

"Water my mother's peonies a lot," said Peter.

Dixie laughed. "How about you, Evelyn?"

Evelyn allowed that she was from Cambridge.

"And what do you do in Cambridge?"

"I teach biology."

"Don't tell me you teach at Harvard," Peter warned.

Evelyn allowed that yes, she taught at Harvard, which instantly put a stop to the conversation. This happened frequently; after fifteen years, she'd never figured out how much to say when people asked where she worked. If she volunteered that she taught at Harvard, she seemed to be bragging. If she held back, inevitably someone would coax it out of her, and then her attempt at discretion seemed snooty.

"I'm glad you don't talk with a Boston accent," Peter said. But before he could start in on *pahking the cah*—everyone felt the need to quote the stale little rhyme—there was a rubbery squeak from the back of the boat, followed by a thud and a cry of distress. Evelyn whipped around to see one of the old man's pale, hairless legs poking skyward, with no sign of the rest of him.

"Lloyd!" his wife cried. In a flash Dixie shipped her oars and hopped back over the gear to help the man up, letting the boat simply float along.

"Are you all right?" Dixie asked.

"Well gee!" Lloyd exclaimed. "I don't know what happened!"

"You have to hold on," Ruth scolded, brushing at Lloyd's sleeve.

"I was!"

"Tighter, then," said Ruth.

Dixie scooted back to her seat and took up her oars again.

"Doggone hot," Lloyd said.

Soon they turned a corner, and Navajo Bridge came into view. Five hundred feet above them, its dark lacy arch spanned the canyon walls. Tiny figures dotted the railing. It was hard to believe that just over an hour ago, Evelyn herself had been standing on that bridge, looking down. Yet here she was now, on the river itself, already initiated into the world of river runners. Evelyn gave a small, insignificant wave to those above. She felt herself dividing the world into *us* and *them,* those on the river and those not, sojourners versus the rest of the world. And it seemed somehow fitting to her, although she couldn't explain why, that this dividing point should be the resting place for Julian's golden heart.

Involuntarily she glanced down into the green water, half-expecting to see a flash of gold, knowing, even as she looked, what a silly, impossible thing that would be.

6

Day One

Miles 4–6

Never in her life had Jill Compson felt the sun burn so intensely. Not in Salt Lake City. Not in Phoenix. Not in Key West, where she'd grown up. It scorched her shoulders and made her skin feel painfully stretched. She splashed water on her arms, but the relief was fleeting, the water so cold that it too burned, and she regretted not wearing one of the long-sleeved shirts that she'd so adamantly insisted the boys wear, back at Lee's Ferry. Sunscreen alone couldn't possibly protect her skin, she thought.

Jill and her family were all riding in the paddle boat today, along with Mitchell and Lena from Wyoming. Jill hoped the boys were making a better impression today than they had the night before, at the orientation meeting. Over and over, she'd had to drag them away from the refreshment table and force them to introduce themselves to the other travelers. What kind of boys didn't know how to make eye contact and greet someone by name? Her boys, that's who.

Although why was she surprised? They hadn't wanted to come in the first place. In fact, when they found out last spring that she'd planned this vacation, they'd made a big scene, claiming they couldn't miss basketball camp. And she barely got any backup from Mark. "Shouldn't you have checked with me before you paid the deposit?" he'd asked, right in front of the boys, giving them even more leverage. Eventually they negotiated a compromise, which included one week of private coaching, plus new video games for the eight-hour drive from Salt Lake City to Flagstaff—a drive that sorely tested everyone's patience, so that by orientation time, Jill just wanted to retreat to a spa for the next two weeks. They had adjoining rooms, and well into the wee hours she could hear the boys jumping on the beds. Four times she had to knock on the wall and tell them to turn the television off. Twice she tried with Mark to have an orgasm. Twice she failed. When she got up in the middle of the night, she looked in the bathroom mirror and wondered how, in the span of thirteen short years, she'd come to look exactly like her own mother: pinch-lipped and stern, and utterly without humor.

But today, like Evelyn, Jill was feeling a distinct thrill as they headed out from Lee's Ferry. In contrast to the oar boats, where the passengers could sit back and enjoy the ride while the guides did all the rowing, the paddle boat required work. The boat was set up for six paddlers, three on each side with a mountain of gear running down the middle. As paddle captain, Abo sat perched in the rear, ruddering the boat with his paddle, calling out commands.

Jill and Mark rode up front, the boys in the middle, Mitchell and Lena in the rear. As they left Lee's Ferry, Abo had them practice their maneuvers a bit, the boat going in figure eights until he was convinced they understood his commands. Then they headed down the river for real. The sun grew hotter, the river greener, and she finally felt with deep conviction that the trip had truly begun. Already the canyon rim seemed to be in another world, a world full of engines and asphalt, clocks and credit cards and news reports that didn't really matter.

After Navajo Bridge, the gorge began to deepen, with blotchy maroon cliffs rising straight out of the river. Jill found herself mesmerized by the bubbling current, by the little whirlpools that spun out from her paddle at the end of each stroke. At some point, she heard Abo telling a story about two young men who swam the canyon with nothing but a kickboard to hold a few supplies. Sam didn't believe him and asked Jill if it was true.

"Honey, if the guide says it's true, then it must be true," Jill replied.

Other than that, she kept to herself, her senses tuned to the dry heat, the shimmering water, the brilliant blue sky, and the stark canyon walls. So lost was she that it came as a shock when Abo abruptly steered the boat toward the right side of the river, where JT had already beached his raft. "Looks like lunch, folks," Abo told them, and

Jill suddenly remembered that the last thing she'd eaten was a crumbly muffin from the hotel breakfast bar at five thirty that morning.

"Forward!" yelled Abo suddenly. "Come on, paddlers, we got a meal to prepare! Sam! Matthew! Let's see a little mojo in those strokes, you want me to starve to death back here?"

The first sign of trouble came when Sam complained for the fifth time about being hot. The guides had set up a table in the small bit of shade and were fixing lunch while all the guests were hanging around in the hot sun with not much to do.

"Well, you know what I said earlier," JT told him as he scooped out an avocado. "If you're hot, you're stupid. Go take a dunk. Keep your life jacket on."

"I'm going in the river," Sam told his father.

"Don't go too far. Do you think it's okay?" Mark asked Jill.

"If the guide says it's okay, it's okay," Jill replied.

So Sam waded into the water up to his hips, and with a great deal of shrieking, he hopped up and down and finally dipped below the surface, but only for the briefest of seconds, during which there was a moment of silence, broken by the boy's explosive burst as he shot back up, screaming. It looked like so much fun that soon everyone was dunking themselves, much to the guides' approval, and there wouldn't have been a problem at all but for the fact that when Sam got out of the water, he somehow managed to trap a fire ant between his toes, and he started screaming and hollering again and threw himself on the beach in a frenzy and pulled off his sandal and flung it into the river, where it promptly sailed away.

JT made a dash, but by the time he reached the water's edge, the sandal was gone.

Jill was mad because it was a good pair of Tevas, brand-new, and Mark was mad because it showed such a lack of foresight, and Matthew was mad because Sam was getting all the attention, and Sam rolled about in agony, kicking sand in everyone's faces as they tried to determine just where he'd been bitten so that JT could dab the bite with the stick of ammonia they kept in the first aid box for just that purpose.

"Right there, I think," Jill said, splaying the boy's toes. "Sam, be still!"

JT poked the ammonia stick between Sam's toes. Sam screamed and kicked.

"For god's sake, Sam," Mark said.

"Try it again," said Jill, but JT held back.

"What happens if you don't use it?" she asked.

"Not much, at this point," said JT. "You have to get it on in the first minute."

People stood around them in a circle, peering down.

"I got bit by a fire ant in Africa once," said Mitchell. "It's no fun."

Matthew dug in the sand, mumbling about how it was just an ant and he didn't see what the problem was.

"Go stick it in the water, kiddo," JT told Sam.

"I'm cold now," said Sam.

Matthew remarked that it was only like two hundred degrees out.

"Just your foot," said JT. "Come on." And he helped the boy up by the arm. With great drama, Sam hobbled over to the water's edge and dipped his foot into the water, his face breaking into a silent scream.

Mark watched with his arms crossed. "Please tell me you brought an extra pair of sandals," he said to Jill.

"Flip-flops."

"Nothing with straps?"

"No."

"Oh cripe," said Mark. "Darn him. He has no sense of responsibility."

"He's twelve, Mark."

"When I was twelve, I had a job."

Jill walked away. Mark's job at the age of twelve was scooping leaves from his neighbor's pool for five minutes every morning. Fortunately, before she could dwell on this, the other guides called out that lunch was ready, and they all shuffled over to the lunch table, where the crew had laid out a glorious banquet.

There were two kinds of bread, and ham, and turkey; slices of Muenster and cheddar cheese, tomatoes, red onions, avocados, cucumbers, pickles, and jalapeños; peanut butter and jelly; wedges of cantaloupe and watermelon; chocolate-chip cookies and nuts and Jolly Ranchers and M&Ms. Many had pooh-poohed the notion of lunch, certain they'd lost their appetite in this heat, but they suddenly found themselves ravenous and ended up packing as much between two slices of bread as they possibly could, then adding a little more for good measure. Susan tried jalapeños with peanut butter; Amy made herself a diet sandwich with turkey and lettuce leaves; Mitchell ate spoonfuls of jam straight from the jar; the boys squirreled away Jolly Ranchers in their pockets. Peter, of course, ate as much watermelon as he could without appearing gluttonous.

Meanwhile, the river flowed on, swiftly, quietly; constant and alive.

7

Day One

Miles 6–8

At the lunch buffet that day, Susan Van Doren was so conscious of people staring at her daughter that she almost confronted them head-on. Had none of them ever been fat? Had a fat friend? Watched the scales go up up up regardless of what they ate?

Get over it, Susan, said the Mother Bitch. *Face it; your daughter's fat because she eats like a horse. And she eats like a horse because you're neurotic about your weight. You drink diet everything. You weigh yourself every morning. For seventeen years, you've communicated your own obsession to her, and now look: two hundred and fifty pounds of maternal fault.*

Susan watched her daughter lumber away from the lunch table with nothing but a slice of turkey rolled up in a lettuce leaf. It broke her heart to see Amy making an effort, on this first day, to set some dietary standards for herself. Susan wished for all the world that the Mother Bitch would go into hibernation and allow her to feel like any other well-adjusted forty-three-year-old woman with a lot to be thankful for: a good job, a nice house, a sweetheart of a daughter. But the Mother Bitch was always there, yap yap yap, making her feel self-conscious about Amy. If she could, she would crush the Mother Bitch to a pulp.

On her personal information form, Susan had written that her goal for the trip was to learn something new about herself. Amy, she'd noted before mailing off the packet, had written that her goal was "to meet people who share a passion for the wilderness and anything outdoorsy and to see the Grand Canyon and above all to have fun ☺☺☺☺☺☺☺☺."

Who could find fault with a girl like that?

Susan carried her sandwich across the beach to join Amy, who had already finished eating. What an awkward situation this must be for her, Susan thought, and a sudden pang of remorse tore through her. Why had she planned this vacation? What kind of mother brought an overweight teenage girl on a trip where you lived in a bathing suit?

"Isn't it gorgeous?" she said cheerfully.

"It's hot."

"Dunk your shirt in the water, like the guides."

Amy stared cruelly at her, then trudged back to the lunch table and took a stack of cookies and headed off to the opposite end of the beach, where the old couple was sitting.

She's really a caring, sensitive, thoughtful person, Susan wanted to tell the others. And really, what were a few cookies, in the grand scheme of things? Nevertheless, she worried that the others might not only judge her for the excess calories, but think she was eating more than her fair share. And Susan thought bitterly, once again, how unfair it was, the way people prejudged overweight people. This time she didn't give the Mother Bitch any chance whatsoever to come back with her snide, fault-finding remarks, but rather stuffed the old hag back into her sack and tied it shut with a double knot.

Ruth Frankel smiled up at the girl and thanked her for the cookies.

"Look what she brought us, Lloyd," she said.

"Who?"

"Amy! Amy, right? Amy brought us some cookies, Lloyd. Thank you, dear," she told Amy. "Now you go sit down and enjoy yourself and stop waiting on us old folks."

"Where did she come from?" Lloyd asked as Amy walked off.

"She's on the trip with us," Ruth reminded him.

"Well, she better lose a little weight or she'll become diabetic. Oreos!" he exclaimed. "My goodness. Did you pack these?"

Ruth sighed inwardly. Even though she'd cleared it back in March with Lloyd's doctor, she still wondered if it was a good idea for them to squeeze in this one last float trip. They'd been making this trip every year since they were a young couple, first running the river back in the 1950s, before the dam was built, when Lloyd was a young doctor working off his medical school debt by volunteering on the Navajo reservation. Ruth had just started painting at the time, and she brought along her watercolors and dabbed splashes of color into her notebook—salmon, mauve, and eggplant, colors she would later reproduce all winter long, wherever she was. Later, they moved to Evanston, Illinois, where they raised their two children, but they returned year after year for two weeks in the canyon. They brought friends. They passed up ski vacations and trips to Mexico to save their money for this particular trip; one year, when both children were in college, they traded Ruth's paintings in exchange for their fare. Didn't they get tired of the same old trip? people would ask. Didn't they want to see other places? The truth was, they both felt a renewal of the soul while on the river, something that their friends in Evanston—churchgoers all—failed to comprehend.

And then, two years ago, at the age of seventy-four, Lloyd began forgetting things. What he'd had for breakfast. What they'd done last weekend. Examining a patient, he found himself repeating his questions, and then he'd go back to his office and find he couldn't remember what he'd just diagnosed. Ruth didn't need a doctor to tell her what was wrong. Last year Lloyd's condition was not so advanced, and they took their river trip as usual, without worry. This year, however, the increasing memory lapses and confusion had left Ruth debating the wisdom of a river trip. Was it irresponsible to take Lloyd? Alone, she visited Lloyd's doctor and asked for his advice. He was an old friend and understood the spiritual significance of these trips for Ruth and Lloyd, and he listened to Ruth ticking off the worrisome incidents with a somber but skeptical demeanor. When she finished, he leaned across his desk and clasped her hands.

"Ruth," he said, "you're a cautious, responsible woman. Go. You'll take good care of him. It will do more for his spirit than keeping him safe in his living room."

So she'd signed them up for what she knew, deep in her heart, would be their last trip together. The hardest part was getting them both packed, because Lloyd kept forgetting that he was going on any trip at all, let alone a two-week journey through the Grand Canyon. Upstairs in their comfortable colonial, Ruth laid out piles of clothes she intended to pack, and Lloyd would wander in and see them there all nice and fresh on the guest room bed and put them on and go out into the garden and stand with his hands on his hips. Ruth bought extra Metamucil biscuits and Lloyd ate them. She bought six tubes of sunscreen, only to have them disappear. At one point she lost her temper, shrieking that she was going to put him in a nursing home and go alone. But Lloyd just replied, "Go where?" and she cried all night, unable to forgive herself.

The biggest moment of relief had come at six thirty this very morning, when they loaded their bags onto the transport bus back in Flagstaff, climbed in, and took a seat; and the driver shut the door; and there was no longer any chance for Lloyd to open up their carefully packed bags, take something out, and lose it.

"I'll bet she's already diabetic," Lloyd said now.

"Don't you say a word," Ruth warned.

"When's Lava?"

"Not for another ten days."

Lloyd shook his head gravely. "I tell them and I tell them and I tell them," he said, "and they just keep on smoking."

After lunch, as Abo and Dixie scrubbed dishes by the water's edge, JT called everyone together and told them their first real rapid was coming up soon.

"How big?" Sam asked.

"Six, on a scale of one to ten," said Mitchell, looking up from his guidebook.

"Well, maybe more like four at this water level," JT said. "But it's definitely big enough. So put on your life jackets, and tighten everything down, and let's go!"

Jill fussed with the boys, making sure their life jackets were tight, their day bags clipped into place with the locking carabiners that had cost five times what she expected at the adventure-gear store back in Salt Lake City. She tightened the chin straps on their hats. (She did *not* want Mark to know that she hadn't packed extra hats.) Finally Abo had to tell her to quit checking on things and sit down herself. She obeyed, slightly embarrassed, and Abo pushed off, and they paddled down the river, three boats in a line: JT in front, Abo and his paddlers in the middle, and Dixie in the rear.

It wasn't long before the river itself changed. Up ahead, the glassy water dropped off abruptly; every so often a sunlit spray danced above the horizon.

"Stop," Abo commanded. "Listen," and everybody fell silent. Sure enough, they could hear the hollow roar of the big water. Ahead of them, JT stood up on his seat to get a better view. His boat rocked a little. The current was rapidly picking up speed; JT waited until the very last minute, then dropped to his seat and quickly angled his boat to the left. Then the boat disappeared into the spray, and all you could see were a few flashes of blue as it bucked through the foam.

Their own boat was now fast accelerating.

"Feet in the stirrups, folks!" Abo yelled. "And pay attention! Sam! What's it mean when I say 'Hard Forward'?"

"It means paddle really hard!" Sam yelled back.

"That's right! Forward!" Abo shouted, and they glided down into the tongue of the rapid, where the water formed a downstream V, dark and smooth and sinuous before exploding into a wall of chaotic white froth.

"Hard forward!" shouted Abo, and Jill dug deep and pulled as hard as she could as they barged on through. She felt the boat tip first to one side, then to the other; water came splashing from all directions, and the paddlers lost their synchronicity and knocked each other's paddles. A long plume of silver spray drenched Jill's face and blinded her for a moment, causing her to gasp for air, and when she opened her eyes another plume was coming and this time she just ducked like a coward, screaming with frantic delight.

Then, just as suddenly, it was over, and they were bobbing in the tailwaves. There were whoops and hollers, and at Abo's direction they all raised their paddles high into a tent formation, then slapped the water with a cheer.

Only then did Jill think to turn around and make sure her children were safe.

She'd gotten drenched, but oddly, she wasn't at all cold; within minutes the sun had dried her arms and legs, and she was grateful now not to have a shirt on because the sun felt so good. She looked at Mark and Mark looked at her, and they both laughed out loud, something they hadn't done in years together, and she glanced back and witnessed a miracle, namely, that the boys weren't fighting and in fact had wide horsey grins on their faces, and she would never have said this out loud but she thought: Didn't I say you would love it? Now, aren't you glad you're here?

Truly, she told herself. Keep your mouth shut.

8

Day One, Evening

Mile 16

They camped that first night on a small beach sloping up to a sandy, rock-studded hillock that overlooked the river. To transfer the massive amount of gear out of the boats and onto the beach, JT had everyone form a fire line, with the guides in the boats unstrapping everything and handing it over, each bag, each box making its way from one set of outstretched hands to the next until the beach was littered with gear. Then, like speedy housewives, the guides whisked about setting up their kitchen, unfolding the long metal tables, hooking up the stove, arranging all the cookware. Abo filled two plastic buckets with river water and slopped them down on each end of the cleanup table. Dixie lugged the large flat fire pan across the sand to an open spot, got down on hands and knees, and leveled things out and wiggled the grill into place for the salmon they would be cooking tonight.

Meanwhile, JT went off to scout out a good place for the toilet system, known in river parlance as the groover. Having camped here many times before, he had a destination in mind and followed a worn path through a thick grove of feathery tamarisk, around some boulders, and finally up onto a ledge blocked off from camp by a huge boulder, with a prime view of dusty pink cliffs rising out of the glassy water. Good views from the groover mattered, a lot.

JT would bring everyone up here before dinner to educate them in the specific how-tos. But now, after a long day in the hot sun, what he wanted most of all was a beer. He hopped down from the ledge and headed back to the camp, his flip-flops kicking up a soft spray of sand behind.

But as he was passing through the thicket, a rustle in the underbrush stopped him in his tracks. Dang if a territorial rattlesnake wasn't going to spoil his groover site. He peered into the brush but saw nothing and warily moved on.

Then he heard another rustle, a quick shake, like dried beans in a pod. Now JT backed away, knowing full well that a snake encounter on their first night would set everybody on edge for the entire trip. *Fine. Keep the tamarisk thicket, keep the ledge site, you bugger. I'll find another place for the groover.*

But as he turned, he heard a whimper, an anxious whine that definitely did not come from a reptile. JT peered into the scrub again.

There, panting heavily on a bed of leaves and sticks, lay a dog. Its fur was gray and matted, its nose crusted, and yellowish goop had collected in the corners of its eyes. Seeing JT, the dog trembled, and with the tremble came a quick chattering of its teeth—the sound JT had mistaken for a rattler. It was some kind of mutt, he wasn't quite sure, but it seemed part poodle, part terrier, with loopy gray curls and a dirty wet wisp of a beard—actually, of the approximate lineage as the dog JT had had as a boy. With liquid black eyes, this direct descendant of the true and loyal companion that had slept in the same bed and shared the same bath and eaten the same bologna sandwiches as a very young JT Maroney now gazed straight into his heart.

JT had seen a lot of animals on his 124 previous trips down the river. He'd seen bighorn sheep and coyotes and countless ringtail cats who crept around camp in the middle of the night in search of leftovers. But he'd never seen a dog. For one thing, dogs weren't allowed below the canyon rim. He'd heard other guides tell of the occasional Navajo cattle dog showing up, especially in this first stretch, where access to the river was easy. But JT had never run into one himself. And this sure as shit did not look like a cattle dog; wash it up and put a collar on it, and it might pass for a Biff or a Molly, with a plaid doggie bed and a personalized bowl nearby. JT couldn't for the life of him imagine where it came from. Definitely not another boating party; they could never have gotten a dog past the ranger up at Lee's Ferry. A renegade hiker, a dog-loving Ed Abbey living in the piñon?

JT held out his hand. The dog sniffed his fingers, then slapped its tail heavily on the bed of branches. It struggled to its feet but could not get up, so it lay back down, setting its chin resolutely between its paws.

"Hey, boy," said JT. "Come on. Get up."

The dog didn't move.

JT knew better than to handle an injured animal; he dug deep into the pocket of his shorts and held out a few oily peanuts. The dog sniffed, then licked them out of his hand. JT moved back a little and held out more nuts, and with a great deal of effort, one haunch at a time, the dog managed to raise himself on all fours.

Now JT could at least see what the problem was, for the dog was favoring its right front paw. JT moved in and, while offering more nuts, tried to inspect the paw. The dog drew back, but JT smoothed his velvety ears and kept feeding him nuts, and the dog calmed down enough for JT to finally locate an ugly cactus thorn lodged between the leathery pads of his paw.

No wonder the dog was whimpering.

"Easy, boy." He cradled the dog's leg and with his stubby fingers tried to pick out the thorn. However, he only succeeded in breaking off the tip. The dog lay down and began licking the tender area.

JT glanced back toward camp. It crossed his mind that he should go back and get Abo and Dixie to come help him decide what to do, but he was still partly afraid that perhaps he was dreaming this all up, and by the time Abo and Dixie got up here, the dog would have vanished, and he, JT, Official Trip Leader, would be the butt of jokes for the rest of the trip.

He didn't give it any more thought but bent down, circled his arms underneath the dog, and hoisted him to his chest. Forty pounds, maybe, no more; JT had certainly carried heavier loads. With the dog in his arms, he retraced his steps out of the tamarisk grove and headed back down the path.

When he reached the hillock that sloped down to the camp, he saw people crowded around Dixie's boat; she'd opened up her drink hatch, and people were fumbling through the burlap bags for their personal stashes. Evelyn noticed him first. Then Lena, who nudged Mitchell, who said, "What *now*?" which caught everybody else's attention, and they all turned to stare up at this grizzled man in a beat-up cowboy hat and a bleached plaid shirt staggering down the sandy slope in the shimmering heat with a dog in his arms.

Dixie shaded her eyes. "Am I on drugs?"

Once on the beach, JT squatted and set the dog on the sand. The two boys fell upon him before either parent could stop them, tussling his ears and trying to rub his belly, and the dog, who knew a good thing when he saw it, forgot about the thorn and happily rolled onto his back and splayed his legs, as though reuniting with his long-lost family.

Dixie hopped down off her raft. "Where did you find that thing?"

"Up in the bushes," said JT. "I heard a rattling sound and thought it was a snake, and then I heard him whimper."

"What's a dog doing down here?" Mitchell asked with a wide smile. He'd taken off his hat; a band of tight curls lay plastered against his skull, making his head seem too small. There was something in his smile that made JT suspect that whatever explanation he offered, it wouldn't satisfy this man.

"And where did it come from?" Evelyn asked.

"I don't know," JT said. "Sam, go fill a bowl with water."

Sam ran off.

"What are you going to do with him?" said Mitchell.

"See if I can get this thorn out of his foot."

"Oh, the poor dog!" exclaimed Amy, falling to her knees beside the dog. She had changed into another large T-shirt, this one dirty white, printed with the red and yellow logo from the Hard Rock Cafe.

"And then?" said Mitchell.

JT put his hands on his hips and looked at the dog, whose hind leg was kicking reflexively from all the petting.

"No idea, Mitchell," said JT. "No idea at all."

9

Day One

Mile 16

The thorn turned out to have a barbed tip, so Abo and Dixie had to pin the dog down while JT wiggled the thorn around with a pair of tweezers, trying to loosen the hook that had snagged itself into the dog's flesh. At one point the dog snapped at Dixie, but eventually JT managed to release the catch and remove the barb. Abo and Dixie let go, and the dog wiggled to his feet, shook, limped over to lift his leg against a bush, and finally retreated to a patch of shade to lick his wounded paw.

JT tossed his hat into his boat, then waded into the water and submerged himself. Dripping wet, he hoisted himself up onto his boat, pulled up the drag bag, and got out a cold beer.

Abo and Dixie joined him. One by one the guests dispersed, except Mitchell.

"Give us a moment, okay, Mitchell?" JT said.

Mitchell turned and retreated.

Abo crumpled dramatically into the well of JT's boat. "Well, this kind of puts a wrinkle in things, don't you think?"

"You're not kidding," Dixie said. "Good thing he's healthy."

"Are you nuts, woman?" Abo demanded.

"Healthy enough so we don't have to feel too sorry for him, is what I mean."

"Ice queen," JT told Abo.

"I'm not an ice queen," said Dixie. "I'm just being pragmatic. Where's he going to sleep tonight, for instance?"

"He can sleep on my boat," said Abo.

"Or maybe with Mitchell," murmured JT. They glanced toward the beach, where Mitchell had spread out a large map and appeared to be cross-checking locations with information in his guidebook. The dog approached warily. Mitchell glanced at the dog, and the dog backed away.

"You think he's a cattle dog?" asked Abo.

"Could be," said JT. "Though he doesn't look like one."

"Maybe he came down in someone's boat," said Abo.

JT shook his head. "I can't imagine anyone getting a dog past the ranger. My guess is some hiker snuck him down one of the trails, then lost him."

Abo leaned over the edge of the boat, pulled up the drag bag, and tossed another beer to each of them. JT set his aside.

"Let's not get sidetracked, though," said Dixie. "This could be a huge pain in the ass."

Abo cupped his hands over his mouth. "Houston, we have a problem!"

"You better call Park Service," said Dixie.

"You think this qualifies as an emergency?" JT said.

"You don't?"

"And what's Park Service going to do?" JT went on. "Stop everything and send down a boat? Then what? Hike him out? With an injured paw?"

"I hate to say this, Boss, but he doesn't look so injured anymore," said Abo, and they all looked back at the beach, where the dog was chasing sticks as quickly as Sam and Matthew could throw them. Every time the dog changed direction, he sent up a spray of sand. JT suspected that as far as the boys were concerned, this was completely normal—why, every time you went down the Colorado River you picked up a stray dog on the first night.

He checked his watch; it was almost seven, and they hadn't even started dinner. "Let's get people fed. We'll deal with the dog later. I sure am not going to worry about it right now."

"What's the menu?" Dixie asked.

"Salmon."

"Oh my god, I LOVE salmon!" Abo shouted.

"Good. Because you're cooking it."

"And I love COOKING salmon too!"

"Tone it down, Abo," said Dixie, "or I am not going to survive two weeks on the river with you."

Abo narrowed his eyes. "Sleep with me tonight, babe."

"Been there, done that," Dixie murmured.

JT tossed his empty beer can onto a tarp near the kitchen area. "Abo, start the grill. Dixie, teach those boys how to bust up the cans." He opened the meat cooler, which was three-quarters solid ice and one-quarter frozen protein. He took out the slabs of salmon, then closed the cooler and looked up to see Mitchell standing at the bow.

"Need something, Mitchell?"

"Just wondering if you knew what you were going to do with the dog yet."

"Nope."

Mitchell set his hands on his hips—not belligerently. "Because some of us are concerned about trouble," he began. "Lena's got allergies. And if the dog's been exposed to rabies or something . . ."

"We'll take care of it, Mitchell," JT assured him.

"I've been waiting years for this trip," Mitchell said.

"I read you, Mitchell," said JT, feeling a certain level of professional tolerance dropping. "But don't worry. The dog's not going to spoil things."

"We've got some gin, by the way, if you fellas want a gin and tonic," Mitchell offered.

"Thanks," said JT. "A rain check, maybe. Gotta get dinner going right now."

And within a mere half hour, they did in fact have a splendid dinner ready. Nobody forgot about the Fourth of July, either: using two oars, twine, and some fancy knot-tying skills, Abo strung up red, white, and blue balloons over the serving table, and for dessert there was a cake decorated like an American flag, which Dixie presented complete with a sparkler, to great applause. The dog, who two hours ago had seemed so seriously crippled, now darted between people's legs in search of dropped morsels; he soon learned that all he had to do was follow

Lloyd, who had a tendency to set his plate down and wander off in search of something else.

"That's three plates of salmon you've taken now!" Ruth scolded him. "Now stay put!"

Although they had known each other just over twenty-four hours, as a group they were already forming tentative bonds. Amy, who had brought a deck of cards, mystified Sam and Matthew with card tricks. Mark and Mitchell found they had skied at the same resort in Canada as boys. Lena convinced Jill that navigating the menu of a digital camera was not as difficult as Jill feared.

Only JT sat by himself, alone on his raft, listening to the sound of water sloshing against his boat. It was dusk, and the color had drained out of the cliffs, leaving them starkly silhouetted against an apricot sky. He did not intend to let the matter of the dog spoil the evening for him; he had faith that it would work out, one way or another. Very few things could rattle JT, which was why he was such a good river guide: he handled the unforeseen with grace, and usually managed to learn something from it and come out ahead.

He looked at the group; people were sitting on mats, logs, or the sand itself, finishing dessert. It seemed to be a good bunch, for the most part. Mitchell had the potential to be a pain, he knew, and Amy's weight troubled him; he'd never had such an overweight person on a trip before. He'd have to think about balancing the boats and scheduling hikes with lots of turnaround options. But so what if she didn't hike as much as the others? The canyon belonged to everyone, regardless of physical limitations. She would still have a good time. And who knew what she might learn about herself?

This was, in fact, what he enjoyed about these trips: watching people discover new sides of themselves on the river. The fearful took risks; the quiet ones opened up; sometimes (though not always), the loud ones quieted down. Egos got checked, life plans altered. You saw a lot of Plan Bs develop on a river trip.

"Last call on dessert!" shouted Abo.

By now the light of a quarter moon was sliding down the western wall. There were dishes to wash, pots to scrub, food to be packed away. Then, a good night's sleep. They would figure out the dog issue tomorrow.

Overall, if you'd asked him to assign a letter grade to the first day, he'd have given it a good solid A.

Fine. A-minus, given the dog.

July 4

Please oh please oh please get me off this trip. I cannot take two weeks of this. Everybody stares at me and I know EXACTLY what they're thinking. What's a FAT GIRL doing on a trip like this? Why isn't she at FAT CAMP? Wonder where she gets those FAT CLUB T-shirts? Quick get in line before the FAT GIRL takes all the dessert!!!

I wonder how sick you have to be for them to call a helicopter. Maybe I could get bitten by a rattlesnake. Then again, maybe not; maybe rattlesnakes don't like FAT GIRLS.

Fine. It's kind of pretty here. But it's unbelievably hot and I have no energy whatsoever. I hope these guides don't expect me to do any work because I can barely move. Mom made me help her put up the tent tonight and I felt like I was on percocet. Oh and by the way, when we were done I went inside to change and guess who takes up the entire tent. Sucks for her but she's the one who wanted to do this trip and if she only has three inches of space to sleep in, she should have thought of that earlier.

Maybe some night I will just float off down the river when every- one else is asleep and never be seen again, the lost whale.

We found a dog tonight. Some people are freaking out but I don't see what the big deal is. I fed him a lot of salmon so he will like me. Maybe I can make him FAT and then I will have something in common with someone else.

DAY TWO

River Miles 16–30

House Rock to Fence Fault

Day Two

Mile 16

JT was leery of naming the dog, but people are driven to name things—especially on a river trip, where you have a lot of time to contemplate things you normally wouldn't. And so the next morning, as Abo and Dixie were cooking breakfast, people stood around proposing names for the dog. Evelyn suggested Glen, after Glen Canyon. Peter came up with Lassie, as a joke. Sam for some reason got stuck on the name Roger. Matthew, already well aware that Sam was getting more attention than he on this trip, countered with the name Groover. Mitchell, who, like JT, knew the danger of naming any animal, remained silent.

But since nobody could agree, for now they simply called him River Dog, which seemed appropriate given his tendency to dash into the water after anything they could throw. Not everyone was enthusiastic about playing with the dog, though; and, it being their first morning on the river, many of them simply milled about, not quite sure what to do with themselves before breakfast was ready—whether to brush teeth and wash, or skip the hygiene and go straight for the coffee. Jill, for the first time since the boys were toddlers, did not insist that anyone do anything; she ladled out a cup of coffee and stood quietly on the beach, taking in the reflections of cliff and sky on the moving surface of the water. She felt an unfamiliar serenity as she stood there, a realignment of nerves that allowed each breath to resonate out through the tips of her fingers. She felt like a lot of things that mattered two days ago no longer mattered. Fleetingly, she wished that she were on this trip without her family.

JT sat on his raft, also drinking coffee. It was six thirty; he figured he would wait until seven to call Park Service and see if they had any boats coming by today that could perhaps take the dog down to Phantom Ranch, where somebody might be able to hike him out. Meanwhile, he opened up his map and planned out the day. Just ahead was House Rock Rapid, rated seven, sure to wake everybody up. Then there was a flat stretch of water, followed by the Roaring Twenties, a five-mile series of nonstop rapids. Tonight, depending on how much time they made, they could camp down around Shinumo Wash or Fence Fault.

As JT was folding up the map, Mitchell strolled over, mug in hand. JT wanted to get off to a good start with the man this morning, so he called out, "Morning, Mitchell! Sleep okay?"

"Slept great," said Mitchell. "So! How far do you think we'll go today?"

"Don't know," said JT cheerfully. "Maybe ten miles, maybe fifteen."

"Think we can go up to Silver Grotto?"

"We'll see," said JT. "No vetoes, no promises."

Mitchell nodded. He sipped his coffee.

"I was wondering," he said after a moment, "if you decided what to do about the dog."

JT checked his watch. "Just about to call Park Service, Mitchell," he said. He reached down into the well of his boat and unstrapped the yellow plastic case with the satellite phone.

"Just worried about my wife," said Mitchell. "Her asthma, you know."

"We're aware of that, Mitchell." JT unsnapped the plastic fasteners and opened up the box. Inside, cradled in a bed of foam, lay the satellite phone, a brick-sized device with a stubby antenna that swiveled up like an action figure. He hated, absolutely *hated,* using the satellite phone—on the second day, no less!—but he really had no choice here. At the very least, he felt he had to report the dog.

As he punched in the numbers for Park Service, Mitchell gazed serenely downriver and sipped his coffee.

"I guess you'd say we're not exactly dog people," Mitchell said to no one in particular.

JT expected the ranger to be more upset about the dog, but in fact he sounded mildly exasperated when JT asked him what he wanted them to do.

"You deal with it!" he exclaimed. "I've got three hikers who refused to listen when I told them how much water they need in this heat, and two of them collapsed halfway down to Phantom!"

The line went dead, and JT found himself staring stupidly at the phone before replacing it in its box. He hadn't eaten breakfast, so he went to the food table and loaded up a plate.

"What'd the ranger say?" Dixie asked.

"He said figure it out."

"So what are we going to do?"

"Keep the dog," said JT. "Find him a life jacket."

"We're taking him with us?"

JT drenched his French toast in syrup. "You want to hike him out yourself? Scratch that. You can't; we need you."

"Can't they send someone down to pick him up?"

"Organize a whole trip to come pick up a dog? I don't think so," said JT.

"Then we should stop one of the motor rigs and get them to take the dog down to Phantom. There's gotta be a hiker who'll hike him out. There's no way we can spend five days with a dog, JT. He'll get into the meat cooler. He'll chew everything."

"We'll watch him," said Abo. "Chill."

"You chill," said Dixie.

JT scratched his chin.

"Fine," said Dixie. "But for the record, he's not riding in my boat."

Abo shot her a wounded look and reached out and caught the dog by the scruff of its neck. "Such a meanie," he crooned. "What's your name, anyway? What do they call you?"

JT set his plate on the sand, and as the dog licked the remains, JT knotted a red bandanna around the dog's neck. "You know what they say," he said.

"What?"

But JT didn't answer. Dog or no dog, he still had a trip to run. Time to clean up. Time to break camp. Time to load up the boats, and make room for the dog. If there was anything JT liked, it was a first, and this was definitely his first trip with a dog.

You name it, you love it, was what he was going to say to Abo, but JT didn't dare articulate the truism, even to himself.

Shortly after breakfast, JT summoned the group for their first morning meeting and told them that for now they were keeping the dog.

Sam and Matthew whooped and roughed him up.

"Until we can figure something else out," JT continued. "It's not exactly what we expected, but hey, this is the river, gotta be flexible, right?"

Mitchell and Lena turned away and conferred with one another. Mark looked at Jill and shrugged; Evelyn glanced from one face to another, as though not ready to commit to an opinion.

Mitchell rejoined the group and asked what hikes JT was planning for the day.

"I was just about to get to that," said JT, and he kneeled on the sand and spread out his map. "If we do North Canyon, you'll see some pretty good geology."

Mitchell pointed out that North Canyon was not a very long hike. "How about Silver Grotto?"

"What's Silver Grotto?" asked Jill.

Mitchell closed his eyes in reverence and shook his head. "Unbelievably beautiful," he told Jill. But he didn't elaborate, which made it seem to Jill that he was casting judgment on her, for not knowing.

"Let's see how the day goes," JT said evenly. He had a name for people like Mitchell; they were known among the guides as copilots. Copilots had done their homework before coming down the river, had studied up on canyon history and geology, had pored over maps and guidebooks and knew where all the best hikes were, knew which waterfalls you could climb behind, which ones you could jump off. JT's method of dealing with copilots was to be as nice to them as possible but to let their chatter go in one ear and out the other.

Now he told Mitchell, "I don't know if we'll make it that far.

Remember what I said yesterday. Gotta be flexible, gotta play it by ear. Right now we're just going to focus on breaking camp. Take your tents down, get your gear packed, put on your sunscreen, whatever."

"I have a question," said Jill.

"Yes, ma'am?"

She placed her hands on her hips. "Do you guides *ever* get a chance to just enjoy the trip?"

There were appreciative nods and murmurs all around.

"Because you work so hard!" Jill exclaimed.

JT didn't like compliments, and he didn't like being in the spotlight. "Abo and Dixie did most of the work this morning," he told them. "I sat and yakked on the phone. Go on. Pack up your things. Let's run this river."

Jill had Mark apply sunscreen to her back.

"Bet these river guides get a lot of skin cancer," he said. He had a slappy, unpleasant way of doing it, and she struggled to keep her balance.

"One of the hazards of the occupation, I guess," she murmured.

"And I bet they don't have very good health plans, either," Mark went on. "If any."

"Sam," called Jill. "Leave the dog's tail alone!" She smelled insect repellent and looked up to see Mitchell spraying his arms with Off. According to JT, there weren't mosquitoes down here. What was the man doing?

Mitchell finished spraying his hat, then joined Jill and Mark. "Of all the things!" he said with a chuckle.

Jill politely asked him what he meant.

"A dog! First day out! If you wrote a story about it, nobody would believe it. I hate to sound inhumane," he confided, "but am I the only one who wouldn't find it totally cruel and unusual to just leave the dog here?"

Jill was taken aback by this.

"I mean, the dog must have some pretty good survival skills," he went on. "We could just leave a bunch of food. Somebody else will be camping here tonight. They'll feed it, just like we did. Why should we complicate our trip?"

Jill wondered if she really wanted to tell Mitchell, on the second day of the trip, that yes indeed, he did sound inhumane. All things considered, she preferred harmony to confrontation.

"Are you just concerned about Lena's allergies? Because we're outside," she pointed out. "There's lots of fresh air here, not like a closed-up room. I can make sure the boys stay away from Lena," she added.

"You don't have to do that," Mitchell said, although it was clear from his tone that he did in fact see that as a possibility. "It's just that after forking out six thousand bucks, I don't want to have to leave the river on the second day."

I forked out twelve thousand, Jill thought, and it wasn't to spend two weeks with someone like you.

Just then JT hollered for everyone to choose a boat. The dog would ride in his boat this morning, he told them. Dixie's boat would be dog-free, for those who wanted. Slowly everyone made their way toward the boats, with the exception of Mark, who hung back.

"Did you bring anything?" he whispered to Jill.

"Like what?"

"Like, you know, bran or prunes or something."

"No, Mark," said Jill. "If you wanted me to bring bran or prunes, you should have told me."

"I was just asking," said Mark.

Day Two

Miles 16–20

High on JT's list of "Top Ten Ways to Make Friends" was to camp directly above a rapid, so as to start the next day with a good wake-up splash. In keeping with this, no sooner had the three boats pulled off shore that morning than they all found themselves gliding into the tongue of House Rock Rapid, where the current ran green and silky-smooth over submerged boulders before exploding in a mass of white foam below.

"Good morning *campers*!" JT shouted as the first icy wave drenched them. "Hold on to that dog!" He leaned into his left oar, and they bucked and slapped through messy, white-crested waves that sprayed in all directions. Up front Jill cowered and gripped the dog's bandanna, and Mark yee-hawed like a seasoned river runner, while in the rear Ruth and Lloyd winced and laughed. The waves rose higher, then higher still, and JT simply followed their lead, making those quick adjustments.

But then one of the waves collapsed on him, and he felt his boat slap against the next lateral at the wrong angle, and the boat tipped precariously—just long enough for Jill, in lurching, to lose her grip on the dog. Like a seal, the dog slid over the edge and into the waves.

JT punched on through the last hungry crests, then shipped his oars and scrambled up on his seat. The dog had quickly gotten caught in a small whirlpool; his life jacket being way too big, it swirled like an empty tent on top of the water with only the dog's nose poking up in the middle.

"Swimmer!" JT yelled. "The dog!"

And Abo, who was having a graceful run right down the center of the rapid, deftly steered his boat toward the whirlpool, just close enough to lean over and grab the life jacket and haul the scrawny animal up out of the water and into the back of his boat.

JT had never witnessed anything quite like it.

Abo guided his boat up alongside JT's.

"You damn dog!" said JT, as Abo hoisted the dog over to him. "Get in here! Siddown! What's the big idea, getting yourself sucked into a blender first thing!"

"That's what we should call him," said Sam. "Hey Blender! Come on, Blender!"

Dixie, whose smooth run through House Rock had gone unwitnessed, glided up beside them. "See what I mean? This dog has *got* to go."

"Thank you," said Mitchell. "At least someone agrees with me."

"Hey Blender!" shouted Sam. "Come on, boy!"

"You *named* him?" Dixie exclaimed. "What are you thinking? I'm not kidding, JT. This dog is going to kill the whole trip."

"Fine. He'll go, as soon as I can find someone to take him. So we gave the dog a name," he said, avoiding Dixie's glare. "So what? It was mostly for Sam," he added, even though Dixie had stopped listening.

With House Rock behind them, with Blender safely ensconced between Jill's legs, the three boats drifted quietly along. They were in the heart of Marble Canyon now, already some two thousand feet below the rim. Here and there, water seeped from cavities in the rock walls, feeding lush cascades of orange monkeyflower. When they'd left camp, they'd been in deep shade, but soon a rich golden wedge of sunlight slid across the river, drenching them in its liquid heat.

Riding in the back of JT's boat, Ruth Frankel lifted her face to the sun. She was amused by their unexpected guest; she had learned long ago that a large part of the canyon experience was dealing with the unexpected. And if the unexpected happened to take the form of a friendly lost dog—well, thought Ruth, worse things could happen.

Her face began to sting; she adjusted her hat and glanced over at Lloyd. He sat perched forward, alert, on the lookout. Already a white stubble was growing on his chin. His lips were chapped, and crusty bits collected in the corners of his mouth. Thank goodness we came, she thought. How awful to have stayed home in Evanston, waiting for him to forget to breathe.

She was glad when JT decided to stop for an early lunch. She was feeling lightheaded and realized with dismay that she'd drunk less than half a liter of water that morning. As a veteran, she should know better. Quickly she guzzled as much as she could before climbing off the boat. The sand was hot and the air twined with insects. The dryness scorched her nostrils, and when she blew her nose, there was blood. As the guides set up a table and began preparing lunch, she waded into the water up to her thighs. She squatted down to pee, and the cold water clamped itself around her hips.

"Don't go too deep, Ruthie," Lloyd called.

Ruth smiled. He hadn't called her Ruthie in years.

Meanwhile, the dog was getting in the way of lunch preparations, sniffing for dropped morsels of food. And he must have picked up the scent of a previous meal, because suddenly he began to dig in earnest, spraying great sandy arcs in all directions, including the prep table with the large open bowl of chicken salad.

"Stop him!" cried Dixie. "Oh, you bad, bad dog!"

Abo lunged and caught the dog by the bandanna.

"Oh, there's sand everywhere!" Dixie wailed.

"You dumb-ass dog," said Abo.

JT spat out a mouthful of sand.

"I hope there's a backup lunch," said Mitchell, peering into the bowl.

"What's going on?" Lloyd asked Ruth.

"Nothing," she said with a sigh. "The dog just got a little excited."

"What dog?" asked Lloyd. "Dogs aren't allowed down here."

"Go tie the dog up," said JT, wiping his mouth. "Dammit all."

The whole group looked on as Abo looped a length of rope through the dog's bandanna and dragged him down to JT's boat and tied him to the bow line. The dog struggled against the rope, whined a few times, then lay down on the wet sand and settled his head dejectedly between his paws.

Glumly the three guides tried to scrape the sand off the chicken salad. The guests looked on and tried to be cheerful. Sam went over and knelt beside the dog.

"Leave the dog alone, Sam," Mark called. "He's being punished." Sam looked up, grief-stricken.

"Call the ranger again," said Dixie.

"Not now," said JT.

"Why not?"

"Because I'm the Trip Leader, and I'll decide when I call the ranger, and right now I want to eat my lunch," and without waiting for the guests to go first, as was the custom, JT slapped a heavy scoop of chicken salad onto a piece of bread and walked off to sit by himself.

Ruth, who as a wife and mother had served many a meal that didn't turn out as expected, knew enough to make the best of things. A little sand wouldn't hurt anyone. She motioned for Lloyd, and they approached the table and made their sandwiches. Out of the corner of her eye she could see JT sitting down on the beach all by his lonesome, and she wanted to go give him a hug. She didn't, of course; it would only embarrass him. Instead, she gave him an encouraging little wave, and he grimly nodded back.

Then she and Lloyd headed to the river's edge, where a flat rock jutted out into the water. Across the river, a great blue heron perched on a wedge of sand.

Lloyd climbed up and settled himself. Ruth handed him her sandwich. She felt around for her footing—so hard to keep her balance these days, especially on rocks and sand!—and placed her hands upon the rock and was getting ready to swing one leg forward when suddenly a flash of red caught her attention. She looked up. A Frisbee sailed over her head. Lloyd looked up too, and then she heard Sam give a shout, and Ruth turned, but by the time she saw the dog careening in her direction, it was too late.

The next thing she knew, she lay sprawled on the wet sand with the wind knocked out of her, water lapping at her legs.

"Ruthie?" said Lloyd, peering down.

Ruth didn't know whether to laugh or cry—that is, until she tasted salt and blood and realized she'd fallen against the rock and bitten her lip; her eyes suddenly filled with tears, and she spat into the water and tried to stand up. The world spun, and then someone's arms were around her and they were dragging her, helping her lie down where the sand was dry. Her tongue hurt; she realized she'd chipped a tooth and its ragged point was cutting into her. She felt herself drooling, and wiped her mouth.

Then she heard JT's low, quiet voice gently telling her to drink; he supported her head and held a water bottle to her mouth, and she sipped and spat and sipped and spat. Dixie appeared by her side, opening up the first aid kit, and she felt someone straighten her right leg out on the sand. She hoisted herself up on her elbows, and it was at that point that she saw the three-inch-long gash down her shin.

"Lloyd?" she said, panicking.

"Right here, Ruthie," and she saw Lloyd's darkened face in a halo of bright sun.

"Let's get her to lie back down," JT was saying, and Lloyd supported her shoulders as she lay back on the sand. She could feel water being poured on her leg. Was it hot or cold? She couldn't tell.

"What happened?" asked Dixie.

"One minute I was handing Lloyd my sandwich," Ruth said. "The next minute I was on my back!"

"Your mouth is bleeding," Lloyd said. "Get my suture kit," he told Dixie.

"Maybe let's take care of the leg first," said Dixie.

Lloyd straightened up. "Don't talk to me that way, missy!"

"We'll get your suture kit, Lloyd," said JT. "Abo, get his suture kit." Abo nodded gravely and shifted positions.

"It'll be all right, Ruthie," Lloyd assured her.

All her life Ruth had punished herself when anyone in the family got hurt. Always she could trace it to some act of carelessness on her part. It was no different now. She should have been watching for the dog. And it was only the second day of the trip!

"I should have been watching out," she said ruefully.

"How'd the dog get loose, anyway?" asked Dixie.

"Where'd this dog come from; that's the important question right now!" Lloyd exclaimed. "What's a dog doing down in the Grand Canyon?"

People exchanged glances.

"JT found the dog last night," Ruth told him, patting his hand. "Remember? In the bushes?"

"Is this all the gauze we have?" JT asked.

Sam tapped Ruth's shoulder. "I'm sorry."

"I'm sorry too," said Matthew.

"Did you boys untie the dog?" Mark demanded.

"Sam did it," said Matthew.

It was true. Sam had actually unfastened the knot.

JT was still fumbling through the first aid box. "Who packed this kit? We usually have tons of gauze. Go check the com boxes," he told Dixie. "How're you doing, Ruth?"

"Oh, me," scoffed Ruth. "I'm doing fine."

"Drink."

Lloyd held the water bottle for her, and she drank again, still tasting blood. She hated being the center of attention, especially for an injury. Whatever it was, it would stop bleeding. It would heal. They shouldn't be fussing over her. She was wasting everyone's time when they should be enjoying lunch.

She sat up and shaded her eyes from the sun and looked at the blood-soaked square of gauze JT held against her leg. "Let me see."

JT lifted the gauze. It wasn't a clean split but rather a raw, messy wound. She saw grit and pink flesh, then a sudden flush of blood. JT pressed the gauze back. Ruth, who had tended to many cuts and abrasions while raising two children, reminded herself that wounds could look more serious than they really were. There was just a lot of blood here. They would clean it and bandage it up, and she would be fine.

She had to be fine.

Because if she wasn't, who would take care of Lloyd?

12

Day Two

Mile 20

After bandaging Ruth's leg, after wolfing down the rest of his sandwich and making sure the dog was tied up and privately explaining to Sam and Matthew how important it was to follow the Trip Leader's instructions, and if the Trip Leader said tie up the dog, it didn't mean let the dog loose—after all that, JT called Park Service again. But now, even more than before, the ranger succeeded in making him feel like an imposition, rather than a guide looking out for the health and safety of his passengers and the canyon itself.

"What'd the ranger say?" Mitchell asked after JT hung up.

"He's got other things to deal with, Mitchell."

Mitchell nodded, reflecting on this for a moment. "Well," he said, "I guess we just roll with the punches."

"That's right, Mitchell."

"You sound tired."

"Nah." Though he was.

"Don't worry," said Mitchell, and he leaned forward and clapped JT's arm. "We'll figure this one out."

JT glanced up. Mitchell's large dark glasses made it impossible to see the man's eyes, but JT could hear in his voice a concern for others that surprised him.

"Thank you, Mitchell," said JT. "Did you get enough lunch?"

"It was terrific. You guys are doing a terrific job."

JT managed a smile. He did a little better with private compliments but still felt bashful.

"Better put some more sunscreen on your nose," he told Mitchell. "You're looking a little red."

———

Their lunch spot was at the mouth of a side canyon, so after cleaning up, Abo and Dixie led a group on a short hike. JT stayed with the boats, mainly to keep an eye on Ruth. He built a kind of hospital bed for her out of sleeping pads, with dry bags as bolsters. Out on the river the kayakers glided by; they waved and he waved back, and then he lay down on his own mat. He positioned his hat over his face, hoping he might drop off for a few moments, but he couldn't stop thinking about the dog. They were five days from Phantom Ranch, where he might be able to convince someone to hike the dog out. But even if he did find someone, was it advisable to send a dog up the trail in this heat? He would require a lot of water, which could add eight, ten pounds to the load. And JT knew the people running the mule trips would balk; mules and dogs didn't really mix on a steep and narrow rocky trail.

All too soon he heard voices and sat up to see the group returning from the hike. He scolded himself for worrying. The dog would be fine. They could keep him tied up all the time, if necessary. No one was going to go into anaphylactic shock.

"We've got the Roaring Twenties up ahead," he told the group as they refilled their water bottles. "So tighten your carabiners, you might get dinged up and batted around, keep the bailing buckets handy, and expect to get very, very wet."

"I won't mind *that*!" Sam exclaimed.

"That's the spirit," said JT. "Okay. Into the boats. Same places as this morning."

And so it was that, as they prepared to head out on this second afternoon, JT found himself tightening an extra strap around the dog's life jacket. Sam and Matthew smacked water into each other's faces; Jill dabbed more sunscreen on her nose; Mark dunked his shirt. Mitchell and Lena quickly reclaimed their seats in Dixie's dog-free boat. Amy and Susan anxiously redistributed the contents of their day bags. Evelyn hiked upriver in search of maximum seclusion in which to relieve herself; Ruth limped toward JT's boat; Lloyd followed, patting his shirt pockets for something.

And Peter Kramer wondered what Dixie looked like naked.

13

Day Two, Afternoon

The Roaring Twenties

From the right front seat in the paddle boat, Peter didn't always have the best view of Dixie; her boat always seemed to be behind them, and he couldn't turn around very often because he was the one setting the pace. But midway through the Roaring Twenties, Abo had them stop paddling so he could get out his kazoo, because he suddenly had an irresistible urge to toot them a song, and Dixie rowed on past, and there she was, in all her loveliness, her compact life jacket zipped up tightly over her red plaid shirt, her warped scarecrow hat on her head, braids peeking out from below.

Peter's head spun, just imagining.

Oh, what a cigarette would do for him right now.

When his girlfriend broke off their relationship last fall after six long years together, nobody was more surprised than Peter. The news came out of nowhere: not only did she not love him anymore, but she had fallen in love with someone else, an insurance agent who drove a Mercedes-Benz and owned a lakefront time-share. A lovable insurance agent? Wasn't that an oxymoron?

Peter didn't get how something like this could happen, how one person could fall out of love without the other person suspecting anything. The words "clueless chump" ran like a news banner beneath his dreams, all night, every night. How had he missed the signs? There was the vacation with her girlfriends last summer, the many late nights with her book club, the mascara she wore when she went to the gym. (It turned out that was where they met: on the StairMaster! How clichéd, how . . . common! He imagined her not knowing how to access the TV channel, and there was John D. Rockefeller, ready to help.) Now they were married, living on a cul-de-sac, where from the looks of all the stray plastic toys littering the yards someone was definitely pumping fertility drugs into the water supply.

But was he going to allow himself to spend any time whatsoever thinking about Miss Ohio and John D. Rockefeller on this trip?

Abo pocketed his kazoo. "Okay, paddlers, we've got Georgie Rapid coming up. Let's stay to the right and follow Peter's lead. Peter! Look alive!"

Peter gripped his paddle. They floated toward the rapid, watching Dixie up ahead.

"And there she goes," Abo murmured. "Looking good, looking good."

Their own boat was now gliding toward the dark V of the tongue.

"Okay now—FORWARD!" Abo shouted as they began to pick up speed. "Come on, paddle, folks, paddle! Let's move this boat! Here we go!" Peter dug hard with his paddle, leaning into the rapid as they plunged down, taking the first cold wave head-on. "Right turn!" yelled Abo. Instantly Peter began back paddling; it was like slamming on the brakes, and the boat went nowhere, and he back-paddled again, this time whacking blades with Sam behind him.

"Right turn, Sam!" yelled Abo. "Right turn—you're *sitting* on the right, Sam; that means you gotta back-paddle, watch Peter! Come on, RIGHT turn, people, HARD right!" But the boat was already angling left, with lateral waves dousing both sides, and Peter, with an instinct he didn't know he had, plunged his paddle down behind his hips, plunged it deep and then pivoted back using all his weight, all 186 pounds, rock hard abs, he was a Viking, Poseidon, Neptune, he was moving oceans. Water soaked his hips, but the boat magically pivoted and slid down into the trough below at a different angle; now they were turning right, narrowly missing a huge submerged rock along the left bank.

"Forward!"

Paddling in sync, they rode the tailwaves out of the rapid to join up with the other boats in the calmer water below.

"Stop!"

Peter froze with his paddle in midair as they bumped up against JT's boat.

"Everybody in one piece?" JT asked.

Dixie was laughing as she swung her boat around. "I almost got stuck going left! Did you see me almost hit that rock?"

"I had to close my eyes, babe," said Abo.

I didn't, thought Peter.

"Mitchell, you might want to tuck that camera away for the next one," JT said.

"That was cool," said Sam. "I hope we tip over sometime."

Abo squirted him with a water pistol. "Let's review a few things, Sam. You're sitting on the right side of the boat. Now, if I say 'Right turn,' do you paddle forward or backward?"

"Back?" said Sam.

"Thank you, Captain Obvious," said Matthew.

"Just watch Peter and do whatever he does," said Abo. "You did great, by the way, Peter. Way to put some mojo into things!"

But Peter wasn't listening. Ten feet away, Dixie was applying Chap-Stick. She rubbed her lips together, then tucked the ChapStick back into the pocket of her shorts. Peter licked his own lips. They were dry. Would it be out of line to ask to borrow her ChapStick?

You are so lame, he told himself.

Look. ChapStick. Right in your own pocket.

It was the saddest thought he'd had all day.

14

Day Two

Miles 25–30

The rapids continued that afternoon in quick succession, with little time in between for even so much as a sip of water. Above them, great gaping cavities dotted the mammoth Redwall; at one point, they spotted a mother bighorn nudging her kid across the rocky debris fan.

Amy, paddling in the back of Abo's boat, regretted that her camera was packed away in her day bag. She would have liked to get a picture of the baby sheep. She also would have liked a granola bar or something. Her blood sugar was low, and she was feeling shaky. Which made sense, as she hadn't eaten lunch. Not because of any sand in the chicken salad, but because of the on-and-off tightening in her stomach. It had begun that morning, shortly after breakfast. Pain? Not really, but it came on quickly, her belly suddenly knotting up, her neck feeling flushed and under pressure, as though she were straining to blow up a balloon. She wasn't sure if she'd ever felt this way before or not. She feared what would happen if things got worse, but then the pain mysteriously stopped just as quickly as it started.

Gas, probably, she'd thought. But then it kept happening, two, maybe three more times over the course of the morning. So that by noon, she'd lost her appetite, and now, in the middle of the afternoon, she was paying the price.

Finally they reached a calmer stretch, and she was able to open her day bag and find a roll of Mentos.

As their boats floated serenely between the soaring canyon walls, Abo brought out a book of Indian lore and began to read. Amy listened for a few minutes, but with the sun so hot, she found her thoughts wandering. Here she was, floating down the Colorado River with a bunch of total strangers, people who knew absolutely nothing about her. She could be anyone, in their eyes: class president, debate champion, winner of the science fair. She could have had the lead in the school play this past spring. She could have placed first in the all-state choral competition. Nobody would know.

Except her mother, of course. Amy glanced across the boat, where her mother was listening to Abo with rapt attention. Her mother was really bugging her, even more than she had anticipated. There was simply too much togetherness down here—*What boat shall we ride in,* and *Where shall we set up our tent,* and *Come sit with me.* Was this going to continue the whole trip?

Because truthfully, she was thinking it might be nice, one of these nights, to go off and camp by herself. Not far, just far enough so she could feel as though she were alone beneath the stars, on her own instead of being safely tucked into bed right there beside her mother. She wanted to sit by herself and write in her journal late into the night without her mother lying there wondering what she was writing about.

And what would she be writing about? High school. Her friends. Her nonfriends. The awful parties she'd made an effort to go to last fall, the ones her mother urged upon her but which turned out to be ugly scenes that Amy had tried to forget, with girls taking their shirts off and guys pouring beer on each other and cops coming and kids running off into the darkness and the few who remained and insisted on sobriety nevertheless getting alcohol tickets for blowing .01. Only once did she herself drink, on Halloween.

Best not to go there. Truly.

Amy knew that if her mother had any inkling of what was going on at those parties, she never would have pushed Amy to go; but Amy didn't want to tell her, for fear of getting other kids in trouble. These were popular kids, with popular parents, and Amy knew her mother would be on the phone quicker than hello, and then she would be even further ostracized at school. And so she began lying, telling her mother she was going to the parties, which made her mother happy, but then simply going to a coffee place, returning only after midnight.

"How was it?" her mother would ask eagerly from bed, setting down her book.

"Good."

"Tell me about it!"

"I'm too tired," Amy would say.

She was not too young to appreciate the irony that here she was, lying to her mother about going to the very parties that all the other kids were lying about *not* going to. And it hadn't helped her lose any weight, either, drinking all that cocoa.

A sudden burst of laughter erupted from Dixie's boat, bringing her back to the moment. She craned her neck and gazed up at the towering walls. High above, two caves had formed right next to each other, like dark empty eye sockets. That was another thing she wanted to write about, this trip and where she was and what it looked like, the colors of the rock, orange and pink and green and gray, and how she felt bad weighing down the boat so much, and how she liked the guides, especially JT and Abo; and Ruth, who was so calm even when she fell and hurt her leg; and how every time she said something to Peter, she got the feeling he was looking straight through her, as though she weren't even there, which she wasn't, because why would a single guy in his late twenties want anything to do with a girl like her?

All this, Amy wanted to write.

Without her mother looking over her shoulder.

Up ahead, the river veered to the right. Abo packed away his book, and as they rounded the bend, they all heard the roar of another rapid.

"Party's over," said Abo. "Last rapid of the day. Pick up your paddles. Get to work. Quit lollygagging. Sam!"

"What!"

"What do you do if I say 'right turn'?"

"Paddle backward!"

"Okay then," said Abo, his voice dropping to its storytelling calm, as though this rapid were nothing much to worry about. "Let's go forward."

And they ran that last rapid of the day as experts, with Abo's serenity infecting them all—even the boat itself—as they glided as one unit straight down the middle of the rapid, right through the petticoat, a neat slice of a run, with only her knees taking an inconsequential splash.

That night there was music. After the dishes were washed, after JT rebandaged Ruth's leg and found the hydrocortisone for Lena's eczema and the Tylenol for Mark's headache and a couple of Ace bandages for the swelling in Amy's ankles—after all this, Dixie brought out her guitar. Somehow she'd gone off and bathed without anyone noticing; her hair was combed straight back in wet ridges, and she'd tied her sarong around her hips. Now, with the light beginning to fade, she knelt in the sand and began tuning and plucking. Her repertoire was sixties folk—good sing-along music for all ages, she'd found in her five short years as a guide.

Tentatively people joined in. Mark, it turned out, had a fine baritone, coupled with a strong memory; he could think of songs and lyrics when everyone else drew a blank. Susan hummed. On the other side of the circle, Amy hugged her knees. Hot air continued to fan them from the cliffs above, and soon the moon rose above the rim, washing them in its clear white light.

Perhaps it was the opening chords of an old Kingston Trio song that inspired Lloyd; maybe it was simply the seduction of moonlight. In any case, he stood up and held out his hand to Ruth. Mistaking his intent, she told him she didn't want to go to bed yet, but he persisted, and finally she rose stiff-legged to follow him to an open space in the sand, where he slipped his hand around the small of her back and drew her close, a lanky old man supporting a wobbly old woman, and together they shuffled in the sand to the soft strums of Dixie's guitar.

July 5 Day Two

It's the end of the second day. I WAS going to write that things were a little better today, but then Mom went and flashed every-one. OMG!!!!! We're going through like a ton of rapids and everybody's getting soaked, and because Mom is so fucking skinny she gets cold so Abo tells her to take her wet clothes off and put on some dry ones. So Mom takes off her shirt—fine—but then she goes and takes her bathing suit top off too! Right in front of everyone! Please don't ever let me see my mother's boobs again! Ever!

Okay, relax. Gotta admit, it's pretty amazing down here. I had no idea. I thought it would just be a muddy river surrounded by boring cliffs. I thought it would be way too hot. I thought I would hate the rapids.

Well, it is hot, and we are surrounded by cliffs, but the water isn't muddy. It's cold and green and the cliffs are all pink and orange, with flowers growing right out of them. The rapids are awesome. Today I got to be in the paddle boat, and we did the Roaring Twenties, and it was like one right after the other. We got totally soaked, and now that's all I want to do, run rapids.

So . . . we're keeping the dog for now. The guy from Wyoming HATES dogs. He says it's because his wife has allergies, but I saw her patting the dog when he wasn't looking and she wasn't like falling down dead or anything. So I don't know what his problem is. The dog is way cute. He fell in the river today so we named him Blender. When he gets wet, his hair gets matted and hangs in his eyes. At some point when Mom's had enough wine, I'm going to ask her if we can take him home.

Most of the people aren't as bad as I thought. There's a family from Salt Lake, and the mom gave me some really good cream for my hands because it is so dry down here my skin is turning into leather. Not gonna lie, the boys are obnoxious, even though I took the time to teach them some card tricks last night, and what gets me is they think they own the dog. The dad is nice but spends all his time either pumping water or scolding the boys.

There's this sweet old couple. They're like ninety. They've been down the river tons of times before, and she got tripped by the dog today and really tore up her leg and chipped a tooth. She's a painter, and he used to be some kind of doctor, and they smile at each other all the time in the cutest way, though I wish he'd use a Kleenex once in a while.

Then there's this kind of weird woman who teaches at Harvard apparently and is always trying to help but always gets in the way, but no one wants to make her feel bad so they don't say anything. Like this morning she wanted to help JT load his boat and he said, oh, just join the fire line with the rest of the folks, and she said no, I'm really interested in how you arrange things, can't I help you in the boat? So he says okay, and then she trips and spills JT's coffee all over his seat. JT has a LOT of patience.

(She's kind of FAT but not as FAT as me.)

Then there's this guy Mitchell. Mitchell thinks he is a really Big Deal because he knows all about some guy who came down the river in a rowboat back in the 1800s. His wife is a teacher, and she needs to learn a little self-assertion if you ask me because Mitchell is always bossing her around. And he's always taking pictures too! Like when we pulled into camp and everyone was *supposed to help unload the boat—well, there's Mitchell, taking pictures. (He took a picture of Ruth at breakfast, and Ruth said, and I quote, "I don't take kindly to being photographed before noon, Mitchell." Go Ruth.) When he isn't taking pictures, he's bragging about all the other adventure trips he's taken. Like he's climbed Mount Everest. Okay. So?*

Finally there's this guy Peter. He wears big baggy swim trunks and a Cincinnati Reds baseball hat, and the back of his neck is already sunburned. Why didn't he read the packing list and bring a bigger hat? Before tonight I thought he was a prick. But then he came and sat with me and Mom at dinner. So maybe he's not such a prick. Can't really tell.

The guides are pretty cool. JT doesn't talk much but he's always got this kind of half smile on his face. Abo is the paddle captain. Definitely hot. Then there's this woman Dixie—I want her body, I want her hair, I want her laugh, and she'll just hang her butt off the boat and pee in the water with everyone looking!!!!! I could never do that!

Even if I wasn't FAT.

DAY THREE

River Miles 30–47

Fence Fault to Saddle Canyon

15

Day Three

Miles 30–39

JT had hoped for an early start the next morning, but Ruth's bandage had come loose in the night, and her wound was still raw and weeping. JT and Dixie washed it with boiled water, while Ruth looked on, grouchy that she was requiring so much attention.

"You have other things to do!" she exclaimed. "Let me take care of this! It's just a cut!"

Just a cut? He wished. Ruth's skin was thin, mottled with spidery veins. Wearing medical exam gloves, he dabbed on antibiotic ointment, spreading it all over the cut and up and down her leg. Dixie placed a large square of sterile gauze on it, JT taped it in place, and then they wrapped Ruth's entire lower leg first in stretchy gauze and finally in an Ace bandage.

"We've only got four squares of this gauze left, you know," Dixie said.

"How many rolls of stretchy gauze?"

"Six."

"Shit. Well, ration it. I want you to wear your rain pants today," JT told Ruth as he helped her up, "so that it stays dry."

"Oh fine," sighed Ruth.

"Can you put your weight on it?"

"Of course I can!"

JT and Dixie both waited, watching. Ruth planted her foot in the sand and bore her weight upon it. She looked at them triumphantly. "You see? It's fine."

It was nine o'clock before they finally glided out into the current. JT found his line of bubbles and let the river carry them along. They were in the shade, and the air was cool. For the next hour, they floated through quiet water, three tiny boats dwarfed by terra-cotta walls. Lush greenery cascaded down the cliffs in places. Sometimes the canyon walls were bleached and striated; other times they were deep red and streaked with black. Sometimes the rim was visible; other times it vanished as the cliffs folded in upon them.

Midmorning they stopped briefly at Redwall Cavern, a vast, clamshell amphitheater cutting into the cliff. As they disembarked, Mitchell was quick to inform them that back in 1869, John Wesley Powell had estimated it would hold fifty thousand people. ("An exaggeration, of course," he conceded.) Some walked and some ran the long stretch of sheltered beach, and they all hallooed back into the throat. Everyone took pictures.

JT, however, didn't want to linger; another rafting party was pulling in, and far upriver, the tiny lineup of kayakers was rounding the bend. "I say we do the dam site," he told Abo and Dixie. "Maybe it'll be less crowded."

And so they loaded up and headed out into the deep green river again, flanked by vertical walls formed by an ancient seabed. JT had the three boats stay close together so he could brief them on the history of the plan to dam the Grand Canyon—how in the 1960s, the Bureau of Reclamation had gone so far as to drill a tunnel straight into the canyon wall at Mile 39.

"But fortunately the dam didn't happen," he said, "thanks to some heavy-duty ads by the Sierra Club."

"David Brower, to be more accurate," Mitchell noted.

"Who's that?" Susan asked Jill, not wanting to publicize her lack of knowledge. But Mitchell overheard.

"Are you kidding? President of the Sierra Club? The man who sacrificed Glen Canyon? Though he was very contrite about it," Mitchell said.

"He was indeed," said JT, catching Abo's eye.

"Said it was his biggest regret," Mitchell continued. "I met David Brower once. Fairly intelligent guy. Look—is that it?"

Far up on the left, a miniature debris fan spilled out of a darkened cavity in the cliff.

"Hope no one's claustrophobic," Mitchell joked.

They headed toward shore, and JT found himself wondering if he should simply let Mitchell take over this side excursion, since he knew so much about it. But his stubborn streak prevailed, and so, as they disembarked from the boats, he heard himself giving orders—telling Abo to stay at the boats with Ruth and Lloyd, reminding everyone else to clip their life jackets to something stable.

"Can the dog come?" Sam asked.

JT didn't see a problem with this. "Here," and he tossed Sam a short length of rope. "Make a leash."

In single file they hiked up a path and headed into the tunnel, gingerly stepping over rocks and puddles and groping each other for balance. As it grew darker they slowed to a shuffle, their murmurs and laughter echoing off the dank walls. It smelled wet and tinny. They rounded a corner, and the last glint of daylight vanished; now there was just JT's flashlight at the head of the line, bobbing in the darkness. The air was cool. Water dripped, unseen. Evelyn stumbled. Mitchell steadied her.

"Thank you," Evelyn whispered.

"Why are we whispering?" whispered Peter.

Eventually JT stopped, and people gathered around as he beamed his flashlight up and pointed out the air shaft.

"Can everyone see?"

"Excuse me," said Mitchell, "excuse me," and he squeezed through the group to crouch and aim his camera straight up. ("Sure hope you'll send me a copy of that," Peter said.) The flash went off, startling everyone—including the dog, who wrenched free from Sam's grasp and trotted back the way they'd come. By the time JT shone his flashlight in that direction, the dog had vanished.

"Oh, well," said JT. "Not a big deal. But maybe we should all head back."

"No, wait! Turn your flashlight off!" said Mitchell.

So JT took the time to switch off his flashlight, to give them a sense of total darkness. The air seemed inexplicably warmer, and with hushed murmurs they craned their necks this way and that.

"Okay," said JT, "party's over. Let's get back before Ruth and Lloyd drink up all the beer."

For some reason it seemed much shorter going out. The air warmed with each step, and there was the strange sensation of traveling from one time period to the next. Mitchell informed them that the Ebola virus originated in bat caves. JT told them this wasn't a bat cave. Mitchell said you never knew about these things but hey, he wasn't concerned. Eventually they turned a corner, and a circle of light appeared.

And with it, the unmistakable smell of skunk.

It rolled over them, thick and pungent, cloaking them in a toxic cloud. There were groans and cries, then pushing and shoving as they all spilled out into the hot white light. And there was the dog, lying on the path with his nose between his paws.

"You're shittin' me," said JT.

Abo came running up the hillside.

"I couldn't stop him!" he said breathlessly. "We were watching the skunk from the boat, we could just barely see it in the bushes and nobody was moving and Ruth was getting some great pictures and then the damn dog comes running and barking down the hill!"

"Sam, stop!" Jill said sharply.

Sam knelt in the gravel, ten feet from the dog.

JT scratched the back of his neck. He didn't know what to say. He stared at the dog. He put his hands on his hips.

"Got tomato juice?" asked Peter.

"You damn dog," JT said. "You goddamn dog."

They had to break into the lower reaches of the drop box to find the case of V8. One by one, JT popped open the cans and poured the juice into a bailing bucket, and with Abo holding the dog's head and Peter grasping his hind end, JT doused the dog and massaged the V8 into his fur.

"I don't think I've ever seen an animal look so absolutely pitiful," Mitchell observed.

The bath did nothing for the stink, and JT silently chided himself.

Of course the dog would get spooked by the camera! Of course he would bolt! If he, JT, had thought to leave the dog with Abo in the first place, this never would have happened.

So much for thinking he could convince one of the motor trips to run the dog down to Phantom.

The delay held them up enough so that they were still at the dam site when the kayakers pulled in. Not surprisingly, they had a lot of questions about the dog, and JT wasn't really in the mood to engage in a lengthy explanation. But the arrival of the kayakers presented an opportunity, for JT happened to notice that their youngest member, a girl of ten or eleven, was busting out of her life jacket.

"I've got something that might be a little more comfortable," he said. "And yours might fit the dog a little better than the one he has. If you're not attached to it, that is."

The girl had indeed outgrown her life jacket, both physically and emotionally, it being bright green with dancing purple frogs. She wanted very much to trade—in fact, she wanted to take a picture of the dog wearing her old life jacket, but JT wasn't going to put *any* life jacket on the dog until the dog had had a more thorough wash. He clipped it to the boat.

"Call the warehouse when you get out," he told the man with the white beard. "I'll mail this one back to you, if you want. What's your name again?"

"Bud. How's the tunnel?"

JT grinned. "Dark."

As the kayakers straggled up the path to the tunnel, JT had a duplicitous thought. What if they simply rowed off without the dog? The kayakers seemed a good bunch; they'd find some way to fit him in their mule boat, and he, JT, could just play catch-me-if-you-can the rest of the trip.

Would that he could be so devious. Besides, Sam had in the meantime found a small towel with which to rub the dog dry, and he was paying special attention to his ears and the straggly beard; and it didn't take much imagination for JT to know that Sam would never, ever let him get away with it.

16

Day Three, Evening

Mile 47

Maybe tonight, Susan thought as she helped unload the boats at the end of the day. Maybe tonight, instead of helping the guides prepare dinner, she and Amy could go sit on a rock, alone, and just *talk*.

Was that really so much to wish for?

Susan knew things could be strained between mothers and daughters, that the last person a seventeen-year-old girl wanted to talk to was her mother. And she knew that everything she herself said came out sounding just as lame as the things her own mother had said thirty years ago. But maybe down here on the river, Amy would open up. Because she felt like she knew so little about her daughter these days! Did Amy have friends—true friends, the kind who would lie for you? Or who would listen without arguing when you needed to say an awful truth out loud? Nobody ever came over to the house; nobody called to ask about a homework assignment. It broke her heart, particularly because back in high school she'd hung out with a big crowd; there were always parties and shenanigans and ditch-days, and she always had a boyfriend, except for two weeks before the start of her junior year. How could her daughter be so different? Where did she come from?

And how did she end up so . . . *large*?

Exactly what I've been asking all this time, said the Mother Bitch.

During these first three days, Susan had made an extra effort to give Amy the space she needed to get to know people on her own, so they could all see Amy as her own person and not merely Susan's daughter. But she was also determined to take advantage of being down here in the canyon, to perhaps pierce some of those heartbreaking barriers.

Maybe a little alcohol would help, Susan thought. And so late that afternoon, as soon as the boats were unloaded and Dixie had opened up the drink box, Susan retrieved her bladder of white wine and went off in search of Amy, whom she found at the water pump.

"No thanks," Amy said, filling her bottle. "I'm going to wash my hair."

"Maybe I should wash my hair too," Susan said brightly.

"Whatever," said Amy.

Smarting at the rebuff, Susan wandered back to the patch of sand where she and Amy had dumped their gear. Their site tonight was disturbingly close to the groover, but by the time she'd gotten off the boat and shaken out the leg cramps and collected her things, all the other flat places were taken. Evelyn, she noticed, always managed to get one of the good spots; tonight, for instance, she'd pretty much dashed across the beach to claim a large flat area with a view, a space that would have been better suited to Jill and Mark and their two boys. Susan glanced over to the spot now; indeed, there was Evelyn, seated cross-legged on her white mat, reading her guidebook, drinking her cranberry juice.

Evelyn noticed Susan and promptly buried her nose in her book again. Susan knew that Evelyn suffered from shyness; she also knew that the nice thing to do would be to go over and offer her some wine. But she simply couldn't bring herself to take the initiative with Evelyn, not right now. Evelyn was so stern, so serious; no doubt she would offer up her critical judgment on something that had happened that day—like how the boys had tried to destroy the lacy spiderwebs on the rock ceiling in the back of the cavern at Redwall. It wasn't a very respectful thing to do; Susan wasn't really defending them—but come on, they were kids.

And besides, Evelyn probably didn't drink, or she would have brought something other than cranberry juice.

Upriver, there was a little cove where people were bathing. Susan saw Amy trudging in that direction, carrying the quilted floral bag that Susan had bought her for the trip. Let her be, she thought, and she headed downstream, away from the busyness of the camp. The wet sand was studded with round pink rocks, and she found it hypnotic to look no farther than a foot or two ahead; she became so focused on this small task that she was startled to look up and see that she had walked right into Jill's private meditation space.

"Sorry," she whispered. She wanted to give this busy mother a little time to herself, but Jill glanced up with a serene smile. She sighed and stretched her legs out and wiggled her toes.

"Oh, you're not disturbing me," Jill replied. "The only people who could disturb me right now are the boys. Sit. Please."

Susan sat down. The shoreline waters lapped softly at her feet; birds chirped and called from one cliff to the next.

"I was going to have some wine," Susan said. "Do you want some?"

"No, thank you," said Jill, which made Susan feel like an alcoholic. She should hang out more with the guides, who drank their fair share.

"You know what's so great about this trip?" Jill said, after a while.

"What?"

"Not having to make any decisions. The kids say, 'Can we jump off the boat?' and I say, 'I don't know; ask the guides.' They say, 'Can we stand up during this rapid?' and I say, 'I don't know; ask the guides.' What a wonderful place to be," Jill said, with the awe and gratitude of one who has been given very little in life.

"You know what I like?" Susan said.

"What?"

"Not cooking!"

"That too," Jill agreed.

"And not going to the grocery store! My goal when I get home is to go once a week, and if we run out, dammit, we run out."

Jill snorted. "The way my life goes, I'll say I'm going to do that, but then the boys will have some project at school that requires jelly beans or marshmallows, and there I am, driving out to Costco."

"Are you sure you don't want some of this wine?"

Jill seemed to think about it for a moment. "All right," she said.

Susan handed her the mug.

"Mark doesn't drink," said Jill, "so I try not to. But every now and then I like a little something."

"With two boys like that, I'd be an alcoholic," Susan declared. Instantly she regretted it.

"Mark's Mormon," Jill continued. "I'm not. I grew up Catholic. My father drank beer and my mother drank whiskey. When Mark and I got married, we had champagne at the reception but no open bar, and Mark and his parents were like, 'Oh, everybody's having just as good a time as they would if there was an open bar,' and I'm like, 'Lady, are you blind? My entire family's out in the parking lot with their brown bags.' What kind of wine is this?"

"Cheap wine."

"Well, it's very good," said Jill. "You know what I think is funny?"

"What?"

"Watching Mitchell with the dog."

They caught each other's eye and laughed, like naughty girls.

"Isn't he a piece of work," Jill said.

"Poor Lena."

"Poor JT, you mean! One of these days he's going to haul off and slug the guy." Jill drained the mug and handed it back to Susan, who refilled it.

"So is Amy your only?" Jill asked.

"She is."

There was a silence, during which the Mother Bitch rustled her leaves in the bushes. *What she really wants to ask is how come Amy's so fat, when you're so thin.*

"How nice, to have a girl," Jill said wistfully. "I always wanted a girl. One of each. I love my boys, of course," she added hastily.

"Would you have any more children?"

Jill hooted. "Not possible. When Sam was born, I had my tubes tied. I'm lying there all cut open, and the doctor's head pops up between my legs and he goes, 'Tubes?' and I go, 'Yes, please!' Easiest decision I ever made. Mark doesn't know," she added.

For some reason, this did not shock Susan.

"He assumes I'm on the Pill," Jill went on. "I'm saving a fortune on birth control. This is very good wine, you know! I think I'm kind of feeling it."

Susan was feeling it too. She thought that Jill had revealed an awful lot of herself in the last ten minutes and that she, Susan, ought to reveal equivalent intimacies. But she didn't know where to start. It suddenly occurred to her that maybe it wasn't just Amy who was responsible for keeping them so distant from one another.

Right then Evelyn passed behind them on her way downriver.

"Evelyn," Susan called over her shoulder, "do you want some wine?"

Evelyn smiled cheerfully. "No thanks! Off for a little walk right now!" She kept heading downstream. When she found a rock that was large enough to hide behind, she squatted.

"She's an odd duck," remarked Jill.

They both watched as Evelyn hitched up her shorts, moved downstream, and squatted again.

"Think she's a virgin?" asked Jill.

Susan turned to stare directly at this upstanding citizen of the suburbs of Salt Lake City. Then she burst out laughing. "Give her credit," she said. "I heard her mention some man back in Boston. But they broke up."

"That explains it. She needs to get laid."

I need to get laid, thought Susan. Amy needs to get laid. We all need to get laid.

"Speaking of which," said Jill, "who do you think's hotter—JT or Abo?"

Susan didn't have to think about it. "Abo. Something about that bleachy-tipped hair."

"I'd say Abo too, except he's got a beer gut. Look at his belly when he's bending over."

"So JT, is that what you're saying?"

Jill didn't answer. She lay back on the sand and closed her eyes. "I wish I were twenty-one," she said. "I'd live on the river and fuck a lot of river guides."

Susan chuckled.

"Do *not* repeat that," said Jill.

17

Day Three

Mile 47

It took Evelyn three squats, three separate boulders, and three hundred feet of shoreline before she could finally pee.

The first rock sheltered her from view of the camp but not from Jill and Susan. Unable to relax, Evelyn pulled up her shorts and hiked farther downstream to the next big rock, where she squatted again—only to glance up and notice that Peter had set up his campsite in a cluster of bushes that put her directly in his line of view. Evelyn traipsed on and finally came upon a slab of rock that offered full protection. And there in its shadow, up to her ankles in the icy water, she dropped her shorts and squatted and finally released the liter of water that she'd been holding since lunchtime.

Exhausted from the discomfort, she remained in squat position, staring numbly ahead. She hadn't expected to have this problem—who would?—but it had descended upon her the first day, when they pulled onto shore for a quick pit stop. "Skirts up, pants down," Dixie had joked, indicating that the women were to go upstream from the boat, while the men were to go downstream. The problem was, there *was* no upstream; it was blocked off by a steep wall of rock, leaving only a tiny cove beside the boat for the three women. Dixie and Ruth quickly went, but Evelyn couldn't. Maybe it was the lack of privacy; maybe it was the time pressure. She tried focusing on the sound of the river (that old trick!), but it didn't work. Finally, convinced that she was delaying the group, she climbed back in the boat, telling herself it wouldn't be too long before they made camp, where there would presumably be a little more privacy.

Which there had been, but the problem presented itself on Day

Two and Day Three: the same setup, only now with the memory of
yesterday's failure adding to her tension. As the day went on, she
watched the men casually relieve themselves over the side of the boat,
while the women either jumped into the water and floated along with
glazed eyes or, as Dixie demonstrated, simply hung their backsides
over the edge of the boat. Evelyn couldn't do either. Every single time,
she had to wait until they were on shore; not only that, but instead of
feeling *more* comfortable with the group as the days went on, she felt
less so, and she was finding it necessary to trek farther and farther
away, just for the fiction of privacy. What was wrong with her? Why,
having done so many backpacking trips with large groups of people,
was she suddenly so shy?

A hummingbird darted in front of her, hovered, then vanished. Red
throat, green iridescence: *Selasphorus platycercus.* Evelyn kept a bird
log and had seen too many hummingbirds to keep track of, but this
was the first she'd seen in the canyon, so it warranted a notation. She
stood and hitched up her shorts. The underwater rocks were slippery,
and she lurched about and finally had to use her hands to crabwalk out
of the water. With the sun still hot on her shoulders, she headed back
to camp; although it wasn't her intent, she glanced toward the bushes
and happened to see Peter bent at the waist, his pale hips exposed.

Without warning, she thought of Julian, alone in his house, watching a ball game.

It was a complicated breakup. When it happened, Julian cried. But
he said that Evelyn couldn't give him what he wanted in life, which
was a partner who wanted to be just that, a partner, someone who
shared his interests and wanted to actually do things together, not
someone who was satisfied to simply come home at night after a day
spent pursuing separate activities. Evelyn liked to canoe; Julian liked
to go to a ball game. Evelyn liked bird-watching; Julian liked reading
the sports page and puttering in the garage. There was very little they
liked to do together, and although he loved her, at fifty-seven, he felt
there was someone out there who could offer him more companion-
ship. Evelyn, for her part, didn't see anything wrong with two people

who loved each other pursuing their own separate interests. In fact, she thought it showed a smothering lack of independence when other couples did everything together.

"Lots of people take separate vacations," she argued. "It doesn't mean they don't love each other."

"But I don't want to take separate vacations," Julian said. "I want someone to go up to Ogunquit with."

"But I'm tired of going to your family cottage."

"Exactly," Julian said.

In the end, she felt too proud to argue with him. If he wanted to find someone else, let him find someone else. She didn't want to stand in his way. But she missed him. They had never moved in together—Julian owned a house in Brookline, Evelyn a flat in Cambridge—but her place seemed empty and quiet without Julian. The batteries in the remote corroded from lack of use. The sports page went straight into recycling. She stopped buying beer to have on hand. She spent way too much time perusing catalogues and eating bagged salad.

When she sent in her deposit for this trip, she contemplated reserving an extra space, on the off chance that Julian might change his mind and decide to try a river trip. But it was a big chunk of money to forfeit, and Evelyn told herself that Julian had probably already blocked out his two weeks with his family, up in Ogunquit.

Back at the campsite, the kitchen was bustling with dinner preparations.

"Can I help?" she asked Abo, who'd tied a purple bandanna around his head. He looked like a pirate, she thought, which gave her a little thrill.

"Yeah, make a cake," he said, and tossed her a bag of cake mix. "There's a bowl, there's the eggs, there's a whisk, go for it," and Evelyn set to work, glad to have a job. She poured the mix into the bowl and added eggs and water. Why was it, she wondered, that it was always the same people helping in the kitchen every night? This was their third night, and she'd already detected a pattern: Jill would go off to do yoga; Lloyd and Ruth would lie down on their mats (although they were to be excused, given their age and Ruth's injured leg); Mitchell and Lena would unfold their padded camp chairs and bring out a large bottle of gin. ("Say," she heard Mitchell ask each night, as if the thought had just occurred to him, "got any extra limes?")

Evelyn thought poorly of people who didn't pitch in. From an early age, she'd been taught to look around and see what needed to be done.

"What else are we having for dinner?" she asked now.

"Ravioli," said Abo. "Meat and/or cheese, with or without sauce, your choice. Never let it be said that we don't offer you people a lot of options."

"Can you believe I thought we'd be eating hot dogs and hamburgers this whole trip?" Amy said, scraping seeds out of a red pepper.

"Over my dead body," declared Abo. "Get out of there," he said to the dog, who was sniffing the garbage bucket.

"Speaking of dead bodies," Peter said. "How many times have you flipped? Be honest."

Abo tipped his head back and roared with laughter, then suddenly went solemn. "Three."

"Dixie?"

Dixie, tending the battered fire pan, sat back on her heels, which were gray and leathery and riddled with cracks. "There are two types of river guides, Peter," she said. "Those who've flipped, and those who will."

"Which are you?"

"You'll have to figure that out yourself," she said. "Evelyn, you ready with the batter?"

Evelyn knelt beside Dixie and tilted the mixing bowl so Dixie could scrape the cake batter into the great iron Dutch oven.

"I'd like to flip, just to see what everyone's talking about," Amy said.

"Ride with Abo," said Dixie with a grunt as she hoisted the Dutch oven over the bed of coals. Evelyn offered to wash the bowl.

"Leave it for Abo," said Dixie.

"Leave it for JT, you mean," said Abo.

Who at that moment came over lugging a full jug of water.

"I'm taking a survey," Peter said. "How many times have *you* flipped?"

JT set the jug on the drink table. The corners of his eyes crinkled. "Why're you asking?"

"I'm trying to figure out the safest boat to ride in."

"Not mine," said Dixie.

"Or mine," said Abo.

"Definitely not mine," said JT.

They were all joking, and Evelyn knew that, but joking was one thing she had never been very good at. She wished right now that she could say something that would make them all laugh, and admire her, and want to ride with her tomorrow.

"How do you tell when ravioli is done?" Abo said, poking a long spoon into the pot.

"When they float," said Amy.

"Oh," said Abo. "Okay. DINNER!"

Amy scraped the pile of red peppers into Peter's salad. They faced one another, beaming, and high-fived.

"WASH YOUR HANDS!" Abo yelled.

Evelyn stood in line and hugged a plate to her chest.

"My oh my," said Lloyd, peering into the pot.

"Get in line, Lloyd," said Ruth.

"Where have you been?" Mark asked Jill, who had rejoined the group.

"Talking with Susan."

"You look very rested," said Mark.

"I am," said Jill. "Oh Evelyn, I'm sorry, were you in line?"

Evelyn didn't understand how it could appear that she might *not* be in line. She told Jill to go ahead, but Jill insisted Evelyn go first, so Evelyn picked up a plate and made her way through the food line. Her shoulders ached from paddling, and as she carried her plate across the sand, she thought of Julian, who kept a set of weights in front of his television set. She should buy a set of weights.

Suddenly famished, she sat down in a central spot and waited for others to join her.

That evening the bats came out. One minute there was nothing; the next minute they swarmed down from the cliffs, fluttering in jerky loops. The air seemed hotter than it had during the day, a phenomenon that Mitchell claimed made no sense but which JT knew could easily happen on a midsummer evening.

Already he could sense the water levels rising for the night; even though the surge from the dam wouldn't come until after eleven or so, the waves seemed to lap more hungrily at the shoreline. They were camped right below Saddle Canyon, at River Mile 47, and before turning in for the night, he enlisted the help of Abo and Dixie to move the kitchen back a few feet, just to be safe.

He was tired but sensed he wouldn't sleep much tonight. He couldn't have said just why. Maybe because of the heat; maybe because of Ruth's leg, which wasn't looking any better when he rebandaged it that night. Then too there was the dog, who—despite a second tomato juice bath—still smelled like skunk. At least they had a better-fitting life jacket for him now.

Wearily he dried his feet, rubbed them with cream, and put on his socks. He stretched out on his sleeping pad and told himself to stop worrying so much. In the grand scheme of a river trip, one scraped shin and a skunked-up dog were minor things. They'd be fine. Letting his weight settle, he sighed deeply and closed his eyes, feeling his boat gently bobbing in the shallows, listening to the reassuring murmur of nearby voices.

Up at Glen Canyon Dam, the engineers opened the spillways, and beneath the stars the river rose.

July 6 Day Three

This morning we stopped at this humongous cavern. People played Frisbee, which I hate, I've never been able to throw it right, it always flies slanted and then rolls away and everyone gets pissed at me. They tried to make me play but I took out my camera and pretended I was busy and they figured it out and were probably relieved anyway.

Then we stopped at this tunnel where they were going to build a dam. This is where things get interesting. We go into the tunnel, and it gets really really dark. At some point Mitchell decides to take a picture, and the flash spooks the dog, and the dog bolts. Sam's dad gets mad at Sam because Sam was supposed to hang on to the dog. Sam's mom yells at Sam's dad for yelling at Sam. Anyway, we head back—and THE DOG'S GOTTEN INTO A SKUNK!!!!!!!!!!! I didn't even know they had skunks in the Grand Canyon!!!!!!!! The dog totally REEKED, and JT washed him with tomato juice, but it didn't help AT ALL. So now we have a dog that smells like skunk.

I love sleeping out in the open. But Mom wants me to sleep near her. What does she think—I'm going to go have sex with the guides?

Like they'd want to.

DAY FOUR

River Miles 47–60

Saddle Canyon to Sixty-Mile Rapid

18

Day Four, Morning

Miles 47–53

It was still dark the next morning when a noise from the kitchen startled JT awake. He sat up. Often the ringtail cats came scrounging for food in the night, and he didn't want to face a mess this morning. Taking care not to step on the dog, who lay curled in the well of his boat, he strapped on his headlamp and hopped off his boat onto the damp sand. The wide expanse of beach was pale against the dark blur of water, rock, and thicket. JT wedged his feet into his flip-flops and headed toward the kitchen, wondering why the dog hadn't sensed anything.

But instead of a ringtail, he saw a human form bent over the kitchen supply boxes.

"Lloyd," whispered JT. "What do you need?"

Startled, Lloyd raised his arm, as if to strike.

"Lloyd, it's JT," he said gently. "What are you looking for?"

"Somebody took my stethoscope!"

"Stethoscope?"

"Somebody stole it," said Lloyd.

"What makes you think that?"

"Because," said Lloyd. "Because."

JT waited patiently.

"I'm going to find out who took it," said Lloyd. "And when I do . . ."

JT glanced around the campsite for signs of Ruth but saw no other movement. "Lloyd," he said. "Where did you sleep last night?"

Lloyd scanned the darkness surrounding them. "I think," he said, "I think it's this way," and he trudged off toward a blurry shape on the sand.

"Ruth," JT said in a hoarse whisper.

A head popped up from the lump.

"I *told* you we were right here!" Lloyd said to JT. "You didn't have to wake her."

"Lloyd, what are you doing up?" Ruth asked groggily, feeling about for her glasses.

"Somebody stole my stethoscope," Lloyd said.

"You didn't bring your stethoscope, Lloyd," said Ruth.

"Yes I did!" shouted Lloyd.

"Ssshhhh!" Ruth tried to stand, but her leg must have hurt because she sat back down. "We'll find your stethoscope in the morning," she told him. "Come lie down, Lloyd. It's too early to get up. I'm so sorry," she said to JT.

"No problem," said JT.

"You'll go back to sleep, won't you?"

JT looked at the sky. "Nope. Time to make coffee."

"My goodness," said Ruth.

"When it's light, I want to check your leg again," said JT.

"Oh, pooh," said Ruth. "It's fine."

"Goddamn hundred-dollar piece of equipment," said Lloyd.

"Get some rest," JT whispered, and as he walked away, he could hear Ruth scolding Lloyd. "You have to tell me when you get up in the night! You can't just walk off like that!"

Returning to the kitchen area, JT clicked the light stick and the stove *whumped* up into a hot blue circle of flame under the pot. The confusion over the stethoscope only confirmed what JT had begun to suspect after three days of Lloyd losing his day bag and forgetting everyone's name and wondering where the dog had come from. It didn't take a neuroscientist. If you'd asked his advice generally, he'd have said without hesitation that a thirteen-day rafting trip through the Grand Canyon was no place for a seventy-six-year-old man with Alzheimer's. But JT knew Ruth and Lloyd. He'd guided four or five trips with them over the years and knew that if any two people depended on the river for their soul and sustenance, it was this couple from Evanston, Illinois. He also knew that Ruth was a capable woman with a good head on her shoulders, who had presumably consulted with Lloyd's doctor and made an informed decision on the matter.

Nevertheless, he was bothered by the fact that Ruth hadn't disclosed anything about Lloyd's condition on his medical form. The guides had extensive training in emergency medicine, but they depended on their passengers to tell them about chronic conditions.

All he asked was that people be straight with him.

Instead of rushing off that morning, they hiked up into a shadowy canyon abloom with the showy white trumpets of the sacred datura. Lacy maidenhair ferns lined the streambed, and orange monkeyflower spilled out of glistening pink walls. Eventually, the canyon dead-ended in a long, narrow slot pool, where everyone—including Peter—dunked themselves.

Back at the river, Mitchell surprised them all with an abrupt turn-about: he and Lena would be riding with JT today. No offense to Dixie, but he was wanting to get to know JT a little better. He'd thought about it long and hard last night, and as long as the dog stayed at the other end of the boat, Lena would be fine.

Thus JT found himself rowing with Mitchell and Lena that fourth morning. And he was glad it had worked out this way, because in his heart, he liked to think that beneath the surface of every pain in the ass was a well-intentioned individual who could probably shed light on some topic that JT had always been wondering about. To this end, as they headed out onto the river, he began to ask questions, and Mitchell was glad to talk, and within the first half hour, JT learned that Mitchell had paddled every mile of John Wesley Powell's 1869 expedition except this last stretch.

"And what'll you do when you finish?" JT asked.

"Write a book," said Mitchell. .

JT was pretty confident somebody else had already written that book.

"I've seen you writing in your journal," he said, to be friendly.

"Oh, he has notes galore," Lena chimed in. "We're running out of space! I tease him. I say, 'Mitchell, when are you going to write the darn thing?' "

"That's an ambitious project," said JT.

"Well, you gotta have a project when you're retired. What about you boatmen? Do you ever retire?"

This was not a question JT could easily answer. Some of his friends stopped guiding when they had families or simply left the river in search of a steady income. Others developed back or shoulder problems. But some kept rowing well into their seventies—wooden dories, rafts, kayaks, whatever they could get their hands on, because keeping them out of the canyon was like keeping them away from food or water.

JT didn't know if he would be one of the old-timers or not. In fact his son Colin, a lawyer with a Phoenix firm, had begun pressing JT to retire from the river. "You're fifty-two, Dad. Get a real job. You need medical benefits, you need a retirement plan." JT would point out that a retirement plan wasn't going to do him much good starting at this late date. "Doesn't matter," said Colin. "You shouldn't be lifting coolers in and out of boats. Who's going to take care of you when you need back surgery? Or when that hernia you've been complaining about starts hollering for some attention?"

JT was moved that Colin was looking out for him, but he suspected that Colin always wished he'd had a more traditional kind of father, not someone who was perfectly happy to fill in with some carpentry during the winter while waiting for the river corridor to open up in April.

"Some of us retire," he told Mitchell now. "Some of us will never leave, though."

"And which are you?"

JT grinned. "Haven't figured it out yet."

"Do you ever get tired of it?" asked Lena.

"Oh," said JT, "maybe there'll be a trip in October that seems to last too long. But generally, no. If I ever get to the point where I feel like I'm shuttling people back and forth, then I'll retire. I'm not there yet."

Mitchell flipped open his guidebook, then scrutinized the cliffs.

"Looks like we're coming up on Nankoweap," he said. "Are we going to stop? I'd sure love to see those granaries."

"We'll see. It's a popular place," said JT. "If there's another party there, I'd just as soon not clog up the trail."

It turned out there was, in fact, another large party at Nankoweap; from the river, JT could see a line of tiny figures inching up the steep peppered hillside to the ancient stone granaries. JT was tempted to skip the hike, but it was already past noon, and people were hungry.

"It's a hot, dry hike," he cautioned them after lunch. "If you come, bring two liters of water, and dunk your hat and shirt. No," he told Sam sternly. "The dog stays here."

Not everyone went; Dixie stayed with Ruth and Lloyd, and Peter opted for a nap. Of those who went, all but Mitchell followed JT's advice and clothed themselves head to toe in wet cotton. Mitchell wore just a T-shirt, a dry one at that, claiming that he really did like the heat, and a wet shirt would just dry out within the first few minutes anyway, and he didn't like that yo-yo feeling of being hot, then cold, then hot again. JT was too hot to argue, and Mitchell seemed to do just fine on the half-mile hike through desert scrub and then up along the side of the cliff, until, just fifty feet from the stone cubbies, he leaned over and vomited, not just once but retching repeatedly, so that JT had to grab on to the waistband of the man's shorts to keep him from tumbling over the edge of the trail. He sent the others on ahead and made Mitchell sit and take small sips of water, but the man's face and neck had turned deep red, and, sensing he was dangerously close to heat exhaustion, JT uncapped his own jug and poured half a liter of good drinking water over Mitchell's head and shoulders.

"Sorry," wheezed Mitchell.

Next time do what I tell you, JT wanted to say.

"This is amazing!" Lena called from above. "Mitchell! Are you coming?"

"In a minute," Mitchell replied.

In a minute my ass, JT thought. "You okay?"

"Better," said Mitchell, just before vomiting again.

Mitchell never made it to the granaries; he couldn't seem to muster the strength to climb the last fifty feet. He didn't seem to care about it, either—a bad sign for someone who'd been so intent on getting up there an hour ago. JT knew the signs of heatstroke and didn't think Mitchell was there yet, but he was dangerously close.

It *was* hot this trip. He reminded himself that all trips in July were hot; but still, he had an elderly couple and an overweight girl and a man who refused to follow directions; and as they headed back to the boats, JT wondered just how hot it could get without these people going really strange on him.

19

Day Four

Miles 53–60

W hoa. Dude. What happened?" Peter asked Mitchell.
Without answering, Mitchell strode into the river and dove under.

"Mitchell got a little overheated," said JT.

"Heatstroke?" asked Evelyn anxiously.

"No," said JT, "but it could have been. Listen up," he told the group. "In case you haven't noticed, it isn't getting any cooler down here. I want you all to drink as much as you can, and then some."

"What's heatstroke?" Sam murmured. He and the dog were lying on their sides, facing one another like spent lovers. The dog's eyes were wide open, and he was panting heavily. Every so often, Sam poured a handful of sand on one of the dog's paws, causing it to twitch.

"Heatstroke can kill you," said Mark. "You better listen to JT."

"And you gotta keep your body cool," JT said. "Jump in the river. Dunk your clothes. I don't care. If you're hot, you're stupid."

There were somber faces all around as they stood in line to refill their water bottles. Peter held the jug, and as he poured for people, he whispered to Amy that JT had spiked the water, and this was just a ruse to get them all drunk this afternoon so he didn't have to cook them dinner tonight. Peter didn't like it when things got too serious. Of course, he didn't like it when people like Mitchell thought they knew more than the guides, who'd only been down the river like four hundred times between the three of them. And he didn't like it when people couldn't apologize for their errors in judgment. He thought a well-timed apology from Mitchell would have done a lot to lessen the tension on the beach. But Mitchell didn't want to talk to anybody.

Peter wasn't one to gossip, but he wasn't one to keep 100 percent of his thoughts to himself, either. And that afternoon in the paddle boat, he let it slip that he hoped Mitchell would chill out. "No pun intended," he added.

"Did you hear he's writing a book?" Jill said.

"About what?" asked Evelyn.

"Us," said Peter. "Ha ha! Just kidding," he told Mark, who looked alarmed.

Susan said, "He told me this trip was a big disappointment to him because he wasn't able to do it in a wooden dory."

"What's so great about wooden dories?" said Peter.

"It's more like Powell," said Evelyn.

"And who's this Powell dude again?"

There were groans all around. But nobody explained.

"My problem is that he's setting a bad example," said Jill. "I'm trying to get the boys to do what the guides say, and then Mitchell does exactly the opposite. Like not wearing a wet shirt for the hike."

"I wonder what he's writing about," said Amy. "Every time I look, he's writing in one of those notebooks."

"Or taking pictures," said Susan, a comment that elicited more groans, and threats to throw the camera in the river.

"Come on, people," said Abo. "The guy simply misjudged the heat today."

"No, he did not!" Jill exclaimed. "He really truly thought he knew better. He did the same thing on the hike this morning! We get to the stream, and JT tells him to keep his boots on, says you can protect your boots or you can protect your feet, and what does Mitchell do? He takes them off! 'They're two-hundred-dollar boots,' he tells JT."

"Be glad you're not Lena," Peter said.

"I would never let myself be bossed around like that," Amy declared.

"Good for you, honey," said Susan.

"Easy forward," said Abo, and they stroked with the current.

"Who was the worst passenger you ever had?" Peter asked.

Abo chuckled.

"Come on," said Peter.

"Fine," said Abo. "Are you ready for a long story? Because this is a really long story. But it's a good story. This guy, he had a bunch of Boy Scouts, and you know how you all got an equipment list before the trip? Well, he told his Boy Scouts it was all bunk, temperatures wouldn't drop below one hundred so forget the polypro, forget the fleece, forget the rain gear even. Then they get down here, and it's monsoon season."

"When's that?" asked Evelyn.

"Late July. Every day it rains. Every day these boys get wet. Every day we're looking at eight hypothermic Eagle Scouts. We guides, we're pulling out every piece of clothing we have, just to keep these kids dry. Then we come up on Bedrock, where there's this YOOGE rock that splits the river, and you have to stay to the right because if you go left you're dead, and who knows what happened, but one of the boats misses the cut and they postage-stamp right up against the rock and these four kids disappear into the water. So! Now we have four boys with hypothermia, and when we get everyone ashore, we tell the boys to strip down and get into sleeping bags together. At which point the scout leader goes totally apoplectic, accuses us of trying to turn his boys into fags—his word, my apologies—and when we get the sleeping bags out anyway, he takes them all and dumps them in the river so they're soaking wet and no good whatsoever."

"What happened to the kids?" asked Jill.

"This is what's so rich. They all warm up! On their own! So the scout leader is now completely convinced that he's Mr. Outward Bound and we're John Wayne Gacy. I thought the trip would never end."

"Wow," said Peter.

"*Yeah* wow," said Abo.

"I guess Mitchell isn't so bad," said Peter.

"Mitchell's nothing," Abo declared. "So I want you guys to be nice to him."

"Did you hear that?" Peter told Jill and Susan. "Be nice to Mitchell."

"We're very nice," they said in unison.

———

Peter couldn't argue with the two women, but he also knew the difference between god-nice and smiley-nice. God-nice was how you acted when a new kid came to school, and his mother shamed him for crying, and so you invited him to play kickball during recess. Smiley-nice was how you acted when your mother made you play with the hairdresser's kids while she got her hair done.

Jill and Susan, he was sure, were being smiley-nice.

As for other matters of group dynamics, Peter was also 100 percent certain that Dixie was sleeping with Abo. He knew this because when they were unloading the boats yesterday, he overheard Abo asking Dixie if she knew what a hernia looked like, and Dixie bent and inspected a very white part of Abo's groin—felt it, even, with her own two fingers. And this afternoon, after they set up camp and Peter went down to Dixie's boat to retrieve one of his beers, there was Abo lounging in the well of Dixie's boat with his feet up in her lap so she could clean his toenails with her pocketknife.

They had to be sleeping together.

Peter took his beer back to his own campsite; he popped it open and savored that first cold, fizzy swallow. Their camp tonight was at the base of yet another rapid, on a small beach walled off by chunky gray slabs rising straight up out of the water. Not a lot of room here, and he'd spent some extra time helping Abo set up the groover tonight; as a result, he'd had to settle for a small uneven patch of sand close to the kitchen area, a site that lacked any privacy—Evelyn as usual having claimed the nicest spot. But Peter resolved to make the best of things tonight—he did, after all, have a full beer in his hand and two more allotted for the evening.

Nothing like cold beer in hundred-degree heat.

Upriver, Jill was trying to convince the boys to wash. They were having none of it, though, and huddled on the sand, hugging their knees. Peter knew he should go down to the river right now with his own bathing kit, horse around, splash the boys, get everybody laughing. He didn't really like kids, but Jill wore such a pinched, irritated look that he felt sorry for her.

And he was all set to gather up his towel and wash kit, when out of the corner of his eye, he saw Amy toiling across the sand in his direction. She was wearing her oversized Jamba Juice T-shirt and carrying her own wash kit, and when she got close, he could see beads of perspiration above her lip, right where a mustache would have been.

"Hey," he said, squinting up at her.

"Hey," she sighed.

"I was just going to go wash."

Amy collapsed on her knees in the sand.

"You don't look so good," he said.

Finally she opened her eyes and breathed in deeply.

"Oh my god," she said. "I've just never been so hot in my entire life."

"Want some of my beer?"

And to his surprise, she took the can and drained what was left.

"Whoa," he said. "Does your mother know you drink like that?"

"I'm almost eighteen," she said, letting out a froggy burp. "When my mother was eighteen, it was legal."

Peter had a thought. He knew it was against the law, but down here in the canyon, the law didn't seem to apply. And based on what he'd seen in Susan, he didn't think she'd mind.

"Don't go away," he said, and he went down to Dixie's boat and gave the guides a goofy wave and got another two beers and came back and opened one and gave the other to Amy.

"Where's your mother, anyway?" he asked.

"Reading. *Not* bugging the shit out of me, for once."

"I can't read down here," Peter said, opening his second beer, which didn't really count as his second, as Amy had drunk most of his first.

"Abo reads at night," Amy said. "Have you seen him? He lies on his sleeping pad with his headlamp and reads before going to bed."

Peter felt scolded.

"I'm supposed to be reading *The Satanic Verses* for my lit class next year," Amy went on. "I'm having a hard time with it, though."

Now Peter was unable to stifle his surprise. "I brought that book too!"

"Are you reading it?"

"No," he confessed. "It's at the bottom of my bag."

"It's just so dense, and I want to like it because I know he's a good writer, but—" Amy bent forward, as though inspecting her toes, and what might have thrilled him in Dixie, repulsed him in Amy.

"I should have brought Tom Robbins," he began, but Amy seemed to have gone into another world, taking shallow hiccupy breaths. He thought she might be crying. Then he saw a little line of drool fall from her mouth to the sand. He suddenly regretted missing his chance to go bathe with the boys.

He cleared his throat. Some people, he'd heard, were allergic to alcohol. "Hey. Amy."

She didn't reply. Peter looked around to see if anybody was watching them. He wanted someone to come over, and he didn't want someone to come over.

Then Amy lifted her head and took a deep breath. She sensed the drool and hastily wiped her mouth.

Peter nudged her. "What was that all about?"

"Nothing."

"Fuck it's nothing."

"It's a stomachache. It's nothing."

Nervously Peter looked around for Susan. "What's your mother say?"

"Do not," said Amy, "do not tell my mother. It's the altitude," she said.

Peter was going to note that they weren't exactly in the Himalayas, but then Amy pointed to the water. "Look," she said. "There are three rivers out there."

Peter looked at the water. She was right. Next to shore were choppy, dancing waves; then farther out, the midstream core, churning downstream; and finally the eddy beyond, floating upstream in a blanket of bubbles.

"You want some Pepto-Bismol or something?"

"No."

"Because the guides have all kinds of shit in that first aid box."

"Jesus!"

"Don't get mad."

"I'm not mad."

"You seem mad."

"Well, I'm not. I'm just wishing I hadn't said anything to you if you're not going to leave me alone about it."

"Fine," he said. "I'll leave you alone."

"Thank you."

Then, just as the mention of lice will cause anyone's scalp to itch, so the mention of a stomachache made Peter feel a little queasy himself. He belched.

"Excuse me," he said, then belched again. He noticed Amy's wash bag. "Is that Vera Bradley?"

"How do you know Vera Bradley?"

"My ex-girlfriend liked those."

Amy picked up the bag and let it dangle from her finger. "My mother bought it for me. I think they're a total rip-off. But it gives her a thrill to see me using it."

"Hundred bucks for a little purse," said Peter. "It used to kill me. But it made her happy."

"How long were you guys going out?"

"Six years."

"Who ended it?"

"She did."

"That sucks."

"Yup."

"Aren't you glad we're not with a bunch of Boy Scouts?" she remarked, after a moment.

Peter finished his beer. "You believed that story?"

"I shouldn't?"

"How do you know when a river guide is lying?"

"How?"

Peter shook his head. "Whenever he opens his mouth! God," he added, "you are one of the most gullible people I ever met."

20

Day Four, Evening

Mile 60

While everyone else was eating dinner, and when she was sure the dog wouldn't come over and start sniffing her leg, Ruth settled herself on a log and rolled up her pant leg. She unwound the Ace bandage, then gently peeled off the gauze underneath. What she saw was not encouraging. The wound was still raw and weeping, and the surrounding skin was red and hot to the touch.

Was it time for the Cipro?

In their medical kit, Ruth had packed a five-day course of antibiotics. It was a practice they'd adopted after one particularly painful trip when she got an ear infection on the fifth night, the kind that could have been easily cured with a course of amoxicillin but which, in the absence of antibiotics, had Ruth clutching the side of her head in agony for the next six days and Lloyd worrying about long-term damage to the middle ear. After that, they always brought along a broad-spectrum antibiotic. It was not something they advertised; although he would have made it available if someone really needed it, Lloyd did not want the responsibility of prescribing drugs to strangers while on vacation.

Now, looking at her leg, Ruth knew she had a decision to make. The redness and swelling indicated treatment; on the other hand, there were no red lines shooting up her leg. If they'd brought along two courses of treatment (and why hadn't they? What foolish oversight!), she wouldn't have thought twice. But with just the one round of pills, she was reluctant. This was simply a surface wound, after all, something that should heal, as long as she kept it clean and used plenty of Neosporin.

JT came striding over. "You should have waited for me," he scolded. "Look, the wind's picking up; your cut's going to get full of sand." He knelt and inspected the wound and frowned. "I don't like the looks of this. Let me see what Dixie thinks." He called Dixie, and she came over and knelt and examined Ruth's leg too.

But Dixie didn't want to decide anything until they consulted Lloyd, so they called Lloyd over, and now Ruth cringed, because she was afraid Lloyd would bring out the Cipro, and she really didn't think it needed Cipro, not yet; she had tended how many cuts and scrapes and gashes over the years? and she knew what infection looked like, and this was not it. But Lloyd came over, duly called, and he first got confused, and Ruth had to explain to him twice how it had happened ("What dog?"), and then, when he finally grasped that it was not a dog *bite,* he shrugged and told her to stick a couple of Band-Aids on it and stop complaining.

So JT and Dixie washed the wound and applied more ointment and bandaged it up, while Ruth sat feeling helpless, and Lloyd wandered over to Evelyn's campsite and began emptying the contents of Evelyn's day bag, in search of a long list of items he hadn't seen since Lee's Ferry.

Yesterday Jill had told the boys in no uncertain terms that they were to try and use the toilet, but by tonight she found herself caring about it less and less. What could happen, medically speaking? Five days wouldn't kill them. Eight days wouldn't kill them. Thirteen days probably wouldn't kill them, but she doubted it would come to that.

Nor would it hurt Mark to go a day without sit-ups. Mark at forty had done well over two hundred thousand sit-ups: fifty per day, three hundred sixty-five days a year, for at least the fourteen years they had been married. At home he did them in their bedroom, upon rising. Here he did them on the sand, in the darkness, after everyone had gone to bed. Jill was grateful to have married someone who wasn't going to let himself go, but she found herself wondering, as she lay on her sleeping mat listening to Mark's little grunts, if he would really develop a set of the dreaded love handles in fourteen days. And so what if he did? The world wouldn't come to an end, she wanted to tell him. She would still love him.

Ten feet away, Sam began to cough. She recognized the succession of sharp dry hacks. She waited for the aerosol hiss, the quick inhalation of his asthma medicine. Nothing. Sam sat up.

"Where's your inhaler, Sam?" said Mark, between grunts.

Sam kept coughing.

"It's in his wash kit," Jill told Mark.

"Where's his wash kit?"

"In his day bag."

She expected the audible sigh of exasperation that Mark made whenever the boys didn't live up to his expectations (be prepared; be responsible; keep your meds available), but instead she heard him rustling in Sam's day bag. Then came the squirt, the deep breath in.

"Okay, cowboy. Go to sleep."

Then Mark came back and lay down on his mat beside her. He smelled of sunscreen. Everybody smelled of sunscreen.

"Thank you," she whispered. *Thank you for finding the inhaler. Thank you for not criticizing him for not having it.*

"I'm glad you organized this," he whispered, after a while.

"Good," she said. "Me too."

"The boys are having a good time, don't you think?"

"Yes." She lay flat on her back, gazing up at the spattered runway of stars; on either side, black cliffs loomed, voiding out the rest of the world. She had never seen anything so beautiful. What other worlds were out there, and where were they all going? She reached out and splayed her palms on the cool, velvety sand. A sense of hugeness, of being able to wrap her arms around the universe, came over her. At the same time, she felt as tiny as a pinhole.

"I hope I get to paddle Crystal," he said, after a while.

She felt jolted. "Why wouldn't you?"

"A lot of people are going to want to paddle Crystal," he said. "I heard Mitchell talking."

"Ssshhhh. He's right over there."

"Mitchell hasn't lifted a finger," Mark whispered, "compared to all the water I've pumped."

She reached over and took his hand. "Look at the stars, Mark," she whispered. "Count them," and he fell silent, as she hoped. And they lay there, floating on the sand, counting stars, while the ever-present sound of moving water lulled them to sleep.

July 7 Day Four

Mitchell is bugging the shit out of everyone. Tonight at dinner he started telling us the dam is going to break. He says it's unstable and the walls are crumbling and when it bursts there's going to be a 500 foot wall of water that'll wash us all down to the Gulf of Mexico. JT was ready to kill him — JT doesn't talk a whole lot, but he finally asks Mitchell if he's an engineer or a hydrologist and does he know about this and that, and he's using all these technical terms and finally Mitchell shuts up. But the damage is already done. Evelyn is convinced it'll happen during our trip.

And he's not very nice to his wife either. Like this afternoon, she got all excited about finding a fossil and asked Mitchell to take a picture of it so she could show her kindergartners, and Mitchell told her it would never come out, it'd just be a picture of a gray rock. I swear she was going to cry. So I took a picture for her. I would NEVER stand to be married to someone like him!!!!! Even if I am FAT!!!!!

Tomorrow I am definitely riding separate from Mom. As long as she is in the same boat with me, I end up saying like two words. Because I know she's evaluating everything I say. Oh Amy, I didn't know you wanted to go to China someday. Oh Amy, I didn't know you wanted to learn to kayak. Oh Amy, I didn't know you were really afraid of flying. I hate revealing myself in front of her. I wish I'd come on this trip alone.

When I get back I have to go visit colleges. I wonder if there's such a thing as drive-through liposuction. Here's my list: State U. Here's Mom's list: Harvard, Yale, Brown, Berkeley, Stanford, Amherst, Princeton. She says anyone who gets a perfect score on their SATs should aim high. If she tells anyone here about my scores, I will KILL her.

Maybe I should go to the University of Alaska, where I can wear a down coat 365 days a year, and no one will really notice that I'm FAT.

DAY FIVE

River Miles 60–76

Sixty-Mile Rapid to Papago

21

Day Five

Little Colorado

It was midmorning the next day when their three boats floated into the confluence of the Little Colorado River. Instantly JT could tell that it hadn't rained upstream, for the tributary was running its strange, aquamarine blue. On a hot summer day, the Little Colorado could get as crowded as a suburban water park, but JT decided to stop anyway, and not just because Mitchell had been talking about it all morning. People of all ages liked the Little Colorado; the water was warm, and they could lounge and play in its series of pools and waterfalls.

There must have been a dozen boats at the confluence that day, and JT had to do some tight maneuvering to find space to pull in. As his passengers eagerly scrambled out of the boats, JT warned them about the crusty travertine ledges; using Abo as a model, he showed them how to fasten their life jackets upside down, diaper-style, to avoid scraping themselves. Then he let them loose, and they ran upstream and joined the throngs, shrieking, splashing, sliding down waterfalls and hitching themselves into clumsy trains that broke apart, limbs in the air, hands grabbing for feet, frenzied laughter the likes of which JT was used to here on the Little Colorado but which most of the adults had not experienced since grade school.

While they reveled in the warm blue waters, JT went from boat to boat in search of gauze, for that morning, Lloyd had taken it upon himself to change the bandages on Ruth's cut. He did a thorough, precise job, wrapping her leg liberally, which would have been commendable in a hospital but was unfortunate down here on the river where they were so low on gauze to begin with. By the time JT realized what was happening, Lloyd had already ripped open the last packet.

Hadn't Ruth remembered they were low on gauze? Why didn't she stop him from using so much? Sometimes it baffled him, how good, intelligent people could get so spacey.

But today he got lucky, for the pontoon crew had a few extra rolls to spare. Thus at least partly replenished, he leashed the dog and hiked up a small hillside to a spot where guides left messages for one another.

It was here, years ago, that he'd left love notes for another guide, a girl named Mac, always a trip behind him, it seemed, until finally they managed to synchronize their schedules, and then it was just a question of whose boat to sleep on, his or hers. After three years together, they drove up to Vegas one night and got married, and within a year Colin was born, taking Mac off the river for a couple of seasons, which she never really forgave him for. JT, that is, not Colin; Colin she doted on, but she and JT never managed to figure out the parenting thing, not as two river guides anyway, and Mac resented JT every time he left on a trip, and JT reminded her it was her choice not to go off for two weeks and leave the baby, he'd be glad to take Colin so she could do a couple of trips each season. But it didn't work. The resentment spilled from her eyes every time he came back from a trip, and they finally decided it was more important for Colin to have two relatively happy parents than one unhappy parental unit, and that was how JT found himself a divorced father with a son to raise, a son he had every intention of infusing with the river spirit but who now worked for a law firm in Phoenix and criticized his father for not having a real job with a retirement plan.

There were no love notes today, just a pink-petaled bathing cap that another guide had left for Abo. "Thinking you might need this," the scrap of paper read. It was clearly a woman's handwriting; JT wondered how long it had been there and where the woman was now. Sometimes he had the feeling that the guides' love-ghosts haunted the canyon, showing up here and there in the form of heart-shaped rocks, or shooting stars—or campy pink bathing caps.

Back at the river, Dixie and Abo were shepherding everyone toward the boats—a giddy bunch, all of them, waddling with their life jackets drooping below their hips. It was while they were unfastening and refastening them into correct position that JT noticed one of Matthew's buckles hanging by a thread.

"What happened to your life jacket, Matthew?"

Matthew looked down.

"How long's it been like that?" said JT.

"I don't know," said Matthew.

The black nylon strap was ragged and stringy; judging from a few other spots that looked suspiciously like tooth marks, JT guessed who was responsible.

"Do you have a needle and thread?" Jill asked.

"Yes, I've got a needle and thread." He didn't mean to sound curt, but he could tell from the look on Jill's face that he did. He got out his sewing kit and mended the strap, and when he was done, he warned everyone to keep a close eye on their gear.

"That dog chews something of mine and he's history," said Dixie.

"When'd you get so evil?" Abo said.

"You're not evil," Peter told Dixie.

"Oh yes I am," said Dixie.

"Load up," said JT. "We got miles to go, people."

" 'Miles to go before I sleep,' " quipped Evelyn.

"Who wrote that?" asked Lena.

"Walt Whitman," said Mitchell.

Amy caught Peter's eye, and they both stifled their smiles.

Jill and Mark remained on the beach while the others got in the boats. Jill was repacking her day bag.

"What *is* it with these boys," Mark said, shaking his head. It was a statement, not a question, and Jill sensed that he expected she would know exactly what he was talking about and fondly commiserate.

Instead she said, "What do you mean?"

"Every time we turn around, they're getting into trouble. They have the worst luck! Sam with the red ant the first day, now Matthew with this. Sheesh," he said, shaking his head. "It's like they're cursed."

Jill didn't think an insect bite and a chewed strap indicated a curse.

"It's not the end of the world," she said.

"Oh, I'm not saying it is! Not at all!" And here Mark laughed, in such a way that was designed to curry her favor, when in fact he really felt he had a legitimate point to drive home. "All I'm saying is, if there's trouble, our guys will find it."

"Ruth got tripped by the dog. Are you saying she was looking for trouble? Or cursed?"

"Don't get snippy," said Mark. "I'm just saying we should look out for the boys a little more, maybe. Nip things in the bud before they happen. I don't see what's wrong with that."

Jill straightened up. "What's wrong with it is that you're kind of ruining things for me, Mark." She didn't know exactly what she was going to say next and hoped she didn't overdramatize. "I really wish you'd relax," she went on. "I'm trying to have this cool family vacation, and you're kind of throwing a damper on things by worrying about every this, that, and the other."

"You completely misunderstood what I was saying."

"What were you saying?"

Mark shook his head and looked downriver.

Jill put her hands on her hips. "What were you saying, Mark?"

"It doesn't matter."

"Do you have to do this? Here? Now? Did we not just swim in the most beautiful place on earth?"

Mark said something about clear mountain lakes.

"Never mind," said Jill. "I'm going to enjoy the trip my way, and you can enjoy the trip your way."

"Well, I just hope we all make it off in one piece," Mark said, climbing into the paddle boat.

Jill stayed behind on the beach for a moment, taking long slow breaths. Then she walked over to Abo, who was coiling his rope. "My arms are kind of tired," she told him. "I think I might take a break from paddling, if it's okay. Maybe ride in one of the oar boats."

"Sure, babe," said Abo.

———

It was late in the afternoon when they pulled into camp for the night. The beach was long and flat and stretched far upriver. People had their routines down by now, and they unloaded the boat and set up their campsites quickly.

JT appreciated their independence at this particular point, but he was still troubled. Ruth's leg had looked worse this morning than it had the day before; twice last night, he'd dreamt of helicopter evacuations. At breakfast, she was limping; at the Little Colorado, she did not go with the group but simply settled herself in a pool with her leg elevated on a dry ledge. She asked Lloyd to stay with her, but he refused.

"No sirree Bob," he said, traipsing off after the others. "I'm going to enjoy myself today."

Also, JT had overheard everything between Mark and Jill back at the Little Colorado. He had watched his share of marriages disintegrate during these trips; the canyon could strip the veneer off a marriage, make placid people restless, suddenly aware of imperfections. Just as you could fall in love at the drop of a hat, so too you could fall out of love. He hoped this wasn't going to happen with Mark and Jill.

In any case, it was not a time for worries, or clefts. They were just above Hance Rapid, entry point to the Inner Gorge, the Land of the Giants, where the walls would narrow in again and they would lose a billion years in geological time as they traveled down into the Vishnu Schist. This was the oldest, blackest rock you would ever see. This was where the river got serious, and unforgiving, where the walls closed in before you could say good-bye to the sky, where a flip meant a long swim before somebody might haul you out of the water. JT had seen real ghosts in this section of the river, ghosts in the water and ghosts in the rock, which was all there was, fundamentally, rock and water—and current. Always the current.

Some people loved this section, and some people were spooked by it. It depended on a lot of things: the weather, the flow, the people you were with. JT couldn't make any predictions with this group. It could go either way.

July 8 Day Five

~~Warm blue waterfalls~~
Turquoise waterfalls
Warm water
Mineral baths:
I ~~bathe myself~~ search for the deepest pool
To bathe my limbs
In these magical waters

Upstream
~~The hobbits~~
Bilbo Baggins grinds his ~~turquoise~~ gemstones
Stirring them into the headwaters
Clouding the water
So that when I immerse myself
There is no
thing but blue.

DAY SIX

River Miles 76–93

The Upper Granite Gorge

22

Day Six, Morning

Miles 76–89

The next day got off to a questionable start when the paddle boat flipped in Hance—this after a thorough scout above the rapid, with everyone climbing to a good lookout point and the guides gravely studying the hydraulics below, noting each rock, each hole, each pourover. Ultimately they decided on a left run, and JT ran it nice and clean and waited below. It was Abo who got into trouble. Piece of cake, Abo had been thinking, but while he was angling the paddle boat across the river to make that left run, a yellow jacket landed on his knee, and Abo, being allergic to bees, took one second to flick it away, one critical moment when he slackened the outward twist he'd been exerting on his paddle, allowing the boat to rotate five, maybe ten degrees to the right. That was enough. Instantly they found themselves being carried into the angry heart of Hance between two sharp pourovers, and even with Peter in front (all that heft, all that mass!), the boat reared up and flipped back, spilling Abo, Evelyn, Jill, Sam, Matthew, Mark, and Peter into the cold, surging waves.

As with most flips, there was no time for dismay; JT went straight into rescue mode, scanning the surface for life jackets. Within seconds, everyone popped up right next to the paddle boat—everyone but Peter, that is, Peter who couldn't swim, and while the others (amid mass confusion) managed to haul themselves onto the slick upturned belly of the raft, JT watched—now with dismay—as Peter got swept down through the rest of Hance and straight into Son-of-Hance, a second wash cycle, as it were, and except for a foot that kept poking up here and there, JT saw no sign of the young man, which didn't really concern him at first, but the seconds kept ticking by, so he was very, very glad when Peter finally resurfaced in the tailwaves, wearing the

127

stunned look of someone who's fallen off a fifty-foot cliff and against all odds not only survived but found his skeletal system intact. JT rowed hard to intercept Peter before the river carried him even farther downstream to Sockdolager Rapid, and when he did haul the young man out of the water, it took a great deal of effort to convince a teeth-chattering Peter that he was still alive, that the life jacket had done its trick and the white light he'd seen while submerged was not the door-way to heaven but the color of the sky as viewed from inside a sea of bubbles by someone in a state of shock.

In the meantime, the paddle boat had roller-coasted upside down through Son-of-Hance, and now Abo was yelling to his five remaining passengers to help him, to stand up and grab hold of the flip line and *lean back*—nothing easy about this, convincing five people ranging in age from twelve to fifty, five people who'd just swum their first major rapid, to get up from where they were lying belly-down, clutching at anything; convincing them to stand up, grab the flip line that ran down the middle of the underbelly, and lean back toward the water. But— and this was what always got JT, how six-day novices could rise to the occasion—they did it, they right-sided the raft with enough time before Sockdolager to settle themselves into place, grab whatever paddles remained, and go.

Finally, below Sockdolager, they found a place to pull in. Cold, shiv-ering, and still pumped with adrenaline, the swimmers peeled off their life jackets, breathlessly pacing and exchanging stories as they let the hot sun permeate as much epidermis as they were willing to expose. Peter was ecstatic, convinced that his survival was due to some innate ability to swim. It had been there all along, and he just hadn't known it! Why, he'd just kicked and flailed and thus defied gravity—he *floated,* he didn't *drown,* he could swim after all—and his mother was going to drop dead when she heard this, just drop dead!

"Do you realize how many lessons, how many swim camps, how many teachers practically tore my arms out of my sockets in an attempt to show me the Australian crawl?" he demanded. "Do you realize how I get sick to my stomach at the smell of chlorine? And here—here on the Colorado River, I can swim!" He arched his back to

the heavens and pounded on his chest. "DO YOU HEAR ME, MOM?
I AM A *SWIMMER!*"

Meanwhile, Sam and Matthew bragged that they had been the first
to surface, and Mark secretly reveled in the fact that it had been
mostly his and Abo's strength that had righted the boat. Jill, for her
part, couldn't seem to warm up, and JT told her to put on a polypro,
and she looked at him blankly and said, "What polypro?" and JT said,
"The polypro top I told everyone to keep in their day bag, just in case,"
and Jill wrenched her eyebrows, and JT sighed and went to his boat
and dug in his own bag and lent her one of his. With the added
warmth, things began to look up for Jill—that is, until she realized that
Sam had lost one of his flip-flops during his swim, one of the ones that
JT had fashioned the straps for out of a piece of rope, and she told
Matthew to let Sam wear one of *his* flip-flops, which Matthew refused
to do out of brotherly concern for Sam wearing a sandal that would be
half a size too big and might, just *might* cause him to trip; which
caused Mark to cuff Matthew, and now things began to look very grim
for the Compson family, until Evelyn finally drew JT aside and confided that she had an extra pair of Tevas that Sam could use, providing
great relief to both Jill and Mark but causing Jill to secretly wonder
why Evelyn hadn't proffered the sandals until now.

All in all, *not* how JT would have chosen to spend his first morning
in the Inner Gorge.

But JT was, in his core, an optimist by nature, and he reminded
himself that a flip and a bit of squabbling was just that, nothing more.
Things like this happened all the time. You couldn't be a river guide
and see the glass as half empty. Shit happened. It was part of the journey. And so when he felt they'd had enough time to warm up, he called
everyone back to the boats, and they headed out once again.

For JT, it was simply yet another morning adventure on the river.
But for the thinking travelers, something had shifted. As they floated
deeper into the gorge, several of them experienced the sense that they
were no longer on the same river—that the canyon, for all its beauty,
had begun to menace in a way it hadn't before. The current ran more
swiftly, and the walls that towered above could have been forged from

a different planet. Gone were the sunny stair-stepping sandstone cliffs; in their place rose more than five hunded vertical feet of glistening black schist, shot through with lightning forks of pink granite. It was dark down here, and it was violent too, and the violence had an inexplicable permanence to it, one that was going to take them some time, as novice travelers, to figure out.

In the meantime, all they could do was simply crane their necks in quiet wonder.

Deep in the Inner Gorge, Phantom Ranch announces itself with a necklace of red balls, strung like jewels across the river at Mile 87.5. This marks the gauging station, which is followed by a large boat beach. Usually crowded with both river runners and hikers, Phantom, like the Little Colorado, reminds you once again that your midsummer river trip is not the wilderness experience you'd anticipated last January back in Cambridge, Massachusetts.

JT had mixed feelings about Phantom. There was a small settlement a half mile up the trail, an outpost of an earlier era, with a general store, a post office, and a dining hall. It was nice to stop at Phantom and get news from other parties, collect whatever mail might be waiting, and find out if there were any surprises waiting for them downstream. And the passengers liked to visit the store, buy a trinket or two, and send a postcard marked "Mailed by Mule" from Phantom Ranch.

But the thing about Phantom was that there was a pay phone. This was of course a nice thing to come upon halfway through a trip, if you really needed to check in on something, but too many times JT had seen one of his passengers make a phone call and hear some bad but not devastating news (the cat vomiting blood, the neighbor's house smoldering); and what could you do with news like that? Worry, that's what you did, for that day and the next seven days, sharing your pall with everyone.

JT had talked about it at breakfast with Dixie and Abo, and although they would have in some sense preferred not to touch base with civilization, they had to stop if they were going to find somebody to take the dog off their hands.

"But we're not going to linger," JT had warned everyone during their daily briefing. "Half an hour, tops."

Now, the red balls of the gauging station behind them, JT aimed his boat toward a wide expanse of sand ahead on river right. Phantom's boat beach, as usual, resembled a crowded parking lot, with a long lineup of bulging rafts. Hot, weary hikers down from the South Rim cooled their feet in the icy shallows, while boatmen rearranged their gear, or bathed, or traded stories and information in front of the bulletin board.

JT beached his boat, hoping that someone here would be just the dog-loving hiker he needed.

"Go charm someone," he told Dixie as he tied his rope. "Tell them the owner's waiting up top."

"You mean lie?"

"Someone's waiting, somewhere," JT said.

So Dixie went off in search of a willing, if gullible, hiker. Meanwhile, half their group headed up to the outpost. Jill and Mark both wanted the boys to send a postcard, but Sam knew his time with the dog was coming to an end and refused to leave; and since Jill and Mark couldn't force Sam to go, they couldn't force Matthew, either.

"Of course we wouldn't dare lay down the law, would we," said Mark. "Far be it from us to exercise our parental authority once in a while."

Sam, in fact, began to engage the dog in an innocent chase game, ducking and darting, sending up soft sprays of sand. JT saw this as a good thing; potential rescuers would see Blender for the energetic hound he was, not some sick runt who'd collapse halfway up the trail. He even took Blender's life jacket off, the better to display his freshly scrubbed coat. In fact, it wasn't long before Dixie captured the interest of a ragtag couple laden with army-surplus gear—the neediest having the kindest of hearts, JT thought. He was all set to walk over and present them with a couple of trip vouchers, when the group who'd trekked up to the store returned with guilty looks on their faces.

"What'd you do, get ice cream?" JT asked.

"Who could resist?" said Mitchell. "You want me to go get you a Fudgsicle?"

"I'll take a rain check," JT said. "Any news from home?"

"The pay phone was out of order," Mitchell reported.

"Darn," said JT.

At the same time, Sam continued to entertain hikers with Blender's tricks. Matthew for his part was drawing an elaborate map in the sand with a stick, but nobody noticed. And so Matthew tried to get in on Sam's game, waving the stick in front of the dog's face, then running a little, then waving the stick again. When Blender didn't respond, Matthew dug in his pocket and found some cookie crumbs. These he held out to the dog. Blender trotted over, sniffed, licked the crumbs. Then he bounded back to Sam.

Who knew exactly what was going on in Matthew's mind? For as long as he could remember, his younger brother had been getting more attention—ever since around the time of Matthew's first birthday, when his gift, so to speak, was a red-faced yawling bundle who from the very start was entitled to more lap time than Matthew. This grabby, blind addition to his world, who stole his mother and kept her bedridden for what seemed like weeks on end, went on to draw better pictures and tell better jokes and end up with the more complicated Lego sets each Christmas.

In any event, while Sam was playing with Blender, Matthew went back to JT's boat and opened up the food hatch and got out the peanut butter. He stuck his finger in the jar and smeared a large glob on the end of the stick. Then he took the stick back to where Sam and Blender were playing and held the stick in front of the dog's nose.

This time Blender gave the stick his full attention. Matthew held it just out of reach, and then, when he knew the dog was thoroughly spellbound, he flung the stick as far as he possibly could out into the river and watched, wiping his hands on his shorts, as the dog bounded, sans life jacket, into the water.

At first it seemed like any other competition between two brothers, Sam outraged over the theft of attention, Matthew smug. As for the stick toss, at first it was just that, a dog chasing a stick into a friendly body of water. And Blender did indeed retrieve the stick, proudly dog-paddling back toward shore.

But the current at Phantom Ranch is swift and strong, and has swept more than its share of hikers to their deaths; and to both Sam and Matthew's horror, suddenly Blender's dog-paddling was doing him no good whatsoever, and his body disappeared, leaving only his head above water, his jaws locked around the stick as he sailed like a toy boat down toward the Gulf of Mexico.

Upon seeing the dog bounding into the river, JT tried to make an immediate dash for the water. However, in accordance with the laws of physics, coupled with the lack of traction, his sudden lunge forward sent his feet skidding out behind him in a violent spray of sand, which in turn sent him sprawling on his stomach. In the meantime, Dixie, with less weight and more forethought, made it to her boat before JT reached his. JT managed to hurl himself at her boat.

"Don't lose him!" she yelled as he pushed them off.

To his left, steep dark walls loomed out of the water; to his right, the sandy boat beach tapered off. And about a hundred feet ahead of them was the dog, his head poking up out of the roiling surface, the stick firmly clamped between his jaws.

"Stay to the left as far as you dare!" JT shouted. On the footbridge ahead of them, hikers were waving their arms and pointing to the dog, who was being carried toward the cliffs. And then, just when it looked as though he was going to slam straight into the ancient wall of pre-Cambrian rock, the invisible current swirled just enough to the right to carry him down under the footbridge.

"Go right!" JT shouted, but it was pretty much beyond their control at this point. JT thought he knew every river-foot of this canyon, but he'd forgotten that just beyond the footbridge, the canyon wall dropped off suddenly to a flat area beyond. Please, he thought, please let there be a nice little eddy. Please let the eddy snag the dog. Please let us all end up on this second beach with its access to the Bright Angel Trail and those nice hikers waiting back up at the boat beach.

But whatever eddy might have existed did not do its job, and the dog continued floating straight down the middle of the river, stick in mouth.

"Switch!" yelled Dixie, and with lightning speed they traded places. JT grabbed the oars but remained on his feet to put the full weight of his torso into each push, because if they didn't catch up to the dog by the end of this second beach, they would have Pipe Creek Rapid to contend with. It wasn't a big rapid, but it was big enough to threaten a dog without a life jacket.

The beach zoomed past. A little island zoomed past. And then the river carried them around a bend, and he could hear the lower frequency of the rapid.

They skittered through the waves, Dixie standing at the helm, shifting to keep her balance. He knew there was a strong eddy coming up at the bottom on the right, so he rowed as hard as he could to stay left, and he was wondering how far down this damn river he was going to go in search of the dog—was he some kind of Ahab or Colonel Kurtz?—when he looked to the right and there, being gently carried upstream in the eddy, was Blender.

JT had just enough time to pull into the small camp below the eddy. Once they hit shore, he yanked free a sleeping pad, tossed it into the water, flopped on top of it, and paddled out to get the dog—who, after all of this, still held the stick clenched in his teeth. His nostrils flared, and his dark eyes regarded JT with an immense sense of calm, as though JT were completely, unquestionably in tune with him, about things in general but specifically about this sixteen-inch stick, which was, as JT must know, the be-all and end-all of life itself; so that when JT grabbed hold of the dog's bandanna and paddled back to the beach and the dog felt solid ground under his feet, he did not run about and sniff, or dance for JT's approval, but rather sat himself upon the sand, head high, stick in mouth, proud of a job well done.

Within a short time the other boats arrived. First out was Sam, who threw himself upon the dog. Jill and Mark followed, looking anxious. Matthew remained in the boat. Slowly the others disembarked and straggled onto the cobbly beach.

"If you're wondering, he's in time-out," Mark declared.

"Who?" asked JT.

"Matthew! For throwing the stick!"

JT looked over at Dixie's boat, where Matthew sat with his back to them.

"You don't need to do that," said JT.

"By golly," said Mark, "he can't keep himself out of trouble."

"He did what any kid would do," said JT, who hated to see people punished (unless by his own doing) on one of his trips. Still, he didn't like to go against parents' directives, either.

"Mark wouldn't want to miss an opportunity to discipline his kid, though," Jill remarked. She tilted her head and began violently detangling her hair with her fingers.

JT's skin prickled; worse than anything was siding with a wife.

Peter came up, followed by Dixie.

"Is this trip jinxed?" she demanded. "Did we piss off Odwalla?"

"Who's Odwalla?" asked Evelyn.

"The river goddess," Dixie informed her, as matter-of-factly as a nun. *Who made the earth? God made the earth.* "Like, what did we do wrong to deserve this?"

Abo looked down, scratched the back of his neck. "It's just a dog, Dixie."

"What's that supposed to mean?"

"You act like he's Darth Vader."

"Well, *sorry* if I'm not thrilled to have the dog along for the rest of the trip," said Dixie. "I told you guys. I told you. Nobody ever listens to me." She stalked back to her boat, waded in a few feet, and squatted.

"Why is Dixie upset?" Jill asked JT.

JT ran his hands through his hair and didn't answer. Because frankly it didn't make a lot of sense to him, what she had against this dog.

Just then, Ruth, dressed head to toe in the beige microfiber that had become her uniform for this trip, came limping across the sand. She knelt on her good leg, and the dog sensed her and came trotting over and sat, panting, so that Ruth could pat him.

"Lloyd," Ruth called, over her shoulder. "Look who survived."

Lloyd was bent over his day bag. "I'd be fine if I could find my keys," he replied.

"Come on, guys," said JT to the group. "Let's fix lunch."

But Mitchell shook out his map. "I think," he began, "if you can make it up over this ledge, you can connect with Bright Angel."

JT assumed Mitchell was confused about something, and he didn't want to take the time to understand his confusion. He ignored Mitchell and headed for the boats to haul out the lunch supplies.

"Do you want me to go?" Mitchell offered, traipsing behind.

"Huh?"

"The dog—someone's going to take him back up to Phantom, right?"

JT stared at the man. A grizzly half-inch stubble had grown in, and his clay-colored shirt hung untucked over his dark swim trunks. JT repositioned his visor. "Say what?"

"Well, look," said Mitchell, shaking the map out.

JT squinted at Mitchell—or rather, at Mitchell's large dark sunglasses. "You can't get to Phantom from here."

"Sure you can," said Mitchell. "See," and he pointed to some dense contour lines on the map.

But JT didn't take his eyes off Mitchell's sunglasses. "Mitchell, are you second-guessing me?"

"I'm just consulting a map is all."

"Well, consult all you want," said JT. "There's no way to get to Phantom from here."

"Then what do you propose to do with the dog?"

"That's easy," said JT. "The dog's on for the duration."

Mitchell expelled a little puff of air.

"That's right," said JT, as though needing to convince himself as well. "I'm certainly not going to make one of us hike him out at Havasu."

"What about Hermit?"

JT didn't answer. Theoretically, it would be possible for someone to hike him out at Hermit Creek, but the likelihood of finding a willing hiker now seemed all too remote. Besides, chasing the dog on this last jaunt from Phantom through Pipe Creek had crystallized something in him, and he didn't like to think of it in terms of ownership, but that's what it was when you came right down to it: the now-clear assumption that the dog was his and would be his, not just now but long after this trip was over. He saw himself putting up a new fence in his backyard, Colin's old sandbox a good place to dig.

"A response would be in order," said Mitchell.

Realizing that they were halfway through their journey and that it was time to level with Mitchell, JT drew him aside. For once, he took off his own glasses, because even though the bright noonday sun burned his retinas, he wanted Mitchell to look straight into his eyes.

"What do you have against me, anyway?" Mitchell began. "You've had it in for me from the start. Are you going to spell it out or just keep pissing me off?"

"Shut up, Mitchell," said JT.

To his surprise, Mitchell fell silent.

"Okay now," JT said, "you've got two options, Mitchell. One, you can stay with us, or two, you can find another trip for the next seven days. That's pretty simple, don't you think, Mitchell? Now I suspect the last thing you want to do at this point is take any advice from me, but I'm your Trip Leader, and that's my job, and so I'm going to advise you to choose option number one and stick with us. And you know why? Because if you don't, you're going to look back on this as the biggest missed opportunity of your life. Because it's not about the dog, Mitchell. It's about learning to let go."

Mitchell folded his arms over his broad chest. His forearms were furred with silvery hairs, which glinted in parallel lines, as though combed.

"And if you stay with us, I promise you two things," JT went on. "Number one, forget about the allergies. Lena's not going to go into anaphylactic shock, unless she cuddles up with the dog, which I don't think she's inclined to do."

Mitchell spat into the sand.

"Stay with me, Mitchell," JT warned, "because here comes promise number two: I guarantee you that book you're writing is going to be a hell of a lot better *with* a dog than *without*. Are you with me here? Think about the opportunities, Mitchell. What would John Wesley Powell have done? You think he would have ditched the dog?"

The riddle briefly tempered Mitchell's fury.

"Hardly a question you really have to ask," JT said. "Now grow up, Mitchell, and let yourself have some fun. Don't take this trip so seriously. Kid around. Be nice. People want to like you, Mitchell. They really do."

It was one of the toughest and longest lectures JT had ever given one of his passengers, more words than he'd said at one time in he couldn't remember how long, and it would not have surprised him if, when the next group of boats came down, Mitchell and Lena invited themselves on board and huffed good-bye, good riddance, once and for all, to JT and crew. But JT didn't wait around to see what Mitchell was going to do. They were two miles below Phantom Ranch on Day Six of their trip. He had a dog, a wounded geriatric, an Alzheimer's patient, a morbidly obese teenager, Cain and Abel—and now a pathological copilot he might have just incensed beyond hope. It was at least 115 degrees. He had lunch to prepare and bandages to change; he was responsible for making sure twelve people kept themselves well-enough hydrated so as not to collapse in this heat. He'd done what he could to send the dog on his way, but the dog was here to stay.

As he'd just told Mitchell, it would make for a much better story someday.

23

Day Six

Mile 89

While JT was off with Mitchell and everyone else was fussing over the dog, Evelyn uncapped her Nalgene and allowed herself four small sips of water.

As of today, Evelyn had started rationing. Yes, she'd heard JT's mandate about everyone drinking enough, but she was confident that she knew her own personal homeostasis well enough to gauge the minimum amount of water necessary to keep herself hydrated without having to suffer a full bladder. JT was recommending a liter every four hours; Evelyn decided she could halve that amount without running any health risks.

It was the simplest of equations:

$$J - B = E$$

Where J = *the amount of water JT was recommending;*
B = *the amount of water that would ordinarily end up in her bladder; and*
E = *the amount of water that she, Evelyn, would have to drink to stay sufficiently hydrated.*

And so today she'd made it from breakfast to lunch on just half a liter. Not being in such intense pain, she found it easier to go. And to check for dehydration, she pressed her thumb to the inside of her forearm, making sure that her flesh bounced back readily. It did. She congratulated herself on her methodology.

Apart from her Problem, though, Evelyn was having a fine time on the trip. She'd seen a peregrine falcon and a California condor, a flock of wild turkeys and too many hawks to keep track of. She'd seen bighorn sheep grazing by the side of the river and funny little mice with big ears scurrying across the sand at dawn. She'd memorized all the layers of rock.

Best of all, she was making friends. Last night, for instance, Jill had invited her to eat with the family, and she'd spent the whole time telling them about her research, which they listened to more closely than her students ever did. The guides in particular were very nice, especially the way they answered her questions so patiently. *Does it ever snow down here? How did that rock get out in the middle of the river? Why did the Anasazi build the granaries so high? What are they going to do about all that nuisance tamarisk? How do you know when the water levels are going to rise? Is the dam really going to burst someday?*

She made sure to take copious notes, writing in her journal at the end of each afternoon while the others drank. (That was the one thing about this trip that she disapproved of, the amount of alcohol consumed, and not just by the passengers but by the guides themselves, because shouldn't they be watching out for the rest of them? Weren't they the designated drivers?) Julian would be interested in hearing about the size of the trout; he liked to fish. And her friends over in the botany department would want details about the flora and fauna. She kept a numerical log of each day's photos too, so she would know just where a particular photo was taken—she didn't want to be one of those people who came back from vacation with a lot of pretty pictures and nothing informative to say about them!

Lots of people were keeping journals, she noticed. Mitchell had a dirt-colored spiral notebook. Amy wrote in something covered with floral fabric. As for Evelyn, she preferred ordinary composition books, marbled black and white, with a blank spot on the cover to note the date and location. She'd always kept travel journals, one for each trip, ever since she was a child. Back in Cambridge, she kept them lined up on a lower bookshelf, in chronological order, her own set of personal abstracts.

———

It seemed to Evelyn that Matthew was being unfairly shunned for his behavior up at Phantom. All he'd done was make a valiant effort to entertain the dog. What was so wrong with that, even if it ended up the way it did?

After lunch she saw the boy sitting forlornly with the dog, while Sam and his father were occupied with something in the boat. Evelyn saw this as an opportunity, not just to comfort Matthew but to try and make friends with the dog. And so she approached them with a hesitant smile. Matthew had taken off his hat, and his scalp looked pale and vulnerable through his buzz cut.

"Mind if I pat the dog a little?" she asked.

Matthew shifted to make room for her. The dog immediately rolled over and splayed his legs. Evelyn hesitated, then tapped his chest.

"Actually, he likes it like this," Matthew told her, and he bent over the dog and rubbed his stomach vigorously. One of the dog's hind legs batted the air.

"Try that," he told her.

Tentatively, Evelyn patted the dog's abdomen. There didn't seem to be much belly room, with all his male apparatus, and she was afraid she might, well, stimulate him.

"Harder," said Matthew.

Evelyn rubbed her fingers in small circles, careful to stay in one area. The dog's leg began to kick in response.

"See? He likes you. Now try this," and Matthew stood up and dug in his pocket and pulled out some Gummi Bears, frosted with sand and lint. He handed one to Evelyn, who hesitated, then offered it to the dog.

"Good job," said Matthew, scrumbling the dog's ears.

"Do you like animals generally?" Evelyn asked.

"I like mammals," said Mathew. "And I love reptiles. I want to go to the Galápagos Islands."

"I've been there!" Evelyn exclaimed.

"I was Charles Darwin for Major Thinkers Day," Matthew went on. "We rented a white beard for me to wear. I made my finches out of feathers from Hobby Village. All their beaks were different," he said proudly.

"I'm very impressed!"

"How come you're on this trip alone?" Matthew asked suddenly.

"Well," said Evelyn, taking the time to think of a good answer, "I like to do things alone, I guess."

"I don't. I hate being alone. My mom likes it, though. Sometimes she wants to be alone so bad, she goes and locks herself in the bathroom."

Although Matthew's hair was no more than half an inch long, Evelyn noticed it was already growing back into its genetic whorl.

"And it's not just me and Sam that make her go in there," he went on. "She goes in there on the weekend, when my dad's home. My dad's not home a lot, though."

"What does your dad do?"

"Something in Japan. One time he brought me and Sam some comic books and he brought my mom a bathrobey thing and she wasn't very nice about it. I hope they're not going to get divorced."

Evelyn's heart lost its balance, and she felt the color rise in her neck. "I'm sure they're not," she said hastily. "Look, they're having such a good time together."

Matthew looked over to where Jill was laughing with JT; Mark and Sam were still off in the boat.

"I guess," he said dully. "If we could just get a dog," he added, scratching the dog's ears.

A spasm of loneliness gripped Evelyn right then. She suddenly wished, with all her heart, that she had urged Julian to come after all. There was nobody with whom she was feeling a real kinship; she was a fifth wheel, unintegrated, both superior and inferior to everyone.

How did you express that, mathematically?

24

Day Six, Evening

Mile 93

That evening, to mark the end of a very long day, JT mixed up a bucket of margaritas. He had just started ladling them out when some hikers came traipsing through the bushes, a weary group of women whose first task upon reaching the river was to shed their clothes and dash into the water. No one was more intrigued than the two boys, who stopped arguing over the can smasher and knelt in rapt attention at the sight of four naked women whooping it up in the river. They were even more impressed when one of them recognized Abo and, after wrapping herself in a sarong, came over to look at some photos he had dug out from his ammo box. The can smasher lay idle.

Eventually, all the women wandered over, and in exchange for margaritas, JT was able to score an extra Ace bandage from them.

"Any of you happen to like dogs?" Dixie asked. "He's really sweet. Doesn't need much water, either."

"Dixie," said JT.

"Might as well ask," Dixie said with a shrug.

"We're not trying to pawn the dog off," JT told the women.

"Oh yes we are," said Dixie.

JT did not want to get into any more confrontations today—even with Dixie. Or especially with Dixie.

"No *way* did I do that," Abo was protesting to his woman friend. "You are such a liar. Don't anyone listen to her."

"Are you Abo's girlfriend?" Sam asked.

Abo looked up. "Sam, you're way too young to be asking those kinds of questions."

Sam whispered something to Matthew, and Matthew shoved him.

Another woman was watching Lloyd as he stood in the shallows, washing his face. "I ought to tell my grampa to do this trip," she said.

"How old's your grampa?" said Abo.

"Older than that guy."

Lloyd finished washing and groped about for his towel, which was floating in the shallows. JT went over and picked it up, wrung it out, and handed it to Lloyd.

"Thank you," said Lloyd, blotting his face.

"No problem," said JT.

"My wife is in love with you, you know," said Lloyd.

Alone in the filtered light of the tent, Ruth unwrapped the Ace bandage, dreading what she would find. Yesterday it had seemed that their careful ministrations might pay off, for the wound had calmed down noticeably. But today it had begun throbbing again, burning hot one minute and ice cold the next; she'd gotten to the point where she wanted to just rip the bandages off and stick her whole leg in the river.

She peeled off the last layer of gauze. Sure enough, the wound was red, slick, cheesy with pus.

Oh, the value of 20/20 hindsight! Regretting her earlier decision to hold off on the Cipro, Ruth frantically pawed through her day bag for the medical kit in which they kept an oblong blue pillbox with the Cipro and all the other just-in-case medicines. If she could take a Cipro right now, then she could tell JT—who was sure to come snooping around any minute—that she'd already put herself on antibiotics.

But when she finally found the canvas kit and unzipped it, there was no pillbox.

She knew she had packed it because she'd taken a muscle relaxant the first night. She emptied her day bag, thinking that maybe she'd simply failed to put the pillbox back into the canvas kit. No luck. She twisted around and emptied Lloyd's day bag. No luck again.

Now Ruth felt a twinge of panic, for there were a lot of important medicines in that pillbox, not just Cipro. Had she left it back at their first campsite? Stuck it in someone else's bag? Had Lloyd taken it? She peeked out of her tent and saw him walking toward the tent, shaving kit in hand.

"Do you know where the blue pillbox is?" she asked when he came crawling inside the tent. He smelled of peppermint, and old coins.

Lloyd looked at the mess strewn all over the tent floor. "Who did this?"

"I did," said Ruth. "I'll pick it up. But I'm trying to find the pillbox. The blue pillbox, with all the little compartments. Try to remember. You said you had a headache yesterday. Did you take some migraine medicine?"

"I don't get migraines," said Lloyd. "You get migraines."

Lloyd had had a migraine two days before they left Chicago. Ruth didn't think it would be helpful to remind him.

"Well, I'm trying to find the pillbox, and I can't," said Ruth. "Do you know where it is?"

"Check with Becca," said Lloyd.

"Lloyd!"—for now she was getting exasperated—"Becca's not on this trip! It's just you and me! And I need the pillbox!"

"Are you saying someone stole it?"

"No, I—"

Lloyd wagged his finger in front of her face. "That's the trouble with you, Ruthie. Always jumping to conclusions."

Ruth told herself to drop the issue. What good would it do to point out that a few mornings ago, he'd been the one jumping to conclusions over his stethoscope?

"I come home late, and you think I'm canoodling with Esther! The teacher doesn't frame David's finger painting, and you think David's flunking out of kindergarten! You have to stop jumping to conclusions all the time!"

Ruth looked away. She was not, absolutely not going to cry.

"I just wish for once you'd get all the facts before you make an accusation," Lloyd said, pulling on a flimsy white T-shirt. It was inside out and backward, so the label curled into the hollow at his throat. "And I don't want another baby until you calm down with all this drama."

Ruth was taken aback by this. She was accustomed to watching Lloyd slip into the past, but for him to raise this particular issue, in this new light? When David was five, Ruth and Lloyd had indeed disagreed over whether to have a second child. Lloyd, busy with his growing practice, wanted to wait. Ruth, on the other hand, didn't want a large age gap between children. But while they'd disagreed, it had never focused on her so-called dramas, as he now put it. Had she really been so irrational?

Ruth liked to think that theirs was a successful marriage. But it had always been a quiet marriage, one without a lot of shouting. Disputes were resolved mostly by the passage of time, as each came to understand, as if by osmosis, the other's position. Loud, accusatory fights made them both uncomfortable, for they knew that things said in the heat of an argument were often said more to inflict pain than to instill truth.

But now, as she listened to Lloyd rant, she wondered if perhaps they'd been too reserved all this time. Maybe they should have occasionally *had it out*, as Becca would have put it when she was in college. Maybe they would have understood each other better.

"What are you looking at?" he demanded.

She didn't realize it, but she'd been staring at his face. He'd missed a dime-sized patch of stubble on his chin, and a few dark hairs poked out of his nose.

"I'm looking at you, Lloyd," she sighed.

"Oh." He seemed to contemplate this, and, sensing a window of opportunity, Ruth placed her palm against his cheek, for touch always seemed to bring him back to the present. His bloodshot eyes skittered through the years.

"Are you having a good time on this trip?" she asked him.

"Of course I am. I couldn't survive without this trip every year."

"Me, either," said Ruth.

He leaned forward to kiss her. His whiskers tickled. "You look pretty cute," he said gruffly.

Ruth smiled.

"Want to fool around?" he asked. "Come on! Who will notice? Becca's out there flirting with the guides and David's got his nose in his book. A little hanky-panky with the old man? A quick roll in the hay?"

Ruth did not remind him that the little blue pillbox had a compartment for Viagra, without which there would be no hanky-panky.

"Tonight," she told him.

"Better keep your word," he warned. "Don't get my hopes up." He leaned over and kissed her again.

"You always had a beautiful smile, Ruthie," he said. "But now I'm going to go and have a beer. Want a beer?"

"In a bit," Ruth said. "After I tidy up in here."

When he was gone, she lay down on her mat and covered her face with her forearm and wept.

She was still lying on her mat when she heard the swish of footsteps in the sand.

"Ruth?"

It was JT. Hastily she smoothed her hair and sat up.

"Are you busy? Because I want to take a look at your leg before we start the dinner circus."

"I'll take care of it," Ruth called out. "If you could just bring me whatever bandages you have."

"Well, I'd really like to clean it myself," said JT. "Are you decent? Can I come in?"

She heard his knees pop as he knelt and lifted the tent flap. "Need a hand getting out? Let's take a look at it in the sunlight. Dixie's got some hot water ready. Aiy," he said as his eyes adjusted to the dimness. "Ruth. What happened?"

"I don't know."

"It wasn't like this at breakfast?"

"I didn't look at it this morning. And at lunch you had the dog to deal with, and Mitchell and all. It's not that bad," she said.

"With all due respect, ma'am, if I took you into a clinic right now, they'd have you on antibiotics before you could blink."

147

"That's just it," Ruth said. "I have some Cipro with me."

"Cipro? As in *Cipro*?"

"We always carry Cipro."

"Why didn't you tell me this before?"

"Because," she began, "because," but she couldn't come up with a reason.

JT sighed. "Okay. So. Have you taken one yet?"

"I can't find it."

JT dropped his head. Ruth didn't think such melodrama was necessary.

"I'm sure it's around somewhere," she said. "I'll check with Lloyd."

"What are we looking for? A prescription bottle?"

"A blue pillbox. About this long, with separate compartments for each day of the week."

"Any chance Lloyd might have lost it?"

It was his emphasis on the word "lost." Obviously he knew. She looked into his clear, blue eyes, then looked away.

"Does everyone know?" she asked evenly.

"Some might. Ruth," he said, "I wish you'd said something."

"The people back in the office might not have let us come."

"But you could have said something to me, once the trip was under way."

"I'm sorry," said Ruth. "Don't be mad."

JT sighed. "I'm not mad. I'm just worried about your leg. And if we have to evacuate you, we'll have to evacuate Lloyd too," he said.

The word was sharp, sudden, unexpected. Evacuate? This wasn't a rattlesnake bite or a broken bone—it was merely a cut, a cut that would heal if she could only find the Cipro.

"Don't say that word," she said angrily.

"Ruth," he said, "I have to do what's right."

"But you can't evacuate us! That wouldn't be right! It's our last trip! Do you know what it would do to Lloyd? Do you know? It would kill him," she said. "One helicopter ride, that's all it would take to erase everything."

"But your leg," he said. "If it gets worse—"

"It's not going to get worse," she said. "We'll find the Cipro, and it'll get better. Stop thinking like that."

"He needs you to be well," said JT.

"He needs to stay on the river!"

"At the expense of your leg?"

"You're not listening," she said. "My leg is going to be fine."

JT ran his fingers through his hair, and despite her anger, she felt a maternal protectiveness toward him. Of course he was worried. Of course he would be thinking about an evacuation. But he didn't know what it was like to be old, to be facing death square in the face, constantly aware of every event possibly being your last: your last Christmas, last time on an airplane, last trip down the river.

She didn't fault him for not knowing this, but she wasn't going to allow the word "evacuate" to be spoken in any form down here in the canyon. Not in her tent, anyway. She scooted toward the door flap, then motioned for JT to go ahead of her.

"Help me up," she said. He gave her his hand, and she pulled herself up. The light was pink; golden dust flecked the air. Down toward the river, where they had set up the kitchen, people stood at the prep table, chopping vegetables. JT led her to a log, where she sat while he went and got the first aid kit, along with a pan of hot water.

"We've had a good marriage, JT," she said when he returned. "We've been good to each other."

JT knelt and pulled on a pair of gloves. "Well," he said, wringing out a washcloth, "not many people can say that."

"And I know what lies ahead." She winced as he dabbed at her leg. "I know it's not going to be pretty. I read the books. I go to the support groups. Sometimes I wish he'd just have a heart attack in the night."

JT looked into Ruth's eyes. They were gray and lashless, but she had penciled a thin line across her upper lid and darkened her eyebrows; and he wondered if there was any other woman he knew, any friend, any lover, or any family member, who would take the time to do this on the river, at her age.

"This trip is our last hurrah, JT," said Ruth. "I don't care if they have to amputate my leg when we get out. Just let us stay on the river."

Quietly, JT wrapped the last of the bartered gauze around her lower leg. Her skin was mottled blue-gray in places, like abstract tattoos, so dry and wrinkled that he could have gathered up handfuls of extra skin.

Around and around the leg he went with the gauze: thick, clean, and white, protection from all things terrible.

25

Day Six

Mile 93

Dude. Have another marg," said Abo.

JT climbed into his boat and took the mug that Abo handed him. The sun had already vanished behind the walls of dark schist, but its heat would linger in the rocks all through the night. Suddenly he found himself exhausted, drained of the usual exhilaration that fueled his trips. He didn't want to be a guide right now. He didn't want to be responsible for everyone and everything. He didn't want to try and figure out how high the water would be running at Crystal tomorrow morning. He didn't want to think about where they would camp tomorrow night, whether to try and nab a spot at Lower Bass or go on and squeeze in a stop at Shinumo Creek and then take whatever he could get below Shinumo. He didn't want to think about what they were going to do with the dog at these popular places or how he was going to accommodate Mitchell's driving desire to hike every fucking side canyon; and had he really noticed the water pump leaking as Mark pumped, and did he have the extra part to repair it if it went out on him?

Most of all, he didn't want to think about what would happen if they didn't find the little blue pillbox.

JT leaned back and closed his eyes. "Where'd the ladies go?"

Abo pointed upstream, where the hikers were setting up their own camp.

"Who's the girl?"

"Friend of mine."

"Same friend who sent you the bathing cap?"

"Different friend."

"You've got a lot of friends, Abo," Dixie said.

Abo grinned.

"Just don't forget you're on for dinner tonight," JT reminded him.

"I'm not going anywhere," Abo protested.

"Not right now, he's not," Dixie told JT.

"Hey. *You* wouldn't sleep with me," said Abo.

"Neither would I," said JT.

"Are you going to marry that guy in Tucson?" Abo asked Dixie. "It really hurts my feelings, you know. Guy's not even a river rat."

"*I* like him," JT told Dixie. "If you need someone to walk you down the aisle, you know who to ask."

"I would never, *ever* recover, babe," Abo said.

"Oh yes you would," said Dixie. "You already have." And as if to prove her point, she wedged herself behind him and began to knead his shoulders. Abo groaned and hung his head.

"JT, you look way too depressed for someone in the Inner Gorge," Dixie said.

JT settled back with a long sigh. "Someday, I'm going to fork out the big bucks and come down as a passenger," he said. "When the guides are fixing dinner, I'm going to sit and meditate. I'm going to write in a journal. I'm going to lie down in the back of an oar boat and ask the guide if these are sedimentary or metamorphic rocks."

"You'd be bored shitless," said Abo.

"Maybe it's getting time for me to be bored shitless."

"Don't talk like that," Dixie said. "Not when we've got the Big Ones tomorrow morning."

"Speaking of which," said JT. "Who'll take Ruth and Lloyd?"

"You will," said Dixie. "And you're going to cheat in Hermit too. Give them a fun, safe run down the right. By the way, I call Amy for the front. What?" she demanded as Abo swung his head around to cast her a shaming look. "Are we going to tiptoe around the fact that she's a big girl, and it'll help to have a lot of weight in the front?"

"I get Amy," said JT.

"Why you?"

"Because I'm the Trip Leader. Ow," he said as Dixie cuffed him.

"Which reminds me, I'm supposed to tell you Amy's been having stomach problems," Abo told JT.

"Says who?"

"Says Peter. Doesn't seem viral, or else we all would have gotten it by now. In any case, she doesn't want anyone else to know about it."

"Keep an eye on her, then," said JT. "Probably heat related."

"How's Ruth's leg?" asked Dixie.

JT told them what he had seen. He also told them about the missing Cipro. And because he was tired of carrying everything on his own shoulders, he told them about Lloyd's condition, which really surprised no one, because they had all witnessed several instances of Lloyd's forgetfulness, and it was an easy conclusion to draw. Still, both Abo and Dixie, like JT, wished that Ruth had disclosed it on the medical forms.

"What a trip," sighed Abo. "Think there's something about the number one twenty-five?"

"Don't even go there," JT said.

26

Day Six

Mile 93

Downstream a bit, over margaritas, Susan was telling Jill about her divorce.

"Out of the blue," she said. "He didn't love me anymore. In fact he never loved me. He didn't want marriage counseling. He was filing papers the next day. Fifteen years," she said. "Just like that. Up in smoke."

"Was it another woman?"

"Of course. Though he denied it at the time. They always do. Then he married her."

"Are they still married?"

"Oh, they're a happy little Brady Bunch," said Susan. "They have a big happy house in Boston and go to Maine every summer."

Jill was about to ask Susan if she herself had a romantic interest, when a shadow loomed behind them. It was Mark. Quickly she drained her margarita.

"Have you seen the boys?" he asked.

"I thought you had them."

"I went to shave," said Mark. "When I came back, they were gone."

Jill untangled her legs and stood up slowly. The canyon walls tilted one way, then another. She reached out to Mark, to steady herself.

Mark sniffed her mug and frowned.

"Mark," she scoffed, "I had like half a mug." Which was not true; she and Susan had each consumed one back at the kitchen and taken a second downriver. She cleared her throat. "Sam!" she called, her voice rattly. "Matthew!"

"I thought you didn't like alcohol," said Mark.

"Well, sometimes I do. Boys!"

"How much has she had?" Mark asked Susan.

"Not too much, really," Susan said.

"Well, they can't have gone very far," Jill said, trudging through the sand. "Did you check our tent?"

"Why would they be in our tent?"

"I don't know, Mark, maybe just because it's there?" Indeed, when they got to the tent, they heard hushed voices coming from inside.

"You go," Matthew was saying.

"No, you."

"They'll notice me. They won't notice you."

"I don't feel so good," said Sam, and Jill and Mark heard that pregnant silence that precedes the surge.

"Not on Mom's pillow!"

Mark cleared his throat, and Jill squatted to unzip the tent flap. She immediately smelled vomit and backed away. Mark finished unzipping things, and there was Matthew sitting cross-legged with the two mugs. Sam retched again.

"Oh, for Pete's sake," said Mark.

"It was Sam's idea," said Matthew.

"How much has he had?"

Matthew began to cry.

"Stop it," said Mark. "Is that Mom's sleeping bag?"

"No," sniffed Matthew. "Maybe."

"Get up, Sam," said Jill. She reached in and wiggled Sam's foot.

"What were you thinking?" Mark said. "I told you boys no. What on earth got into you two? Hasn't there been enough excitement for one day?"

"It was Sam's idea."

"So? You're older. You're responsible for him. What, I can't go down and shave without keeping an eye on the two of you?"

Jill reached underneath Sam's arms and hauled him out of the tent. She propped him in the sand, struggling to keep him upright. The boy's eyes were half closed, and he mumbled something.

"What?" asked Mark.

"I said I'm sorry!" cried Sam.

"What's the problem?" said JT, joining them.

"Sam and Matthew got into the margs," Jill sighed.

" 'Margs'?" Mark asked Jill. "Up on the lingo, aren't we?"

"We told them no," Jill said to JT, "but then Mark went down to the river to shave."

"It doesn't take much when you're that size," said JT. "Sam! Sam buddy!"

"Hey," said Sam, struggling to keep his eyes open.

"How much did you drink, Sam!?"

"I don't know," said Sam.

"Stand up." JT helped Sam to his feet, and Sam took two steps. "I'm fine," he said, and then he sat down again.

JT sighed. "Let's get a little coffee going. I'm sorry about this."

"It's not your fault," said Mark. "These boys. I just don't know."

"They're kids," said JT. "I've seen much worse."

Something about this comment caused Mark to bristle. "Actually, that doesn't really comfort me a whole lot," he said. "And I do think it's your fault, frankly."

"Mark," Jill said.

"You guys must have underage kids all the time on these trips," Mark said. "Haven't you figured out a way of monitoring things?"

"He was dealing with Ruth's leg," Jill said.

"Abo wasn't," said Mark. "Dixie wasn't."

"I think I'll get the coffee going," JT said.

"I'm just accepting his apology," said Mark when JT was gone.

"You're being a jerk, Mark."

"The boys are twelve and thirteen!"

"I know how old our children are."

"There's research now that says if you drink when you're that young, you're more likely to have problems later."

"It was one time, Mark."

"Which can change your whole brain chemistry."

Briefly Jill had the sickening feeling that because of this, the boys would in fact turn into alcoholics.

Before she could figure out what to say, Peter and Amy approached them. Amy had on a large blue T-shirt with a high school swim team logo. Jill herself didn't mind them coming over, but she knew that Mark would think it snoopy and rude. He would assume that they came to judge. And she would hear about it from him later.

Glances flickered: grim, helpless, empathetic.

"Everyone does something like this at least once," Peter finally offered.

This did not console Mark. "Are you Mormon?" he asked Peter.

"No, sir," said Peter.

"Then it doesn't matter what you did," said Mark. "Mormons aren't everyone."

"Mark, please," said Jill.

"Come on, Sam," said Mark, pulling the boy to his feet. Sam's arm was long and skinny, and his ribs showed. "A dunk in the water will help. You too, Matthew."

When Mark and the boys were out of earshot, Jill apologized to Peter and Amy. "He tends to overreact."

"So did my father," said Peter.

This was a first for Jill, one of her children getting drunk, and she was eager for advice. "Did he ever lighten up?"

"Well," said Peter, digging in his ear, pausing, "actually, he died when I was sixteen, so no."

Jill felt the color rise in her neck, for making such a faux pas. "I'm sorry." Not knowing what else to say, she asked if his mother was still alive.

"Yup."

"Is she well?"

Peter shrugged. "She has stomach ulcers and diabetes and high blood pressure, and she doesn't wear her compression stockings and won't even talk about selling the house, which has three floors and a huge garden out back full of peonies, which have to be watered daily, and guess whose job that is? Other than that, she's well."

Jill looked down to the water's edge, where Mark had hold of both boys' hands and was standing between them, ankle deep. A strong, solid man, flanked by two Gumbys.

"The thing is, my sister's kids go to a public school back east," she said. "They're sixteen and seventeen. My sister tells me stories. I worry that we've got some rough years ahead of us."

Peter nodded knowingly. "Sex, drugs, and rock 'n' roll."

This did not comfort Jill.

"Is it like that at your school, Amy?" she asked.

Amy colored.

"She can't say because her mother's on the trip," said Peter in a dramatic whisper.

Without a word, Amy turned and lumbered away.

"Hey! I was kidding!" Peter called after her. "Oops," he said to Jill.

"Maybe it's a sore point," Jill offered. "I don't imagine she goes out very much." There was an odd way in which Amy was walking, Jill noticed, stiff and dragging, with one hand pressed against her lower back. How awful to be that heavy, she thought.

"I didn't think she'd take it that way," said Peter. "And actually, she's kind of hinted she has a social life. But maybe you're right; maybe it's a sore point."

Jill and Peter might have speculated a little more about Amy's social life, but the discussion ended because Mark was calling her. Both boys were sitting in the wet sand, refusing to budge. Jill steeled herself and headed to the shoreline. Amy was Susan's responsibility, not hers; she had her own kids to worry about at the moment. And she had to fix things with Mark too, so they wouldn't be blaming each other for this. *You went off to shave. Well you went off and got drunk.* Things like that: they didn't help in the short run or the long run.

But he really was being a total shit.

I hate this trip. I hate these people. I hate my mother. I hate Peter, for thinking he knows me. Sex, drugs, and rock and roll? He has no clue.

Everyone's eating dinner now. I hate food. I hate being fat. I hate my mother for always telling me I look fine the way I am. I never look fine.

Crap—here he comes—

27

Day Six

Mile 93

Peter didn't know what he had said to offend her.

"I'm writing," she told him.

"I brought you another margarita."

"No thank you."

Peter shrugged, and took a sip himself. "You eat yet?"

"No."

"Why not?"

"I'm not hungry. I'm trying to write," she reminded him. She waved her notebook, but Peter sat down anyway.

"Oh my god, are you blind?"

Peter handed the mug to Amy. Amy set it on the sand and hugged her notebook to her chest, as though trying to prevent him from peeking. He kept forgetting she was only seventeen, and then she'd do something like this, like someone in fifth grade.

"So when are you going to put the moves on Dixie?" Amy said.

"Excuse me?"

"It's *so* obvious."

Peter snorted. "Dixie's got a boyfriend."

"So what?"

"Well, maybe I will, and maybe I won't."

"Are you scared? What, are you a virgin or something?"

"What do you think? Are *you*?" As soon as he said it, he kicked himself. Can of worms! Change the subject! Sure enough, Amy tucked her pen between the pages of her journal. She squinted at JT, who was working in his boat.

"Tell me about your first time," she said. "How old were you?"

"Are you serious? I am definitely not having this discussion," he said. "There are laws against this."

"Did you like her?"

"Like I said. Not having this discussion."

"I'll ask Mitchell then," said Amy, and she waved to Mitchell, who hesitated, unsure of the invitation.

"Oh, for Christ's sake. Fine," Peter said in a low voice. "It sucked."

"Why?"

"She cried."

"I was too drunk to cry," she said. "Would you fuck a girl who was drunk?"

"Jesus!"

"Would you?"

"What do you *think*?"

Amy was silent.

"You going to elaborate?" he demanded.

"No."

"Good. Because I don't want you to."

"Good."

"Then we're in agreement."

"We are."

"Good." Peter carried his plate over to the wash table, scraped it clean, dunked it through the series of buckets. Then, against his better judgment but motivated by some vague sense of brotherly concern that pissed him off yet couldn't be ignored, he returned to the spot where Amy was sitting. He kept his voice low.

"You shouldn't let yourself get drunk like that. Guys can be assholes, you know."

"Thanks for the tip."

He was definitely angry now—at himself, at Amy. He didn't want to be hearing any of this, yet he couldn't walk away.

"What got you in such a pissy mood back there with Jill?"

For the first time in all of this conversation, she turned and faced him. "Because you shouldn't go telling people you know what high school is like for me! You have no idea what high school is like for me!"

"And this has something to do with your getting drunk?"

"No clue at all," she continued.

"Sorry."

"Absolutely no clue."

"Okay! Fine!"

Amy lay back on the sand. "I didn't think I would like you, that first night, in the hotel."

"Well, I didn't think I'd like you, either."

"Because I'm fat?"

"No. Because of your Jamba Juice T-shirt. Jamba Juice sucks."

"It was because I'm fat. That's okay. A lot of people do it. I'm used to it. Sometimes I think I should just walk into the river at night while everyone's sleeping."

"Oh, how goth."

Amy sat up and glared at him, and he sensed he'd gone too far. But then, to his surprise, she burst out laughing. Peter felt like he had either just gotten away with something hugely significant or said something brilliant. He didn't want to know which; he wanted to leave it at that, with a laugh the two of them could share, even if it might be for very different reasons.

In any case, he was most thankful to see Susan walking toward them, carrying two plates of something fruity and crumbly.

"She doesn't know, by the way," said Amy under her breath. "Hi, Mom," she said brightly.

"I thought you'd want dessert," Susan said, handing them the plates. Peter took his gratefully. The cherry filling was thick and gluey and probably came straight out of a can but tasted so, so fine, down here on the river. And when Susan told them that Ruth might have to be evacuated because of her leg, it barely registered, because between three margaritas and a plateful of cherry cobbler and whatever he'd eaten in between, Peter wasn't feeling so very great himself.

———

Late that night, while others slept, Evelyn headed upriver in the dark to find a good place to pee. Most people at night simply waded into the shallow water by the boats, but Evelyn felt too self-conscious with the guides so close by. And she wasn't going to punish herself over this anymore, either. She was who she was, and so what if she needed her privacy?

She didn't want to go too far upriver, though, because she didn't want to intrude upon the hikers' camping space. What a bunch of women! Stripping down like that! Once she and Julian had gone skinny-dipping in the ocean up in Maine. The moon was out, and Julian's little white rump bobbed in the surf. They were both afraid of getting caught, but it was early in their relationship, when they felt emboldened by love to commit risqué acts. The dark water pounded and tossed her around, but when she came up sputtering, Julian was right there.

Eventually, Evelyn reached a small cluster of rounded rocks, full of little pools and inlets. She was about to squat when she heard a woman sigh. Evelyn glanced up. Just beyond the rocks, away from the water's edge, a form shifted on the sand. Two forms, actually, and Evelyn quickly looked away, but not before she saw the woman stretch her arms out to the sides, like a snow angel, as the man moved on top.

Evelyn felt her stomach flutter. She didn't think they had heard her, but all the same, she had witnessed them. Which was all that mattered here, because it seeded in her a yearning she thought she had disposed of when she dropped the necklace off Navajo Bridge. She flashed back to that night in Maine. She and Julian had been too scared to make love on the beach that night. But down here . . .

For the rest of the trip, Evelyn kept imagining what it would be like, lying naked on the warm sand, with the sound of the river and a slight breeze and Julian between her legs, whispering terrible, lovely things in her ear.

DAY SEVEN

River Miles 93–108

Granite to Lower Bass

28

Day Seven, Morning

Mile 93

During breakfast the next morning, JT told everyone to look for Ruth's pillbox, impressing on them the gravity of the situation. Ruth was no practicing Catholic, but she found herself saying a prayer to St. Anthony, patron saint of lost things. She ate quickly and went back and ransacked their tent. She turned their sleeping bags inside out. She pawed through the plastic bag of dirty clothes. She searched through the pockets of all their pants and shorts. Tears stung her eyes, but she blinked them away. She was not, she was *not* going to let JT evacuate them.

But her search was to no avail, and soon she heard JT calling her. Reluctantly she climbed out of the tent and followed him to a clear space in the sand.

"Sure looks like flesh-eating strep to me," she declared when he unwrapped the gauze. "In which case it won't matter if you evacuate us because I'll be dead by tonight. Might as well die down here where it's beautiful." She cringed at her sarcasm. She was acting like a sulky teenager. But she couldn't help it.

"Lloyd will jump out of the helicopter if you try to evacuate us," she informed him.

JT sat back. "Look, Ruth. I know it's your job to think about Lloyd. But it's my job to think about you and Lloyd and everyone else. I've got a trip to run. I'm liable for your health and safety."

"I'll sign a release."

"*Ruth.* I could lose my license over this. And do you really want to risk having your leg amputated? Who will take care of Lloyd if you're stuck in a wheelchair?"

It seemed to Ruth that she had reached the very depths of despair, hearing this. She was damned if she stayed and damned if she went. But JT was right. As a responsible adult, she should be thinking of the long-term consequences of her actions.

"I don't know how I'll tell Lloyd," she said.

"If you want, I'll tell him," JT said. "I'll tell him I called my boss, and it's out of our control."

"We'll miss Crystal and Lava," Ruth said.

JT squeezed warm water over her leg. "You get your leg healed up, and we'll find you space on another trip this summer."

He'd gone too far, here; he'd lost his credibility, for they both knew another trip would never happen. But before she could call him on this—and make him feel twice as bad—they looked up to see Susan hurrying toward them.

"It was under a towel in JT's boat," she said breathlessly, showing them the pillbox. "I got as many pills as I could find, but the rest were half dissolved. I don't know what's what." She handed it to Ruth. It had been gnawed ragged, and the pills that remained were all mixed up in the various compartments. Ruth dumped everything into the palm of her hand. Greedily she poked through them, separating out four of the oval tablets.

"How many were there supposed to be?" JT asked her.

"Ten."

"Go back and look some more," JT ordered Susan. "Give me the pillbox. God damn it," and he held the pillbox in front of the dog's nose. The dog panted and wagged his tail.

"You bad dog," JT said, "you bad, bad dog," and in a moment of temper, he swatted the dog's nose with the pillbox. Blender yelped and slunk away.

"God damn it," said JT. He felt as close to wanting to punch something as he'd felt in a long, long time.

Meanwhile, Ruth had already uncapped her water bottle and taken one of the pills.

"You stop that, JT," she said, wiping her mouth. "We found the pills. Don't yell at the dog."

"Four out of ten!"

"Enough to get me started."

"You can't just take half a course," he said.

"I can when I'm on the river!" she said angrily. "Stop being such a gloomy Gus! I'm on antibiotics now! You're off the hook!"

Sam came up, holding a few more pills, including another Cipro.

"See?" said Ruth triumphantly. "Now we have five! You can't call for a helicopter when I have half the medicine I need! And who knows, we may find even more. Come," she ordered the dog, and he slunk around JT to sit at Ruth's side. He nuzzled her face and licked her neck.

"He was just doing what a dog does," she told JT. "Now say you're sorry for smacking him. Come on," she said. "Say you're sorry."

"I'm not."

"Oh, but he is," she told the dog, smoothing his ears back. "He can't say it out loud, but he is."

Without replying, JT set about re-dressing Ruth's wound, using the new bandage they'd gotten from the hikers. Ruth felt chastened by his silence. She wished he would say something. Was he still thinking of evacuation?

It seemed not, because when he was finished wrapping her leg, he stood up and brushed the sand off his knees. "Let's get this show on the road," he shouted to the group. "I want everyone ready to leave in ten minutes sharp! Pack it up!"

He turned and offered her a hand. She pulled herself up and watched as he repacked the medical kit.

"So . . . ," she began.

JT latched the kit. "No helicopter," he said flatly. "Not this morning, anyway."

"Thank you," Ruth said meekly. JT shrugged and walked off. Ruth looked down at her leg.

Heal, you old coot.

29

Day Seven

Mile 93

It's not about the rapids, JT always emphasized to his passengers. It's about the side canyons. It's about sleeping beneath the stars. It's about layers of rock, and quiet currents, and jungles growing out of hot red rock.

But try convincing twelve people not to get too excited about running the biggest white water on the continent. Try telling a parent it doesn't matter how much experience a particular guide has. There's no getting around it: ninety-three miles downriver from Lee's Ferry, it's about the Big Ones.

That morning it was clear that most everyone already had a certain seat in mind. Mark wanted to paddle—in fact, he felt entitled to paddle, having spent so much time pumping water instead of, say, drinking gin and tonics. Mitchell felt entitled too, not just because he knew more than everyone, but because he was sure his brawn would be needed for whatever split-second commands Abo might fire at them. Jill wanted to paddle, but she wanted the boys to ride with JT because she was sure he was the more competent oarsman; which raised the question of whether she should be in the same boat as her children, for perhaps she could somehow prevent them from falling overboard, should it come to that. And Peter was torn between wanting Dixie to see just how skilled a paddler he was in the Big Ones, and being available to rescue her should she happen to fly overboard.

After settling things with Ruth and her leg, after sending everyone off to pack things up *pronto*, JT drank the last of the muddy coffee and broke down the kitchen. Then he gathered everyone back together and spread out his map on the sand. The hikers had already left, and

Abo and Dixie worked in their boats, lashing gear with somber looks. JT found a stick and squatted.

"First one coming up is Granite Rapid," he told them. "It's got a good strong lateral that we'll try to side-surf toward the right, just enough to avoid the hole at the bottom. What we don't want is to hit the cliff over there, but if we do, keep your hands in the boat. I don't want any broken bones."

"Can I stand up in this one?" Sam asked.

JT squinted at the boy. "If you even *try* to stand up, I will put you on groover duty for the rest of the trip."

Sam smiled sheepishly, but with pride, for once again he had gotten noticed, and Matthew hadn't. JT turned his attention back to the map.

"Now: right after Granite comes Hermit, one of my favorites, with some very nice roller-coaster action." He did not tell them that he personally was planning to cheat this one and run it to the right to avoid the wave train. This was not the trip to play around with that fifth wave, not with Ruth and Lloyd in his boat. Abo and Dixie, they could decide for themselves.

"Next up is Boucher," he went on, "not too big, just a read-and-run. And then it's Crystal. That's right," he said, holding up his hand to forestall an eruption of chatter, "the one you've all been waiting for. We'll scout from the right, although I don't expect much has changed since three weeks ago. Big thing is to avoid the Hole and hang on tight."

A low murmur of excitement stirred through the group. A Monster, some of them had read. King Kong. The Maelstrom. Its nicknames were well earned. Crystal was one of the two biggest rapids on the river, a hydraulic traffic jam that could make even the most seasoned guide quake with fear.

"There's a lot of hype with this one, and it's well deserved," JT told them. "But more often than not, we manage a nice smooth run down the right, and it's over before you can blink. Ruth and Lloyd, I want you in my boat. Abo? Did you figure out who's paddling?"

Abo sprang from his boat onto the sand. "Yes, I did, Boss," he declared, wiping his hands on his shorts. "I want Peter and Mitchell up front. Susan and Jill, you're about the same weight, you take the middle. Mark, I want you in the rear. That leaves one space. Who wants it?"

As it turned out, a lot of people wanted the space, so Abo had them draw straws—or rather, strips torn from an empty cereal box. In the end, it was between Sam and Evelyn. Abo fanned the two strips. Sam wiggled his fingers, then drew. Then Evelyn drew, and they compared.

"Whoo-hoo!" Sam shouted.

(Have I not taught my children any sense of grace? Jill wondered.)

Evelyn made a valiant effort to disguise her disappointment. "Fair and square," she said brightly. Then she sat down and took her sandals off and focused intently on a complicated strap adjustment.

"I tried really hard to picture the strips next to each other," Sam told Jill as he buckled his life jacket. "I closed my eyes and looked into my brain really hard, and there they were, lined up right beside each other. I think I have ESP. Do you believe in ESP?"

"Jill?" said Mark. "Can we have a word?"

Frowning, Jill followed her husband away from the group. As he spelled out his concerns, she simply listened. She thought she knew her husband well, but as she heard his proposition, she was taken aback.

"So we're in agreement on this?" Mark said. "Trust me," he said before she could reply. "It's the right thing to do. Trust me and we'll talk about it later."

"But it's—"

"Just trust me, Jill," he said, and he walked back to the group. Jill followed, seething, and she wanted to say something more to him, but Mark had already put his arm around Sam's shoulder.

"Sam," he began, "we want you to rethink this."

Sam eyed them both warily.

"See, Evelyn's been waiting a long time for this trip."

"So?"

"And she's older."

"But I won."

Now Mark placed both hands on Sam's shoulders. "Sam, I want you to put this into context," he said. "You're twelve. You're going to have other chances to come down the river. But Evelyn's fifty. This may be her only shot."

"You said fifty wasn't old."

Mark scratched his neck.

"So she might have another chance," said Sam. "And *I* won," he reminded his father.

Mark straightened up. "Just because you won doesn't mean you have to claim the prize. Right, Jill?"

Jill felt herself seething inside. In a way she knew Mark was right, but in a larger way she thought that Sam had just as much right to the spot; and this feeling of hers had less to do with age and chance and more to do with simple filial loyalty, something Mark, she now saw, obviously found morally wrong.

She repositioned the boy's baseball cap. "Well, Dad's got a point," she said, "but it's up to you. If you really want the spot, you can have it."

Sam, sensing the cleft, crossed his arms.

"But you know what would be the right thing to do," Mark added.

He cast a dark look at Jill, and suddenly she found it impossible to censor herself. She nudged his arm—actually, batted it was more accurate—and stalked away from the group again.

"Look at it from Evelyn's perspective," Mark said as he followed her. "She's not going to have unlimited chances to do this trip."

"And Sam is?"

"Sam only wants it because everyone else wants it."

"Easy for you to say," said Jill, "you with your sure spot in the paddle boat."

"Are you forgetting about last night? Someone puking in the tent?"

Jill stopped. "What in god's name does that have to do with Sam giving up his seat?"

"He could stand to be punished," Mark said.

"Sam drinking and Sam paddling Crystal have nothing to do with each other!"

"The seat is a privilege. When you screw up, you lose some privileges. But put that aside for now. Mostly what I'm saying is, I think it means a whole lot more to Evelyn than it does to Sam."

"And I care about Evelyn because why again?"

"Grow up, Jill," said Mark, lowering his voice. "Be a parent for once. Say no to your kid. It's not going to kill him. In fact, a kid his age—"

"Stop," Jill said, and she whipped around to face him. "This has nothing to do with age. It has nothing to do with Sam. It's really all about you, Mark, or haven't you noticed?"

Mark looked skeptical, bemused. "Want to educate me here? Because I'm missing something."

"Fuck *you*."

"Hasn't happened lately," he remarked.

"Oh FUCK you! FUCK *YOU*! And don't tell me you don't know what I mean! You know exactly what I mean! You're so caught up in looking good to others, Mark! You've got to be the good parent all the time, be the generous soul and teach your kids to do the same! Make them give half their Christmas presents to the shelter or pledge half their allowance to the church! Jesus, Mark, don't you ever want to be selfish?"

"That's an interesting perspective on parenting."

His calmness fueled her rage. Like he was above it all.

"I mean, it all comes back, doesn't it?" he went on. "You give up something, and something else comes back to you? Isn't that what people call karma?"

"You don't believe in karma, Mark; you're a Mormon."

Mark laughed.

"Laugh all you want. But I want you to know, I plan on enjoying myself a little more after this trip. You want to keep giving things up, fine. Give up alcohol. Give up skiing because your knee hurts. Why don't you give Evelyn your seat, if you think it means so much to her? Oh, because you didn't get drunk and therefore don't need to be punished?" She was rambling, and she hated rambling in an argument. Especially with her levelheaded husband.

"No," said Mark patiently. "Because kids ought to defer to adults. It's thoughtful. It's respectful. It's a nice thing to do. Now let's go back."

"I'm not finished."

Mark sighed. He took a nail clipper from his pocket and began to clip his nails. That did it. She snatched the nail clipper and threw it as far as she could out into the river—a quick sparkle in the air, then gone forever.

But before she had a chance to enjoy any childish satisfaction, she looked over his shoulder and saw the rest of the group watching them. They all looked away quickly, but it was too late: they had seen everything; they had heard everything. Not only that, but as she stood there cringing about what she had revealed about herself and Mark and their marriage—as she stood there feeling just about as naked as she'd ever felt, she saw Sam walk over to Evelyn and begin gesturing.

Mark headed back. Jill wanted to dig a hole and bury herself. She knew she should go back and help load up, but she couldn't face anyone, and so she stood on the sand, alone, as everybody else started loading up the boats. They could cut her some slack right now, she felt. Because inside she was still livid. All she wanted on this trip was for her family to break their routine, to grow and have fun and see themselves as more capable than they might have thought, back in Salt Lake City.

Was that really too much to ask for?

After some time she saw JT heading toward her. Everybody else was in the boats. This is just too rich, she thought.

"I'm fine," she told him.

"Sam can paddle Lava, if he wants," he said.

"I littered."

"Huh?"

"The nail clipper. I threw it in the river."

"Oh. Well, it's not a huge deal."

"I can go look for it. I can find it."

"Actually, you probably can't. Don't worry about it."

"Where's Sam?"

"Dixie's boat."

"I'm really, really sorry you had to witness this," she said.

"Oh," said JT, "I've seen worse."

He probably had. But it didn't make her feel any better.

30

Day Seven

The Big Ones

Miles 93–98

It *was* fun; there was no doubt about it: for all his chatter about appreciating the smaller moments on a river trip, JT couldn't deny that sometimes a thirty-second thrill in big water could trump everything else.

Pushing off above Granite Rapid, he hoisted himself into his boat, took his seat, and wiggled into place. The air was spiced with honey, and the sun was working its way down the cliffs. He shoved a stick of gum into his mouth, pulled a few strokes, then pivoted around to face downstream. He had Ruth and Lloyd safe in the back, with Amy up front gripping the dog.

Once his boat was out in the current, he stood to get a better view. Strong lateral waves boiled toward a steep wall on the opposite side, rebounding back on themselves. Farther down to the left, a smooth, dark hump of water bulged above an explosion of silvery backwash—the hole he wanted to avoid. His goal was to ride the laterals across, just far enough to avoid the hole but not so far as to slam up against the black wall on the other side. To this end, he picked out a focal point to aim for, and just before they dipped toward that first lateral, he dropped to his seat and grabbed his oars to steady his entry and *whoosh*, they scooted up and caught the surf, which seemed to hold them in one place, moving but not moving, except that anyone could see they were plowing toward the wall; and now he had to heave with his right arm, muscling everything from the core to turn the boat downstream—there was the hole on his left, fine, they were going to miss it, but the wall came looming forward and he shouted to Amy to keep her hands in the boat and he pulled and pushed on his oars, and they cruised on by the wall with only a couple of inches to spare.

And as they swirled downstream, Amy twisted around to mouth the words "Oh my god." JT managed to steady his boat, and they watched Abo and his paddlers narrowly skirt the hole, all six wooden paddles jabbing randomly in the froth, and then Dixie ran it exactly as he had, coming a little too close to the wall, but everyone made it through safely, and JT allowed himself the thought that they were going to have good, safe, fun runs all day long today; luck was on their side, the sun was hot, and the water was fine, and he could already hear Dixie playing her guitar under the starry sky tonight, when it was all behind them.

Amy knew it was the wuss boat, with Ruth and Lloyd in the back and herself up front. She told herself it didn't really matter. And she was able to believe that, until she looked over at the paddle boat after they ran Granite and saw that Abo had handed out whimsical hats, colorful foam visors in the forms of ducks, frogs, and birds; at which point she could no longer deny that they'd been chosen as an exclusive little club, and she wasn't in it. She'd been allocated like a meat cooler.

Amy stroked the dog's ears. She told herself not to dwell on it. And she reminded herself that even if she'd been chosen for the paddle boat, she might have had to decline, for her stomach was still bothering her. She started to open up her day bag for the Tums, but JT warned that they were coming up on Hermit. Was Hermit the one with the wave train? What exactly *was* a wave train? She looked downriver to see a long chevron of white water. She hugged the dog tightly, ready for what lay ahead. She wanted the ride of a lifetime.

But instead of heading straight into the rapid, JT angled the boat, and Amy found that they were skirting all the big waves. She looked back in disbelief. Did JT mean to do that? Then she looked over and saw the paddle boat, the A Team, taking it right down the middle, bucking through the giant waves, whooping and screaming as they rose and fell; she looked back at Ruth and Lloyd and realized: of course JT meant to take this route.

Wuss boat, she thought. Gramma boat.

But Amy was good at putting things behind her. She'd done her job this morning by keeping the dog in the boat, and she reminded herself that silly hats didn't make an A Team. She thought of high school and how it was full of A Teams and B Teams, and it seemed to her that being here, deep in the heart of the Grand Canyon, she could certainly escape that high school habit of classifying everyone. Where else would it have such *little* relevance, as down here?

They ran another rapid, and then she saw that JT was steering the boat toward a rocky debris fan on the right. Across the river, jagged cliffs rose out of the water, glossy black, shot through with glittering veins of pink granite. Second by second, the volume of the roar rose, doubling upon itself until it had drowned out all other sound.

"Is this Crystal?" she shouted to JT.

But JT was already out of the boat, looping his line around a rock to anchor the boat.

"Keep your life jackets on," he instructed everyone as the other two boats pulled in. "Anyone wants to take a quick scout, follow me. Hey. Dog. C'meer." He slipped a rope through the dog's bandanna.

The paddlers clattered out of their boat. "Hey, honey!" Susan exclaimed. "How'd it go?"

In the wuss boat? "Fine," Amy replied.

"Wasn't Hermit a blast?"

No. We skipped Hermit. Because we're the WUSS BOAT. "Hermit was cool," she said.

"Let's not dawdle," said JT, and he led them up through prickly brush that clawed at her legs. When they reached the edge of the overlook, Amy followed JT's gaze. Large rocky snags tore the river apart, shredding it into long fingers of white water. How did the guides tell one section of chaos from another?

". . . punch on through and keep hugging the right," JT was telling

Dixie. He had one arm around her and was pointing with the other. "There's your marker. Stern first."

"Could you fill us all in?" Mitchell asked.

The plan, JT explained, was for a run down the right side, where the water was not so rough. This meant avoiding the entry tongue that angled off to the left at the top of the rapid—for the tongue would carry you straight down into the Hole. Which was not where you wanted to go.

"Why don't we just hug the shoreline?" Evelyn asked.

"Because it's not a quiet shoreline," JT replied, "and if you actually *hit* the shoreline, you could ricochet off, and one of those diagonals will take you into the Hole." The safest route at this water level, he explained, was through a narrow channel that ran to the right of the Hole but avoided the shore.

"That's the plan, at least," he finished with a grin.

"Where's this Hole you keep talking about?" Amy asked.

JT pointed. Amy searched, but still, the whole river looked wild and messy and mean below that first drop-off—until she realized that that *was* the Hole; she was looking straight at it, a gaping cavity where the water rolled back upon itself, a geological vortex that could swallow you in a second.

For the first time on the river, Amy was able to picture, clearly, how very small she would be, at the bottom of that vortex.

The plan was for Dixie to run it first, and then Abo. JT would go last, running rescue if needed.

He sculled with his oars and watched the two boats ahead of them. "There she goes," he murmured, watching Dixie's boat pick up speed. The boat pivoted and cut to the right and then vanished into the waves. Fifteen seconds later, it bobbed up at the bottom of the rapid, all passengers on board. Dixie stood up and waved.

JT maneuvered his oars to steady their direction. "Okay, Abo," he murmured, "show your stuff," and now the paddle boat followed in Dixie's wake, with Abo in back sitting up so straight that he seemed to have grown an extra few inches. He dragged his paddle, angling it now and then, and the paddlers stroked calmly, and then suddenly Abo gave a shout and up front Peter shot forward from the hips, the others quick to follow: torsos, arms, and paddles all moving in synchrony to guide the boat down along the right side of the river, disappearing and then emerging from the spray to join Dixie at the bottom. Over the din of the rapid, Amy heard faint whoops and hollers.

JT braced his feet. "Okay, guys. This is it. Hold on tight. Amy, got the dog?"

All around, skirmishes danced on the surface, and everything seemed pretty harmless—until Amy looked over and saw the long lean muscle of water broaden slightly and then drop off at a sharp angle, down into a huge ragged pocket of foaming backwash, a monstrous upstream wave that had probably been breaking nonstop ever since the first flood rolled the giant rocks into the river. It was twenty feet wide and who knew how deep, bigger than anything she could have imagined from shore, and she knew in an instant just what all the fuss was about.

The boat rocked to one side. A wave splatted against her shoulder. They were cruising close to shore now, but everything was racing by, a blur out of the corner of her eye. She tightened her grip on the dog.

And then maybe the river relaxed. Maybe JT overcompensated for something. But in the middle of one of his heaves, they broadsided a great ridge of water that drenched them. Amy crouched and with her free hand tried to wipe her lenses. Then there was a sharp jolt from below as they snagged on something—something hard, because Amy could feel it under her knee. The boat buckled, and water began pouring in over the tubes.

"Highside!" JT yelled, struggling to hold on to his oars. "Amy! HIGHSIDE!"

Amy lurched forward—or up: it was hard to tell with the boat rising at a forty-five-degree angle. Her foot slipped, and she heard the squeak of rubber as she sprawled forward. She tried to get a foot brace but couldn't find anything firm except the downside tube—and if she pushed against that, it would bring in more water.

"Highside!" JT kept yelling. "Get up there!" Ruth scuttled across to join Lloyd, but JT waved her back. "Stay where you are!" he shouted to Ruth. "AMY! HIGHSIDE! NOW!" Amy grasped the chickenline and pulled with all her might, but she simply couldn't move, and the boat continued to rise.

"The dog!" Ruth cried.

Then Amy heard a clunk as JT dropped his oars. In a flash he scrambled up, braced his feet against the pile of gear, and leaned forward to grab the shoulders of Amy's life jacket. He gave a swift yank, and at the same time her feet found the edge of something firm. The next thing she knew, she lay sprawled on top of JT. Their hats knocked brims, and she was afraid she was going to crush him, but he squirmed and wiggled them up over the tube as far as he could. Now she was looking straight down into rushing water—water that suddenly came looming toward her as the boat dropped and leveled out.

And that was all, basically, that Amy remembered of Crystal. She wasn't aware of JT scrambling back to his seat. She didn't hear Lloyd hollering gibberish. She was only aware of ducking down into the damp well of the boat as they thrashed about, with someone's dirty socks floating loose, water bottles dangling, a pair of Teva sandals swinging from their clip.

Then all the thrashing stopped. The boat kept spinning; dizzily she peered over the edge into calm, blue-black water. They glided up to the other boats, and the guides all stared at one another. Then they burst into laughter.

"How did *that* happen?" Dixie exclaimed.

"I was sure you guys were gone," Abo declared. "I told my paddlers, 'They're gone. They're toast. They're history, folks.' Dude," and he shook his head. "You were two feet from the Hole!"

Amy whipped around. "Where's the dog?"

"I've got him," Ruth called out. There he was, plastered against Ruth's leg, panting happily.

JT picked up his water jug and drank deeply. "The water got squirrely on me," he marveled. "Then I hit that rock."

"What rock?" said Dixie.

"Well, it sure felt like a rock," said JT.

"Your hat, doll," said Abo, tossing Amy her pink baseball cap. She caught it and put it on and wished she could vanish, for she had just figured it out. It was *her* weight that caused the boat to snag, *her* weight that made them tilt. Any minute JT was going to start yelling at her, for being such a FAT PIG. They should never have allowed her to come on this trip in the first place.

As if on cue, JT asked her how she was doing.

"I'm sorry. I couldn't get a grip," she said meekly.

"Hey. You did great."

"No, I didn't!" Amy exclaimed. "I almost made us flip!"

JT shrugged dismissively. "It's never one person's fault."

It was in this case, Amy wanted to say. And she flashed back on the image of her lying on top of JT—smooshing him, really, all 237 pounds of her; of burying her face against his neck for the briefest of moments (warm skin, creased and tacky and smelling of maple); and she thought that he was an awfully good man, a better man than any she had ever met, the kind of man she hoped one day would see her for the person she was, underneath all this flab.

31

Day Seven, Evening

Mile 108

It astonished Peter how easy it had been for Abo to get laid last night. Pretty girl shows up on the river and boom, off she goes with the paddle captain. He saw it with his own eyes, Abo heading upriver after everyone else had gone to bed. Was this their first time? Or had they already slept together?

Peter sensed there was an awful lot of sex in the life of a river guide. Probably every time you went down the river, you fell in love with someone and had a lot of great sex. It occurred to him that he might inquire, while he was here, about getting his guide's license. It couldn't be all that hard; the way he saw it, you simply made friends with gravity and let the water do the work.

It was early evening on the day they'd run Crystal, and Peter and Amy were, at the moment, sitting on the edge of Dixie's boat, drinking beer and listening in as the guides talked about their day in the Big Ones. Peter could barely keep his eyes off Dixie, who was twisting herself into a pretzel on the side tube. Her blue sarong lay crumpled in the well. Peter wondered, were he to get a sunburn, if Dixie might lend him that blue sarong to drape over his shoulders.

"So are we stopping at Shinumo tomorrow?" Abo asked.

"That's the plan," said JT. He was wearing a pair of black drugstore glasses, which sat crookedly on his nose as he made notes in a three-ring binder. "Everybody loves a waterfall."

"Prime Christmas photo op." Dixie untangled her limbs and popped open a can of Olympia, nearly causing Peter to swoon. Eyes closed, can tilted to her lips, a quick sparkle of lager—Dixie was the girl on a greeting card he'd received long ago. He felt like God had just invented the five senses, for him alone.

"How much you want to bet we get a card from the Compsons next Christmas," said Abo, "all four of them, standing in front of Shinumo Falls."

"Maybe Mitchell would like to take another group photo," Dixie suggested, which prompted a chuckle from JT and Abo.

JT twisted back to Peter and Amy. "Cover your ears," he told them.

"Lemme ask you," Abo said. "Is Mitchell really writing a book? Because if he is, I'm worried. What if I'm in it? What's he going to say about me?"

"He'll say you drink too much," said Dixie. She turned on her side and began doing leg lifts. Peter had to use all the self-restraint he could muster not to look at the hollow at the top of her thigh.

"You think I drink too much, Boss?"

"Only after Crystal and Lava," JT replied.

"Oh! Well, then it doesn't count," said Abo, opening another beer. "Peter. Amy. Catch," and he tossed a can to each of them.

"Mitchell drinks a lot of gin," Amy volunteered.

"We know," said all three guides in unison.

"And he doesn't share," Abo grumbled.

"Okay, Abo," JT said. "That's enough."

"I'm just saying."

"Zip it."

"We don't mind," Peter said.

"Well, I do," said JT.

"Speak of the devil," said Dixie.

Up on the beach, Mitchell and Mark were doing push-ups, clapping between lifts.

"Hey, Mitchell!" Abo shouted. "Are you trying to embarrass us or something?"

Mitchell grunted but kept going.

JT turned to Peter and Amy. "We like Mitchell," he confided, "but Mitchell can be a little intense. And you're not hearing any of this."

"Twenty more, Mark!" Abo called.

"*You* like Mitchell," said Dixie. "Mitchell takes himself way too seriously for me. We need to put Mitchell in his place. A few practical jokes wouldn't hurt. Maybe I should get out my bugs."

Here, finally, was the chance Peter had been waiting for since stepping off the bus back up at Lee's Ferry.

"What bugs?" he asked pleasantly, immediately regretting it, for it sounded sexual, though he couldn't say why.

"Show Peter your bugs, Dixie," said Abo.

And that sounded even more sexual! Wait! Did Abo intend a double meaning? Had Dixie said something to him in private about what a skilled paddler Peter was or how brave he'd been while swimming Hance? He swung his legs around and climbed across the gear. Dixie, meanwhile, had brought out a baggie of plastic bugs—not the neon-colored ones you'd get in a gumball machine but lifelike versions, the kind you might find at a museum gift shop. She picked out a scorpion and tossed it to Abo, who jumped and screamed in a falsetto.

"Bed or day bag?" said Dixie. "Coffee mug maybe?"

Peter felt so privileged to be a part of this plot that he had to restrain himself, for he had a lot of practical jokes up his sleeve, his sister could attest to that, and if the guides wanted to put Mitchell in his place, Peter would be only too glad to help.

But JT was shaking his head. "Forget the jokes, people," he said, slapping his menu book shut. "I don't need Mitchell having a heart attack. He's a pain, but we're not going to play around with him. That's all I need, is more shit on this trip."

"Boo," said Abo. "Hiss."

They all fell silent. Peter picked through the bugs and found a centipede and laid it on his thigh and admired it.

"Speaking of which," Abo said after a moment, "how's Ruth's leg?"

"Terrible."

"Even with the Cipro?"

"Doesn't work that quick."

"Think we'll evacuate?" asked Dixie.

"God, I just don't know! I sure wish she'd started that Cipro earlier," JT said.

"Why didn't she?" asked Abo.

"Saving it for something important, probably," sighed JT. "Isn't that always the case?" He got up and balanced his way across to his own boat, where he opened up the cooler and began gathering the ingredients for the night's dinner.

This had the effect of breaking up the group, for Abo and Dixie were on dinner duty, and Amy trudged off to her campsite. Peter stayed there, alone on Dixie's boat. She'd left her ammo box open, and there was a creased picture of Dixie and her boyfriend, taped to the inside of the lid. The boyfriend barely had any hair at all. Peter wished he hadn't seen the picture because he didn't want to imagine Dixie with a guy who had no hair.

He tucked the centipede in his pocket and smoothed his hand over the rubbery surface of her sleeping pad. He thought of her lying on this pad at night, with her blue sarong loosely covering her hips. He pictured that twisted silver amulet, the ancient horse, warm in the hollow of her throat—which opened the floodgates, and Peter finally allowed himself to wonder what it would be like to make love on a raft in the middle of a smooth stretch of dark water, floating to Baja.

"Not at all, honey," Jill assured Sam. "Dad just wants to sleep by the rocks, and I'd rather sleep by the water tonight."

"Well, he *looks* mad," said Sam.

"Silly goose," said Jill, rubbing his back.

July 10 Day Seven

I'm the only one up, and I'm sitting on a rock where no one can see me. Very peaceful. Everyone else is asleep, even Mom. I think I'm having a better time than she is at this point. I will make a point to be nicer to her. She's so pathetic.

Today we almost tipped over in Crystal, thanks to FAT GIRL. Do the guides actually think we're going to <u>remember</u> what to do when there's an emergency? We hit something, the boat goes up, and JT's yelling at me to highside. WTF!? How am I supposed to remember what that means? Of course, even when he told me what to do, I still couldn't do it. So he does it himself and yanks me up so I'm lying on top of him.

I probably broke his ribs, and he's too nice to say anything.

DAYS EIGHT AND NINE

River Miles 108–150

Lower Bass to Upset

32

Days Eight and Nine

Miles 108–150

Aside from Jill and Mark barely speaking to one another, the next two days were glorious. For one thing, by now they'd all pretty much internalized the routines of life on the river, so those baffling challenges of the first few days—packing bags, loading and unloading—were now automatic. Expertise bred confidence, which in turn bred a collective good mood, no small factor on a river trip.

For another thing, after the Big Ones came a relatively gentle and magical stretch of the river, and JT made a point of letting them stop and play in the shady waterfalls and pools that were such a contrast to the harsh landscape of the last several days. The Compsons did indeed get a Christmas picture of all four in front of Shinumo Falls (a terrible photo though, wooden smiles, stick postures); farther down at Elves Chasm, the cool mossy rocks and trickling water soothed everyone's nerves, still raw from the day before. The only moment of ill will came when Mitchell climbed up on a big boulder and dove into the pool below, reminding JT how quickly everything could change.

"I told you guys the first day, NO DIVING!" he exclaimed. "You want to crack your head open?"

("Did you get a picture of me?" Mitchell asked Lena.)

But there were other, more unique twists of fate that were helping too. The Cipro seemed to be working, for starters. Evelyn stopped trying to be so useful all the time. And Mitchell's dreaded camera ran out of memory, at least until the end of the day when he could retrieve the spare memory card from his overnight bag.

In any case, those two days went more smoothly than any since leaving Lee's Ferry. Or so it seemed to JT. He'd done too many trips to read much into this and knew it portended nothing, really; but he definitely enjoyed the good luck that extended through Day Nine, especially when Mitchell figured he had more than enough liquor for the rest of the trip and offered gin and tonics to everyone who was of legal age. Also when Jill spoke a few words to Mark, which gave him hope that he wasn't going to witness another marital bust-up on this trip.

The most magical moment came just before bedtime, when Lloyd experienced a mysterious window of lucidity and told them all of early trips on the river, when they wore canvas sneakers and cutoffs, and there was no such thing as sunscreen, and Glen Canyon Dam hadn't been built, and the water was warm and wild and the tamarisk hadn't yet taken over the corridor and jets were nonexistent and at night, if it was cool, you could build a campfire and fall asleep to the snap of embers sparking up through the chimney of cliffs into the starry sky above.

Only Susan was having a hard time at this point. Although she appreciated the ease of routine, a certain weariness was creeping in. Dare she call it boredom? Sometimes the rapids all seemed alike; sometimes the canyon walls felt closed in. Was she the only one who was getting tired of all this beauty?

By now her wine tasted like plastic, and it was never cold enough. The coffee was muddy. And to be perfectly frank, she was tired of group camping. Everyone snored, it seemed, and the mats were so thin that every morning she woke up with sore shoulders and a knot in her neck and a pain in her lower back that didn't disappear even after Dixie showed her how to stretch. There were scorpions to worry about, and red ants, and rattlesnakes.

She was dragging her overnight bag down to the boats that morning when the obvious occurred to her: *There was an end to all this.* Had she forgotten? In five days she'd emerge from the canyon heat and walk into an air-conditioned hotel room, with a pillow-top mattress and cool sheets and her own personal refrigerator. There would be a clean robe hanging in the closet, chilled wine in the little refrigerator. She would step into a hot shower, stand beneath the silt-free spray, and wash thirteen days' worth of grit down the drain.

"How do the guides do it?" she asked Jill the next afternoon. They were riding in the back of Dixie's boat, lounging with their feet up. Peter was rowing; Dixie herself was riding up front, advising Peter as needed.

"Do what?" asked Jill.

"Stay so enthusiastic! I can't imagine making this trip twice, let alone a hundred and twenty-five times."

"Oh, I could live down here," Jill said. "No laundry, no grocery stores, no carpools . . ."

Susan would have agreed with her the first few days. But not at this point. At this point, she wanted a bath. She wanted to see a street lined with fat-leafed maple trees.

"I miss my bed," she said. "And a mattress—what a concept! Air-conditioning, a quiet room to myself . . ."

"But hasn't this trip been good for you and Amy?" Jill asked.

"Amy wants absolutely nothing to do with me down here."

Jill didn't reply, which disappointed Susan, for she'd hoped Jill would have some inside knowledge about Amy's feelings that would contradict her.

"Amy would rather spend her time with Peter," Susan said.

"But that's good, isn't it? She's seventeen, after all. Don't discount the power of peer relationships."

Peer? thought Susan. He's twenty-seven.

And he's always giving her beer, if you haven't noticed, said the Mother Bitch. *If Amy weren't so fat, you'd think he was trying to take advantage of her.*

Susan felt her eyes smart. With two fingers, she reached under her lenses and dabbed at her lower lids.

"What's the matter?" asked Jill.

Susan smiled ruefully. It was hard for her to put her finger on it. She felt like such an awful mother for thinking the thoughts she had sometimes. But there they were. Perhaps this mother of two from Salt Lake City would understand, down here on the river.

"Did you have a mental image of your children, before they were born?" she asked.

"Sure! They were going to look just like me."

Susan laughed in spite of herself, for the Compson boys didn't look anything like Jill, being pink-skinned and blond, as opposed to Jill with her olive complexion and dark, wavy hair.

"Well, *I* envisioned a little girl with a Dutch cut and bangs," Susan declared. "She would be able to sing. We would harmonize on long car rides. She would want a horse too."

"I don't know about the singing, but I take it the horse didn't pan out?"

"Or dance, or team sports, or tennis." Susan wanted suddenly to tell Jill about Amy's SAT scores. But she was afraid it would sound braggy.

"Still, she's awfully nice," said Jill. "I noticed it the first night with the boys—teaching them card tricks and all. And she's smart. You can tell. She and Peter were talking about Virginia Woolf. I was impressed. Does she know where she wants to go to college?"

"Possibly Duke," Susan said. "Maybe Yale."

"You see? You should be proud of her!"

"I *am*. I just . . ." Susan put her hands over her face. "Nobody tells it like it is," she cried. "The doctor calls her heavy. Her father calls her large. Everyone tiptoes around the fact that she's just terribly, terribly overweight. And she never, ever talks to me!"

The water lapped gently against the side of the boat as they began to pick up speed. Jill leaned over and patted water on her arms. "When I was a teenager, I had acne," she said. "And my parents denied it. They said, 'Oh, it's just a pimple here and there. Dab a little makeup on your face; you're the only one who notices it.' Which was not true. I looked like I had the chicken pox. And it must be especially hard, with you being so trim and all."

"Sometimes I think that's what did it," sniffed Susan.

"Why?"

"Because I watch my weight. I like eating healthy. I like being thin. So maybe I made too big a deal over it, while Amy was growing up."

Jill snorted. "Matthew's sensitive—does that mean I mollycoddled him? And Sam's a clown—does that mean I didn't give him enough attention? We mothers certainly blame ourselves too much."

The boat dipped down into another rapid. Jill and Susan barely noticed. It was too noisy to talk while they were in it.

"So what happened with Mark the other day?" Susan asked, once they were through.

"Oh," said Jill, and she raised her face to the sun. "Too much togetherness, I guess."

Susan knew that wasn't the case.

"Fine," Jill said. "We bicker about the kids sometimes."

"He's Mormon, isn't he?"

"Right."

"And you're not."

"Right."

"So how do you deal with that?" And Susan, who usually bent over backward not to pry too much, was able to marvel at her boldness. How long, she asked herself, might it have taken her to ask Jill these things, if they hadn't been on the river together?

"You mean, am I the lost soul of the tribe? Mostly it's a problem for his parents," said Jill. "We get together at holidays, and they want to see my pantry, and I show them my pantry, and they say, 'That's not a pantry; we mean a *ree-ul payantree*,' and Mark steps in at that point and reminds them that we've had mice and don't really feel like storing a hundred pounds of rice in our basement."

"That's nice, that he sticks up for you."

"I suppose. Although being the bitch that I am, I always focus on what he *doesn't* do for me, instead of what he *does* do."

Both women chuckled, in mutual recognition.

"Remind me again, where's Amy's father?" Jill asked.

"Boston," Susan replied. "Amy goes and visits him in August. He has a cottage on a lake. She babysits his kids." It suddenly seemed pathetic to her, that that was what her daughter did for the month of August at age seventeen.

"What's high school been like for her?" Jill asked. "I know when I was in high school, kids were pretty cruel. Is it still as bad?"

"It was worse in middle school," Susan said. "Now they just ignore her. Although I will admit that she's gone to a few parties this past year, like last Halloween. But then she didn't go out much after that. Not sure why."

"Well, it's a start," said Jill. "Does she have a boyfriend?"

Susan wanted to throw her arms around Jill, simply for asking. None of her friends back in Mequon had ever thought to wonder.

"Be careful what you wish for," Jill declared. "From what my sister says, sometimes it's best that we don't know everything our kids do."

Just then, the boat bumped against something solid, and they turned around to find themselves nudging up against a steep shoreline alongside JT's boat. The sun was dipping toward the rim. A long, drawn-out canyon dusk would follow. Peter shipped his oars.

"*You* got us here?" Jill said.

"Available for hire," said Peter. "Anytime."

Dixie slid off the bow of the boat and stood in the water, grasping the rope and bracing them against the current as they unclipped their day bags.

"Let's continue this over wine," Susan said.

But Jill was already climbing over the massive pile of gear. "I swear to god, if Evelyn takes the biggest campsite tonight, I am going to wring her thick little neck."

33

Day Nine, Evening

Mile 150

Upset Hotel, as their campsite was called, was a difficult one to access. The water was deep and swift here, and sharp chunks of limestone made pull-ins tricky. In addition, the camping area itself was situated up a steep embankment, a daunting climb even without all their gear.

But JT didn't want to chance going farther downriver. If the next two camps were already taken, there would be no place large enough for them before Havasu, and since no camping was allowed at Havasu, they'd have to continue on downriver.

JT didn't want to *think* about the prospect of Mitchell missing Havasu.

So they tied up the boats at Upset and, in keeping with the spirit of the last two days, everyone rallied cheerfully, spacing out the fire line and hauling up the tables and the stove and the Blaster and the groover and the kitchen supply boxes and the can smasher and the first aid box and the twenty-four large blue dry bags and the twelve smaller white ones, with everyone joking all along about how easy it would be to get the gear back down to the boats the next morning. Soon they had the kitchen set up, the steaks defrosting; and those who appreciated geology were able to take a moment and enjoy the view.

Mitchell being among them. He'd dressed for dinner tonight in a bold turquoise Hawaiian shirt with a few lost buttons that revealed a hairy belly when he moved about. "Things just keep getting more and more beautiful," he murmured, gazing downriver, where gray-green cliffs, furred with sage and cactus, tilted out of the river. With a few quick twists he set up his tripod. "Whoever would have thought I'd get so interested in rocks?"

"How many pictures have you taken, Mitchell?" asked Peter.

"Twelve, maybe thirteen hundred."

"You could publish a book," said Amy.

"I intend to," said Mitchell.

He fastened his camera to his tripod and concentrated on photographing the downstream landscape—although by changing the angle, he was also able to photograph the guides, who had remained down on the boats and seemed to be in no hurry to start dinner. People began to quip that the guides were on strike tonight, and for once they appreciated Mitchell's efforts, because they would remember the scene fondly: the night the passengers got dinner going while the guides had a little R & R on the boats.

But then Sam called the dog, and the mood changed. Evelyn especially looked anxious. "Maybe the tripod's not a good idea," she said as the dog darted about.

Mitchell glanced up with surprise, as though Evelyn had just solved the world's oldest mystery. He pointed jauntily at her. "You know what? I think you're right, Evelyn," and he unscrewed his camera, dismantled the tripod, and slid it back into its sleeve. "I've probably got too many pictures of rocks, anyway. Hey, doggie," he said as Blender sniffed at his sandals. "What's the matter; do my feet smell?" He laughed loudly.

The dog wagged his tail, and Mitchell stooped and deposited one tidy pat onto the dog's head. Evelyn, Susan, and Jill looked on nervously. Last night, when they were sitting around together, they'd taken turns sharing their fears, and Mitchell had confessed to being afraid of dogs. "When I was a kid, I got bit," he'd told them. "Some yappy little thing. And I have to admit that's the real reason I didn't want this dog on the trip. I should have been straightforward with you all. I'm sorry," he said. "Maybe on this river trip, I can get over my fear."

So now they were all remembering Mitchell's confession and worrying he might go overboard in an attempt to undo years of trauma. Blender had been keeping his distance from Mitchell for most of the trip, of course; dogs can sense when someone is not inclined to offer a belly rub on short notice.

Sure enough, just as they feared, Mitchell squatted and held out his hand. "Hey, doggie," he said. "Come here, puppy dog."

It quickly became clear that Mitchell, like Evelyn, didn't really know how to play with a dog. In fact, he treated the dog like a cat, trailing a bit of rope through the sand in front of the dog's nose. Blender sat down.

"Go like this," said Sam, and he took the rope and tied a thick knot, then dangled it above Blender's head. Blender instantly latched onto the rope. Sam tugged. Blender growled and planted his feet and tugged back. Sam released his grip with a flourish; Blender fell back, recovered, and danced in front of Sam.

"Good dog. Now you try it," Sam told Mitchell.

Mitchell wiped his hands on his shorts, took the rope, and dangled it in front of the dog's nose. When the dog latched on, Mitchell laughed and looked around at his audience before tugging lightly at the rope.

"Grrr," he said. "What a toughie. Who's your best friend, huh? Who's your best friend now?"

He played with the dog for a while, tugging and tossing and holding the rope aloft so Blender could jump for it. You could tell he thought he had invented the game.

"Be careful, Mitchell," said Lena, watching.

Mitchell ignored her. "I think this dog actually likes me," he observed with satisfaction. "This is a first. Maybe he's trying to tell me something. Come here, buster," he said, snapping his fingers. "Want to come home with me after the trip?"

Sam looked stung. Mitchell got down on his hands and knees. He held the rope in front of his mouth and growled and pretended to bite the rope.

"Honey, not so close," Lena protested.

From down on the boats came whoops of laughter. "Who wants another beer?" Peter said.

Mitchell stood up. "Hey, that's an idea. Okay, doggie, that's it for now," he said sternly. "Good doggie. All good things must come to an end. Time to go play by yourself. Time for Mitchell's gin and tonic."

Blender barked.

"All yours, Sam," Mitchell said. He held his hands up. "I don't have it, doggie! Look! Sam's got the rope!"

But the dog was not convinced. Nor was he about to be dumped so easily. He circled Mitchell, barking, and Mitchell backed up.

"Don't raise your hands like that," Sam told Mitchell. "He thinks you've got something in them."

"Well, I don't! Look! Hands! Empty!" And he fluttered his fingers above his head.

"That excites him," said Sam. "Put your hands down."

But Sam's instructions didn't register with Mitchell—either that, or it was simply too strong an instinct to hold one's hands up when a dog was barking. And from the dog's viewpoint, what was he to make of this large man with the half-grown beard and the dark glasses and the Hawaiian shirt, standing at the top of a steep riverbank, waving his hands above his head in some kind of primitive dance?

Blender sprang forward, knocking Mitchell back, and the two of them went tumbling down the hillside, a ball of fur and gaudy fabric, here and there a well-tanned limb jutting out, pinballing against rocks and prickly shrubs, only to be stopped, finally, by the rubble at the water's edge.

JT was sitting on his boat enjoying his second beer of the evening when this happened, and he was mellowed out enough that the descent seemed to occur in slow motion, during which time three things occurred to him:

One, the dog was surely going for Mitchell's jugular;

Two, far be it that Mitchell might be lucky enough to score a soft landing against the rafts;

And three (this realization occurring just as Mitchell collided head-first with the rocks), they'd run out of gauze two days ago.

Mass confusion ensued as Lena raced down the hill and JT leapt out of the boat and Mitchell struggled to right himself from the crotch of two boulders.

"Grab my hand!" Lena cried, extending one of her sparrow arms.

Mitchell bicycled his legs in the air, and Peter finally had to reach down and lend his arm so that Mitchell could haul himself up.

At which point JT couldn't help but wince, for Mitchell's forehead was covered with blood. He tried to stop Mitchell from touching it, but it was too late. Mitchell stared at his fingers.

"The dog bit me," he marveled.

By now almost everyone was crowding around to see how badly Mitchell was injured. Even Ruth came hobbling down.

"He was teasing the dog," Sam reported.

"I wouldn't call it teasing," said Lena.

"Well, he was holding his hands up in the air, and the dog jumped," said Mark.

With all this chatter, JT felt like his head was going to burst, this at a time when he needed to stay calm. Was it him, or were they having more medical crises than usual on this trip? He was grateful when Dixie squatted beside him with the first aid box.

"Is he up-to-date on his tetanus?" Dixie asked Lena.

"I can hear every word you're saying and yes I'm up-to-date on my tetanus," said Mitchell. "Now could someone please bring me a mirror?"

"You don't need a mirror, Mitchell," said Dixie. "Let me look."

With great stoicism, Mitchell raised his head. JT and Dixie and Lena all peered closely. There were many small abrasions on his forehead, but most of the blood was coming from a small split near his hairline. It did not look like a dog bite.

"I think you cut it on a rock," JT said, sitting back.

"Besides, Blender would never bite anyone," said Sam.

"He would me," said Mitchell. "I told you, dogs have been biting me my whole life."

"Lie back, Mitchell," said Dixie as she opened up the first aid box. "Hey. Where's all the gauze?"

"We're out," JT said. "Use paper towels." And Abo, as though having already read JT's mind, handed him a roll from behind.

"How can you be out of gauze?" Mitchell demanded.

"Lloyd used it."

"And what, he thought we were right around the corner from Wal-Mart?" Mitchell spat into the sand. "I pay three thousand bucks and you can't provide me with a five-dollar roll of gauze?"

All this time the Mother Bitch had been sitting off to the side, flossing. *Shoot this guy*, she said. *Tie him to a rock. Let him fry.*

At that point, Lena spoke up in what seemed to everyone to be the first time she'd said much of anything the entire trip.

"Mitchell," she said. "Behave yourself. We're a group, and someone else got hurt, and we used up the gauze. We didn't mean to but we did." Her use of the first-person plural reminded everyone that she did indeed teach kindergarten. "Now give me your handkerchief, and take this," and she handed him a paper towel.

"Do I need stitches?" he asked her.

"No," said Lena. "You don't need stitches. There's a lot of blood, but trust me, it's a small cut. Head cuts are like that."

"Lie down, Mitchell," said Dixie.

"I'll bet if I walked into the ER right now, they'd give me stitches," Mitchell said. "Now I'll have a scar. But hey, what's the big deal? Fifty-nine-year-old guy, why should he care about his face?"

"Come on, Mitchell. Lie down," said JT.

"I wouldn't be surprised if this dog has rabies," said Mitchell.

"The dog does not have rabies," said JT.

"And you're an expert on rabies how again?"

"Mitchell! Lie down and SHUT UP!" said Dixie.

Lena held up her hand. "I think it would help if everyone took a deep breath. Mitchell, you don't need stitches. The dog doesn't have rabies. Dixie and JT have everything they need to bandage you up. Now it's time to cooperate."

"Thank you, Lena," said Dixie.

"Please, Mitchell. Lie back," said JT wearily. "I want my beer."

Mitchell lay back with a grunt. JT cradled the man's head in his lap. His beard was rough, his skin craggy. Mitchell closed his eyes, and JT was thankful for that. Lena told Mitchell to think of a nice place.

"I'm in a nice place," he grumbled.

"A nicer place," said Lena.

"On three, Mitchell," said Dixie.

Mitchell grimaced as Dixie poured peroxide directly onto the wound. JT blotted it, then Dixie swabbed it with antibiotic cream and taped three Band-Aids over it.

"Okay, kiddo," she said.

Mitchell opened his eyes.

"All in the anticipation," Dixie said. "Isn't that right, Sam? Sit up, Mitchell. Take a look." She found a small mirror in the first aid kit. Mitchell peered at Dixie's bandaging job. He did not look too terribly unhappy, but he was not going to begrudge anyone anything at this point.

"If this gets infected, you are going to regret this decision like no other," he told JT.

JT stood up and cuffed sand off the back of his shorts. "Which decision might that be?"

"The decision to keep the dog," said Mitchell. "What are you guys governed by, a state licensing board? I imagine it doesn't screw around with decisions like this. One hundred and twenty-five trips, did you say? Maybe that's a nice round number to call it quits."

Stake him to an anthill, said the Mother Bitch. *Want me to do it? No qualms here.*

"Oh goodness," said JT. "I wouldn't go that far."

"Don't test me," said Mitchell.

Afterward, Evelyn made her way down to the boats and hovered about until the guides looked up.

"I'm not second-guessing you," she said, "but peroxide is no longer the disinfectant of choice. You should use Betadine."

"Oh. Okay," said JT. "Thank you, Evelyn."

Evelyn turned and toiled back up the slope.

"She's a good lady," said Abo. "Even if she is a fuddy-duddy."

"She is," said JT.

Dixie leaned back and closed her eyes. "JT?"

"What's that?"

"Have you ever wished for any of your trips to be over?"

"Are you counting the days, Dixie?"

"Nope," said Dixie. "But I'm glad I'm not the Trip Leader right now."

34

Day Nine

Mile 150

It was a tense dinner that night. Mitchell went off and ate by himself; Lena, having received a testy rebuke when she tried to follow him, stayed with the group for once and got a stern lecture from both Jill and Susan that she really didn't need to take Mitchell's bullying for the next thirty years.

"I wouldn't call him a bully," said Lena.

"Somewhat overbearing?" prompted Evelyn, and Lena didn't correct her, and Evelyn felt good, for being definitive. Their site was narrow and hugged the cliff, and they all sat together in a long line, looking down upon the river, glassy and dark. Evelyn scooched closer to Jill.

"Mitchell has a hard time with groups," said Lena.

"You don't need to make excuses," said Susan.

"And he's wanted to do this stretch of the trip for so long," Lena went on. "The city council wants him to give a slide show at the library, after he's finished Powell's journey. And he knows someone who used to work for *National Geographic* too. He might do a story for them. That's a long shot," she added.

Far below, a lone kayaker glided silently down the center of the river. They waved. She waved back.

"Still," said Jill. "A little common courtesy goes a long way."

"I would never argue with that," said Lena. "But you people don't know Mitchell the way I do. You've known him for eight days. I've known him for thirty years.

"He can act like a boor," she said, "but he's not a boor at heart."

———

Peter for his part could deal with the fact that he wasn't going to get any blow jobs on this trip, but he didn't think he had it in him to tolerate four more days of Mitchell.

He dished himself a plate of food and walked over to join Amy and didn't even offer a lead-in sentence. "I'm thinking in the middle of the night," he said, sawing at his steak. "We stuff a sock in his mouth. We tie his hands. We drag him down to the river and give him the old midnight heave-ho."

"Better if we could make it look like he fell," said Amy.

"Because it's me or him," Peter went on. "One of us has got to go."

"I'll bet my mother will help," said Amy. "She's strong."

"I don't care if I even have to go to jail," said Peter. "I am so sick of this guy making himself the center of attention. What, you're not eating?"

"Not hungry," said Amy.

"This isn't the time to try and lose weight."

"Thank you, Dr. Atkins." She reached over and took the piece of meat he'd just cut. "Happy now?"

"Maybe we should put some of this steak in his sleeping bag," said Peter. "Let the dog do the rest of the work."

"Find a scorpion and put it in his hat," Amy suggested.

"Or hot sauce in his coffee."

They watched Mitchell take a picture of Dixie bending over one of the kitchen boxes, in an unflattering pose. "I swear, if that guy takes one more picture of me," said Peter.

Amy sat up.

"What?"

"Oh, my, god," said Amy.

"Tell me!"

"This is so perfect."

"*What's so perfect?*"

"I have *the* best idea." And she proceeded, then, to tell him about the idea that had just popped into her head. Peter thought at first it was too simplistic, that it wouldn't be mean enough and nobody would pick up on the nuances; but as she gave him one example after another, he marveled at the girl's ingenuity. Ten days ago he'd assumed she was merely somebody to tolerate. Now he was filled with admiration.

"You can be really mean when you want," he told her.

"I'm in high school," she reminded him.

July 12 Day Nine

So today Mitchell cut his head on a rock and was a total asshole and snapped at everyone, including Ruth. Peter and I were having dinner afterward and figuring out ways to kill Mitchell, and I had this idea. It just came to me in a flash. OMG. We are SO going to get him back.

Here's the plan:

So Mitchell's been taking pictures of everyone and everything the whole trip. Sam with the red ant. Mark and Jill fighting. JT bandaging Ruth's leg. Evelyn in her sports bra, (Okay, she shouldn't be wearing a sports bra, but it's the RIVER and EVEN I CAN WEAR A SPORTS BRA DOWN HERE IF I WANT, JUST DON'T TAKE A PICTURE OF ME IN IT!!!!)

Anyway, Peter and I are going to take pictures of Mitchell! They'll be totally innocent pictures, but they'll remind us of what an asshole he's been. A picture of him taking pictures, for starters. I definitely want to get one of him without his shirt on, if I don't puke in the process. Oh, and talking to Lena, so we can all remember how <u>not</u> to be treated by our husband someday.

Then we make an album and post it online.

Am I not the biggest bitch in the universe?

DAY TEN

River Miles 150–168

Upset to Fern Glen

35

Day Ten

Miles 150–157

And so the next day, Peter and Amy set about taking lots and lots of pictures—of everyone, but especially of Mitchell. It was, as Amy maintained, all innocent stuff. Mitchell stirring up the grounds in the coffee. Mitchell with his hand up his shorts, adjusting things. Peter took a close-up of Mitchell's well-marked guidebook. Amy caught him as he slipped while getting into the paddle boat, and then she took another shot of him sitting straight-backed in front, ready to go when everyone else was still getting settled.

She would look at that picture next winter and hear his voice clear as day, wondering out loud what was taking everyone so long.

For his part, JT counted his blessings when they managed to get the boats loaded without anyone falling down the steep slope of Upset Hotel. There were basically two big days left, Havasu Creek today and Lava Falls tomorrow, and if he could get through them with no mishap, he might not look back on this trip as a giant migraine.

Jill would always look back on Havasu as The Day Sam Jumped Off a Cliff and Saved Her Marriage.

Everything she'd heard about Havasu Creek was true. Turquoise waters and tropical flowers spilling out of glistening rocks—it was, as Mitchell had promised, a paradise, and as she made her way through thickets of wild grape, as she waded across the stream under the shade of giant cottonwoods, she felt like she'd stepped into the ancient botanical gardens of a long-gone culture.

"You want me to wait?" Mark asked politely, once she started to fall behind, and just as politely, she told him to go on ahead. The last thing she wanted was Mark lingering, keeping her company just so he wouldn't look like a shithead for abandoning her.

She was, admittedly, still angry with him. They'd said as little as possible to one another after their fight above Granite; and her lingering grumpiness now had as much to do with the fact that everyone had witnessed her outburst as with the substance of the fight itself. Everything was so public, down here on the river!

In any case, she ended up hiking by herself that afternoon, a quarter of a mile or so behind everyone else. Eventually she caught up with them at Beaver Falls, where the creek opened up to a series of broad waterfalls, each cascading into a succession of deep green pools. A jungle of vines drooped over the banks, and the air smelled of cloves and oranges.

"You feeling okay?" JT asked. "Drinking enough?"

She liked the way he was always checking on them. She felt taken care of, watched over; she felt safe.

"You're such a parent," she told him.

"Well," he said, allowing his half smile, "I guess I try."

She'd planned on swimming but suddenly found herself chilled. Out in one of the green pools, Mark and the boys ducked and swam and splashed one another. Jill watched them without envy; they were doing what a father and his two sons ought to be doing on a trip like this. It was good for them to horse around. She found herself thinking back on all their family squabbles, the stupid everyday things—which kind of pizza, how many videos, who called shotgun, where all the money went, why did you wait until the night before the assignment was due?—and it all seemed ludicrous now. How could any of it matter?

And as for their fight over Sam yielding his seat to Evelyn: What was wrong with a father trying to instill a sense of grace and generosity in his son?

But she was still mad. What an odd, fickle day, she thought.

When it was time to head back, JT led them along an alternate route, one that followed the narrows of the creek itself, which meant wading up to their hips and clutching the underside of great overhanging boulders to guide themselves along. Once through the narrows, they all scrambled up onto a small ledge to dry out and congratulate one another on their maneuverings.

"Hey, Mitchell," said Peter. And he took a picture of Mitchell hoisting himself up from below, grimacing with effort.

Jill squeezed into a sliver of sunshine to warm up. Mark came up close.

"How come you didn't swim?" he asked.

"I was cold."

"The water was warm."

"Not warm enough for me," she said meanly.

Mark rubbed her arms briskly, and she tolerated it. But in truth she wanted to go back to the boats. All this luxurious greenery was overwhelming her. She wanted rocks, river, sky. And some of Susan's wine, frankly.

"Where's JT going?" Mark asked.

Dixie chuckled. "Up to his ledge."

Jill looked up to see JT squeezing through a narrow slot. Then he vanished.

"What ledge?" she asked, for she saw no ledge from which anyone could jump.

Dixie pointed.

The reason Jill wasn't seeing any ledge was because she was looking only halfway up the cliff. She looked further, and then, squinting from the sun, she saw JT's silhouette appear on a tiny lip of rock far above them. Jill was lousy at estimating distances, but she would have guessed this to be a hundred feet up.

"He's going to *jump*?"

"Every trip, rain or shine," Dixie said. "He calls it Continuing Education."

Matthew, cold by now, came up and huddled against her. She put her arms around him. She hadn't held him close in a long time and now noticed that his bones were lumpy and knobby at the joints. She wondered if this was normal for a teenage boy.

She kissed his head. "Where's Sam?"

But before Matthew could respond, Peter gave a low whistle. "Wow," he said. "Way to go, Sam," and Jill and Mark both looked up to see their second-born son poised on the lip of JT's ledge.

Jill's legs went wobbly, and at the same time she had the sensation of biting on metal. Her eyes dropped to the pool below. Maybe a hundred feet was an exaggeration, but still: the pool was small. There was no room for error.

"Yikes," said Susan, joining her.

"Is Sam actually going to jump?" inquired Evelyn.

"Lucky Sam," said Amy. "I'd jump too, if I weren't so fat."

"Oh, honey!"

"Shut up, Mom," said Amy.

"*Whoa* that's high," said Mitchell.

Jill wished they would keep their comments to themselves, because she knew what they were hinting at. *Are you actually going to let him jump?* Which infuriated her. Whose business was it anyway if Sam jumped?

"What do you think?" Mark asked in a low voice.

It shocked her that he wasn't automatically vetoing the idea. Mr. Safe. Mr. Cautious. Mr. Always Wear a Helmet. She looked up again. In the dappled sunlight JT was standing right behind Sam. He'd placed his hands on Sam's shoulders, and now he bent down so that his face was level with Sam's as he pointed to landmarks below.

"Hey, Sam!" Mark shouted, and when he had the boy's attention, he held out his hands in a questioning gesture. Sam made a small indeterminable movement in response. *Yes, I'm going to jump. No, you can't stop me.*

And Jill recalled a time long ago, senior year in high school it must have been, upstate New York, a sunny afternoon at a gorge. She watched her friends jump, one by one. And when she finally jumped, she felt her limbs go loose. She saw the blurred stone cliffs, bodies sunbathing on the ledges below, the sparkle of sunlight filtering through fat green leaves; and then she felt the hard, cold smack of the water. Her legs stung, and she swallowed a lot of water, and after she hauled herself up onto the warm rocks, she discovered a large plum-colored bruise on her thigh. But the thrill was palpable and lasted long into the night—the thrill of a reasonable, sensible girl living dangerously for one short moment on a warm spring afternoon.

Still: she'd been eighteen. Sam was twelve. And JT should have checked with them first. She felt that wobbly feeling again. If they had any chance to stop Sam, they would have to decide quickly.

"What do *you* think?" she asked Mark. She felt shy doing this, as though it were their first major decision together. Their house, their friends, their whole life in Salt Lake City seemed very, very far away.

"It's just that there isn't a lot of room for miscalculation," Mark said. "Dixie? Is this safe?"

Dixie had no qualms. "JT wouldn't take just anyone up there," she told Jill and Mark. "He's been watching Sam the whole trip. Sam's a coordinated kid. He'll be fine. And JT's done it a million times. He knows this spot like the back of his hand." She paused to wave at Sam. "Of course, it's up to you and Mark. But I'd trust JT."

That was the thing, Jill thought. You had to trust the guides. You had to trust them when they told you *not* to do something; but you also had to trust them when they gave you the go-ahead—not just because it was safe in their eyes, but because they knew you'd be better off for having done it.

"I think it's okay, then," said Mark.

"I think it's okay too," she said. And she found his hand and squeezed it.

Everybody was looking up now. JT had stepped back, and Sam stood poised at the edge of the lip. Jill waved to him. He wrung his hands at his side. She thought of changing her mind. Then Sam took a small step back and leapt straight out.

A collective gasp rose from the group.

Sam flailed in the air before hitting the water dead smack in the middle of the pool. The impact sealed in upon itself. The surface foamed; ripples rolled swiftly to the edges of the basin and then back in upon themselves. And then, five feet from the bull's-eye, the water broke and Sam's head popped up, his eyes wide with shock as he sculled about in a moment of disorientation before spotting the group on the nearby ledge. He swam toward them, and Dixie leaned over and extended an arm.

"Come on up quick, so JT can jump!" and she hoisted the boy up onto the ledge. His teeth chattered as he huddled against Dixie, and Jill had the good sense not to put her arms around him at this time. They all craned their necks again, and there went JT, falling in a half-seated position, hitting the water thuddishly in the exact same spot as Sam. Within seconds his head emerged and he gave it a shake, and with three strong breaststrokes he swam to the edge of the rock, where both Dixie and Sam extended their arms.

"So what'd you think, kiddo?" said JT, water dripping from his baggy shorts. It was clear he viewed Sam as a member of an exclusive club now.

"It was pretty cool," said Sam nonchalantly. "Didn't you want to go, Matthew?"

"No," said Matthew. "I don't like heights." And Jill was flabbergasted at this level of maturity in her son, that he wouldn't try to go just because his younger brother had gone.

"Grab your water bottles, gang," JT called out. "Fun's over. Keep up the pace. We still have some river miles to make when we get back."

"Were you scared?" Mark asked Sam as they headed down the trail.

"Nope."

"What was JT saying up there?"

"He was telling me to hold on to the family jewels," Sam said, with dignity and pride.

Jill had to think a moment, to figure out the meaning.

"And did you?" Mark asked Sam, man to man.

"Yup."

"Good," said Mark, tousling the boy's head.

Up ahead, Susan, Evelyn, and Mitchell stayed close together. Jill sensed they were talking about her and Mark and their decision to let Sam jump. She could understand Evelyn and Mitchell being quick to condemn, but she was a little mystified by Susan. After all that wine they'd drunk together, she thought they were in agreement on most issues. She felt a little betrayed, like she did whenever Mark voted Republican.

The hell with them, she thought. They don't know Sam like we do.

"Were we crazy?" she asked Mark as they ducked through the leafy thicket of wild grape.

"Nah," said Mark. "Sam was great."

Jill smiled. "He was, wasn't he?"

"It meant a lot to him. If we made him come down, think how humiliated he'd have been. You can't do that to your kid. Not on the river. Not at age twelve."

"You can if it's a mile high."

"But it wasn't."

"No, it wasn't. I really went by what Dixie said," said Jill, feeling a weight suddenly lifting. "I figured if JT thought it was safe, then it was safe. But I don't think some of the others felt that way."

"That's their problem, then," Mark declared, and it gave her a thrill to hear him say that. If they'd not been in such a rush to get back, if they'd not been in such a heavily used area, Jill would have grabbed her husband's hand and dragged him off behind a tree for the quickest fuck in the history of their marriage.

As it was, she had to wait until after dinner that evening, when JT got out his book of poetry and read to them all, and Jill and Mark were able to slip away unnoticed. Years later she would still be able to recall kneeling in the sand, Mark's fingers fluttering on her skin, the tacky warmth of his neck, the black river moving soundlessly in the night as they lay down together.

36

Day Ten

Mile 157

In Susan's view, it was the remoteness of their location that made Jill and Mark's decision so imprudent. What if the boy had cracked his head open? It wasn't like they were at a city park, with a hospital just down the road.

"I personally don't think even JT should have jumped," Evelyn confided as they headed down the trail. "He's our Trip Leader. What if he got hurt? Where would we be then?"

"Up shit creek," Mitchell declared. "He could have jeopardized the trip for everyone. Gotta remember, we're paying two hundred fifty bucks a day. That's a lot of money to waste just waiting around for a helicopter."

"Maybe Jill and Mark weren't thinking clearly," said Susan. "They haven't been speaking much. Maybe neither one of them wanted to call the shot."

"But it's the first thing you learn in wilderness school," Evelyn said indignantly. "You don't take unnecessary risks. And how was JT so sure that things hadn't changed since the last jump? What if there was a boulder he didn't know about? What if Sam was off by a couple of inches?"

Mitchell grumbled his agreement, and he and Evelyn continued to imagine worst-case scenarios as they continued down the trail. Susan herself wondered what she would say at happy hour tonight. She really didn't feel like going off to drink wine with Jill, because she was afraid she wouldn't be able to keep her mouth shut. *What kind of a mother are you, letting your son jump off a cliff, miles from nowhere?*

For once, Susan felt like she was on the same side as the Mother Bitch.

Peter and Amy tromped along the trail, Amy in front, Peter behind.

"I should have jumped," Peter kept saying. "Why didn't I jump?"

"Would you shut up?"

"I would have been fine. Sam did it. Sam was fine. It was my only opportunity. I'll never be back here. Hey!" he exclaimed as a branch snapped back in his face.

"Sorry."

"This is why I hate hiking," Peter said. "I'm always getting hit with branches. That and poison ivy. Is there poison ivy here, do you think?"

"I don't know."

They went twenty, thirty steps in silence.

"I wonder what's for dinner," Peter said. "Do you know what's for dinner?"

Amy shuddered. "I have like *no* appetite."

"You're really a world-class whiner, you know? Have you always been this much of a whiner?"

"It's the heat," said Amy. "I'd rather just drink beer. How many beers do you have left?"

"Five."

"Five each or five total?"

"Each."

"Good."

"I hope you're planning on reimbursing me, when we get back to civilization."

"My mother will," said Amy. "She's so happy I'm drinking beer with you, she'll pay you double."

"She didn't look too happy the last time I checked."

"When was that?"

"When Sam jumped."

"Oh, you mean how she looked like this?" Amy turned around and pursed her lips fiercely. "Probably she thought Sam shouldn't jump. My mother can be very critical of other mothers' decisions."

Peter was so hungry he was beginning to feel a little light-headed. He peered among the giant grape leaves for real live grapes.

"My mother would have loved for me to jump," he said. The leaves were as big as dinner plates, and neon green. There were no grapes, though. "She probably would have pushed me."

"Shut *up.*"

"She would. My mother's mean."

"She's lonely, from what you tell me."

"And that's my fault?"

"Just water her flowers," sighed Amy. "Sit with her. Drink a glass of lemonade. That's probably all she wants."

"Like you're going to be so nice to your mother when she's old. I'm going to come and chew your ass off then," said Peter, "and remind you of how judgmental you were of me, once upon a time."

"You won't even remember me two weeks after this trip."

"I'll remember you. You think I'm Lloyd?"

"Lloyd's so sweet," said Amy. "We should save our money and do this trip next year, with Ruth and Lloyd. Without my mother, of course."

"Or Mitchell."

"Especially not Mitchell."

They climbed out onto a ledge that overlooked the mouth of Havasu. Down in the fjordlike inlet, plump rubber rafts jostled against one another. Just outside the mouth, the candy-colored waters of Havasu melted into the brackish Colorado.

"Speak of the devil," said Amy—for down in JT's boat, there was Mitchell, fumbling with his shorts. Amy took out her camera and snapped a picture just as Mitchell arced back slightly.

"Mitchell's not going to want to go anywhere, not after he sees our pictures posted all over the net," Peter said.

"Can he sue?"

"For what?"

"Invasion of privacy?"

"*You* he could sue," said Peter. "Not me."

JT couldn't help but notice the new alliances that night. Mitchell and Lena were eating dinner with Susan and Evelyn. Mark and Jill sat comfortably braced, back to back; and it didn't escape JT's notice that for much of the time their hands were interlaced. He was amused, later, when they snuck off during Poetry Hour. He just hoped they knew to watch out for snakes, because there was a big mean one that lived around here, fat from mice.

He made sure they were back before everyone broke up to go to bed.

Two more nights, he told himself as he prepared for sleep. He lay back on his mat, letting the wisp of a breeze cool the bare skin of his belly and the undersides of his arms. He dropped his hand down to the dog below and fingered the rubbery flesh of his ear.

"I suppose you're too spoiled to sleep in one of those crates," he murmured. "Probably have to sleep in a man's bed, don't you? Whether he's got a girlfriend or not. Yeah," he said, "well, we'll see about that."

July 13, Day Ten

I would love, I would just love if they all could have seen me at Havasu today. If they could tear themselves away from Victoria's Secret and look up from Facebook and the three hundred photos from last night's party, and see me with everyone else wading out into the pool, and JT telling us we had to just trust him and hold our breath and dive down, and not open our eyes, but feel along the sharp edges of this rock and keep your hand on your head because if you're a little off you can hit your head as you come up. And there we are, surfacing in this underwater cave, like being in an agate, water trickling, no other sound until JT tells us it's time to leave, and we have to dive down again and feel our way along that rock, and now when we come up the air is warm and yellow —

What I would give not to have to spend another 180 days of school with those people —

take me away
take me far, far away

DAY ELEVEN

River Miles 168–179

Fern Glen to Below Lava

37

Day Eleven

Miles 168–179

On the morning they'd be running Lava, JT brewed the coffee twice as strong. While the grounds were settling, he got out his sewing kit and mended one of the straps on his life jacket. He clipped his fingernails and washed his face well. Finally, he dug through his dry bag and got out his Lucky Lava shorts, which thus far had taken him safely down Lava Falls 124 times.

When the coffee was ready, he brought three steaming mugs down to the boats. Dixie wrapped her sheet around her shoulders and blew on the coffee. Abo sat like a bullfrog, blinking.

"Rise and shine," JT said. "It's Judgment Day."

He didn't have to tell them, for they'd dreamt of it as they tossed and turned in their boats that night. Lava Falls, Mile 179, rated ten on a scale of ten. Lava, with a sharp drop-off at the top followed by the Ledge Hole, which could suck you straight down into the center of the earth.

Dixie took a sip of coffee and winced.

"And take these." JT handed them some vitamins.

"It's just *Lava*," complained Abo. "What's the big *deal*, everybody?"

JT knew he was kidding, but there was an element of truth in what he said. Lava was unquestionably the Big One, but it got more than its fair share of horror stories. Which naturally Mitchell had passed on the night before—near drownings and broken limbs and wooden dories getting ripped to splinters. Swim Lava, Mitchell promised, and your hair will turn white.

"Mitchell's got Susan scared to death," Dixie said now. "She asked me if she and Amy could walk around it."

"Nobody's going to walk around it," said JT. "We're going to have good clean runs. We'll take it from the right, hit the V-wave, get drenched, bail like hell, and be through in twenty seconds."

"Mitchell's just trying to scare people off so he can get a spot in the paddle boat," said Dixie.

"I call Not-Mitchell," Abo said promptly.

"Not-Mitchell," Dixie echoed.

They both looked at JT.

"That leaves you, Boss," said Abo.

"I'll take Mitchell," he said with a shrug. "Abo, you want to let Sam paddle?"

"Why, SURE I do!" Abo declared.

Dixie closed her eyes. "Abo? You're here," she said, leveling her hand up high, "and you want to be here." She dropped her hand.

"And Evelyn," said JT. "I think it's really important to her."

"Evelyn can paddle," said Abo. "As long as I have Peter up front. This quiet enough for you, darlin'?" he asked Dixie.

"Now cover up your butt."

Abo glanced over his shoulder, then pulled the bedding farther up around his hips. "Who's taking Ruth and Lloyd?"

"I am," said JT. There was no argument here. The fact that he had more experience than either Dixie or Abo didn't guarantee anything. It did, however, make him feel prudent.

"How's Ruth's leg doing, anyway?" Dixie asked.

Fair is how JT would have characterized it. Holding. No more Cipro had turned up, so Ruth had only taken half the course, which meant they'd probably contributed to the global problem of antibiotic-resistant bacteria.

However, he wasn't going to ship her off the river, not on Day Eleven. Two more days, and the Flagstaff ER could take over.

"I've seen worse," JT told them. "But this is definitely Ruth and Lloyd's last trip."

"That's so sad," said Dixie, blowing on her coffee.

At breakfast JT had to tell Mitchell to shut up with his stories. Despite the apprehension, everyone ate heartily. Yesterday's rift over Mark and

Jill's parenting judgment had healed for the moment in the presence of excitement over Lava. They all applied sunblock liberally today, as though it would protect them from the rapids themselves.

"I am so sick of groovers," said Peter, relaying the roll of toilet paper to Jill.

"Anyone seen my water bottle?" Mitchell called out.
  "Mitchell," said Peter, holding his camera. "Smile."
  Mitchell smiled broadly.

There are no real rapids to speak of in that stretch of river above Lava Falls, and without them, the guides and the paddlers had to work extra hard to keep up their speed. They passed a landslide, with boulders perched precariously atop towers of rubble. Then they entered a vast volcanic field, with glistening black basalt dikes and lumpy beds of lava. Soon they rounded a bend, and a huge black rock rose up from the middle of the river—Vulcan's Anvil, a malevolent ship in placid water.
  And with its appearance, the guides pricked up their ears for the sound of Lava Falls.
  JT looked over at Dixie, and they grinned at each other. It was there. It was always there: loud, wide, and hungry.
  Twenty minutes later they pulled into shore on the right, along with the cluster of kayakers and several other rafts.
  "Everybody out," said JT. "Time to scout."
  "Is this Lava?" Sam asked.
  "This is Lava," JT replied. "Let's see if it's got any surprises for us today. Wet your shirts; it'll be hot up there on the lava bed."

"Got your camera ready?" Peter asked Amy as she dunked her baseball cap. "Got enough memory? Want to take mine, as backup?"
  Amy positioned her hat, letting water drip down her neck. "I'm going to use my waterproof camera."
  "Excellent idea," said Peter.

―――――

Ruth and Lloyd traipsed up the path behind JT. "Ruthie," said Lloyd, "this is such a beautiful place. I'm thinking we should come back here sometime."

"Do you think JT would kill me if I took just one teeny tiny chunk of this lava rock home with me?" Susan whispered to Amy as they climbed up the hillside.

Lena peered down the steep drop-off. "It doesn't look that big," she said.

"Shouldn't Amy buckle the bottom buckle on her life jacket?" Evelyn asked Abo.

JT stood at the edge of an outcrop, tight-chested from the intense heat that radiated off the black rocks. In the five minutes it took to get up here, his shirt had already dried. Down on the river, one of the kayakers headed for the drop.

"Too far left," JT said. But he was wrong; the kayaker bulleted through the rapid, spinning in triumph at the bottom.

"Anyone else having trouble with the eggs from this morning?" Abo inquired.

"Because—I don't know, I'd just feel more comfortable, riding with the boys," Jill said to Mark.

"I totally understand," he replied.

"Oh golly," breathed Mitchell, gazing down at a tiny raft in the maelstrom of waves. "Yikes."

"No wonder it's a ten," said Evelyn.

"Holy fuck," Mitchell said.

38

Day Eleven

Lava

Mile 179

Amy tried to keep up with the group as they hiked up the short trail to the scouting point, but with her feet so swollen, every step made her wince. She felt like she was walking on cacti. The rocks were black and hot, and the trail was overgrown with prickly bushes that clawed at her legs. When she reached a small lookout, she stopped. Lena was right; Lava didn't seem all that big. From the way Mitchell was talking the night before, Amy expected something along the order of Niagara Falls. This looked like any other rapid, only wider.

Then she watched a fat white pontoon boat slide down into the mess and plow through a standing wall of water, and she calculated that the wall was as high as the boat was long.

Oh.

Peter, who had been up with the rest of the group, now came slapping back down the trail to join her.

"Go up and see it from there," he urged her. "You get a much better view. Hey. You okay?"

Amy didn't want to tell him about her feet. She didn't want to draw attention to them. She crossed her arms. Her breasts hurt, and she felt off balance. "So where's that stupid ledgie thing?"

Peter pointed to a long irregular interface near the top of the rapid, where the dark, smooth-flowing river exploded into white chaos.

"The dark part's the Ledge," Peter said. "And all that white stuff below, that's the Hole."

"And the Hole is where we don't want to go?"

"Where we definitely don't want to go," he said. "Even if you can swim. Like I can. If you remember, I learned to swim on this trip. But I don't want to swim in that hole."

"I just want to get it over with," said Amy. "It's so hot here."

"How many shots do you have left in your camera?"

Amy took the waterproof camera out of her fanny pack. It was school bus yellow, sheathed in hard plastic, with a blue rubber wrist strap. She squinted at the dial. "Seven."

"Well, listen. This thing is bigger than I thought. There won't be much time. Twenty seconds, JT says. If you get a shot of Mitchell, great. If not, no big deal. We've got a lot of other good pictures of him."

"I definitely want a picture of him in Lava," said Amy. "He's been talking about it the whole trip. If there's going to be one picture of him that sums it all up, it'll be Mitchell at the helm in Lava Falls."

"You are *such* a bitch," Peter said proudly.

"Thank you," said Amy.

Back at the boats, JT gathered everybody together and waited for their full attention. A hush fell over the group.

"Okay now," he said, looking around. "From the looks of it, things seem pretty normal. There's a lot of hype here at Lava. And for good reason. This is big stuff. But I want everyone to stay calm. Keep your wits about you. Listen to your paddle captain. Listen to Dixie. Listen to me."

"Where's Blender going to ride?" Sam asked. He stood hopping from one leg to the other. The dog had ridden in the paddle boat that morning, much to Sam's delight.

"My boat," said JT.

"Who's in your boat?" asked Sam.

"I've got Ruth and Lloyd, plus Amy and Mitchell."

Sam stopped dancing. "So who will hold on to the dog?"

"Well," said JT, "well, I guess Mitchell will."

"*Moi?*" said Mitchell.

"That's right," JT told Mitchell. "You're going to be riding up front, so you're in charge of the dog."

(Way to make things as hard as possible, he thought.)

But Mitchell shook his head somberly. "Well then, this hombray will rise to the occasion."

Once again, JT reminded them to check their life jackets. Solemnly they all boarded their respective boats as the guides stood knee-deep in the water and coiled up their bow lines. There was a kind of informal queue among the parked boats, and their group was next.

When Amy, Mitchell, Ruth, and Lloyd were in their seats, JT pushed off.

"Here's the deal," he said, rocking the boat as he climbed up and settled himself on his seat. "Main thing is to just stay low and hang on tight." He reached back and tightened the retainer strap on his sunglasses. "And listen closely! We're going in on the right and in two seconds I'm going to shout 'V-wave!' "

"What's a V-wave?" asked Amy.

"It's just a huge backward wave. Anyway—when I yell 'V-wave,' I want you to duck—and then I want you to *immediately* start bailing. I mean *immediately*! And with the buckets—don't bother with the bailing pump; there isn't time. Just bail like hell. Then there'll be another huge wave, and then we're through. Whole thing takes twenty seconds. Pretty simple. Not a lot to remember." He snapped the latch on the ammo box at his feet. "So, Amy . . . What is it you're going to do?"

"Hold on? Duck when you say 'V-wave,' and bail?"

"That's what I like," said JT. "A passenger who listens."

"What do I do with the dog?" Mitchell asked. "Should I hold on to his bandanna? Put him on a leash? What should I do?"

All this time the dog had been sitting patiently at JT's feet.

"You're going to squeeze him between your legs, as close to your crotch as possible," JT said. He gave the dog a nudge. "Go see Mitchell."

"Come here, doggie," said Mitchell. "Don't bite me again. I'm a nice guy." Gingerly he stretched his arm over the stack of dry bags. JT gave the dog another nudge. JT knew he was pushing things here, but he didn't have any alternative. Ruth and Lloyd were out of the question, and Amy—well, he recalled Amy sliding around in the

231

boat during Crystal. Amy had to hold on with both hands, good and tight.

"No time to hold a grudge," JT said to the dog. "Go on now." Blender slunk toward Mitchell. He sniffed the man's fingers, thumped his tail, then settled at Mitchell's feet in the front of the boat.

"Wrap your legs around him, Mitchell," said JT. "Squeeze him like you're a woman."

Mitchell laughed nervously but corralled the dog between his thighs. "So—where's this V-wave?" he asked, craning his neck.

"You can't see it from here." JT took up his oars and pounded down the safety pins for good measure. "Only when you're right down in the middle of things."

"Want me to be on the lookout for you? Act like an extra set of eyes?"

"No, Mitchell," said JT. "I want you to stay low and hang on, just like everyone else. Keep the dog between your legs. Ruth? Lloyd?" He wrenched around in his seat. "You set on instructions?"

"I am happy to report that I moved my bowels today," said Lloyd, tightening the strap on his hat.

Ruth looked at JT and shrugged.

"So are we ready?" JT called over to the other boats.

"Ready," said Dixie.

"I'm ready," said Abo.

"Then let's rumble," said JT.

In the front of the boat, Amy crouched down, squatting against her heels. She was glad to get off the hot black rocks, to be out on the water again; the perpetual puddle in the bilge felt cool against her swollen ankles.

She wasn't scared. JT knew what he was doing. He had, after all, run this rapid 124 times.

"Everybody got a good grip?" JT asked them. "Got the bail buckets handy?"

Amy slipped her right hand through the wrist strap of the camera, then took hold of the chickenline, shielding the camera from JT's view with the bulk of her arm and shoulder. With her left hand, she worked her fingers under the tight web of straps.

Mitchell was watching her closely. "These straps are tight as guitar strings, aren't they!" he exclaimed. "Sheesh! Wow! Here we go! Look out Lava!"

Amy could tell that Mitchell felt uncomfortable with her, and she suspected it had to do with her being so fat and him not approving but trying to hide it with jovial chatter.

"Now wouldja look at that kid?" Mitchell said.

"Who?"

"Sam!"

Amy glanced at the paddle boat, where Sam had taken up the middle post, right behind Peter. Sam was sitting up straight, alert as a soldier. His shirt cuffs were buttoned, and his chin strap looked tight enough to choke his skinny adolescent neck.

"A far cry from the boy who lost his sandal the first day, don't you think?" Mitchell asked. "I'm actually glad he got to paddle today. He'll remember this run for the rest of his life. And boy, will he have earned bragging rights back home."

Amy was tempted, for one second, to take a picture of Sam and Peter. But she didn't want JT to know that she had her camera out. And she didn't want Mitchell to know, either, lest he request that she take his picture. She couldn't say why, but she felt that an authorized photo would lack meaning and value. It had to be taken on the sly.

She mentally planned out the composition of the picture. She wanted to catch Mitchell at his most alert, maybe a silhouette of his head, with all that foamy water in the background. She felt the silhouette angle would capture his pomp. Man at the Prow. Captain Mitchell. Maybe they could photoshop a different hat on his head. What would John Wesley Powell have worn?

The oarlocks creaked as JT rowed away from shore. Abo's boat was up ahead, Dixie's behind. Far above, on the hot rocks, another set of scouters gazed down. Now Abo's boat began to pick up speed, and suddenly Abo gave a shout. Six torsos shot forward. Paddles flashed. The boat dipped down, nosed up, then rocked dangerously to one side before disappearing into the ocean of froth below. Amy couldn't tell if they were safe or not. And she couldn't hear anything because the roar of the water was increasing exponentially. She wondered how JT would know if Abo had had a safe run or not, before it was their own turn.

Which it was, now. Amy crouched lower. She could see nothing but silky dark water, yet the roaring was just below, and it grew more deafening with each passing second. The fact that there was no turning back, that they could only go forward—that they were now committed to the run, like it or not—suddenly seemed profound to Amy, and she felt as though the river was sharing some ancient, simple secret with her, one that only those who'd slid down the tongue into this particular rapid could comprehend.

Next to her, the dog panted a happy dog grin from between Mitchell's clenched knees. Amy glanced up at Mitchell. She should take the picture now, she realized, before they dropped. And it was a perfect shot: Mitchell's small head topping a vastly distorted orange life jacket.

They were picking up speed, and Amy knew she had only seconds to take the picture. With a flick of her wrist, she caught the camera in her hand and scooched down further. She squinted through the viewfinder.

It was, indeed, going to be a perfect shot.

Later, JT would ask himself if he'd left something out of his safety instructions. Did he not tell them all to hold on? With both hands? Tight?

And wouldn't a normal, reasonable person put it together that unless you had three hands, you couldn't simultaneously hold on with both hands and take a picture?

Did he have to spell everything out?

It happened to Ruth every time in Lava: that primal, gargly scream coming from the bottom of her belly as the V-wave came crashing down upon her. It was cold and powerful and right on target, a free-standing waterfall in the middle of the river. She just screamed and screamed and screamed, and then remembered to pick up the bucket and bail.

Mitchell was squeezing the dog between his knees so hard that he thought he was going to crush the poor animal. Still, with that first big downward lurch, he was unable to keep the dog from skidding out of his grip when he shifted his feet to keep his balance.

He never even saw the dog go over.

39

Day Eleven

Lava

Susan was so thrilled to be a member of the paddle team for Lava that she forgot to give Amy the customary hug before they boarded their separate boats. By the time she remembered, the lip of the rapid was fast approaching, and she scolded herself for being superstitious. A mother's hug wasn't going to keep Amy safe at this point. Amy was going to keep herself safe.

Beyond the lip, the water dropped off into a mad, boiling sea. Sitting in the front left, Susan wedged her foot into the footcup and watched Peter, who was sitting across, for the slightest twitch—for although in theory she expected to hear Abo's commands herself, she trusted her eyes more than her ears.

Nevertheless she heard Abo's first command loud and clear.

"Forward!" he shouted, and in one smooth motion Susan dug her paddle deep into the last bit of sinuous black water. They hit the first wall of backwash, which left them jabbing blindly with their paddles. Okay, Susan thought. We can manage this.

And then the boat plummeted straight down into the deluge of the V-wave.

In all the other big rapids, they'd been able to plow straight through the waves. But Lava's V-wave captured them in its curl. Oceans of water poured down upon them. Susan screamed as the force seemed to erode her flesh. They didn't go forward or backward; nothing moved, and everything moved. She felt utterly useless; the one time she probed with her paddle, the force yanked it back, so rather than risk losing her paddle or getting her arm torn from its socket, she clutched the shaft and hunkered down and didn't even bother to try.

"Don't let up! Come on! Hard forward!" Abo yelled. His voice came from high above, as though he were standing over her—and maybe he was, maybe he wasn't, Susan had no way of knowing whether the boat was pointed up or down or level. Then they slammed into something and the V-wave lessened; now the water merely sloshed over her shoulders. The boat pitched again, and Susan felt her foot get wrenched from its cup. Frantically she wedged it back in.

"Keep going!" Abo yelled. "Hard forward!"

And then, drawing on some reserve that she didn't know she had, Susan straightened up and dug down with her paddle one more time, taking the next blast head-on, and found that by doing so she regained both her balance and composure. Again and again she dug her paddle deep into the oncoming waves, and at some point, she felt the resistance that told her that her paddle was catching; she was helping to steer the boat, to propel them out of the chaos and into the smooth black current where it was calm.

A collective cheer rose up.

"Fucking Maid of the Mist!" shouted Abo, standing and jouncing the boat like a child. "You guys are awesome!"

"I thought I was going to drown!" Sam crowed.

"That's one heck of a lot of water," Mark observed.

"Buckets!" Evelyn cried. "Buckets and buckets and buckets!"

Breathlessly Susan searched upstream. From where they were now, Lava looked like the open spillway of a vast industrial dam. Had they really paddled through all that?

Sam was asking if they could drag the boat up and run it again.

"Sure we can," said Abo. "Long as you do the loading and unloading."

"Seriously?" said Sam.

"I'm never serious, Sam. Haven't you learned that by now? Everybody watch JT," said Abo.

Their amusement park hilarity fell silent as they watched JT's boat vanish into the curl of the V-wave. It reared up, then disappeared again. All they could see was the occasional flash of an orange life vest. Hang on, Amy, Susan thought.

Then like a beast JT's boat rose up out of the froth, water draining off all around, and there was JT half-sitting and half-standing as he struggled with the oars.

"What's he yelling?" asked Evelyn.

Susan couldn't hear anything. Upstream, scouters were racing down the path to the water's edge. Suddenly there was a thump and clatter in the back of the boat as Abo dropped to his seat.

"SWIMMER!" he shouted. "Paddles in the water! Move it!"

"Who is it?" shrieked Sam.

Susan tried to locate Amy by her pink hat. JT's boat was bucking so much she couldn't see anything.

"Forward! Left turn! Stop! Goddamn it! Left again! Follow Peter, you guys, come on! Forward! Stop!"

The contradictory directions came so rapidly that, try as she might, Susan couldn't keep up. In fact, nobody could coordinate any kind of group effort at all. They needed to break out of the eddy fence, that boundary between upstream and downstream currents, which in this case was sharp and distinct, two rivers scraping by each another in opposite directions. But their paddling was clumsy, and every time they neared the edge, they got caught and dragged back upriver. She kept trying to get a glimpse of JT's boat, to make sure Amy was safe.

"Don't watch JT!" Abo shouted. "Just paddle! Come on! Put some more juice into it!"

Somehow, somewhere, they found a collective burst of energy, and in three communal strokes, they broke through. The boat shot forward and swung around, and they were headed downstream. Gone was their elation. They were on the biggest river in the world, and someone had fallen overboard, and Susan was doing a pretty good job convincing herself that it wasn't Amy; it was probably Ruth or Lloyd, who were old and infirm and had misjudged their capacity for strength—

Until she saw the flash of pink, bobbing in the water less than twenty feet away.

Peter saw it too. He leaned over and extended his paddle out as far as he could, and with a bit of maneuvering, he caught Amy's cap on the fat wooden blade and swung it around and dropped it on the pile of gear in the middle of the paddle boat.

40

Day Eleven

Lava

The main thing Amy was aware of when she slid off the boat was the sudden cessation of earthly noise. Everywhere there were bubbles: gray and white, big and small, spinning like another galaxy all around her. She felt somebody grab her ankle, skin against skin; then, whoever it was let go, and she flailed some more and managed to bob up to the surface. The boat, however, was gone. She looked this way and that and tried not to panic.

Then, right smack in front of her, two stories high and wide as a city block, loomed a giant wall of water.

Down she went, tumbling and swirling and spinning into a cauldron of darkness. She felt like Alice going down the rabbit hole. She had no idea which way was up and which way was down; she felt her shin hit something sharp and saw a flash of yellow. Something punched her in the stomach, then it swung her around and punched her in the back. She needed air, but only once did she surface into that sea of sloppy waves, gasping and swallowing water before getting sucked down again. Without any air, her lungs felt shredded, the emptiness so excruciatingly painful that she would have sucked in anything—water, air, light, the vapors of Mercury—just to fill them up and erase the pain.

This is it.

I cannot hold my breath any longer.

She was all set to give in to the urge, to breathe in gallons of cold, dark water, when some force grabbed both of her feet, spun her around and around, and in doing so sucked her down where no human being had been before. This was no rabbit hole; this was the inside of the inside, deep and dark and bottomless. And at that point, her initial panic gave way to terror, as a spidery black creature muscled its long tentacles around her tiny body.

This is what it's like to die, she marveled.

What happened next, she would never know. Maybe it was a fractal of light. Maybe it was a lone bubble that happened to catch under her chin on its way to the surface. Whatever it was, the water turned gray instead of black, and then it turned white instead of gray. Oblivious to the pain in her lungs and her gut and her leg and now her head as well, Amy kicked and flailed and pulled at the water and finally broke through the surface, where the ragged, enginelike bray that filled her ears seemed to come from a herd of wild animals, rather than from her own windpipe as she sucked down that first lungful of silvery bright air.

Nothing would ever, ever taste so sweet.

Only after filling her lungs repeatedly did she remember JT's instructions that first day. *Look for the boat,* he'd told them; *put your feet up and lean back,* and so she looked for the boat. She looked for *any* boat but saw nothing except a blurry-looking shoreline that tilted one way and then another. Another wave sloshed over her, and she panicked that she was going back under again. But it was a little wave in comparison, and she stayed above water, sculling and riding the giant waves: this was one time when it helped to be so fat, another time being in the Minnow class at swim lessons and everyone saying, *Look at Amy float, it's so easy for her,* and Amy feeling proud, she was only seven and didn't have any clue what was making it so easy for her, but of course her mother did, and her mother looked embarrassed—

A flash of red.

It vanished, then loomed up beside her face. A silver paddle, a black-gloved hand, a white beard beneath a yellow helmet. He was yelling something, tipping and sloshing, and she couldn't understand. Then his hand grabbed hers and folded it over a knotted lump, and she found the power within herself to hang on, and they were slicing through the ocean, and the shoreline stopped tilting, and the fat white tubes of a raft appeared just as a gaggle of hands reached for her life jacket and pulled, pulled harder, and finally hauled her up over the tubes, letting her slop down into the soupy well of the boat, where among the buckets and the straps and the Nalgenes and a floating tube of sunscreen and a cluster of hairy ankles, she lifted her head and began to cough.

And didn't stop coughing, it seemed, through all that was yet to come.

41

Day Eleven

Below Lava

Below Lava, on the right side of the river, lies a long sandy beach. Often river runners will pull in here, stoked high on the rush of running Lava; they might finally eat the lunch they couldn't seem to manage earlier, or pop a beer as they recounted their twenty-second, adrenaline-laced ride.

But there was no middle-of-the-day beer drinking in JT's party that day. The guides beached their boats and hammered their stakes, and everyone else unzipped their life jackets and tried, though it was not possible, to stop the ringing in their ears.

The last time JT had had a swimmer in Lava was three years ago, and it barely counted because, after getting washed overboard, the man popped up near the boat and was able to hold on for the rest of the ride. But Amy's experience definitely counted as a swim; she'd gotten sucked down deep, and when he saw her head vanish, he knew she wouldn't be coming up for a while. Nevertheless, he had a boat to row, and he did his best to alert the others on the river while seeing his boat safely through to the bottom of the rapid, albeit one passenger short.

The kayakers had landed farther down the beach, and JT wanted to thank Bud for rescuing Amy. But right now he had to attend to the girl. Something was definitely wrong. He saw it as soon as she tried to climb out of the boat: she couldn't even stand, she was so doubled over with pain. His first thought was a broken limb. They helped her up onto the beach, where she fell onto her hands and knees and put her head down in a kind of yoga pose. She'd unclipped her life jacket, and the buckles dragged on the sand as she let her hips sway back and forth, moaning, seemingly deaf to the guides and her mother and Peter standing around asking if she was all right. Then she fell onto her side and drew up her knees and made an awful face by baring her teeth and sucking in a great deal of air.

Peter and JT exchanged looks.

Then slowly she emerged from her trance. She opened her eyes and looked at their faces. "What?" she said irritably.

Peter squatted and brushed his fingers against her shoulder. Susan, who had been hovering close, sat back on her heels. Amy rolled onto her back and propped herself up on her elbows. Beads of sweat glistened above her lip, and she licked them off and plucked her wet T-shirt away from her middle and said, "Can't you guys find something better to look at?"

JT's first order of business was to get her out of the wet clothes. Even thirty seconds in the Colorado River could send a person into shock. And granted, Amy had a lot of padding, but he was still worried, especially with the way she was acting.

"Let's get your life jacket off," and he held the jacket open, and Peter guided Amy's arms out of the armholes. Then Susan helped her take her T-shirt off, so that she was exposed down to her bathing suit.

This was the first time JT had seen her without a T-shirt, and it took every ounce of willpower not to stare. Her breasts were like melons, straining at her pink halter-style top. Her vast, doughy belly folded over onto itself in several places. For bottoms, Amy simply wore a pair of baggy black shorts with the waistband rolled down low, beneath the folds of flesh. Susan quickly tugged the shorts up an inch or so; from the look on her face, JT guessed that it had been a very long time since she had seen her daughter without a T-shirt too.

In the meantime, Abo had gotten a sleeping mat, and they all helped Amy lie back. Then Abo draped a sheet over her, for although her skin was dry and the temperature was well over a hundred degrees, she was shivering.

"Is that comfortable?" JT asked.

Amy shrugged.

Though worried, he wanted to make light of things. "You're on the Lava Swim Team now, you know. Pretty elite."

"Are there T-shirts?"

"Are you kidding? T-shirts, hats, duffel bags, the whole shebang."

"Good," said Amy, closing her eyes. "I was never on a team."

Susan tucked a small towel under Amy's head, and JT was going to suggest that she try and drink some water, but Amy got that look in her eyes again. She covered her face with her hands and bent her knees and wiggled her toes in the sand.

"I think something's wrong," Evelyn ventured, from over JT's shoulder.

"Amy," said Susan. "Amy, look at me."

Amy rocked her head from side to side and gouged her heels into the sand.

"Amy?" Susan said. "Honey?"

Amy didn't answer, and JT wasn't happy about this. "Any history of seizures?" he asked Susan.

Susan shook her head.

"I don't think this is a seizure," Evelyn offered.

Then Amy went limp again. This time, however, she didn't open her eyes. She kept her elbow crooked over her face. JT glanced down and saw a large circle of wetness under her hips. He didn't know if she sensed it or not.

"I'm not a fucking epileptic," Amy said in a muffled voice.

Susan stood up and hugged her arms to her chest. Evelyn shifted to give her some space. The others—JT, Jill, and Peter—just sat there beside Amy, not knowing what to do. JT himself was hoping the whole problem would just go away, when Bud walked up.

"Thanks for the help out there," said JT.

"How's she doing?"

"Not good, actually."

"What's wrong?"

"Not quite sure."

Bud squatted down. "Hey. Remember me?"

Amy opened her eyes. She looked at Bud and his big white beard and then looked around at all the other faces. Then she closed her eyes again.

"What's the matter," she said. "Haven't you guys ever seen a fat person before?"

It wasn't a seizure, Evelyn knew that much. Julian had seizures. This wasn't a seizure. She wished people would listen to her. How was it that she was fifty years old and a full and tenured professor of biology at Harvard University, and still people didn't listen to her, unless she was up at the lectern? And even then.

Peter's fear was that it was appendicitis. She'd had it for days, and he should have known, and now the tiny useless organ had ruptured. He thought of all the appendicitis scares his mother had had—all those stomachaches, high up, low down, deep in the belly, dull, sharp, throbbing, incessant. Always he'd taken her to the hospital; always the pains turned out to be gas. Peter had grown to think of appendicitis as something from the 1940s, old-fashioned and extinct, like polio. Now, with it staring him in the face, he'd done nothing.

Thinking of his mother's trips to the hospital made him think of hospital beds and clean sheets. How nice it would be, to crawl into a freshly made bed. And then he thought about Miss Ohio folding linens in her sun-drenched laundry room, telling her pimp-husband how Peter was still tied to his mother's apron strings.

An odd thought, but there it was.

Mitchell traipsed along the shoreline, whistling for the dog.

It was Jill who put it together. She watched Amy go rigid, watched how she dug her heels into the sand and made little gasping noises. She saw the long slow leakage underneath Amy's hips on the sand. She thought back to the night that Sam and Matthew drank the margaritas, when Peter said something and Amy got mad and left. That walk. That waddle.

She told herself it couldn't be possible. A girl would know. Her mother would know.

Then she remembered stories she had read in magazines over the years. Lack of education. Denial. Overweight to begin with.

Susan had gone off to get Amy some water. With Susan gone, Jill gave herself permission to look at Amy's stomach. And she knew. She didn't know how she knew; she just knew. She put her hand on Amy's forehead.

"Could you give me a moment?" she asked JT and Peter.

JT seemed relieved. He stood up and went over and conferred with Dixie and Abo. Peter stayed and Jill didn't argue.

"Amy," said Jill, "is it your stomach?"

Amy nodded her head.

"How bad?"

"Really bad."

"Amy," said Jill, "would you mind if I felt your stomach?"

Amy opened her eyes and looked at Peter. Then she closed them again. "Fine."

Jill laid her hand on Amy's belly. The skin was warm and sticky, and there was a raisin-shaped mole just below her navel. She felt around. She was wanting to feel nothing so that her suspicions would be wrong. But just below Amy's diaphragm, a little to the left, she felt a lump. It was roundish, maybe the size of a plum. Jill pressed, and it rolled beneath her fingers. An elbow, perhaps a foot; Jill couldn't be sure.

She took a deep breath and, not knowing what else to do, gently began to massage Amy's belly. She had never rubbed another woman's belly before, she realized; in fact, it was possibly the most intimate thing she had done to anyone lately, except Mark.

"Does that feel all right?" she asked.

"It feels fine. Anyway, I don't hurt right now. I'm not an epileptic, and don't anyone call a helicopter."

"The pain comes and goes?" Jill asked.

Amy nodded.

"For how long?"

Amy shrugged.

Jill was trying to keep her face calm, but inside she was in ER mode.

ER mode was where she went when Matthew broke his leg up at Alta and they looked at the X-ray and said, *Actually, it's a lot worse than we thought, and see this little spot on the bone?* ER mode was when Sam spiked a fever and got a stiff neck and then went limp in her arms; when Mark had chest pains, and they hooked him up to machines and wires and a counselor came and asked if he had a living will. She had always thought that ER mode was a place she only went when it involved her immediate family, but now she realized that was wrong.

She thought she could deal with telling JT what was going on, and she even thought she could deal with telling Amy. But she didn't think she had it in her to deal with telling Susan—in whom she had confided so much on this trip—that her seventeen-year-old virgin daughter was going into labor on the Colorado River, miles from the nearest emergency room.

42

Day Eleven

Below Lava

Jill stood up in the hot sunshine. Her knees were stiff from crouching and her mouth was dry. She touched Peter on the shoulder and motioned for him to join her out of Amy's earshot.

She'd noticed over the course of the trip an unlikely alliance between these two. She recalled meeting Peter back in Flagstaff the night before they left—noticing how he had a kind of snotty attitude toward everyone, especially Amy. Jill had left the meeting wondering how she was going to hold her patience for two weeks with this frat boy, who was obviously more interested in getting laid than enjoying his time on the river—she could read the disappointment in his face when he looked around and saw the likes of Amy and Evelyn, Susan and Jill, little Lena and ancient Ruth.

So she wouldn't have guessed that he'd have chosen Amy to spend so much time with. She wouldn't have guessed he'd had it in him, to develop a friendship with a woman with whom the possibility of a sexual relationship was not the first thing, quite frankly, that leapt to mind.

Now Peter stood with his eyes cast downward, head cocked toward her, waiting.

"Has Amy told you anything?" she asked him.

"She's had these stomachaches," he said. "I guess I should have said something, but she didn't want me to."

Jill glanced around Peter's bulk to where Amy had rolled on her side again. And she wished suddenly that her wristwatch wasn't buried at the bottom of her overnight bag. It would be helpful if she could time the contractions, and she would need a watch for that, because after ten days on the river, she didn't trust her sense of time in the least.

"It's not a stomachache," she told him.

"What is it?"

"She's in labor."

She waited, then, for it to sink in. And this frat boy, whom she expected would back away nervously, folded his arms across his chest and nodded gravely, as though he had expected nothing less bizarre.

She had to hand it to him.

"Are you sure?"

"I've gone through this twice. I'm sure."

"I knew it wasn't just a stomachache," he said. "But I didn't think it was labor. Did you tell JT yet?"

They both looked over to where JT was listening to Mitchell, who was speaking and gesturing with agitation.

"No," said Jill. "But I will in just a minute. I thought maybe you could explain to Amy what's going on."

"She doesn't *know*?"

"If she knew, she wouldn't be so terrified," said Jill. Then she reconsidered. "Fine, she'd be terrified, but she wouldn't— She's clueless, Peter. Trust me. She has no idea."

Peter looked dumbfounded. "How can this happen? Don't girls miss their periods? Don't they notice they're getting kind of big?"

"It's definitely bizarre, but it happens," said Jill. "When a girl's seventeen, she might not be keeping track of her cycle. And when you're as big as Amy, well, sometimes you just don't notice things. There was a girl in my high school twenty years ago. She was like Amy—really, really big. And she didn't know. Honest to god she didn't know. And then one day she went to the bathroom in between math and science and—"

"Okay," said Peter. "I get it."

"So it can happen," Jill finished.

"How close is she? To, you know, actually having the baby?"

"I don't know," said Jill. "I don't think she's that close, but she might be. I don't know."

"So what do we do now?"

"JT's going to have to radio for help. Because we have to get her to a hospital. And in the meantime, we're going to keep her very very still and try and slow down the contractions. But I want you to tell her what's going on. She likes you."

Peter scratched the back of his neck. "Of all the gin joints in all the world," he murmured. "Fine. I'll tell her."

"Just think of how it's going to be for Susan," said Jill, by way of consolation.

Peter went back to where Amy lay propped up on her elbows again. Her legs were extended out in front of her, dimpled and thick, and he tried to look at her like nothing was different but found it impossible. He wished he had said something directly to JT about her stomachaches, but he also realized there was no good to come of him scolding himself, so whenever that thought came into his mind, he pinched a little fold of skin on the back of his hand. Hard. It was a trick he'd learned from his shrink when he was trying to get over Miss Ohio. The shrink told him to pinch himself whenever he thought of her, and it would decondition him.

"The whale surfaces," Amy said, feigning drama as she tried to sit up.

"How do you feel?"

"Crappy."

Peter looked upriver to Lava Falls. It seemed small and far away and unimportant. This was going to be hard, and he could think of no better way than to just say it.

"Jill thinks you're having a baby," he said.

Amy looked off, like she was remembering something that amused her.

"I'm sorry," she finally said—and her voice was cheery—"but I thought you said that Jill thinks I'm, like, having a baby. What did you really say?"

"That's what I really said." He waited. "Are you?"

"Uh, *no?*"

"She thinks you're in labor," Peter went on.

"How could I be in labor if I'm not pregnant?"

"Are you not pregnant?"

"No," said Amy. "Yes. I'm not pregnant. Look at me. Do I look pregnant? Oh god. Don't answer that. Of course I look pregnant. I always look pregnant. Well, I'm not *preg*nant," she said, emphasizing the first syllable, as though it would sink both the word, and its truth, into the river.

Peter wished Jill hadn't chosen him to be the messenger. This should be JT's job. JT was their leader, and he had all the authority. By this point in the trip, JT could tell them all to go run Lava on boogie boards, and they'd have done it, they trusted him that much.

He looked over at the boats, where Jill was talking to the guides. Jill had one hand on her hip and with the other she was shading her eyes as she talked to JT. JT glanced over at Amy, and Peter felt like he wanted to pull a curtain around her. She deserved privacy, in this land of giant openness. He moved to block their view.

"I guess it's because you get these stomach pains, and they come and go," he said. "She said she felt your stomach. She said it felt like her stomach when she was having Sam and Matthew. She's had two kids," he added, as though this were determinative.

But Amy had gone off into her other world now—or rather, Peter reminded himself, she was having another contraction.

"I think you're having another contraction," he told Amy.

Amy groaned.

Peter had seen women in labor only in the movies and on sitcoms. "Breathe?" he suggested.

But Amy held her breath. Not knowing what else to do, Peter held her hand, and she squeezed so hard he thought she might break his fingers. He prepared himself for this contraction to convince her that she was indeed in labor, but when it was over, she sat up and spat into the sand. She jerked herself forward with her arms, trying to stand up. But she couldn't.

"This is all just bullshit," she said. "I'm sorry I ever told you anything."

"It was Jill who figured it out," said Peter. "It wasn't me."

"Go get me some Tums," she grumped.

Peter wiggled his finger in his ear. Part of him wondered why he was putting up with this. What tie did he really have to this fat girl? He could go over and horse around with Abo and Dixie, and let Susan (who was the girl's mother, after all) take care of whatever was going on. And maybe Jill was wrong. Who gave her the final say?

But another part of him recognized himself as the same person who went over to his mother's every Saturday and watered her peonies, who cleaned out the Weber grill and threw away the vegetables that were rotting in the back of the refrigerator, who picked up his mother's medicine at the pharmacy and made sure she had enough refills authorized for the coming month. That was the kind of person he was. He might complain about it, but he did it, because it was the right thing to do.

Had Miss Ohio not appreciated that?

"Be nice to me," he told Amy.

Amy glared at him. He glared right back. Out on the river, a train of yellow rafts floated by, with everyone waving and shouting, and why shouldn't they be? They had just run Lava without someone in their group going into labor.

Twenty feet away, Jill was still talking to JT. Peter doubted that JT would be as incredulous as Amy, but still, this couldn't have been one of the things he routinely dealt with on his river trips.

"All I want are a couple of Tums," said Amy. "Is that too much to ask for?"

"You know what? It is," he told her. "It is too much to ask for. All *I* want is for you to admit that you're pregnant, you're in labor, you're going to have a baby, and this is going to be a very big deal for the rest of us, because we're down on the river, and there isn't a hospital for miles around. And so a lot of people's plans are going to be altered for you. Which I'm not complaining about, but you should give up on this Tums thing and help people help you. Because as I understand it from Jill, the last thing we want is for this baby to actually be born down here. I don't know what can go wrong, and I don't want to know. But I imagine it can be pretty bad. So quit asking for Tums."

Amy didn't reply. She looked over to where JT and Jill were talking to Susan now.

"Is Jill over there telling my mother I'm pregnant?"

"She is," said Peter, and indeed, right at that moment, Jill put her arm around Susan's shoulder as all three of them looked over at Peter and Amy. Peter tried to imagine what this must be like for Amy. He tried very hard but couldn't come up with anything that would be quite so humiliating. And his heart went out to this girl whose sexual history was about to become the topic of conversation among a group of people who, until eleven days ago, had absolutely no connection with her. Lena the kindergarten teacher, wondering if it had been a serious, meaningful relationship; Evelyn the biologist, wondering how it could have possibly escaped a girl's radar for six, seven, eight months; Mitchell, thinking this would make his book that much more interesting; and Mark, wanting to know how old the father was and whether statutory rape laws would apply.

And all of them who, against every last shred of conscience, would at some point in the next twenty-four hours find themselves shamefully yet inescapably challenged by the notion that somebody like Amy might have had a serious boyfriend.

Amy reached for her T-shirt, which was lying nearby on the sand, and laid it over her stomach. "Don't let my mother come over here."

But Susan, Jill, and JT were already walking in their direction. JT was carrying a beach umbrella over his shoulder, and when he reached Amy, he opened it to reveal dazzling panels of turquoise, pink, and purple. He twisted its post into the sand to shield Amy from the hot midday sun, and there in this small circle of shade, with her mother and three strangers looking on, and another ten wondering what the problem was, Amy covered her face with her hands and began to cry.

43

Day Eleven

Below Lava

Once JT was able to grasp the full implications of the situation, he was able to act with astonishing speed. He told Abo to radio for a medevac. He told Dixie and Evelyn to string up a tarp for shade, for they would need more than a tiny beach umbrella. He told Mitchell to pump water and Mark to get out a kitchen table and set up the stove and start boiling whatever water they already had in the jugs. He told Sam and Matthew to go tell everyone pulling onto shore that they had a serious medical emergency and see if anyone was a doctor. He told Lena where the lunch materials were kept, in which cooler, in which boat, and asked that she set up the lunch buffet. He told Mitchell to put away his camera, please. And he told Ruth and Lloyd to find themselves a place in the little patch of shade by the tamarisk bushes, because it was going to be a long afternoon.

Lloyd recapped his water bottle and wiped his grizzled chin. "I'm a doctor," he said. "What's the problem?"

"Lloyd, come and sit," Ruth urged, taking his arm. But Lloyd brushed his wife's hand away. He planted himself before JT. His tattered beige shirt was half tucked in and the shirttails sagged loosely around his hips. His beard was patchy and his eyes, when he removed his sunglasses to look directly at JT, were rheumy and yellow.

"If I can be of some assistance," he said.

And JT, who was willing to grasp at any straw that appeared before him, told Lloyd about Amy's situation.

Lloyd nodded. "Well," he said carefully, "it's not my area of specialty, but I might be able to be of some use."

"Come with me, then," said JT.

"I seem to remember a few things from my medical school days,"

Lloyd said, trudging along beside JT. "That and being on the reservation. Do you know how many weeks along she is?"

"I don't think anyone knows."

"Even her husband?"

It occurred to JT that this might not be a good idea, getting Lloyd
involved. On the other hand, what harm could he do? Even a confused
mind could offer comfort, at the very least.

"There is no husband," he told Lloyd.

Lloyd nodded somberly, one doctor in on confidential information
with another. "I trust this is her first child," he said. "But babies can
come quickly, even in a young primigravada. You never know. Ruth,
for instance, delivered our first child in five hours."

JT wasn't happy to hear that. He also couldn't help but think back to
twenty-five years ago, to Mac's labor with Colin at the hospital in
Flagstaff and how they went for thirty-six hours before the doctors
finally agreed it was time for a C-section. The memory of that C-section
right now sent an electric zing up the backs of his legs. Mac had lost a
lot of blood, her life was at risk, and they were both terrified. But all
the doctor had to do was order up a few pints of blood, and they
appeared like magic; the IV was already in place and within minutes
the color returned to Mac's face—all this while his newborn son was
off being weighed and washed and swaddled in a soft, hospital-issue
blanket. JT remembered how he had almost wanted to kiss the floor of
the delivery room: for things could have turned on a dime, and yet in
the end he had a happy wife and a fat squalling baby boy to take home.

And he looked at his surroundings here—the beach littered with
all their equipment, the coffee-colored river, the band of cliffs, a hot
white sun overhead—and wondered just what they were going to do if
Amy's baby decided it was going to go ahead and rush itself out into
the world before a helicopter could get here.

"Has her water broken?" Lloyd asked.

"I don't know. Have you ever delivered a baby, Lloyd?"

"On the reservation, I delivered a set of twins. But I might be a little rusty," he said.

"Don't be rusty, Lloyd," JT told him.

"Don't sue me," Lloyd replied.

And JT marveled at the human brain, that it could become so entangled with the plaquey ropes of Alzheimer's, yet still find a clear line to a quick, snappy retort.

By now a makeshift trauma station was taking shape on the beach. Using stakes and rope and a triangular nylon tarp, Dixie and Evelyn and the boys had constructed an open-air tent that provided both shade and ventilation. Mitchell had lugged one of the five-gallon water jugs over and set it in the shade, and Evelyn, in between helping Dixie with the tarp, had managed to find the unopened twelve-pack of cotton bandannas that she'd stashed in the bottom of her overnight bag.

In the meantime, another party had pulled in, and a motley crowd had gathered outside the tarp area—young strappy guides, lizard-skinned oldsters, throngs of passengers in their clownish rubber-toed sandals. And the kayakers, all of them. Unless there was a doctor, JT didn't really want an audience, so he designated Mitchell to shoo everyone away.

"Tell them if we need any help, we'll ask for it." He was annoyed, even though he knew he had no reason to be. Anyone would be curious; anyone would want to help.

"What should I say?" said Mitchell.

Do you tell a crowd of strangers that a seventeen-year-old girl who didn't even know she was pregnant was going into labor? This question had never arisen before.

"Find out if there's a doctor," he told Mitchell.

Mitchell marched out into the sunshine and cupped his hands around his mouth. "Is there an obstetrician in the house?"

JT groaned inwardly.

"Well, now they know," Peter said.

There had been several times during the course of this trip that JT would have said that he was nearing the end of his rope. Back at Phantom, watching Blender get swept beneath the footbridge. Or two nights ago at Upset, when Mitchell and the dog went somersaulting down the hill.

Now it seemed that the rope had no end, that it was just a long series of knots and tangles, a kind of Jacob's ladder into a bottomless hole. It had no meaning, being at the end of one's rope; you were either on it or off; nothing much mattered, except keeping everyone alive. And he flashed on Mac once again, because Mac was one of those people who could always find another rope to grab, when all else failed.

They had once made such a good pair, JT thought. And he felt a sudden stab of grief, to think that his marriage hadn't worked, that all his years on the river had passed without the one sweet love of his life by his side.

But obviously he couldn't focus on Mac right now. Sitting back on his heels, he took a long drink of water from his Tropicana jug. At the same time, Susan returned with Amy's water bottle. She hovered near the circle of people, not sure of herself. JT moved aside to make room for her.

Lloyd was in the process of taking Amy's pulse. "One hundred and ten," he called over his shoulder.

"Somebody write that down," said JT.

Evelyn promptly recorded the number in her journal, and Amy began making little rocking movements with her hips.

"Here we go again," Lloyd announced.

"Note the time," JT told Evelyn.

Susan held one hand, Jill the other, while Peter, who was stationed by her feet, gripped her ankles.

"Breathe, Amy," warned Jill. "Remember how I told you? Breathe before it starts to hurt. Deep breath in, long breath out. You can do it."

"It already hurts!" Amy groaned.

"You can do it," said Jill. "Come on. Deep breath in. That's a girl. You can do it."

Amy managed a deep breath in but couldn't control her exhalation, and she exploded in a loud, ragged scream.

"Try it again!" Jill exclaimed. "Deep breath! Follow me!" and she wheezed in a long, noisy breath to demonstrate. Susan looked on, paralyzed. Amy ground her heels into the sand.

Then it was over.

"Two minutes," Evelyn announced.

"Honey," Lloyd said, bending over Amy. "You're going to be okay. We're going to take good care of you and your baby. Are you hoping for a boy or a girl?"

Amy's eyes darted about in terror.

"I know, I know," Lloyd said. "You don't care as long as it's healthy. Don't you worry," he assured her; "we'll take good care of you."

JT decided that the best thing to do with Lloyd was to go along with him. "Lloyd's right," he told Amy. "You'll be fine. All you gotta do is breathe. Just like Jill showed you."

Just then Mitchell ducked under the tarp, out of breath. "I found a doctor!"

JT almost leapt up. He strode out into the sunlight to find himself face-to-face with a man wearing wraparound sunglasses and a ten-day beard.

"This is Don," said Mitchell.

JT gripped Don's hand. "What kind of a doctor?"

"GI," said Don. "And I'm only a resident. I don't know if I can really help."

"You can definitely help," said JT. Same quadrant of the human body, he thought. Good enough for me right now.

"Are you sure she's in labor?"

"Yep."

"How many months pregnant?"

"We don't know. She's only seventeen," JT said. "Until an hour ago, she didn't know she was pregnant."

"How far dilated?"

Dilation! JT hadn't thought of that. And his mind envisioned Mac's knobby knees poking up out of the sheet and the doctor down between her legs, sticking his arm up to her throat.

"Nobody's checked that," said JT. "Move aside, folks!" he said, ducking back under the tarp. "Don's here. Don's a doctor."

Lloyd finished blowing his nose into an old bandanna. He wadded it up and stuffed it back into his pocket for the next century.

"Lloyd's a doctor too," JT told Don.

"And what's the girl's name?" Don asked.

"Amy."

"Hello, Amy," said Don. He knelt close and moved a strand of hair off her forehead. "I'm Don."

Amy simply stared back.

"Amy," said Don, "do you mind if I feel your stomach?"

Amy shook her head. Don placed his hand on the wide pale swell of her stomach. His face remained solemn as he felt around, pressing gently. JT imagined him looking up with a surprised frown, saying, *Why, this girl isn't pregnant! This girl just has to lose a little weight!*

"Your assessment?" Lloyd inquired.

Don sat back. "I can't really tell a lot. I did a rotation in obstetrics two years ago, so whatever I know is based on that. I can't say exactly how many weeks along she is, but obviously she's pretty far. And I'm guessing the baby's head down. Which is good," he told Amy. "You want your baby to be head down."

Amy's expression didn't register this. He might just as well have told her of a new mathematical proof.

"But what I'd like to do is see if I can figure out how far dilated you are," he went on.

Again, Amy's face remained blank.

"When you're in labor, your cervix dilates," Don said. "Do you know what your cervix is?" He explained it in clinical terms, then told her to think of an upside-down pear. "And where the stem would be, that's the cervix. Anyway, it has to stretch so that the baby can come out. That stretching part is called dilation."

Amy flicked a bug off her leg.

"The more you're dilated, the closer the baby is to being born. And the less you're dilated—well, it means you have some more time."

"Time! Oh, please," Susan whispered.

"You might want to explain how you check for dilation," Jill suggested.

"Oh! Well, to tell how dilated you are," Don said, "I would have to do an internal exam. And what that means is, I'd have everyone clear out, and I'd insert a few fingers into the birth canal and measure your cervix."

At this point he paused. Amy's face still held no expression, and he looked from person to person, as though waiting for another prompt. Jill leaned forward and cleared her throat.

"Amy," she said, smoothing the girl's hair, "this is something we need to find out. It might be a little uncomfortable, but it's nothing you can't deal with. Not compared to these contractions, anyway."

"Who gives," Amy murmured, without opening her eyes.

"She's right," Susan said. "We have to find out."

"Shut up, Mom," said Amy.

Susan sat back. Without a word, she stood up and walked out of the tent.

"Let's clear out," JT told the small group that remained. "Let's give Amy and Don some privacy. Lloyd, how about if you go check on Ruth? Make sure she's drinking enough. I don't want her getting dehydrated."

"Certainly," Lloyd said.

"Peter, go see what the boys are up to."

"Yessir," said Peter.

JT felt happy to be able to delegate jobs again. But as he shook the tingles out of his legs, he saw Lloyd out in the sun, smoothing the corners of his mouth. He walked over to the old man.

"Check on Ruth?" he prompted.

Lloyd took his hat off, ran his fingers through his hair, and put his hat back on again. JT pointed to the lunch table, where Ruth was busily rearranging the remains of deli meats into something that would look palatable to those who had not yet eaten.

"Oh yes," said Lloyd, trudging toward the table.

"Lloyd," said JT.

Lloyd stopped and turned, squinting.

"I'll bet you were a great doctor," said JT.

Lloyd shrugged. "I did my job."

44

Day Eleven

Below Lava

It was the timing that made it so bad, Susan told herself. That plus the context, being on the river and learning your daughter was, oh, in active labor. Whatever the reason, when Susan heard Amy tell her to shut up, she felt like she'd been stabbed.

Well, it wasn't the nicest thing for her to say, said the Mother Bitch.

Oh, it was rude; definitely it was rude. But the thing was, Amy was always telling her to shut up, and usually it didn't bother her in the least. When Susan complimented her on a new T-shirt, for instance, or tried to commiserate about the stress of taking five AP classes. *Shut up, Mom.* Susan always saw it as an affectionate warning that she was laying it on a little thick; and while she didn't like to admit it, sometimes it made her feel like part of a privileged club.

But not today. Today the three little words sent a jolt through her heart, so swift and damaging that she had to flee the tent.

She felt not only rejected by her daughter but humiliated and incompetent as well. What kind of mother didn't know her daughter was pregnant? Didn't she notice Amy gaining weight? Didn't she notice they weren't going through tampons at the regular rate? Didn't she wonder why Amy was throwing up before school?

Why, she hadn't even wondered if Amy was having sex! And what kind of mother didn't wonder about that nowadays, with all the news reports, all the magazine articles about hooking up and STDs and middle-school girls giving blow jobs in the school bathrooms? What kind of mother didn't at least speculate?

Susan, that's who. And why? Because Amy was fat. Fat girls didn't have boyfriends and didn't have sex.

It made her want to throw herself into the river, to think she'd fallen for such a stereotype.

Oh, stop it now, said the Mother Bitch. *It's not like she has cancer.*

Susan knew that. She also knew that this was not the time to beat herself up for her mistakes or to cower from a few sharp words—not with Amy about to give birth under a makeshift tent at the bottom of the Grand Canyon. But she couldn't stop hurting. All the other times, *Shut up* meant *Oh mom, you dork you.* Today, it meant *Go away. I truly hate you. I don't want your help. Ever.*

"Susan?"

She turned to find Jill standing behind her. Susan instantly flashed on their foolish little cocktail hours, all their so-called meaningful talks about kids and husbands and whatever. This while her own daughter was walking around in labor.

Jill put her hand on her shoulder. Susan folded her arms tightly across her chest and moved away.

"It happens," Jill said. "I've read about it. Anyone could miss it. Anyone—"

"Stop. Just stop. I'm her mother. I should have known."

Jill fell silent, but if Susan had spoken too sharply, she didn't care. Everyone could offer explanations, everyone could excuse her, but they weren't in her position. Jill certainly didn't know how it felt to realize you'd been so blind that you could fix your daughter breakfast and drive her to school and visit colleges and sleep next to her in a tiny pup tent—and not know. Jill had boys, not girls, and didn't understand that from the moment Amy was born, consciously or not, Susan had been waiting for the day her daughter announced she was intentionally, happily pregnant, so that she, Susan, could exult, commiserate, advise. And now—to suddenly learn that an unplanned pregnancy had happened without either of them knowing!

A movement caught her eye, and she saw Evelyn shuffling toward them, a water bottle dangling from her finger. Susan bristled; she didn't think she could bear the presence of this odd, serious woman who held a PhD in molecular biology but possessed no sense of how to commune with the human race.

Evelyn hesitated, then said, "Abo chipped off some of the ice from the cooler, and I gave Amy some ice chips to suck on."

"Thank you, Evelyn," said Jill.

Evelyn hovered.

"Don't say it," warned Susan.

"All right," said Evelyn.

Startled, Susan looked at Evelyn, who was standing there awkwardly.

"What do you want?" Susan said harshly.

Evelyn thrust the water bottle at her. "It's mostly ice," she said. "I thought it would help you too."

Shamed by this token of kindness, Susan held the bottle against her breastbone. It made her feel cool all over.

"Thank you," she managed.

"Let's sit," Jill said.

Susan shook her head in misery, but then she sat and hugged her knees to her chest. Jill and Evelyn sat down on either side.

"All right," Jill began. "You didn't know. You missed the signs. But Amy needs you right now."

"Amy doesn't need me," said Susan. "Amy doesn't want me, either."

Evelyn looked anxious. "I don't think that's true," she said. "Of course Amy needs you. Of course she wants you. How can you say she doesn't?"

"Maybe because I've got some experience with a teenager, Evelyn," Susan said. Evelyn looked down, and Susan knew she had hurt this childless woman who was never going to face these muddled issues. But Susan didn't care. Hot tears spilled out.

"Why didn't she tell me?" she cried.

"She didn't know," Jill said.

"But she didn't even tell me she was having sex! Did she think I would scold her? Tell her she was too young? She was—is—but I would never have scolded her! I would have taken her to the doctor, and then the doctor would have examined her, and we'd have known, and we wouldn't be here on the Colorado River with her going into labor!"

Jill and Evelyn both laid a hand on Susan's shoulder.

"I'm a failure," Susan sobbed.

"Phooey," said Evelyn.

"In fact, I'm such a failure that not only do I not know my daughter is pregnant, but when she's suddenly going into labor, all I can think about is how bad a parent I am. Isn't *that* rich!"

Evelyn looked thoughtful for a moment. "So what you're saying is, you're a failure because not only have you failed your daughter, but in the process of failing her, all you can focus on is how you've failed?"

Susan sobbed harder. "And I've done this all my life too. I always make everything all about *me*. No wonder Amy doesn't open up—she knows she'll just have to sit and listen to me talk about how it was for me me me, way back when."

Evelyn and Jill pondered this.

"I've just been trying so hard to connect with her," Susan said. "And nothing works."

"Maybe not until now," Jill said gently. "But you can't just walk away when she needs you the most. You have to be the strong one right now."

"You certainly do! I'd lay down the law with that girl," Evelyn declared, and she smacked a fist into her palm. "I'd say, 'Amy, I don't care what you say, I'm going to be right here by your side from start to finish!' "

Susan smiled wanly, for she'd had yet to witness this passionate side of Evelyn. She thought she would like to watch Evelyn teach a class sometime. Once she'd had a teacher who was passionate about wind patterns over the Pacific. By the end of the class, everyone else was passionate about wind patterns over the Pacific too.

She wiped her nose. "I'm not usually so thin-skinned."

"I think it's being on the river," Evelyn said.

"Watching your daughter go into labor might have something to do with it too," added Jill.

The three women helped each other stand up. Susan inhaled

deeply. Her eyes stung from salt and sun, and she wanted again to walk into the river and float away.

Instead, she gave a shaky little laugh. "My heart," she said hoarsely. "I feel like it's right here," and she patted her arm.

"Well," said Evelyn, "well, you just keep it right there, if that's what you need to do."

"How soon for the helicopter?" JT asked Abo.

"We're next in line."

JT drew a deep breath.

"Doing a swell job, Boss," said Abo.

"Keep telling me that."

"How can a girl not know she's pregnant?" Abo asked, after a while.

"No clue."

"Ever delivered a baby in the canyon?"

"Never delivered a baby, period. But we're not going to deliver a baby. The helicopter's going to come and it's going to fly her away to the Happy Hospital and we're going to have our Lava Falls Boating Club party tonight."

"Do you really think we'll be in the mood for a party?"

"No."

Abo paused, frowning. "I just don't get it," he said. "How can you not know?"

Ruth twisted the cap of the mustard bottle and wiped off the little brown disk that clung to the nozzle.

"He's probably just stuck in an eddy," Mitchell told the two boys. They were standing at the downstream end of the beach. Matthew was looking through Mitchell's binoculars.

"Do you see anything?" asked Sam.

"No," said Matthew.

"Can I look?" said Sam.

Matthew handed the binoculars to Sam. Mitchell patiently showed him how to adjust them to fit. "Just look for the red bandanna," he said. "That would make it easy to spot him."

"He had his life jacket on," said Sam, screwing up his face behind the lenses. "Didn't he?"

"Of course he did," said Mitchell.

"He's a really good swimmer," said Matthew.

"Then we'll find him," said Mitchell.

45

Day Eleven

Below Lava

The man's eyes were kind and gentle, and the first thing he did was to cover her with a fresh cool sheet from the waist down. Then he pulled on an exam glove.

"I want to do this in between contractions," he said. "Can I slip your shorts off?"

Without answering, Amy lifted her hips. She was in the Grand Canyon, people thought she was in labor, and she was going to have to let a doctor examine her to prove she wasn't pregnant. She had a cyst, a cyst the size of a grapefruit, just like a girl she'd read about in *Glamour*. Now she was in the process of expelling it. Probably like a kidney stone. Anyway, to get through this exam, she would pretend she was someone else—a college girl, say, someone who had a boyfriend and rode her bike across campus for the kind of female checkup that college girls get.

Sitting at her side, her mother laid a damp T-shirt over her chest. The cotton jersey was cool and soothed her skin. She found it hard to imagine that she had been so cold, after swimming Lava.

"How are you doing, honey?" Susan asked.

"Crappy. Is he a—" She couldn't think of the right word.

"I'm not an obstetrician," said Don as he folded her shorts and set them aside, "but I think I can help you through this. Scooch toward me a little. Draw up your knees. Try and relax. Sorry," he said, looking up sheepishly. "I guess that's like telling someone to relax in Lava."

Amy tentatively let her knees fall apart. She was a college girl. She did this all the time. Her mother sat calmly beside her. Amy was impressed that she wasn't flipping out.

"I hear you took a pretty good swim," Don said. "And I'll bet your baby said the hell with it, I'd be safer on my own."

Amy wanted to remind him that it was a cyst, but she didn't want to make him feel dumb.

"Let's see what we've got," said Don. "Nice and easy. Deep breath. Here we go."

For Amy, it felt like he was sticking a baseball bat up inside her. And when she thought he wouldn't push any further, he did. And it hurt. It felt like another whole contraction. Or rather, that thing they said was a contraction but that wasn't really a contraction.

"Okay," Don murmured, placing his other hand on her stomach. "Okay," and he gazed off toward the river. Amy could feel continents shifting inside her. She waited as long as she could.

"So?" she said.

The worst thing in the world during a doctor's exam is sudden silence. Amy tried to think back to what Don had told her, about what he was going to check for. Something about dilation. Something about her cervix. He was expecting a baby, and she was expecting a cyst, but a third possibility suddenly occurred to her: Maybe it wasn't a baby *or* a cyst! Maybe it was something much, much worse!

Don removed his hand and pulled off the glove and placed it on top of her shorts.

"You said you've been having stomachaches?"

"They weren't that bad," she said.

"For how long?"

"I don't know. Maybe a week."

"Nausea? Diarrhea?"

"A little."

"Back pain?"

"Some."

Don stood up and squeezed her knee. "I'll be right back," he said, and he motioned to Susan, and they both ducked out from under the tarp. Amy watched as they went over to where JT and Jill were standing together. He said something to them, and her mother made a sudden movement in the direction of the tent, but Don took hold of her arm and held her back.

I'm dying, she thought. They all know it, and they're wondering how to tell me.

I should have drowned in Lava.

The next contraction came without warning, while she was still alone. One moment there was a twinge of tightening, and before she could call for help, her stomach had frozen into an alien, rock-hard dome. Heavy machinery began scouring her insides. The pain was worse than before, something she wouldn't have thought possible. Someone shrieked, and immediately people were kneeling beside her. Somebody cradled her head, and she turned and vomited all over somebody else's knees, the stench hanging heavily in the air. She was afraid she was going to lose control of her bowels. She felt something cool on her cheek and grabbed whatever it was and bit down hard and pounded the ground with her fists. All this with a cork plugging her windpipe.

Then all the heavy machinery went still, and she was able to breathe. When she opened her eyes, her mother, Jill, Don, and Peter were all kneeling around her. Peter gently extricated the bandanna from between her teeth, and her mother held a cup of cool water to her lips.

"Go ahead, tell me," she said flatly. "I'm dying, aren't I."

"No, you're not dying," Don said. "As it turns out, you're about nine centimeters dilated. Which means your baby is pretty eager to make its entry into the world. I didn't expect to find you so far along. But I think you've been in the beginning stages of labor for a day, maybe even a few days. That back pain? The stomachaches that came and went? I'm actually surprised you stood it so well."

"I'm not pregnant," Amy said. "I have a cyst."

Don leaned forward. "It's not a cyst, Amy," he said. "You're one hundred and ten percent pregnant. And you're about to have the baby."

"No," said Amy. "No, I am not!"

Her mother's face appeared. "Yes, you are, honey," she said. "We're going to walk you through it."

"No," said Amy, feeling the panic rise up. "You guys don't understand! I'm not pregnant!" She refused to give in on this. It simply couldn't be. She was not going to try to remember anything—not when or who or where. And she wasn't going to give in to the humiliation that would come if she had to admit something like this. Because for a girl to go nine months without knowing she was pregnant seemed like the ultimate in cluelessness. And she was a smart girl. She'd scored 2400 on her SATs. She was going to be applying to good colleges this fall. She was going to be that skinny college girl, biking across campus to meet her boyfriend.

"Amy, listen," and now Don's face appeared in her circle of vision, and he looked directly into her eyes. "You *are* going to have a baby. Soon. It's already on its way. There's no other way out. It's like going down a rapid. Once you're in the tongue, you're committed."

Amy shook her head.

"You can do it," said Don, "because you have to do it. Try and rest because there will be another contraction coming."

"No," Amy sobbed.

"Don't cry!" Don said sharply. "You can't cry right now. When we get this baby out you can cry all you want, but right now, you can't cry."

Her mother squeezed her hand. "He's right. Save your strength. This is the worst part. Make it through this, and you can make it through anything."

"How do you know?" Amy snapped.

Her mother laid a freshly dampened bandanna across Amy's forehead. "Because I've been there. Once you get to ten centimeters, then you can start to push, and it'll hurt too but not like this. This part is hell. The contractions are long and intense and come one right after another."

Indeed, another one was starting—the tightening, the choking sensation, the deep imploding pain. She felt like she was being disemboweled. She tried to hold back a sob, but she was too afraid—afraid of the pain right now and also afraid of all the pain to follow. Don was right: there was no way out of this. Everywhere she looked, there was pain.

Voices shouted but they were in the next world over. "I can't do this!" she screamed.

"Yes, you can," said her mother. "Breathe!"

"I can't!"

"Amy," and she felt her mother's hands upon her face, turning her so that she was looking into her eyes. Her mother held up her index finger, right in front of Amy's mouth. "Amy. Look at my finger. See my finger? I want you to pretend it's a candle. Now blow it out!"

Amy wrenched her head away, but her mother turned it back and continued to hold up her finger.

"Blow," her mother commanded.

Amy pursed her lips and managed a little puff.

"That's right! Blow! Blow the candle out, honey! Deep breath in! Now little blows! That's great, honey. You're doing great!"

Amy squeezed her mother's finger and tried to blow. The pain was both within and without, evil, twisting and stretching, and there was no letting up, no lessening of the force.

"Blow," her mother said, and Amy was so angry at the pain that she grabbed her mother's finger and bit down hard.

Afterward her mother sat back and wrung her hand.

"I'm sorry," Amy said. "Did I break the skin?"

Her mother held up her finger. There was no blood, just a row of pink molar tracks. "Next time maybe just blow?"

"Next time she gets a stick," said Peter.

Amy didn't laugh. "More ice."

Susan stood up. "I'll be right back. Before the next one."

Amy didn't want to be reminded of the next one. She closed her eyes and tried to go limp. The strangest images came to her from far away: her chemistry teacher's voice as he handed out their final, the smell of rain on hot pavement. The lack of pain right now was cool and sweet. She had already lost all sense of time, but now she felt herself floating as well, and she heard a humming sound. Then she felt something touch her lips, and she opened her eyes and saw that Peter was holding a cup for her. His beard was bristly, and his hair rose in sweaty spikes from his forehead. Everyone else was gone.

Amy tried to take a sip, but it made her nauseous, and she belched loudly.

"It's so bad," she told him. "It's unbelievably bad."

"You can do it."

"How?"

"You will," he said. "You just will."

Amy had heard those words many times, but hearing them from Peter was different. For the first time, she believed them.

Although if anyone—Peter included—asked who the father was, she would get up and walk straight into the river and never return. She would. She really would.

"The camera!" she said, suddenly remembering. "I lost it! All those pictures!"

"Fuck 'em."

This made sense. "Did you see what I did to my mother's finger?"

"Hell yeah. Stay away from me."

Amy closed her eyes. Peter held her hand, and as she began to pant (and no, she wasn't getting good at it, there was just no other way to breathe), she sensed other people gathering around her.

But something different was happening now. Instead of feeling like she was being torn apart inside, she felt like she had to go to the bathroom. The pain was back just as strong as before, but now she needed to get to a toilet. This was terrible. The timing was awful. What were they going to do if she made a big mess on the sand? JT had made them be so careful the whole time, to protect the river ecology. And now she was going to pollute the whole beach.

But it was already coming, and there was nothing she could do but bear down and grunt like a beast and push.

46

Day Eleven

Below Lava

JT could feel it before he actually heard it, the thrumming in his chest that always put his nerves on edge when he was on the river. Automatically he looked up into the sky. Abo looked up too.

"Right on schedule, Boss," he said, just before the sound of gunfire ripped through the canyon. Everyone on the beach craned their necks and shaded their eyes. In the next second, the helicopter materialized, a sparkling bubble sashaying up the river corridor.

"Get back!" JT shouted, waving his arms. "Over there, by the bushes! Sam! Matthew! Get out of the water!"

He and Abo ran out and rolled up the orange panels they'd laid out earlier to mark their location for Search and Rescue. The helicopter hovered, then lowered itself onto the beach, spraying sand and rippling the smooth waters of the shoreline eddy. The pilot cut the motor, and a man and a woman hopped down out of the cockpit and ran, crouching, over to where JT and Abo awaited them.

"Is there a baby yet?" the man shouted.

"No!"

They hurried toward the tented area. "I'm Andy," the man said. "This is Barb. What's going on?"

"Seventeen-year-old girl," JT told them. "Swam Lava and went into labor."

"When did she start?"

"Three hours ago. But she's already pushing. Listen, I don't want that baby getting born down here," JT said. "Just so we're clear on that."

Before Andy could answer, Amy let forth another scream, and JT had to summon every bit of emotional strength not to cover his ears like a child. He had a strong stomach, and even in emergencies he could usually remain calm, but Amy's scream released a sickening flush of adrenaline.

Because of this, he stayed outside the tented area while Andy and Barb ducked inside. He crossed his arms and shoved his hands into his armpits and wondered what to do. Abo and Dixie were back at the helicopter, talking to the pilot. They didn't need him in the tent, and they didn't need him at the helicopter. JT felt like an extraneous uncle, so he was caught off guard when Jill stepped out from underneath the shade of the tent.

"Please tell me they're going to be able to get her out of here before she delivers that baby," he said.

"I wish," said Jill.

"The Flagstaff ER's less than an hour away," he said. "That's not very far."

"A lot can happen in an hour."

"Don't say that."

"You're the Trip Leader," she reminded him. "You have to be prepared."

She was right, of course; he was captain of this voyage. But never had he felt like such a passenger on someone else's boat.

Jill seemed to sense this, because she took his arm and led him away from the tent, toward the water's edge. JT stood where the sand was soft and wet and let his feet sink down into the cold. He wanted to wade in and dunk himself until the water filled his ears and made his head ache, just to drown out the bad thoughts.

"I don't mean this in a disrespectful way, JT," she began, "but I don't think you have any clue what it's like for Amy right now. And it's kind of been a while for me, Sam being twelve and all, but when I was pushing my babies out, if you had told me you were going to load me into a helicopter, I'd have put a gun to your head."

"But it's up to the paramedics, isn't it?"

"In theory," said Jill. "But if I have any vote in the matter, you know where I stand."

The back of his throat felt bitter and dry, and JT found he could not look at Jill any longer. Here was a woman who, twelve days ago, had been but a name on a list, a thirty-eight-year-old mother from Salt Lake City with no allergies and the stated goal of making her boys forget about basketball camp for a few days. Yet now, here, below Lava, on her first trip, she seemed endowed with Solomonic wisdom. And what did that say about him? What had he learned, on 125 trips? How to run Crystal? Anyone with any sense could do it. How to feed large crowds in the wilderness? Read a book. Why, Jill could have done all that, and more—she could have delivered this baby herself if the paramedics hadn't come.

What he'd learned, on all his trips, was how to be alone. And right now, he wasn't even very good at that.

"Are you drinking enough water?" Jill asked. "Because you don't look so great."

JT repositioned his visor.

"Do you always smile when you're flipping out?"

JT put his hands on his hips. How was it she knew him so well? She held his gaze until he himself broke it and looked out across the river. He felt on the verge of tears, and he wasn't a man to cry. He picked up a rock and threw it in the river and watched the current swallow the rings.

"I've spent half my life on this river," he said. "I've seen heart attacks. I've seen appendicitis. I've seen rattlesnake bites and broken legs with the bone sticking out, and I've even had one guy pull a knife on me. But I've never had anyone go into labor."

"Well, I don't mean to scare you. This baby seems to have a mind of its own, but everything will turn out fine."

"Or not."

"If you're going to be thinking like that, then you should go for a walk."

"I'm not going anywhere," said JT.

"Then calm down," said Jill. "Have a beer if you need it. But shame on you for saying that. We've got a doctor and two paramedics with Amy. Things may go a little faster than we'd hoped, but they won't go wrong. And you can't keep thinking like they will. Because you know what happens if you do?"

"What?"

"When you lose your confidence, you lose everything. You said it yourself."

"I said that?"

"Several times."

JT knew he'd said it, but it sounded far more convincing coming from someone else. Half in jest, he asked if she wanted a job. "Pay kinda sucks," he admitted.

"You guys are such bullshit artists."

"I'm not kidding. I can teach you everything," said JT.

"You already have," said Jill.

And this embarrassed them both, so they turned their attention to Sam, who was arguing with Abo.

"No, you cannot take one of the boats," they heard Abo say. "Go play with the dog."

"But that's the thing," Sam said.

Of course, one look at Amy and the paramedics knew they weren't going anywhere. Not until after the baby was born, anyway. They weren't going to move her out of the tent, they weren't going to load her onto a stretcher, they weren't going to risk being in the air when this baby decided to make its entry into the world.

While Barb looped oxygen tubing around Amy's ears, Andy radioed the hospital in Flagstaff. Then he inserted an IV into the back of Amy's hand. Peter, who had not left Amy's side since she started pushing, sat and held her other hand as she gasped for air between pushes. He didn't know what to say to her to make her feel better. The whole thing looked like torture to him, and he was trying his best not to imagine what was going to have to happen to her body for this baby to get from Point A to Point B.

Meanwhile, the paramedics had opened up their bags and removed an entire closet of medical supplies—pads and kits and masks and more plastic bags of clear fluids than Peter wanted to imagine the need for. Susan, who was cradling Amy's head, asked Don if, now that they had the IV in place, they could give Amy something for the pain.

"Actually, I'm going to defer to the paramedics on that," said Don.

"But you're the doctor," said Susan.

Don allowed a hint of a smile. "I'm going to guess these guys have more experience delivering babies than I do. In fact, I'm going to move aside," he told them, "and let you two take over. Just let me know how I can help."

Andy stationed himself between Amy's legs while Barb continued to monitor the IV bag and the oxygen.

Susan looked at Barb expectantly. "So? Can she have something?"

"I'm not trying to be sadistic about this," Barb said. "But I'm afraid it'll slow things down."

"But maybe that's what we want to do," Susan said. "Then we could get her to the hospital."

"No way am I taking a chance on delivering a baby in a helicopter," said Andy.

Just then Amy began groaning again. Peter, who by now considered himself an expert on the warning signs of impending pain, announced to all that another contraction was coming on.

"Okay, Amy," said Andy. "Make this one count. I want to see the baby's head."

Amy moaned as Susan slid her arms underneath Amy's shoulders from behind, bracing her so Amy could put everything she had into bearing down. Peter and Don each did the same from down below, hooking their arms around her legs. It was a most awkward, animalistic position, and yet Peter found that it didn't faze him in the least to be doing this. As the contraction bore down, Amy brayed for ten, fifteen, twenty seconds.

"She's crowning!" Andy announced.

"You can see the head?" Susan cried. "Amy, did you hear that? He can see the head!"

"Lotta hair," Andy murmured.

"Hair!" Susan cried in wonder.

Amy took another breath and made that awful squeezing, grunting sound again.

"Push!" everyone shouted. "Push, Amy, push! Keep pushing!"

"Okay, stop now," Andy said. "You want to take a look, Gramma?"

Scrubbing the tears off her cheeks, Susan scooted down to where Andy was positioned, between Amy's legs. "Oh," she breathed. "Oh, Amy. There she is. Or he! Oh," she said. "Honey, you're going to have a baby!"

"I know that, Mom!" Amy shouted. "Get back here and hold my arms!"

Susan scooted back up to position herself by Amy's head again. But she bent her face down to Amy's ear. "It's beautiful, honey," she whispered.

"I don't care if it's beautiful!" Amy shouted. "Get it out of me!"

"Want to see?" Andy asked Peter.

"No thanks," said Peter.

"Okay then, Amy," said Andy. "Next push, I want the head out. But not too fast. I don't want you to tear."

"Scissors?" Barb asked.

"Not yet," said Andy.

"You really should see it, Peter," said Susan.

"Oh!" cried Amy. "It's half in and half out!"

"Not quite yet," said Andy calmly. "But we're getting close."

"Just take a peek," Susan urged Peter.

"Mom! Shut up!" Amy screamed. She began to pant, and Susan, Peter, and Don took up their counterpoint positions again, and Amy took a deep breath, and for Peter it seemed as though Amy was trying to pull them all into her heart. She folded and squeezed and grunted, and suddenly Andy shouted, "The head's out! Now hold! Don't push anymore! Suction!" and Barb handed him a little blue bulb, and Peter couldn't see what Andy was doing with it and didn't really want to see.

"I can't hold it!" Amy cried.

Andy said, "You have to! Just pant!" Peter, who suddenly felt more like part of any team than he'd ever felt in his entire life, relayed this command to Amy and told her again to pant, and he was amazed when she followed his command. Her eyes were wild with fear now, and she seemed completely dependent on his instructions. "Pant!" he kept telling her, over and over, and when this contraction had ended and

Amy was still looking terrified, he thought, What an awful, awful thing, to have a baby half in and half out of you!

"It's okay!" he whispered to her. "I think you're almost there."

"One more push, Amy," said Andy.

"Oh!" sobbed Amy. "I can't I can't I can't," but then she drew in the longest, deepest breath she'd yet taken and squeezed so hard that Peter couldn't look at her face for fear that something would pop, and then—just like that—this *thing* torpedoed out from between her legs, this blue-gray seal with a rubbery corkscrew tail, shooting out so fast that Andy almost failed to catch it. But he did catch it, and the next thing Peter knew, Andy was cradling the waxy limp thing in his hands. It was a boy, and it was still and lifeless, alien and quiet, and what was first and foremost on Peter's mind had nothing to do with the miracle of birth but rather who in this group was going to have the courage to tell Amy that her baby was dead.

Andy laid the baby on his side across his lap. He worked quickly and with both hands at once, suctioning the baby's nose and mouth and vigorously toweling him dry.

"He's not crying," said Amy.

Andy said something under his breath.

"What's happening?" said Amy, looking from Susan to Peter. "Somebody tell me what's happening!"

Peter knew that the right thing to do at the moment would be to give Amy a running narrative of what he could see, since she was lying flat on her back and her stomach was still just as big as it was before the baby came out. But all he saw was Andy rubbing the baby so hard that it looked like he might be giving the baby a flesh burn.

"Just look at those balls," Lloyd announced, peering over.

"Why isn't he crying?" Peter whispered to Don.

"Like you think I can't hear?" Amy screamed. "Why isn't the baby crying!"

Just then there came a faint trebly sound, a feeble little wail that seemed to string its way from ear to ear among those in the group. And then it came again, louder now, and a cheer erupted. The baby's skin flushed pink, and moments later, with a big smile, Andy reached over and placed him on Amy's stomach.

Amy looked stunned. "Do I touch him?"

Andy laughed. "Of course."

Amy shifted, and Peter had the good sense to help her partially sit up so she could hold the baby. He had done a pretty good job of not looking at Amy's breasts during this whole ordeal, but he could not help but look now as Amy cradled the baby. He had never seen breasts that big before. Nor had he ever felt so free to stare.

Susan bent down so that she was cheek to cheek with Amy. "A boy, honey," she said. "A baby boy."

Amy, still in a daze, stroked the baby's hand with her pinkie, and the baby grasped it. Peter sat back. He felt frayed and raw, exhausted and exhilarated, even a little proud of himself for his role in the birth.

In the meantime, Andy had placed a blue plastic clamp on the umbilical cord. He must have assumed Peter was the father because he handed him a small pair of scissors. "Cord?"

But this was a privilege that Peter didn't feel entitled to. He handed the scissors to Susan, who wasn't even making an effort anymore to wipe her cheeks. She sniffed loudly and took the scissors and held them against the rubbery tube, paused momentarily, and squeezed. The long tail fell away and Barb dabbed the translucent stump with a wipe.

Meanwhile, a crowd had gathered around the tent, for they had heard the shouts a few minutes back.

"Lloyd?" said Don. "You want the honor?"

Lloyd solemnly put his watch into his pocket and went out into the sun. He cleared his throat and searched among the faces. "Ruthie?"

Ruth stepped forward. "Right here, Lloyd."

The crowd waited. Lloyd was wheezing slightly. He shaded his eyes and kept looking from face to face.

"Lloyd," said Ruth, touching his arm.

"I'm so confused," he told her. "Who are all these people?"

"Was the baby born?" she asked gently.

"Yes."

"Is it healthy?"

"Oh yes."

"Is it a boy or a girl?"

There was a long silence as everyone waited.

"It's a boy," he finally said.

"Oh, how wonderful," said Ruth, smiling broadly.

The announcement seemed to have wrung every last bit of strength from the man. He hobbled across a patch of sand to sit on a rock nearby. He took out his handkerchief and wiped his brow. He patted his pockets, and when Ruth handed him her water bottle, he drank deeply, then wiped his mouth, making little sighing sounds, as though having a bad dream.

"Are you all right, Lloyd?"

The old man's face had grown pale. He dabbed his chest with his handkerchief, and Ruth could see now that he was sweating profusely. All sorts of worries ran through her mind.

"Lloyd? Can you see me?"

Lloyd gazed around.

"Can you hear me, Lloyd?"

He patted his pockets again and frowned.

"Where are we?" he asked, looking up. "How did we get here? I'm so confused, Ruthie," he said. "I don't understand any of this."

"Now now," said Ruth. "I'm right here."

"Don't leave me alone like that! I don't know any of these people!"

"There, there," she said, stroking his temple.

From a short distance away, Peter watched the old couple together. It pained him deeply to see Lloyd like this, but at the same time he thought about how lucky they were, to have each other right now. To take this trip, to manage the ins and outs of old age together. And he tried to imagine himself in their shoes, and found it was not as difficult as he might have thought two weeks ago, even if it wasn't Miss Ohio taking his hand and leading him off to sit down and collect himself.

47

Day Eleven

Below Lava

They had no diapers, of course, but the blue high-tech towels everyone had brought along were just the right size. Duct tape held things in place, and thus the baby was kept from squirting all over as the paramedics readied things for Amy's transport.

There was momentary confusion when Susan insisted on going, for the helicopter would not hold mother, daughter, baby, and two paramedics. But Barb volunteered to stay behind and wait for the pilot to make a second trip.

Everybody gathered around the stretcher to say good-bye. Jill leaned over and kissed Amy's forehead. Dixie draped her blue sarong over her, and Peter fussed with the edges, straightening things out. Evelyn smiled broadly, grasping for words that never came. JT stood back and gave Amy his thumbs-up.

"Time's a-wastin'," said Andy.

They hoisted the stretcher up into the helicopter; Susan followed, and when she was settled in her seat, Andy handed her the baby. He was light as a doll, his mouth a tiny pout between fat round cheeks, and Susan just stared and stared into his funny, angry little face. She was full of questions for Amy—who and when and how and where, for starters—and as she gazed at the baby's features she couldn't help wondering who among Amy's classmates he looked like. She scolded herself because it didn't matter; besides, it was futile, because what baby really looked like his father an hour after birth? All newborns looked like little Russians to her.

But wonder she would.

And what would happen next? Would Amy want to keep the baby or put him up for adoption? If she kept him, how would she manage her senior year, with college on the horizon? How would she manage college itself, for that matter? Susan thought with a twinge of guilt about some of the plans she'd had for herself, once Amy left home—training for a marathon, for example, or taking Spanish. If Amy kept the baby—well, Susan imagined herself doing a lot of babysitting.

And finally, all those unanswerable questions. Was love a factor, or had this been a simple hookup? Had Susan failed to pass along some fundamental biological facts? And still: How could she herself have missed all the flashing lights? Fool!

The helicopter motor started up, drowning out any chance for conversation. Andy climbed up and buckled himself into his seat. With a slight jolt, the helicopter lifted straight up into the sky. Amy strained to look down but winced as she did so and lay back as they swung up over the canyon rim and headed east. Susan cradled the baby to her chest and peered down. The view was already panoramic, a vast branching tableau of tan and pink and dusty green, with a tiny silver ribbon weaving in and out. It was just like what the Grand Canyon was supposed to look like, and nothing like what it really was, down on the river.

"See Lava?" the pilot shouted over his shoulder, pointing to a fingernail of white.

Amy now managed to hoist herself on her elbows to look down. Instinctively Susan threw out her arm to guard her daughter. It was sudden and unnecessary—and wouldn't have been effective anyway—and it reminded her of her own mother years ago, throwing her arm across the front seat when braking quickly, to keep Susan from flying through the windshield.

Just then the baby's face broke, and he began to yawl. Susan jiggled him a little. Amy looked on, her eyes flat and expressionless. The baby continued to cry.

Then Amy reached out and stroked the baby's cheek, almost as much out of curiosity as anything else. He scowled in her direction, and without giving it much thought, she slipped the tip of her little finger into his mouth, and he grew quiet; and Susan glimpsed in Amy's face something that she, Susan, had forgotten: the sudden, wondrous awareness of one's innate maternal magic.

Emboldened by this, Susan leaned forward and tucked a strand of hair behind Amy's ear. And just as boldly, Amy gazed back without flinching.

Below, on the beach, everyone stood in a daze as the helicopter lifted off. Some, like Jill, felt the emotion finally hit them, like delayed thunder. Others recounted to one another their small roles in the birth sequence—Dixie giving Amy her blue sarong, for instance, when she started shivering; Evelyn recording every single contraction in her notebook.

Only the two boys seemed eager to put it behind them. They were glad to see the fat girl go, because it meant they could finally get back on the river again, and find the dog.

48

Day Eleven

Below Lava

Post-Lava Night was usually a time for celebration. The guides were glad to have made it safely through; the passengers felt as though they'd been initiated into a new club; and everyone had an intense need to keep recounting the run—the V-wave, the whirlpools, the bailing and sloshing and screaming and slipping and lurching about in between. Often it was a time to dress up; Abo had packed an entire duffel bag of costumes, including a hula skirt and a horned Viking hat, and Dixie had a collection of nail polishes, which she'd planned on setting out for a toenail-painting contest. Oh, things could get jolly after Lava, with songs and skits and the presentation of goofy awards, and people stumbled off to bed feeling like true river runners.

But tonight, the Post-Lava party never materialized. JT had decided to camp there below Lava, since they'd already unloaded half their gear. The bucket of margaritas was well received (Mark declined, though he filled a mug for Jill); but mostly they were still too overwhelmed by the events of the afternoon to celebrate. At times, some of them wondered if they'd imagined the birth; but then they would look around, and Amy and Susan's absence would erase their doubts. Jill and Peter, who'd served as coaches, both agreed they felt a little cheated—they'd worked so hard alongside Amy that they felt personally vested in this new family, and now they had nothing to show for it.

"I just wanted to hold him a little more," said Jill wistfully. "He was so tiny!"

"I thought he was dead," Peter declared. "Are all babies that gray?"

Then, of course, there was the matter of the dog. Sam and Matthew refused to give up hope that he would come loping over the rocks, tail wagging, panting, in a scene straight out of a Disney movie. They were certain he'd survived the swim, and no one really wanted to convince them otherwise.

"They shouldn't get their hopes up, though," JT told Mark. "I think he would have shown up by now if he came ashore in this area. My guess—my hope—is that he got carried farther downstream. He had his life jacket on good and tight. With some luck, we'll find him downstream tomorrow."

The fact that he hadn't seen the dog go overboard disturbed JT greatly. As an experienced guide, he prided himself on knowing where each and every member of his party was at all times—especially when they were on the water itself. But he'd been so focused on Amy going overboard and then getting his boat safely through Lava, that he hadn't even noticed the dog was gone until they'd pulled onto shore.

"What are the chances?" Jill asked. "Be honest."

"I don't know," he said.

Jill nodded somberly. "I just want to be prepared," she said. "I just want to know what we might be dealing with if he doesn't show up. The boys haven't had anyone or anything die on them before, and I want to be able to say the right thing."

Mark drew her close. "We don't need to cross that bridge."

Everyone just felt so *off.* Mitchell and Lena quarreled publicly over who had lost the eco-shampoo, and Ruth and Lloyd retired to their tent for a nap that went on for so long that JT eventually went and rustled the front flap. Oh dear *god,* he thought, then realized he couldn't finish the thought. Fortunately, Ruth peeked out and groggily confessed that it was the margaritas, and JT, who usually didn't let himself worry too much about his guests' alcohol consumption, felt like scolding them as though they were Sam and Matthew. *You're on medications! You're old and thin and fragile! What were you thinking?*

For dinner there was Thai food, and Abo got a little slapdash with the recipe and added a big dollop of peanut butter to the green beans, which caused Lena's throat to start itching. JT was angry at Abo, not just for being careless, but because now he had to figure out whether they should give Lena the EpiPen; she was over there coughing, and the Benadryl didn't seem to be working, and Mitchell was going to blow, just blow; but then Mitchell came walking up, the light from his headlamp jittering in the dark.

"I gave her the EpiPen," he told them. "She threw up, and she's breathing better. She says her throat doesn't hurt anymore. I'll stay up with her tonight," he told JT. "She'll be fine."

"I'm really sorry this happened," Abo said.

Mitchell shrugged. "We all make mistakes. I've certainly made my share."

JT was so surprised to hear this that he couldn't come up with a gracious response.

"I gotta say," Mitchell went on, "I was so impressed this afternoon, watching you guys deal with Amy and all."

"We just called for help," said JT. "The paramedics did everything else."

"But the real hero is Amy, isn't she?" Mitchell said. "I have to hand it to the girl. She really rose to the occasion. Not that she had a choice. But what a trooper. Seventeen years old. I just hope it doesn't get in the way of her college plans."

"Are you going to put this in your book, Mitchell?" Dixie asked.

"No," said Mitchell. "Nobody would believe it. Well, I'm going to go sit with Lena. But I really think she's going to be okay."

JT watched Mitchell walk off into the darkness. He thought to himself that if they'd given out awards that night, Mitchell certainly would have earned the award for Most Changed Passenger. Because to go from someone who refused to follow directions and insisted on scaring the shit out of everyone and threatened to sue the guides when things didn't go his way—to go from that to someone who could lift the iron chains off the Trip Leader's shoulders at the end of a really difficult day didn't count for nothing, down here in the ditch.

They quickly washed the dishes and stowed away the kitchen supplies. JT retired to his boat and laid out his sleeping bag. He didn't want to let himself think about the fact that the dog wasn't there at his feet, but he couldn't help it. Were the boys hoping for too much? Was he? Because he had to admit that a part of him expected to find the dog tomorrow, alive and well. He knew it was a piss-ass thought and hated himself for having it, but there it was.

He unclipped his sandals, dipped his washcloth into the water, and washed his feet. He got out the tube of cream and unscrewed the cap and squeezed out a dollop and rubbed it in between his toes. He could be thankful that he hadn't gotten the foot fungus on this trip, at least. He could be thankful that the stomach flu hadn't ripped through camp. He could be thankful that he'd had ten good days with a dog who came out of nowhere.

He had a lot of things to be thankful for, but none of them helped him go to sleep that night.

The next day JT took Mitchell and the boys in his boat so they could all scour the shoreline for signs of the dog—a flash of green, maybe, or a red bandanna in the bushes.

Sam and Matthew rode up front, sitting high on the tubes with their legs dangling over the side. The water was calm, and they did not need to hold on to anything. They weren't wearing their hats, and from the back they looked like twins, with their skinny arms poking out of their life jackets, their baggy swim trunks ballooning out below.

There were several false sightings, and the boys' hopes soared, then plummeted.

"We'll find him," said Mitchell after the third time. "I'm sure we'll find him."

Sam whipped around to face JT and Mitchell. "How do you know?" he demanded. "Why should I believe you? You're the one who let go of him."

"Sam," cautioned JT.

"You didn't like this dog from the start! You wanted to leave him on the beach where we found him! I heard you say that! You've been try-ing to get rid of him the whole trip!"

"Come on, Sam," JT warned.

"Sam's right, though," said Matthew, and something in his voice served as a further reminder that they were brothers; that despite the fact that they had been arguing since the day Sam was born, they were, fundamentally, on the same cosmic side of all the things that really mattered. And when it came to a dog and the possibility that some grown man might be responsible for its demise, they were going to stick together.

"Lava was a wild ride," JT reminded them. "I wouldn't go blaming Mitchell for losing the dog."

"But the boys are right," said Mitchell. "I did lose him. He was my responsibility, and I let go. But I didn't mean to. I really didn't mean to."

The boys turned to face downstream again, without answering.

"I really didn't," Mitchell told JT.

"I know you didn't, Mitchell."

"But I want them to believe me."

"They will at some point," said JT. "Maybe just not right now."

There were a few moments of silence as Mitchell shuffled around in the back of the boat. When JT glanced back, Mitchell was ruminating over his unopened journal.

"How'd you get to be so patient, JT?" he asked. "Were you born that way?"

"Hundred and twenty-five trips, I guess."

"How do you get to be a guide, anyway?"

"You interested?"

"Only when I'm feeling adventurous. But I wish I'd done this trip when I was a little younger, you know? Before the old body started breaking down."

"You're never too old to start something new," said JT.

"What about you? You going to keep on doing this the rest of your life?"

JT grinned. "Med school, I'm thinking. Obstetrics."

Both men were silent, remembering the strange events of the previous day.

"I gotta hand it to her," Mitchell said. "She came through with flying colors."

JT didn't want to get into a man-to-man evaluation of Amy's labor and delivery. He glanced at Mitchell's notebook. "What are you going to name this book, anyway?"

"Haven't a clue," said Mitchell.

For the next half hour they floated. The boys kept an optimistic conversation going, convincing each other of the dog's safety. He was wearing his life jacket; he knew how to swim; he knew how to take care of himself in the desert. QED: he would show up at the campsite tonight.

JT didn't want to say anything, but he grew less and less hopeful as the morning wore on. Even with a life jacket, the dog would have been sucked down immediately and remained underwater for who knows how long. In any case, it wouldn't take much time for an animal that size to drown.

He felt it his duty to start preparing the boys, but they were busy concocting elaborate theories about the dog's tracking abilities. They factored in upstream and downstream winds, the need for shade and rest; Matthew, who was good at math, calculated that based on the speed of the water, and depending on where they set up camp, the dog should arrive sometime between five and six o'clock tonight.

"Dogs are so smart," Sam told Matthew.

"Should we keep his name?"

"We can probably come up with something better, if you want."

"I guess I like Blender."

"I like Blender too."

Matthew kicked at the water. "Mom'll never let him sleep in our bedroom, though."

"Nope."

"We'll have to sneak him in."

"Dad'll help, I bet," said Sam.

"When he's not in Japan."

"He told Mom he's not going to spend so much time in Japan," said Sam.

"That would be cool," said Matthew.

49

Day Eleven, Night

Flagstaff

In a small, dimly lit room on the second floor of the Flagstaff hospital, Amy sat propped up in her bed and tried to read the pamphlet on breast-feeding. Beside her, the baby lay in his Plexiglas bassinet, swaddled in flannel. He had been sleeping for half an hour. The nurse had told her she should try and sleep when the baby slept, but she wasn't tired. Her mother had gone out to get them some food, so Amy was alone.

Be sure the baby has a good latch; otherwise you will develop sore nipples. See illustration.

Amy studied the tasteful drawing of the pretty mother's pink round breast, with the Gerber baby sucking away as they gazed lovingly at one another. Amy glanced down. Her boobs were huge and white and veiny and dimpled. And her nipples were *scary;* they'd turned into these big, brown pimply saucers, each with its central rubber knob. If she were a baby, she would take one look and run.

She'd tried nursing him earlier; he'd clumsily batted his head and kissed and sucked, but she didn't know if it counted as a good latch. Whatever that was. Supposedly there would be a lactation consultant coming to visit in the morning. They told her to nurse him even if she didn't know if she was going to keep him or not. Amy wished the night nurse would come and tell her if she was doing it right, but the night nurse had three other mothers to take care of.

Tickle your baby's cheek to stimulate her sucking reflex.

She sat up and peeked into the bassinet. Her baby's head was elongated and pointy and, she wasn't going to lie, pretty ugly. In a slot by his head was a blue card with her name and the name of her doctor;

where the baby's name would have been, they had written simply "Baby Van Doren."

She thought it wise not to think of names.

Drink a full glass of water or juice each time you nurse.

They'd given her a large insulated mug decorated with the hospital's logo and kept it filled with ice water, which tasted good. The drinking water on the river was always warm, and she'd forgotten how good ice water was, and she drank and drank and drank. She'd been so thirsty in the helicopter! During the flight, she'd tried to get a view of the river, but she was trapped on her back, and all could she see were blue sky and a few wispy clouds. She'd never been in a helicopter before and was disappointed that she wasn't in a condition to appreciate the ride. When they landed at the hospital, she felt like she was in a television show, what with all those people running out to meet them. Before she could say anything, they whisked the baby away, and she panicked that she hadn't put some kind of a mark on him to prevent the kind of mix-ups you read about in *National Enquirer.* What if they switched babies on her? Would she know the difference? Had she looked at her baby long enough to recognize a switch?

Spicy foods can affect the taste of your milk. If your baby seems fussy, consider eliminating these foods from your diet.

She'd been hoping her mother would bring back enchiladas; now she wondered if that was a good idea. On the other hand, she might as well test it out and see if it bothered the baby. Maybe he would like enchilada milk.

Soon she heard footsteps in the hallway, and Susan appeared with a bag from Subway. She was still dressed in her river clothes, but she'd taken off her hat; her hair was matted and darker than usual, and a white rim of skin banded her hairline.

"Turkey," she told Amy, handing her the bag. "You'll want to go easy at first."

Hungrily Amy unwrapped the sandwich and took a large bite. It tasted of refrigeration, but it still tasted good. Shreds of lettuce dropped on her chest, and she picked them off and ate them.

"Where's the nurse?" Susan asked, drawing up a chair.

"Busy," said Amy between bites.

"How long has the baby been sleeping?"

"Half an hour."

"Did you get any rest?"

"No," said Amy, "but I read about how much liquid I have to drink. Did you get me a Coke?"

Susan handed her a large cup with a straw. Amy took a long drink, then glanced at her mother. "What about you?"

"I got a sandwich. I already ate it." Susan straightened the blankets on the bed, and Amy watched her slender fingers and recalled their touch earlier, in the helicopter. She could never have said this out loud, but she'd wished her mother would not only move the strands of hair off her forehead but run her fingers through her hair, starting at her temples, over and over, like she used to do when Amy was sick.

"How are you feeling?" Susan asked now.

"Okay."

"Sore?"

"Kind of."

"Maybe they'll let you take a sitz bath."

Amy pictured the plastic basin she occasionally found set upon the toilet bowl in her mother's bathroom. It had always mystified Amy, but suddenly she saw its value.

"You know, I wonder," her mother began, and Amy thought, Here it comes:

Who's the father?

How did this happen?

Didn't you notice your periods stopping?

And what are you going to do with it?

But instead, her mother said, "I wonder if they have a whirlpool. They had a whirlpool in the hospital where I had you. I think I'll go check. I'll be right back."

No, stay, Amy wanted to say, but her mother was already out of the room.

Now the baby stirred. Amy looked over and watched as he arched his back and made a face. What was the theory of swaddling them so tightly? She leaned over the bassinet and slid her hands beneath the little bundle and carefully lifted him up. He weighed absolutely nothing! She untied her hospital gown and held him to her breast and tickled his cheek, just like the book said, and he twisted his mouth to the side, like a little gangster. She stuck her giant nipple in between his lips, but he made funny breathing noises, and she was afraid she would suffocate him, so she held him up, and he began to cry, and she began to cry, and her breasts felt prickly all over, and she wished her mother had not left the room, and she wanted to go back to yesterday, the day before Lava, when she was not a mother, she was not pregnant, there was no baby, it was just a stomach problem, annoying but temporary.

She heard the swish of Kleenex and opened her eyes. Her mother was standing by her bedside, and Amy saw the saddest thing she'd ever seen in her life: the sight of her mother crying. Which made Amy cry even more.

Susan took the baby while Amy blew her nose. But Susan didn't hold him very long; as soon as Amy was ready, she handed him back. Then, using her own finger, Susan gently opened the baby's mouth and at the same time guided his head to Amy's breast and helped work her nipple into his tiny mouth. He clamped down, and Amy felt an inner tug as the baby's jaw worked up and down.

"That's what they mean by latch," Susan said gently. As the baby nursed, she dabbed at the corners of Amy's eyes, which made Amy start crying all over again. Amy stroked the baby's downy hair, feeling more naked than she'd felt while giving birth.

"Why should I nurse him if I'm not going to keep him?"

"Because it's good for him," said Susan.

"If it's good for him, then I should keep doing it, which means I shouldn't give him up. And if I keep nursing him, I won't be *able* to give him up. I'll want to keep him even more."

"Shhh," and Susan handed Amy another Kleenex. Then she told Amy to lean forward a little. She moved around behind her, and after removing a comb from a plastic wrapper, she began to gently work the snarls out of Amy's hair. "All these things will fall into place," she said. "There's no rush to decide."

"I don't know who the father is," Amy whispered.

"That's all right."

"No. It's not."

Susan set down the comb. "Do you want to tell me about it?"

"No. Because that means I'll remember more than I want to remember."

But it was already there, whether she wanted to remember it or not.

"I won't flip out," Susan said. "I promise."

"Yes you will." And it suddenly hurt Amy, to think of how much it was going to hurt her mother, to hear what had happened.

"Amy," said Susan, peering around to face her, "I just helped you deliver a baby. My mind's already imagining the worst. You might as well tell me."

"About how I got drunk? You realize I probably don't have all the details, because of that."

"Believe me, honey, I probably don't want all the details."

Amy adjusted the baby, who had fallen back asleep and was sweating against her breast. She was grateful that her mother was standing behind her. "So last Halloween?"

"Okay," Susan said, "okay," and her voice sounded guarded, and Amy wished she hadn't begun the story but knew there was no way to stop at this point.

"I wasn't even going out that night. I was going to stay home and hand out candy. But then you got dressed up as Pippi Longstocking."

Susan stopped combing. "I liked that costume!"

"Except you wanted me to dress up too. You had a Little Orphan Annie wig you wanted me to wear."

"I did?"

"Yes, you did."

There was no way she was going to stay home and wear a Little Orphan Annie wig. And so Amy had left the house and gone to a coffee shop, where she ordered a hot chocolate and read a chapter in *Walden*. Around ten, some guys came in; one of them was in her math class. And they must have taken pity on her because they asked what she was doing there alone, and she said she was reading ahead for lit class, and that's when they joked about kidnapping her.

People didn't usually joke with her, and it made her feel cool. She didn't say that out loud to her mother.

"So we went to a park," she went on. "They had vodka. They weren't trying to be mean; they just figured I knew how to drink."

"How much did you drink?"

"Like I'd know?"

"Do you remember calling and telling me you were staying at Sarah's?"

"Is that what I told you?"

"You did. And I believed it."

"Sorry."

"That's okay. It's not like I never lied to my parents."

Things got even fuzzier after that. She remembered being in the backseat of someone's car and people helping her walk into a house. She remembered the scratchy carpet against her face, and some girls helping her to her feet and taking her into the bedroom, where there was a king-sized bed piled with coats. She woke up in darkness with a cottony mouth and cold feet. Her pants lay on the floor; her legs were damp and sticky, and her underwear was on backward.

She had the sense there'd been more than one.

She told all this to her mother, except the part about the underwear. And the number. Which she really didn't know. It was just plural.

"Who was it?" Susan said, after a while.

"You said you wouldn't ask."

"No I didn't."

"Mom."

"Honey, we—"

"*Mom.*"

At home she took a shower, and everything stung, and yes, it occurred to her, but only fleetingly, and she put it out of her head because there were more pressing things to think about, such as college visits during the winter and SATs and AP exams in the spring.

"Didn't you feel yourself gaining weight?" Susan asked.

"I'm always gaining weight."

"But didn't it feel different?"

"No. Yes. I don't know." *Don't worry,* she wanted to say. *Next time I have sex with the football team, I'll make sure to get a pregnancy test.*

"And those girls didn't stay to help you?" Susan said suddenly. "Didn't they know they shouldn't leave you alone like that? Whatever happened to the idea of girls looking out for each other?"

"It doesn't work that way, Mom," said Amy.

"I want to wring their little necks," said Susan. "I want to wring that boy's neck too."

"Mom. You told me you'd be able to handle it."

"I didn't say I wouldn't get mad, though," said Susan. "It infuriates me. Not just what the boy did to you. Didn't anyone look in on you? You were passed out! You could have choked on your own vomit! What's *with* these kids?"

Amy shrugged. She'd been the subject of whispery speculation for about a month—until Thanksgiving, actually, when someone else did something dumb and provided new gossip for the high school tabloids.

Now she lay against her hospital pillow, watching her mother pace. She wanted desperately to comfort her mother right now. *I'm alive,* she wanted to say. *I survived.* But she knew her mother's heart was broken, and nothing she could say would help. And she hated herself, for getting drunk that night and doing this to her mother.

"Mom. Stop. I'm all right."

Susan took a deep breath and sat down beside Amy and searched her eyes.

"It isn't easy, hearing this," she said. "But you're right. I promised you I wouldn't flip out. I *feel* like I'm going to flip out, but I won't. I just need to vent a little. But I'll deal with this. You'll deal with this. It's not going to wreck your life. You're not going to punish yourself forever. We're going to figure out the best solution, and it might not be clear for a couple of days, or even weeks, but we're going to get through this. Remember what JT said? You lose your confidence, you lose everything. My goodness." She sighed. "What if we had never

297

come down the river? What if this had happened back in Mequon? I don't know if I would have been able to get through all this and come out whole. Maybe I would have. But I don't know." She took Amy's face between her hands and shook her own head in a way that meant yes.

"We'll figure it out," she said again.

"Okay," said Amy.

And even Amy thought that particular word, "okay," sounded different, when spoken for once without anger or sarcasm.

DAYS TWELVE AND THIRTEEN

River Miles 179–225

Below Lava to Diamond Creek

50

Days Twelve and Thirteen

Miles 179–225

Everyone had a theory about the dog.

Evelyn was sure he was dead. She recalled Lava Falls, and how much water there was. Automatically she computed numerous factors in her head—volume, body weight, time, and temperature—and knew there was simply no way the dog could have survived.

Jill thought he was dead too. Not by any calculation of the odds, but because of her ingrained belief—despite this river trip—in her own personal Murphy's Law: if something could possibly come along to make her boys forever happy, it wouldn't. She began to regret not letting the boys get a dog earlier—perhaps if they already had a dog, they wouldn't have grown so attached to Blender. She wondered how much grieving time she should allow before suggesting they visit the animal shelter in Salt Lake City.

Mark, on the other hand, was convinced the dog had survived, that it was only a matter of time before he caught up with them.

"That dog has nine lives," he declared, right in front of the boys, which made Jill wince for all its false hope. At the same time, she envied his optimism.

Please, just don't let us find a body, she thought.

Ruth, who had buried a yardful of pets, was more philosophical. Perhaps because she had seen so many animals come and go; perhaps because she knew it was, after all, just a dog, and at the moment other things—childbirth and degenerative illnesses, to name a few—seemed more compelling. And Lloyd had already forgotten completely about the dog; he couldn't understand what the fuss was all about. "Dogs aren't even allowed down here," he kept reminding people, implying that fourteen people had hallucinated Blender's existence.

For his part, Mitchell was racked with guilt, and he retreated into morose silence. He kept revisiting the run through Lava. Just when had he let go of the dog? Was it in the V-wave or below? He sat in the hot sun in the back of JT's boat and stared at his hands, trying to understand how they had released their grip. And why hadn't he clamped his thighs around the dog more tightly? Why didn't they think of tying him to one of the lines, for that matter? There were a thousand decisions that Mitchell, in anguished hindsight, would have made differently.

By the end of their last full day, there was still no sign of the dog. They pulled into a camp with a large open beach, and their attention was briefly diverted when Evelyn went off downriver in search of a more isolated site for her last night and came running back, hollering that she had seen a four-foot rattlesnake coiled in the sand; and every-body wanted to see it, which JT didn't recommend, but they all trooped off anyway to see the beast, cameras in hand, and came back shaken up enough to move their sleeping mats in toward the center of the clearing for the night.

Over dinner they managed to focus on JT's tales of past mishaps, blunders, and pranks. They all laughed. But during cleanup, when the dog would have been scrounging for scraps, they missed him as though they'd raised him from puppyhood, and they grieved at the thought that they might never know just exactly what had happened to him, on the river.

"Because he might show up in the night," Sam explained to his father, after Mark asked him why he was keeping his headlamp turned on, even as it lay on the sand.

"Of course," said Mark.

"Dad?"

"What's that?"

"If somebody else picked him up, they'd take him to a shelter some-where after their trip, right? They wouldn't just keep him?"

Mark said he guessed that any good-souled person would do that.

"So we might find him when we get back to Flagstaff?"

"We might. I don't want you to get your hopes up, though."

"I won't, Dad. Can I leave my light on?"

"Sure," said Mark, and when he bent down to kiss his son good night, Sam wrapped his arms around his neck and didn't let go for a long time.

"I hate to give him false hopes," Jill said when Mark came to lie down beside her.

"What would you tell him?"

Jill thought for a moment, then sighed. "I guess I'd tell him the same thing." She felt across the sand for Mark's hand and laced her fingers with his. "But I'd try not to feed things."

"I don't think I have," said Mark.

"No. I don't think you have, either. You're pretty sensitive to nuance."

"You think?"

"Yes, I do," she whispered.

"Thanks," he whispered back. "You know, I really do think he's alive."

"Keep thinking that, then," she said, squeezing his hand.

Before going to bed, Peter walked down to Dixie's boat.

"Hey, Peter," she said as she restacked gear. "What's up?"

Peter stayed on the sand.

"Everything all right?"

"Oh sure," he said.

"Do you need something?"

"No. I just wanted to say thank you."

"Don't mention it," she said cheerfully. "It's been quite the trip, hasn't it?"

"I don't mean it like that, although thanks for that too," Peter said. "What I mean is, well, maybe you noticed and maybe you didn't, but I've had a crush on you the whole trip. I think you're one of the most beautiful women I've ever known. And you're a river guide! I was a goner as soon as JT introduced you to us all, back up at Lee's Ferry."

Dixie sat down.

"But I'm not telling you this for the reason you might think. I know

303

you have a boyfriend down in Tucson. I know we're going to say good-bye tomorrow, and I'll probably never see you again. But I just wanted to say thank you, for letting me be in love with you for two weeks."

Dixie fingered the twisted wire horse at her throat.

"That's all," said Peter.

Down on his boat, JT settled himself on his sleeping mat. The air was still, and the moon, now in its last quarter, bathed the river in its pearly light. Tomorrow they would row the last few miles to the takeout at Diamond Creek. They would unload the boats; there would be a bus and a truck and a big lunch spread waiting for them. After lunch the guides would load up the truck, and the passengers would file into the bus—

And that would be it. Trip over. Finito.

JT laced his fingers beneath his head. Ordinarily he was always looking forward to the next trip: a few days off, then the mass load-up again, a new list of passengers, introductions, and lessons about the basics of life on the river. Ordinarily he didn't let himself get too senti-mental at Diamond Creek, knowing the river would always be there, knowing that he would always be back.

But a large part of him was feeling way too fragile on this trip. He was afraid to say good-bye to these people, for reasons he couldn't explain. In the middle of the night, he woke up with a start. His heart was pounding. And a new thought came to him: he was a fraud. Who was he, to think that he could guide people down the river? Oh, he knew the water, he knew the hikes, he knew enough stories and his-tory to write a book. But in the end, he was just a guy who loved the river, who made a pact with the stars every night, who woke up every morning with the current tugging at his soul. For people like him, going down the river wasn't just going down the river. It was some-thing so much grander, a journey into a simpler time of a simpler soul, and JT suddenly had the feeling that in taking people down the river, he broke something in them, something that perhaps needed breaking but needed reconstruction as well; and while he was good at the breaking part, good at taking them to the other side of chaos, he felt like he gave them nothing with which to reconstruct themselves after the journey.

Fraud with a wrecking ball.

The takeout at Diamond Creek the next morning went as smoothly as possible. Everyone was as quick to help as they'd been on the first day at Lee's Ferry—only now they weren't trying to impress anyone; now they were simply getting the job done, stacking every single piece of gear into neat piles on the rocky beach. When all the gear had been unloaded, they rinsed off the boats, dragged them up onto shore, and opened the valves; and then the boys had an exhilarating ten minutes of flopping about to squeeze out every last cubic centimeter of air.

Jill looked on with dismay as the guides rolled the eighteen-foot rafts into three tight little bundles. Was this all it boiled down to?

"Lunch!" yelled Abo. "WASH YOUR HANDS!"

As people crowded around the picnic table, JT coiled up his ropes and straps and stashed them along with his carabiners in a worn zippered duffel. He was hot and hungry and felt a sudden craving for an ice-cold Coke. He was about to head to the shade of the picnic area when he looked up and saw the kayakers floating down the river. Six toy boats bobbing on top of the sparkling water, followed by the fat mule raft. Even from far away JT could spot Bud, with his full white beard.

As he neared the beach, Bud signaled to him with his paddle, so JT waited. Bud's kayak glided swiftly toward shore and collided with the pebbly beach. But instead of unhooking his skirt and climbing out, he rested his paddle across the top of the cockpit.

"Señor," said JT, nodding. Something about the man's posture disturbed him. "Everything okay?"

"I thought you should know," he said, squinting up at JT. "We found our life jacket."

"Your life jacket," said JT.

"The one we lent you," said Bud.

"The dog's, you mean."

"Right."

"The green one?"

"Yeah."

JT felt his mind speeding up. He was already arguing with himself, that it didn't mean anything, that the dog could have slipped out of his life jacket and still be alive. Why, he'd even thought about this yesterday, the possibility that the dog might have lost his life jacket right off the bat, up there in Lava; it didn't clinch the issue yesterday, so it shouldn't clinch the issue today.

"Listen, I don't know if I should pass this on, but somebody on another trip was talking about a bunch of turkey vultures, back up around Pumpkin Spring," said Bud. "I don't know what they were circling."

JT thought for a moment. "Could have been a dead ringtail," he told Bud. "Could have been any number of things."

"It could have," said Bud. "But I thought you ought to know."

JT felt his ears begin to ring. He did not want to share Bud's news with the group. But Mitchell had already spied the kayakers, and he came down to the shoreline holding a messy sandwich.

"Greetings," he said.

"Greetings," said Bud.

"You haven't by any chance seen the dog, have you?"

Just then the mule boat skidded up against the shoreline. There, on top of all their gear, was the green life jacket.

"Hey! That's—" Mitchell broke off and glanced around at all the faces.

JT tried to draw Mitchell aside, but the word "dog" must have resonated, because instantly the boys came running down. When they saw Mitchell's face, they slowed to a walk and came to stand by the nose of Bud's kayak.

JT placed a hand on Sam's bony shoulder, smooth and warm from thirteen days of sun.

"You don't have him, do you?" Sam said to Bud.

Bud shook his head.

"That's his life jacket."

Bud nodded.

"Well," said Sam staunchly, "well, it doesn't mean anything."

"No, it does not," said JT, and he could see the boy's mind processing the evidence, just as he himself had done. An empty life jacket alone did not equal a dead dog. Bud didn't say anything about the vultures, and JT decided then and there to offer Bud a free trip down the river, at his convenience, for this little bit of discretion.

By now the other kayakers were pulling in, and JT could tell from their faces that they'd discussed the matter and drawn their own conclusions. One by one, the people in JT's group came wandering down from the lunch table. A solemn quiet fell upon them as JT explained that the dog's life jacket had been found.

"It doesn't mean anything either way," said JT. "I don't think anyone should jump to conclusions. On the other hand, I guess we're just not going to know anything for sure."

The group waited.

What, do we do a rain dance? JT wondered.

"Nine lives," Mark murmured.

"Even so . . . ," said Evelyn.

"Perhaps if we leave a note on the picnic table," Ruth said.

"Use our phone number," said Mark.

"Mark, don't," Jill said quickly.

"Dogs aren't even allowed down here," Lloyd reminded them.

It was Sam who noticed that Mitchell had disappeared. They looked around and finally saw his floppy tan hat bobbing through the tall thickets along the bank downriver.

Then his head vanished, and in another moment they heard the terrible sound of retching. Under other circumstances, there would be speculation of a stomach virus, or too much to drink the night before, or gluttony at the lunch table. Not today.

Sam headed toward the thicket.

"Give him some space, Sam," Mark called.

But Sam kept going, in search of the man who was most in need of comfort.

51

Day Thirteen

The Road Out

The road out of the canyon at Diamond Creek is steep, rocky, and deeply rutted from flash floods. It's an eighteen-mile trip that can take an hour, even when weather conditions are good; and after gliding down a river for two weeks, the bumps and jolts can take their toll on a person's joints.

Abo and Dixie rode in the back of the cab, and JT rode up front with the driver. He was trying to figure out what he would say tonight, when they all met for a farewell dinner at a pub in downtown Flagstaff. He had a pretty standard speech, but this had not exactly been a standard trip.

He thought of getting sick. A sore throat. A stomach bug. He thought of telling Abo that Colin was in town, just for the night. A robber had ransacked his house.

"Hey, Boss," said Abo from behind. "How much of this trip are you going to write up, when you make your trip report?"

"The whole truth," said JT. "Nothing but the truth."

"Don't write about how I put peanut butter in the green beans."

"What's going to keep you from doing it again?"

"Well now, I LEARN from my mistakes!" Abo declared.

Dixie sighed. "Tone it down, Abo?"

Abo wrapped his arms around her and firmly smooched her cheek. "Let's do another trip together!"

"Maybe next year," said Dixie.

As they climbed, the truck lurched dangerously from side to side. The driver had to hold tightly to the steering wheel, for the cobbled ruts had a will of their own and threatened to pull the truck off course if he wasn't careful. At one point, he had to hug the right edge to avoid a boulder that had fallen, and JT found himself looking straight down into the dry canyon bed.

A shadow. Moving.

"Hey. Stop the truck," JT said.

"I can't stop," said the driver. "I'll never get going again."

"Stop the truck," said JT. The truck lurched forward with a shriek, then sank back with dust rising all around. JT opened his door with a loud creak and stepped down onto the hardened dirt. There was less than a few feet of space between the truck and the edge of the drop-off. When the dust cleared, he looked down, thinking he'd imagined it.

There he was, loping along the creek bed.

"What is it?" Abo said, climbing out of the truck. "What do you see?"

JT strained his eyes to make sure. How the fuck?

Dixie poked her head out of the window. "What is it?"

JT shook his head in wonder.

"You damn dog," he breathed.

ACKNOWLEDGMENTS

This book never would have happened if I hadn't fallen out of the boat in Deubendorff Rapid during my first Grand Canyon trip. Which might seem odd, given the fact that my so-called swim lasted for just thirty terrifying seconds. But with the terror came an exhilaration I hadn't felt for ages, and before I even dried out, I was already writing about it. I wouldn't know there was a novel here until much, much later, but the experience has fueled most of my writing since that day.

And so right off the bat I give a tremendous amount of thanks and blessings to Ed Hasse of Arizona Raft Adventures. Ed was my paddle guide that day, and we got off course in Deubendorff. As the boat reared up, I toppled over the back; Ed grabbed onto my ankle for the briefest of seconds, then let me go, physically and spiritually, down into the deep. A lot of people have written very eloquently about what it's like to swim a big rapid; the most accurate comparison for me lies in the expression "getting maytagged." I was sucked down and spun around and finally ejected back into the sunlight, after which I truly felt like an unexpected rebirth had taken place. And so thank you, Ed, for letting go. Thank you, too, for all your advice and detailed comments on the manuscript.

That first trip jump-started a continuing passion for the river, and several years later I had the opportunity to go down again—this time as a guide's assistant. Thanks to Arizona Raft Adventures' Rob Elliott, Diane Ross, and Katherine Spillman for this last-minute offer, which gave me a much-needed inside view of a guide's life. A warm and heartfelt thanks to my magnificent guides: Bill Mobley, Jan Sullivan, Jerry Cox, Jessica Cortright, and Jon Harned. With a great deal of patience (and a lot of ribbing) they taught me how to rig a boat, read a rapid, set up a kitchen, and cook a bang-up meal for twenty-five in one of the most exquisite environments in the world. May you all continue to welcome other travelers into the magical world below the rim.

My entire river education has been supremely enriched through a deep friendship with artist Scott Reuman, Zen Master of Flowing Water. Thanks to Scott for reading and critiquing the manuscript, and for always being available to answer questions both banal and profound. Why do you use four buckets to wash the dishes? Ask Scott. What's so cool about a river trip? Ask Scott.

And to another invaluable source, Maureen Ryan of Grand Canyon Dories—thank you for pondering my "what-ifs" and offering so much insight into a guide's thought process. I am forever grateful for our sessions at Vic's, for your careful reading and commenting on the manuscript in progress, and for your continuing friendship.

To all the members of my fabulous writing group—Marilyn Krysl, Gail Storey, Julene Bair, Lisa Jones, and Janis Hallowell—what would I have done without you? My love and heartfelt thanks for your critical ears and wise comments, week after week after week. More love and thanks to Lisa Halperin and Laura Uhls, too, for reading and critiquing the manuscript in its final stages.

Some people may not have realized they played such an important role in this project, and I wish to extend my gratitude to them: my in-laws, John and Madeleine Schlag, for suggesting the trip in the first place; Graham Fogg, professor of geology at UC Davis, for steering me away from an implausible premise; Artie and Patty and Renee and Kees and Scott, for taking me down the Green; and, above all, my beloved parents, John and Betty Hyde, for all those trips in the red canoe, which despite its unfortunate disappearance is out there on some lake or stream, making someone happy.

To my New York Crew: down-on-my-knees thanks to my agent, Molly Friedrich, for including me in her very busy life; to my editor, Jordan Pavlin, for having confidence in this novel when it was just a phrase in my mind; to Lucy Carson, for such careful readings of numerous drafts; and to Leslie Levine, for handling all the details at every stage of publication.

Thanks to Vic's Café in Boulder, not only for all the caffeine but also for the anonymous workspace. (You senior noontime ladies rock!)

And finally to my husband, Pierre, whose central role in this project goes back to a lunch on our deck one summer day. It was about a year after our first river trip, and I was still obsessed. Since I was writing *The Abortionist's Daughter* at the time, I was trying to turn one of the characters into a river guide. Suffice it to say that I had trouble figuring out how a river guide would end up a criminal detective, and sought Pierre's help. We brainstormed for an hour.

"Give it up," he finally said. "Go write a whole novel about the river."

So I did.

RESOURCES

FOR GENERAL INFORMATION

National Park Service, http://www.nps.gov/grca/planyourvisit/river-
concessioners.htm
Grand Canyon River Outfitters Association, http://www.gcroa.org/

RAFTING COMPANIES

Arizona Raft Adventures/Grand Canyon Discovery, http://www.azraft.com/,
1-800-786-7238 (my personal favorite!)
Arizona River Runners, http://www.raftarizona.com/, 1-800-477-7238
Canyon Explorations/Expeditions, http://www.canyonexplorations.com/,
1-800-654-0723
Canyoneers, http://www.canyoneers.com/, 1-800-525-0924
Colorado River & Trail Expeditions, Inc., http://www.crateinc.com/,
1-800-253-7328
Diamond River Adventures, http://www.diamondriver.com/,
1-800-343-3121
Grand Canyon Dories, http://www.oars.com/grandcanyon/dories.html,
1-800-346-6277
Grand Canyon Expeditions Company, http://www.gcex.com/,
1-800-544-2691
Hatch River Expeditions, http://www.hatchriverexpeditions.com/
default.aspx, 1-800-856-8966
Moki Mac River Expeditions, Inc., http://www.mokimac.com/,
1-800-284-7280
O.A.R.S., http://www.oars.com/, 1-800-346-6277
Outdoors Unlimited, http://www.outdoorsunlimited.com/,
1-800-637-7238
Tour West, http://www.twriver.com/, 1-800-453-9107
Western River Expeditions, http://www.westernriver.com/, 1-866-904-1160
Wilderness River Adventures, http://www.riveradventures.com/,
1-800-992-8022

PRIVATE TRIP PLANNING

Professional River Outfitters, Inc., http://www.proriver.com/, 1-800-648-3236

RIVER GEAR

NRS, http://www.nrsweb.com/, 1-877-677-4327
Red River Sports, http://www.azraft.com/redriversports/, 1-800-786-7238
Red Rock Outfitters, http://www.redrockoutfitters.com/, 1-800-566-2525

A NOTE ABOUT THE AUTHOR

Elisabeth Hyde is the author of four previous novels. Born and
raised in New Hampshire, she has since lived in Vermont, Washing-
ton, D.C., San Francisco, and Seattle. In 1979 she received her law
degree and practiced briefly with the U.S. Department of Justice.
She currently lives in Colorado with her husband and three children.

A NOTE ON THE TYPE

This book was set in Caledonia, a typeface designed by
W. A. Dwiggins (1880–1956). It belongs to the family of printing
types called "modern face" by printers—a term used to mark the
change in style of the type letters that occurred around 1800.
Caledonia borders on the general design of Scotch Roman, but
it is more freely drawn than that letter. This version of
Caledonia was adapted by David Berlow in 1979.

COMPOSED BY
Creative Graphics,
Allentown, Pennsylvania

PRINTED AND BOUND BY
Berryville Graphics,
Berryville, Virginia

DESIGNED BY
Iris Weinstein

MAP BY
David Lindroth

HYDE   Hyde, Elisabeth.

In the heart of the canyon.

DATE			

BAKER & TAYLOR

JUL

2009